CU00693085

Laura

Love and Deadly Consequences

Copyright 2016 © Marianne Roberts

The rights of Marianne Roberts and her work has been asserted by her in accordance with the Copyright, Design Patent Act 1988

All rights reserved.
No part of this publication may be reproduced, stored in a retrieval system, or transmitted, in any form or by any means electronic, mechanical, photocopying, recording or otherwise, without prior permission in writing of the copyright holder or publishers.

All views and comments printed in this book are those of the author and should not be attributed to the publisher.

Published by Arc Publishing and Print
166 Knowle Lane
Sheffield
S11 9SJ

Telephone: 07809 172872
e-mail: chris@arcbooks.co.uk
www.sheffieldbooks.co.uk

Acknowledgements

With my grateful thanks to
Mike Gardner, without whom this
book would never have been written.

Chapter 1

A pale winter sun tried desperately to lift the mist hovering over the river. Laura Sogar stood at the window of the second floor apartment and sipped appreciatively from the cup filled with hot, sweet coffee. Restless, she knew that today something would happen that would change her lonely life forever. How she longed to see the green band of the greatest waterway in Europe; full of working barges, ferries and trading boats. From May onwards, the pleasure steamers carried people up and down the river, decks awash with pennants fluttering in the breeze and she would hear the music floating up to her as they passed and wished she too was on the boat.

Laura gazed out over the small patch of roof garden and saw the spring bulbs well advanced in their containers. Soon it would be warm enough to take table and chairs outside to watch the activities below. She'd miss that if they had to leave this place.

"Peter! Breakfast" she called out to her son, to be rewarded with a muffled sound coming from the bedroom.

Across the water the peaks of the hills were clear of the mist, the ruins of a castle perched on each. Once the splendid homes of petty barons and dukes, who had fought bloody battles with the nobility on the opposite range of hills behind the town, the banks of the mighty river a natural boundary.

"Peter!" Laura called out again. "Get up. You can make your own breakfast if you're not out in ten minutes!"

"OK, mum! Ten minutes!"

She wondered if she'd be here when the hikers were trekking up the slopes, like colourful ants. Probably not! Rema House was up for sale. This beautiful building would be a Ladies College in future.

Here she had cried for her father, the gentle eccentric Professor of Literature who had tried to be father and mother to his only child. Here she had cried for Jack, her husband, in the dark of the night, when the loneliness became unbearable. Jack, who didn't have to go to war, but needed action to fill his days. Leaving her and Peter, convinced it would be over soon and that he was invincible. 'Big Jack' was not, nor were any of his friends.

Startled, Laura turned away from the window to see her son standing in the doorway of the kitchen, yawning loudly.

"Morning, mum!" Peter bent down to kiss the top of her head, about ten inches taller than his mother, this was a constant source of amusement to him. Smiling broadly, he asked, "Breakfast?"

"I've been waiting for hours," Laura laughed, raising her hand in a mock attack. "Must've been some party. I'll do the eggs. You make fresh coffee!"

Peter, whistling softly, refilled the coffee pot. "We really painted the town red last night."

Breaking eggs into a pan, Laura remarked "I heard the bike. You shouldn't ride that machine if you're drinking. It's dangerous!"

"I wasn't that drunk. We just had a good time. Stop worrying, mum!" Peter took the pot to the table in the corner, slid onto the bench seat and poured coffee for both of them. He picked up the morning paper and removed the inner pages, leaving the outside for his mother to read. Laura placed breakfast and buttered fresh rolls in front of him, biting with pleasure into the crisp crunchy bread and scanned the front page.

"Listen to this, mum!" Peter said, an urgent tone in his voice.

"I'm listening"

He held up the page of adverts and read.... "Joining other emigrants to America, Josef Schumann and his family will depart from Hamburg on the seventh of May. I hereby wish potential buyers of the property at 10, Annsberg Road, Dettingen, to contact me as a matter of urgency...." Peter looked expectantly at his mother. "What do you think? We passed those houses last year on the way to the football match. Remember? You liked them. We've got to leave here sooner or later!"

Laura hesitated for a moment, gazed out of the window and noticed that the mist over the river had lifted.

"Yes, I know. It's never been the same without your father. Better to move away altogether. Make a clean break. I remember the houses, they looked different, but I only want the one at the end with the big white building in the garden."

She remembered whizzing through the village just after Peter bought himself the new bike. He had promised to take her for a ride on that Saturday afternoon, then remembered he was also supposed to be at the football match between Dettingen and Annsberg. There he felt at home and held long conversations with Father Michael, the parish priest, when they

4

met on the football field or the teams local. Sometimes Freddy von Dettingen-Annsberg would join them, and she wouldn't see her son until the next day, when he would stay at the Baron's lodge or with the priest at the Presbytery. Peter told hilarious stories of his exploits abroad and was generous in providing beer for his friends. They respected his work and reputation as one of Martin Ryker's best engineers, where he had almost attained the stature of his father before him.

Peter waved the paper in front of her face. "OK, mum!" he said, getting excited. "We'll go and have a look."

"Hold on a minute, son. Where's the money coming from to buy a big property like that?

Laura looked worried. Peter carelessly waved his hand in the air and laughed. "Money? Don't worry about money. We've enough. Martin's seen to that. Get yourself into some warm clothes. I'll phone from downstairs, then we'll go shopping for a new home!"

Laura watched her son disappear through the door, heard him running down the stairs, whistling. He was so like his father. Unruly brown hair bleached into streaks. Bronzed and fit and so handsome with a smile to melt a heart of stone. Brown eyes full of laughter in his lean face. Her son was the best legacy Jack could have given her. She loved him so much, as she had loved his father and remembered the first time they had met...

It had been a month after her seventeenth birthday. As the librarian at the University, she had stood on top of the tall gantry, the feather duster removing minute specks of dust from leather bound volumes of rare species. She'd almost lost her balance as the high steps jolted. At her exclamation of an un-lady like 'Damn' she'd heard a pleasant voice saying, "I'm sorry!" and looked down into anxious brown eyes. 'Big Jack' Sogar had entered her life. Jack was an expert on blowing up mountains, building tunnels and highways in foreign places in the company of men. The slender girl with the mischievous expression in her grey eyes left him standing below with his mouth gaping, his head in a whirl. Jack observed the curvaceous figure, accentuated by the simple cut of the blue serge dress, a colourful scarf tied around the neck. 'Wow' Jack murmured, still gazing in amazement, wondering what it would be like to take the pins out of the golden hair and feel it. He loved the curls that escaped and hung about her face, the soft lips with that impish smile. To kiss that mouth would be heaven. And that delicate complexion; enhanced by eyebrows and lashes as black as a ravens wing. He wanted her in his arms and hoped she couldn't read his mind.

"Er..I'm looking for a map," he mumbled and felt hot under the collar at the amusement in her eyes.

"I'll be down and help you find it," she'd said and stepped off the platform of the gantry, giving him a glimpse of slim ankles. He extended his hand to help her off the ladder and she smiled at him. Jack was in love.

Laura looked up into laughing brown eyes, a clean shaven lean face tanned by foreign sun, noticed the unruly, brown wavy hair that hung over his face like a boy's. He was a large man, broad and muscular, unlike the pale gentle creatures that inhabited the University. They'd had little appeal to her, except as escorts. Laura too, fell in love...

They'd married a year later. Jack came home two or three times a year and she'd had Peter while he was blowing up another mountain. Their love had not diminished with the years but Peter remained their only child. He enjoyed the visits of the amusing stranger, but never really got to know his father. Laura and Jack experienced a perpetual honeymoon until July 1914 when talk of war became reality.

Jack, confined to home territory was getting restless. He and his friends left three weeks later, so handsome in their uniforms. They solemnly vowed to bring the war to a swift end. Jack came home for a few days in October and by the middle of November he and his friends had been blown skywards like obscene pieces of flotsam and jetsam. Cannon shells are no respecters of human flesh. 'Big Jack' Sogar was no exception. Ten years without Jack had been lonely. She'd had three proposals of marriage, liked her suitors, but never felt more than affection for any of them. Perhaps she needed a new direction in her life...

The sound of Peter's voice floated up the stairwell and brought Laura back to the present. He was joking with someone below, laughing. Laura cleared the table, then walked into her bedroom and looked out of the window, across the town in the valley. She saw the range of hills in the distance, they were not peaked like the ones across the river, but flat on top. She knew the plateau stretched as far as the French border. There would be much to explore on her doorstep if they bought the house. The two villages met at the foot of the hills. Each having an existence in its own right, its core the tall spires of the church with their golden weather vanes. Staunch Catholics all, Laura wondered how they would be received by the people. As Protestants they might remain outsiders, but Peter was liked and the Priest he spoke of sometimes sounded a liberal, understanding man.

Dressed in her warmest clothes, woollen hat, scarf and mittens, Laura was ready for the ride on Peter's motorbike. Peter, resplendent in his leather outfit, called out. "Come-on, mum. They're waiting for us!"

He pushed the bike out to the pavement and Laura took her place on the pillion seat.

Chapter 2

The roads from the river pointed in a direct line to the churches. No-one could miss them if one walked long enough over the grey-black tarmac surface, bubbling in summer with the intense heat. Across the tram lines skirting the periphery of the town and over the railway line, the first isolated houses of Dettingen came into view; to Laura it seemed a long way off from the water, and lonely. Peter turned the machine to the left, along a gravel lane, turned right, rode down a narrow path which ran beside a small stream and presently stopped at the end, the nose of the motorbike protruding into Annsberg road.

"Here we are!" he said, a big grin on his face. Laura realised they had taken a route well known to him and missed out the heart of the village. She could see the properties on her right, at the south end and almost like an appendix to the main body of the village. Five terraced dutch-type properties on either side. A small piece of Holland. In the other direction the road stretched away into the distance towards Annsberg, not a house in sight, only meadows and long gardens with neat huts.

Getting off the pillion seat, Laura looked up and down the road. As he watched his mother trying to get her bearings, Peter pointed towards Annsberg.

"You can see the two flag poles of the football ground on the right. That's the boundary of Dettingen and Annsberg. They share the field and one of these days they'll kill each other," Peter informed her as he dismounted from the machine. "Let's find number ten," securing the bike on its stand at the curb. They walked past a meadow and a large garden with the white building sitting in the middle of it. Laura saw Peter glance at the number plate of the house, disappear up three steps and press the bell.

Mara Schumann, rosy cheeked, round and smiling happily, opened the door. "You must be Peter Sogar." She stretched out her hand to give a hearty shake to Peter's. "And Mrs. Sogar. Do come in. Josef is waiting for you," shaking Laura's hand vigorously. Laura liked what she saw. The hall was light with a door at the far end. She loved the impressive oak staircase spiralling up and around to the first and second floors. Following Mara Schumann, they entered a large comfortably furnished room in the middle of the house. Part dining, part living room, it felt homely. Josef Schumann stood at the high window in the corner of the room, looking out over his garden. As he turned to greet them, Laura was startled to see a kind, gentle face almost covered by beard and moustache. A dark scull cap on top of the greying hair. Conservatively dressed, his appearance contrasted sharply with Mara Schumann's bubbly and flamboyant personality. Shaking hands, Laura smiled at him as he motioned her to sit down. She wondered why they were selling this lovely house and leaving everything to go to America.

"Do you have any other family, Frau Sogar? This is a large property," Josef enquired.

"No. There's only Peter. I lost my husband in 1914," Laura explained. "This house will not seem so big if Peter gets married and has a family of his own."

Mrs Schumann brought in a tray with coffee and biscuits, handed them round and sat down in one of the large leather chairs. Laura asked "Do you know who built these houses? They don't fit the general pattern of properties around these parts!"

The face of the little Jewish woman lit up with pride. "My father built them. He came from Holland and wanted a bit of home, here in Germany."

"They look very impressive," Laura said, genuinely pleased. "But this house feels warm and comfortable."

"Let's proceed with your inspection," Josef invited them, after they had finished a second cup of coffee. He led the way to the sitting room at the front of the house. Large, high, lived in. Laura felt pleased.

"You have beautiful furniture. I love this room!" She looked out of one of the tall windows at street level. "It's nice here!"

Josef turned to Peter, "I will be sorry to leave this house and my country. The persecution at the moment is surreptitious but will gather momentum as the new breed of hooligans gain more and more power. We won't wait for that day. Perhaps America will be kinder to us!"

Peter looked at the gentle man in front of him. "Do you really think it will be as bad as that?"

"I'll show you the kitchen," Mara told Laura. "The men are going to talk politics," and ushered Laura out of a second door into the hall. She pointed to a door under the stairwell. "That one leads to the cellars and the other onto the patio." She opened the half glazed door, went down two steps and they stood on a long, wide flagged patio. "When the children were small, they used to lead me a merry dance running round in circles. In and out of doors, hiding. Come!"

Laura visualized children being chased by the plump lady and laughed. "I see what you mean!"

Mara opened the door to the kitchen. It was the domain of someone who cared about food and liked to be there. Friendly and welcoming, like its mistress. Peter and Josef joined them, still talking about foreign affairs.

"If you'd like to explore the garden and other rooms down here, please do so," Josef said.

Laura and Peter walked out to the paved area outside the kitchen. The buildings continued in an 'L' formation, with lofts above. Opening a door with a heart cut out, Peter grinned at his mother. "Useful!" he said.

Next to it, a large laundry room. Zinc baths hung by the handle on large hooks on the wall. A huge copper boiler and three shower heads running along the ceiling amused Peter. "Do they take communal showers?" he whispered to Laura.

"Not at this time of year, I shouldn't think. It'd be lovely in the summer, though," Laura remarked.

A double door took up the short end of the 'L', and revealed a long room that stretched behind the laundry, windows that looked out over meadows at the back. Bicycles stacked neatly at the far end. Garden tools hung from the walls. In the centre a wide open-tread stairway went up to another room. Light and airy windows faced the back and side garden.

"It's a pigeon loft!" exclaimed Peter. "Hasn't been used for a long time! Janus might like it up here. I don't think he'll move into the house with you."

"This'll be perfect!" said Laura. "The floorboards will clean up beautifully."

They closed the doors securely behind them and leaned on the low wall. The garden stretched away in all directions.

"I guess it's about an acre. Maybe more," Peter said. Laura stared at the white building.

"I'm going to see what's in there. You have a look at the garden."

She opened the gate and ran down a gentle slope, followed the gravel path and stopped before a wide blue door. The key turned easily, the door swung back on well oiled hinges; chinks of light revealed four shuttered windows. The room was as large as the pigeon loft, the speckled flooring of blue and cream tiles identical to the surfaces of hall, kitchen and outbuildings. Overhead thick beams spanned the length of the room and pretty lanterns hung from them at intervals.

Laura sat down and wanted to open the shutters. Somehow she felt she had come home.

Peter entered the room, "This is some garden. More like a small holding. You'll need Janus to help with the work, mum. From the lay-out you could make yourself some money growing fruit and vegetables to sell. It's good soil. He looked around him. "This is nice. Big enough to have parties in!"

"Yes, it is nice. Shall we buy it?" she asked Peter and he laughed out loud.

"I don't think they'll sell this without the house to go with it, mum!"

"I know that, silly!" Laura chuckled. "I like it here!"

"OK!" Peter commanded his mother. "Let's go and see the rest of it."

Mara and Josef Schumann were waiting for them in the kitchen with fresh coffee and a plate of delicious home baked cakes. "Did you like the summerhouse, Mrs. Sogar?" asked Mara. "I saw you go in!"

"Oh yes, very much."

After coffee and cakes, Mara led the way up to the first floor with three large bedrooms, then on to two attic bedrooms. All had wash basins, but there was no bathroom. Peter and Laura looked at each other. They went over to the window, Peter leaned out. Laura joined him and saw his finger pointing downwards to the patio below. "Chamber pots or 'That' down there?" he whispered.

His mother dug her elbow into his ribs and whispered back. "We'll sort that out later. What will you do with the furniture?" asked Laura, as they returned to the ground floor.

Mara looked at her husband and sighed. "We cannot take any of it. It will have to be sold!"

"We don't have enough to furnish a house this size. Will you sell them to me if we can agree on a price?" Laura ventured, looking at Peter, who nodded in agreement.

"I'd like that very much. If I can think of my belongings staying here, leaving this house won't be so bad," Mara told Laura.

Two hours later, Laura and Peter were the virtual owners of number 10, Annsberg Road, Dettingen, Bonn South. Mother and son said goodbye, almost skipping out of the door.

"Let's have a ride through our new place of residence, Peter!" begged Laura.

"Hop on. I'll show you the essential, important buildings. We'll start with Jochen's around the corner. I'm very thirsty, madam."

Laughing, Laura mounted the pillion. "You're right, son. A small glass of wine, I think, to celebrate."

Andreas Sachs, the football coach said, 'hello' to Peter, asking if he'd like to bring his girlfriend to the match that afternoon. Laura, seated at a table by the window liked the atmosphere of the small inn, the people were friendly and most of them knew Peter.

"I'll go and ask her!" Peter said to Andreas, who was still unmarried at forty. Not ugly, nor handsome, he had a pleasant face, red hair and a tendency to eat too much. No amount of running about on the football field with his team would reduce his weight. Some said he drank too much beer, others told the tale that he consumed six large sausages and a whole loaf at breakfast. He was fat and cheerful. Peter walked over to his mother and whispered: "Andreas thinks you're my girlfriend. Fancy coming to the match later?"

Laura shook her head and smiled as the waiter put their drinks on the table. "Sorry, darling. We've got shopping to do and I must get back. You'd better tell your friend who I am, but thank him for the compliment. I'll come some other time!"

At the bar the speculation of who she was went on in hushed tones. Andreas barely concealed his admiration for Peter's companion.

Laura fastened the woollen scarf around her neck, put on her mittens and said, "We've got to go if you want to get to the match in time," and waved to the men at the bar. Peter followed, calling to Andreas.

"I'll see you later. Sorry, my mum can't make it today. Bye!" and laughed at the astounded face of Andreas and his friends.

Peter straddled the motorbike and waited for his mother to get on the pillion seat. A tall, blackrobed figure waved to Peter from the pavement opposite. After having said goodbye to one of his parishioners, the Priest crossed over to greet them, a happy smile on his face.

"Good day, Father Michael. Coming to the match?"

"Hello, Peter. I'll try, if there is no urgent business to attend to. I'd like to hear your latest exploits abroad!" Father Michael shook the outstretched hand with genuine pleasure. Laura's face, muffled in scarf and woollen hat, was only partly on view and while the two men exchanged greetings she observed the Priest, aware of the intense blue of his eyes in the saintly face. He reminded her of one of the apostles. As tall as her son, with dark hair under the round hat, a smooth thin face, and a beautiful smile. He was a man, and yet he conveyed the innocence of a child. Laura felt strange, uneasy, then became aware that Peter was talking to her.

"Mum. This is Father Michael. He's the parish priest. You'll probably see a great deal of each other."

Father Michael stretched out his hand. Laura removed her mitten and placed hers into his, they both greeted each other with a polite 'how do you do?' Blue eyes met grey ones and for an instant Laura saw a flicker of fear in his eyes. Then it was gone. Father Michael, suddenly ill at ease, excused himself with unseemly haste.

"I shall be there this afternoon."

He inclined his head towards Laura, murmured "Goodbye," a confused expression on his face and hurried away. Peter looked at the retreating figure, puzzled, then turned to Laura.

"Strange, he's usually very talkative," and started the engine, "Ready?" Laura gazed after Father Michael and felt like a sixteen year old having met a tongue tied youth for the first time.

* * *

They arrived back at Rema House just after one o'clock. Peter left the bike on the pavement. Kick- off was at 2:00 pm and he'd have to hurry. He was pleased with himself, whistling some modern tune. They'd done well this morning, and he liked the new place. It wouldn't be too bad leaving here. Laura deposited the shopping on the table, packed the food away and told her son, "I'll make something to eat before you go."

Peter, on his way to the bedroom, waved. "Thanks, mum. I'll be late back. We'll sort out the details tomorrow."

She watched him disappear through the door. The dark leather outfit seemed for a moment to resemble the black cassock of the Priest and his thin face, with the extraordinary blue eyes floated into her mind. He certainly was a handsome man. And why not? They didn't have to be ugly to be Priests, did they? The Protestants had their own good looking clergy. They could fall in love and marry. 'Fathers' could not...

Suppressing the fluttering within her breast, she reached for a packet of assorted cold meat, and concentrated on the lunch she promised her son.

13

Chapter 3

It had been a bitter winter. March was still cold. The Schumann's had 'open house' to say farewell to their friends in Dettingen. From two 2:00 pm onwards it would be bedlam, so Father Michael was invited to lunch.

Seated at the dining table with his friends, he watched Mara put another piece of duck on his plate, protesting mildly that he'd really had enough. She just laughed and told him to get on with it. There wouldn't be any more lunches or suppers in future and she didn't believe him anyway... Josef poured more wine into his glass and smiled fondly at his wife. Father Michael remembered the pleasant evenings spent in the house, the lively discussions on their respective religions, politics and local affairs. He would miss them both.

"You've been my most valued friend, Father Michael and I'll miss you sorely. I just hope I'll meet a Rabbi who will entertain me as much as you did!" Josef said, a wistful note in his voice.

"And I'll miss you both. Mara for her cooking and you my friend, for your stimulating conversation. Here's to a happy future in America!"

The catholic priest saluted his Jewish friends, looked at them both with affection and sadness, then added: "I wish you luck!"

Lent was a quiet time for Father Michael. He sat at his desk, trying to focus his thoughts on work he should do and found it difficult to concentrate. Easter. formal and solemn. Whitsun. a joyous occasion. The church filled with his parishioners. The older ones attending the early service, sporting new hats to brighten up their conservative attire. But at ten o'clock the church would be overflowing with people showing off their new suits and bonnets. He didn't begrudge them that one morning of vanity and always found it fascinating to watch the pleasure women took in outshining each other. They would talk outside on the green after the service. Would she be there? He was curious and excited at the news circulating in the village that Peter's mum was moving in at the end of the month. Her image would not leave him and he was finally going to find out. See that tantalizing face again. This hell was worse than the one he left behind in 1918.

Sometimes he wished he was back there. Clean, unshackled and free from earthly desire. Memories of that hell replaced Laura's image...

He'd already been at the front for three years before he met Freddy in 1917. Attending to the dying, writing letters, comforting the wounded. He had not believed such carnage could be possible. But his faith in God never wavered.

When Baron Frederick von Dettingen-Annsberg arrived at the front to take the place of a wounded officer he had marvelled at the courage of the priest. Unhurried, unflinching, he walked the trenches. What was he made of? Was he not afraid to die? Did he think he was God? Freddy had asked him.

They met often after that. During the last year of the bloody war, Freddy could tell Father Michael that he was scared and know he wouldn't think any less of him. They talked of his home in Dettingen, of the hills, the river, the people and Freddy wanted him there as the parish priest. To Father Michael it sounded almost like heaven itself. He needed somewhere peaceful to mend his soul and cleanse it of the rivers of blood that flowed about them every day. He would say 'yes' if the bishop allowed it. Freddy said his father would see to it if they survived this lot.

Two months before the surrender, twenty four year old Freddy stepped onto a disk shaped object half buried in the ground and his left leg was ripped from his body. Father Michael stemmed the life blood pumping out of Freddy, promised to come and see him in hospital. The young baron had been lucky. All he lost was one leg. He was pleased to see his friend, convinced he still had two legs. He asked Father Michael to confirm that but the priest shook his head: "One of them will be a wooden one, Freddy!" he regretfully informed his friend.

"Never!" said Freddy. "I'm going to spend the rest of my days in a wheelchair."

"Fine," Father Michael remarked calmly, "Then I'd better find myself another parish to live in."

Freddy had sulked for days, then told the surgeon he needed two legs to walk on and would they please hurry up as he and the priest wanted to go home. Father Michael suffered as much pain as Freddy, but on Easter Saturday 1919 he proudly watched Freddy walk with his stick to greet his father, Baron Cornelius von Dettingen, waiting at the station in Bonn. He heard Freddy say; "Papa. Meet Father Michael Schiller, our new parish priest and my best friend."

Grateful, the old Baron embraced the priest. "I am forever in your debt, Father. Welcome to Dettingen."

They had spent three weeks on the estate at the top of the hill. A good horseman, Father Michael explored the forest which stretched for miles and gradually the trauma of the war lessened. He moved into the presbytery a week before Whitsun and gave his first service on Whit-Sunday. Freddy had already introduced him to the villagers. Father Michael became honorary member of each club in Dettingen. He attended them in strict rotation so as not to offend anyone. A football fanatic, he would referee if called on to do so.

The parishioners grew fond of their priest. Father Michael smoked slim cigars, drank in moderation, judged the pigeons and adjudicated with Freddy at the big races. He played an excellent game of poker, donated his winnings to the kitty and could shoot with the best of them, taking part in the culling hunts in the Autumn in tweeds and high boots.

His very presence commanded respect. There was nothing he didn't know about them and nothing they didn't know about him. He did not molest boys or girls, had no liaison with his young chaplain, kept his distance from the nuns, except on church business and what was more astonishing, Clara Shelton, his housekeeper, went home every evening after leaving his supper for him.

To the men he was a friend, good looking, but no threat to their women; to the women he was beautiful and desirable, they considered it a sin to have the handsome priest go to waste. So unlike many of his predecessors. Sneaky, leacherous priests, all of them!...

They asked him what had he done in the war and all he would say was 'he had seen it and hoped never to live through it again.' Father Michael was not in the habit of talking about himself, but listened attentively to anyone else's story, compassion and humour reflected in his sensitive face.

Until now, he had been content with his fellow men and enjoyed in moderation the adoration of the women. He had not been tempted to break the vow of chastity as most of his fellow priests had. Perhaps he had been too arrogant. Thinking he'd passed the time of temptation. Thinking it only belonged to the young. He was thirty nine years old and felt sixteen. Foolish, sinful, for no-one knew his days and nights were haunted by a pair of soft grey eyes, with long black lashes. And no-one guessed he could still feel the electrifying touch of the small hand in his. Oh, God, help me...

Father Michael stared at the large crucifix on the wall opposite his desk, but received no answer.

Tonight it was the turn of the football club. As Father Michael entered the room at the back of the public bar, the fifteen members already present shouted a jovial greeting. Andreas was in full flow and the conversation had a buzz, a sparkle and Father Michael wondered at the reason. He sat in his usual place by the window, a glass of beer in front of him. Andreas revealed the latest instalment to excite the assembled company. He told Father Michael "I saw her! At the house!" and Father Michael's body tensed instantly with a feeling of curiosity.

"Who did you see, Andreas, and where?" he asked. Nothing could subdue the chubby football coach.

"Peter's mum, she came to the house on that motorbike of his. What a woman!" Admiration gave his face an animated glow. Father Michael looked concerned.

"Surely she wasn't driving the machine herself?"

"No, but I wouldn't put it past her," Heini Wagner said, having met Laura on her first visit to the pub.

"Then who drove it?" Father Michael was insistent. "Peter's not due back for two months." He needed to know and Andreas obligingly provided him with the answer.

"Some fellow was driving. Not decked out like Peter. Youngish bloke, but his hair's all white. They stayed a long time looking around the place and the garden. I wanted to say 'hello' but couldn't stay. I needed to collect the accounts for tonight!"

Father Michael could not explain the sudden tremor he felt at the mention of the man, and wondered who he was. They must know him well enough to allow him to drive Peter's machine. He made an effort to concentrate on the conversation buzzing around him, listening to Andreas.

"What I'd give to run my hands over that lady!" accompanying his desire with the appropriate gestures. Normally Father Michael took no notice of all the exaggerated tales of the more attractive females in Dettingen. Most of it was just wishful thinking, and he knew they were harmless enough. Tonight was different. Andreas was talking about the woman who had invaded his mind, his life and it disturbed him.

"That hair!" Andreas continued excitedly. "She took her scarf off. It all hung loose down her back, like the girl in the fairy story. The one who sold her golden hair, you know! Curls everywhere, beautiful!" Among shouts of 'tell us more' and 'what else did you see?' Andreas got really worked up. "For her I'd give up at least four sausages at breakfast!" reducing the assembled company to momentary silence.

Father Michael was equally silent, his mind filled with an image of the face surrounded by golden hair, and wondered who the stranger was, driving Peter's motorbike.

Chapter 4

Laura had ordered the removal van for the last Friday of the month. Janus had promised to help her settle in, but to her request to come and live in the new house he gave no firm commitment. They'd taken the bicycles and looked over the property and gardens after Peter left. Janus approved and was impressed with the space and light of the pigeon loft. Laura felt certain he would come with her.

After two years of having to guess what his reactions might be to any request she had learnt to use her intuition where the silent man was concerned. He didn't talk much, but she knew he could. Peter and Janus had long conversations, she had heard them laugh and her son found him interesting to talk to. At any other time, Janus listened to everybody's tales very politely, smiled, but showed no emotion and they had got used to him...

Back in 1922 it had taken him almost two months to acknowledge her existence. She had noticed him at the end of the winter, sitting on that small bench at the river bank. A solitary, forlorn figure, staring into the water. He was there every day when she returned from work, wearing a tattered army uniform. Like so many of them, he looked undernourished, abandoned after a war they hadn't wanted in the first place. Desperate to survive not only defeat, but the humiliation of poverty, displacement and suffering pain they couldn't put a name to. Their world had crumbled and the shame of it all did not sit well on the shoulders of brave soldiers. Four years later something evil was emerging. It spread it's insidious tentacles even to this quiet town.

The University was a hot bed of conflicting loyalties and ideologies. The new party promised the people dignity and hope. They didn't mention the price that had to be paid. Follow us, they said. Nationalism will be your salvation.

The lonely man disturbed Laura. As the weather got warmer, he discarded the jacket and sat in a grubby army shirt. She'd wondered where he lived and if he had any other clothing. It was really none of her business. But then again. What if that had been Jack sitting somewhere, or Peter? He was older than her son, but not old enough to have white hair. What horrors had he experienced?

On impulse she sorted through her son's clothes and made a neat pile of shirts, trousers, jackets, socks and a pair of nearly new boots. If they didn't fit, he could always sell them. Quality clothes might give him a few square meals.

Laura packed everything into one of Jack's old suitcases and took it to work with her. On the way home he was there. Placing the suitcase at his feet, Laura just said, "Please don't be offended, but perhaps you can use what's in there."

As if he had to make a conscious effort to take his eyes off the water, the face turning towards her was that of a man in his early thirties. War had mutilated him. The thick hair, snow-white, should have been as dark as the well shaped eyebrows, the brown eyes of the man reflected nothing at all. He had left his soul in some hell or other. As he stared at her, she could feel this mans pain as if it was her own.

Laura remembered Jack. Had he looked like that before the shell ripped him apart? Had he seen hell? Oh, God. How many more were there like him?

She blinked to stop the tears from flooding her eyes, said: "Good day," and walked quickly towards Rema House and home.

Saturday afternoon she shopped in town. The girl in the delicatessen asked: "Going on a picnic, Mrs. Sogar?" when Laura wanted a separate food parcel.

Smiling, she'd said "I'm thinking about it!"

If the man wasn't there, she'd have one on the roof garden, the sliced bread, cheese, butter and cold meats looked quite appetising.

She found him in his usual place. Taking the parcel out of her basket, she placed it on the seat. "Enjoy the food," Laura said and did not wait. She did not know how many hours he sat there. No-one ever joined him. It was almost as if they were afraid of him.

He was there every night. To her greeting, she neither expected nor received any response. On the following Saturday she purchased another parcel of food. As she placed the parcel at his side, the stranger lifted his face, looked at her for a long moment and said quietly: "Thank you!" then turned his face back to the water. Laura smiled and walked home, pleased with herself.

She worried what would happen to him in the winter. Maybe Peter could try and talk to him on his next leave. She knew the stranger had a voice, he must also have a name.

* * *

Janus and Daniel, the thirteen year old orphan living at the mission, were sweeping out the dormitories. A strange kind of resolution had been going round and round in Janus's head since he'd woken this morning.

"I'm going to have a bath," he said in a firm voice. Daniel stopped sweeping and stared at him, took in the ragged clothes and stubble on his face, and recovered his wits.

"Yes, sir!" he shouted, dropped the broom and rushed out of the room. Janus could hear the boy's boots hurrying along the lino in the corridor. He wondered where he'd gone to in such a hurry and carried on sweeping. The footsteps sounded again and Daniel, a big grin on his face, called out, "Your bath is ready, Janus. Come on!"

Dazed, the man followed the boy down the corridor and into the bathroom. Steam was rising, obscuring the mirror and window panes.

"I found a new bar of soap for you. Don't tell Sister Mary, though. She'll flay me alive," Daniel said, grinning cheekily.

"Thanks, Daniel. I won't tell," Janus promised as the boy left the bathroom, closing the door. The man locked the door and undressed, then stepped into the steaming water. He contemplated the long handled stiff brush for a moment.

Janus wallowed in hot water, scrubbed away dirt and grief and misery, and when he had done, he lay back to think of the beautiful 'She'. His mind conjured up a string of names that would fit the image. Long forgotten feelings flooded into his soul. He was warm and alive, surfacing from the depths of an icy lake.

With a sudden burst of curiosity, Janus left the bath and wiped away the steam on the mirror. He stared at a face he remembered. That of his father. A thin face topped by wet, silver hair. He gazed intently at the reflection and saw that the hand running through his hair was his own, but couldn't recall when his hair had turned to snow. Maybe he'd remember one day? Right now, he was grateful that the noises in his head were receding a little each day, leaving room for other thoughts to travel around in his mind.

Janus dried himself, combed his thick hair and tidied the bathroom. The clothes he had discarded suddenly seemed offensive to him. How long had he been wearing them, he wondered? He put on trousers and vest, walked along the corridor to the dormitories and his locker, where he chose from the items given to him by the 'She'. Whoever had had them before must be about his height. The clothes were loose, but then, he was very thin. The boots fitted snugly around socks without holes in them.

The boy Daniel had followed him and stood open-mouthed, astonished at the transformation. The man in front of him looked tall and dignified, a man on the threshold of a new life. Janus placed his hands on the boy's shoulders saying, "Thank you, Daniel. For being my friend. I think, you've just saved my life with that bath," and a huge smile spread over the face of the boy. Janus pointed at the heap of clothing on the floor. "Burn them, Daniel. I won't need them anymore."

"Yes, sir," the boy said. "You look grand, Janus. A real gentleman."

In the evening, the astonished crowd in the Tavern stopped their conversation as he walked in.

"Who did you murder for those togs, Janus?" someone called to him.

"Have you found yourself a rich mama?" asked another.

"Did you rob the store in town?" called someone else. And Lotti, the new barmaid looked at him with something else but pity in her eyes, as he walked tall and straight to his usual table. There were still voices in his head, but he listened to the heated debates about growing fanaticism, political ideology and let more thoughts come in. What was the new order they were all talking about? He had a lot to learn.

Lotti took the beer Nell, the landlady, had just pulled for Janus. "Doesn't he look handsome, Nell?" she asked the vivacious, well-built woman behind the bar.

"He's a fine looking man, Lotti," she agreed. "Maybe now he'll start to get his brain working again. Don't lose your head, girl. He's not for the likes of you," Nell remarked kindly.

"Thanks, Lotti," Janus said politely, when she placed his beer in front of him and all she could do was stare at him in surprise.

"That's alright, Janus," she replied, wishing he would talk some more, as she liked the sound of his voice, deep and mellow. But he remained quiet, enigmatic, listening intently and drinking in knowledge he had not absorbed for four years.

* * *

Peter came home for three whole weeks. He asked what had happened to his boots and Laura told him about the stranger, mentioned that he'd be wearing his clothes. "I don't mind about the clothes or the boots, mum. You shouldn't get involved with men that sit on a bench by the river all day. It's dangerous. Hasn't he any work to go to?"

"You're not here long enough to see what is happening in this country," Laura had reminded her son, "and I'm not getting involved. That man's suffering inside. If your father had come back, he could have been like him. The Karitas and Red Cross tell me there are thousands like him. Nobody knows what to do with them. They're so damaged they can't get work, if there was work to be had!" determined to make her son understand. "I can't leave him there!"

"Knowing you, you'll think of something. Just don't give him my leather things," Peter told his mother.

Laura looked at him, pleading: "Go and talk to him, Peter. Find out who he is and if he's got a family, please. This afternoon!"

"Sorry, I'm going to the match!" then looked at her disappointed face, a note of resignation in his voice. "OK, mum. I won't stay on after, I'll be back at four." and gave her an affectionate hug. "When you want something, you certainly know how to appeal to a man's better nature. I'll try!" Peter was rewarded with a dazzling smile, a hug and a kiss.

"You can give him the food this afternoon!" Laura said.

* * *

It had been very late when Laura heard footsteps coming up the stairs. She opened the door and saw Peter holding up the stranger, almost too drunk to walk.

"Tell you later. I'll have some black coffee, mum!" He guided his companion towards his bedroom, coming out with pyjamas and a pillow, and flopped onto the sofa. Peter said, "He's out like a light. I'll sleep on here tonight."

23

"What happened?" asked Laura, handing him a coffee.

"I found him on the seat, gave him the food and introduced myself. He never said anything, so I just sat there and talked about dad. Suddenly he said his name was Janus. I asked if he'd like to go for a drink, which he must have considered for some ten minutes or so, then he packed the food into his haversack and said 'yes'. He got up and I just followed him!"

"Where did you go!" asked Laura.

"To some dubious tavern at the waterfront. Not very smart, but the natives were friendly. He seemed to be well known there. The barmaid said he was 'touched' and only drank two beers all night. She reckons he's afraid to get drunk. Tonight he did and he talked a lot. There were some strange people in there. Seemed very interested in what Janus had to say. They watched him all the time. Made me feel uncomfortable, as if they waited for him to say something he shouldn't. Funny crowd. I took him to the mission where he sleeps, but they wouldn't have him in that condition, so I brought him home. Sorry, mum, hope he's not going to be any trouble?"

"Well, at least we know his name and where he goes."

Peter looked at his mother in horror. "I hope you're not thinking of looking for him in THAT place, mum. You keep away from there, do you hear?" he insisted.

"Alright. I'm not likely to go there, son. Did he say anything else?"

"Oh, yes. His parents came to live in Cologne before the war. Janus worked on the railway, like his father, and volunteered for the Army in 1914. After his parents died, his younger brother joined him at the front. The boy got hit by a shell just before the war finished. Janus went berserk, he wouldn't let go of the pieces. They discharged him last year. He likes to sit by the river. Says it's peaceful there!" Peter gave his mother a strange look, then carried on: "He likes you. Calls you his beautiful lady. Everybody was quite agog, until I explained you were my mother. They probably think you're some old do-gooder, doling out charity!"

Laura smiled at her son. "Maybe he is looking for a mother?"

Peter, an amused expression on his face, told Laura. "Janus is a man, he doesn't think of you as a mother, believe me!"

A puzzled frown appeared on Laura's forehead. "But I haven't exchanged more than the time of day with him in the past months."

Peter laughed "Mum. You don't have to talk to a man to make him fall in love with you. They just do. You ought to get married. It's such a waste of a beautiful woman!"

"Peter! You're being silly!" A faint blush appeared on her cheeks.

* * *

The sun was warm on his face when Janus opened his eyes and quickly closed them again. The light was too bright and his head was hurting. He felt uneasy, the place was too quiet. This couldn't be the mission. Tentatively, he opened his eyes again, blinking several times. He was in a room that belonged to a man. It was big, the bed was big and he wondered how he had got here. Concentrating hard, he remembered that a nice looking young man had brought him food yesterday afternoon. He'd said his name was Peter and that his mother couldn't come. The boy had talked about his father who got himself killed in that same bloody war that messed up his head, and he understood now why his beautiful Lady had shown so much compassion, why she appeared lonely.

The boy, sunburned from working in far away places, hadn't mentioned anything about him wearing his clothes. They had gone to the Tavern, where the son of his Lady looked out of place. He remembered drinking with the boy called Peter because he liked him and they had a lot to talk about. By the feel of the explosions going on in his head, he must've drunk a lot more than the usual two pints he allowed himself, because he couldn't remember anything after that. Was his Lady here? What would she think of him? Janus sat up in Peter's bed and wondered what to do next, when the boy came in, looking fresh and grinning all over his face.

"Good morning, Janus. Brought you some coffee." Janus drank it greedily, hoping it would make his head feel better. "The bathroom is next door, you'll find all you need in there. Mum left you a clean shirt on the basket," Peter said cheerfully. "Breakfast'll be ready when you are," and left him.

The face looking back from the mirror didn't seem any different from yesterday, only the eyes looked troubled. He would meet her here, have breakfast and talk...

Laura was in the kitchen and smiled at him as he stood in the doorway. "Come and have breakfast, Janus. Sit over there," pointing to the benchseat where Peter was reading the paper.

"Thank you. I'm sorry for making a nuisance of myself. Please forgive me, Mrs..."

"Laura Sogar. You and my son seemed to get along fine," she said graciously. "You're not a nuisance at all. It's nice to have you."

Janus sat down, watching the slim figure of his Lady pouring the coffee.

"How's the head, Janus?" Peter asked, winking at him.

"Fine," Janus lied, knowing he had the biggest hangover in the world. "It's fine."

So her name was Laura. She didn't look much older than her son and he felt very strange listening to the lilting sound of her voice.

"How would you like to live at Rema House, Janus? There are two empty rooms at the back. It's the old coach house. You could make them into your home, look after the boiler and the garden, and do the usual things that need doing to a property."

All he could say was, "Yes, I'd like that," feeling as tongue-tied as a silly school boy.

* * *

Janus moved in. He was polite, worked well and did more jobs than was expected of him, but kept himself to himself. Peter taught him to ride the motorbike and was the only one Janus was at ease with, even laughing heartily at his tales from abroad. At any other time, the only emotion that showed in his eyes was at the sight of Laura. He was in love, completely, and he knew he would love her for the rest of his life.

And sometimes, during the next two years, when the longing for her drove him to despair, he'd accept Lotti's invitation and went up to the attic, where she took him to her bed and he pretended to make love to Laura. Lotti never minded, never asked questions. She was just pleased to have him for a while and make him happy.

But Janus always came home a little after midnight to watch the light go out in the bedroom on the second floor.

Chapter 5

The last Friday in April 1924 marked a new beginning. The removal van arrived about midday; so did Janus on the motorbike. Curtains twitched and people took to visiting friends in Annsberg Road. They made unnecessary trips to Walter's shop at the end of the road until the men had emptied the van and left. The motorbike was wheeled up the side of the house; it and the man disappeared into the door below the pigeon loft. The stranger took in boxes and suitcases, but did not leave. Dettingen began to speculate where he slept and nudged each other. Wives informed their husbands.

It was Father Michael's poker night, the speculation went on there as well. He did not have his mind on the cards and lost heavily that night. Feelings he had never known and could not put a name to tormented him.

* * *

Laura was pleased with the house. All she had to do was unpack and arrange Peter's room. Janus seemed to be happy in his new quarters. He took the spare key to the kitchen door, volunteered to attend to the cooking range in the mornings and make his own breakfast until he got organised. They had only brought the best of the furniture from the apartment at Rema house and most of it was to go into the large back bedroom on the first floor to make Peter feel at home. The surplus furnished the attic rooms. Laura was happy with the two bedrooms at the front of the house, only changing Mara's flock mattress for her own softer one. Her writing desk fitted neatly in a corner of the smaller room. She knew she had come home...

On sunday morning she woke with a start. "What on earth?" Laura muttered. The sound of church bells seemed to be everywhere and his blue eyes and gentle smile went round and round in her head. "Blast him and his bells!" Was this what it was going to be every Sunday? Next week she'd keep the windows shut and close the folding shutters inside. The bells had sounded so pleasant at Rema house, but they had been a long way off...

Janus had insisted on bringing the pot-bellied stove he had used at Rema house. The long black enamelled pipe went up and out of the wall in the loft, smoke curled lazily away over the meadow at the back. He could use the stove to keep the copper kettle boiling, or simmer a thick stew in the heavy cooking pot. Janus liked order. The iron stove gleamed like pewter. No squalor for him. He'd seen enough of that...

Laura had been his inspiration. She liked nice things around her. He'd seen it at the other house and it hadn't taken her long to make this one feel as if she'd lived here for years. Now it was his turn to show her what he'd done to his place. Maybe later they could talk about making themselves independent with a market garden. Times were not going to be easy and just now they all lived in a fool's paradise. He would ask her to marry him soon. He could wait for her to grow to love him. Hadn't he waited two years already?

Janus, sitting on the bed, his face softened by a smile that gave the nicely defined mouth a sensuous look, glanced at the alarm clock on the bedside table. Collecting together the many pages, covered with his neat handwriting, he placed them into the old suitcase Laura had given him two years ago, then locked and pushed it under the bed. Now that he had finished the room, he would have to devote some time to this business. Already he had missed several meetings and would have to check all this information again, just to make quite sure they hadn't got the wrong people. He really didn't like all the indiscriminate secret persecution going on and would have to insist on more evidence. He had promised THEM he would co-operate and make neat files. It took longer now to get to the tavern on the bicycle and the path along the stream was convenient. He could miss out the village altogether and the side gate gave him access to his room, without having to go through the house. He smoothed down his fine hair in the mirror, stared for a moment at his reflection, murmuring. 'There'll be a future for me, one way or another...'

He heard Laura call from below and as he left the bedroom, he looked round once more to make sure all was in order. Laura climbed the few steps and knocked on the open door. Janus tried hard to be frivolous and made a bow. "Welcome to my home." She was never quite sure if the slight accent was of working class dialect or a legacy of his early years near the Polish border. Wherever it came from, it was pleasant.

"Thank you, Janus," Laura said with equal formality, then grinned at him, eyes full of amusement. "A present for you." She handed over a parcel. "Four pairs of curtains, a tablecloth and two covers for your chairs. All matching and not too bright, I hope!"

Janus unwrapped the package and looked pleased as he touched the yellow and brown striped linen. "Thanks, they are nice. Did you make them?" he asked.

"Naturally. What do you think sewing machines are for?" she said, gazing around the room. "You've worked hard, made it homely!" She admired the stained floorboards and gleaming windows. A large rush mat was in front of the stove, which stood on red quarry tiles. A table with two chairs matched the newly stained shelf arrangement, which was filled with an assortment of books and ornaments. Laura pushed the rocking chair and made it sway. "Can I try it?" Janus nodded his head and smiled as she rocked back and forth.

I never knew he read any books, she thought, he had never invited anybody to his room at Rema House. "I like this chair. So restful!" said Laura and glanced at the closed door of the bedroom, but Janus did not extend an invitation for her to go and see. Well, a man's entitled to his privacy, she conceded. "It's all very nice. You could have moved into the attic, you know!"

Janus stood by the stove and lit a small pipe. The pleasant aroma of sweet tobacco smoke mingled with the lingering residual odour of woodstain. He looked at Laura for a moment and she saw a strange expression in his eyes. He turned away and looked out of the open window. "I'm comfortable here, thank you."

Laura noticed the dark brown belt hanging behind the stove. The handle of a heavy revolver peeked out from the holster. She suddenly felt uncomfortable. "Janus!" Laura addressed the broad back, muscular now from working outdoors for the last two years at Rema house. "Why do you need a gun?"

He turned round, but did not answer immediately as if he seemed to search for a suitable explanation. Then said simply, "I promised Peter I'd protect you."

"Protect me from what?" queried Laura, aware that his eyes had taken on a curious intensity.

"Anything!" he answered.

"That's very kind of you, Janus. I just hope you're not going to shoot any visitors that come calling?" Laura said jokingly.

29

Janus saw nothing funny in her question. "It depends on what they want."
Laura, puzzled at his reply, shook her head. "Be careful with that. I think
you need a licence." she told him.

For the first time she had known him, Janus' face distorted with fury and
his normally pleasant voice was raised in anger. "Why? I didn't need one in
1914 when they taught me to kill the enemy and I don't need one now." He
stormed out of the door, down the steps and disappeared into the garden.
Laura stared after him.

The younger women of the neighbouring homes called on Laura. She was
glad of their company. She missed work and her friends, but that was
compensated for by the task of getting the garden ready for planting. In the
evenings Laura experimented with baking in the huge oven. Janus always
gave his verdict when they had coffee or an evening meal in the kitchen.
She usually talked, and he would nod or make other suggestions. She
missed Peter. He could always make him laugh.

Today, Katrin, Annie and Erika from next door had come with a
proposition. Katrin, in her mid-thirties, plump and full of fun, tucked into
Laura's creme torte. "We know you're not a Catholic," she said between
mouthfuls, "but wondered if you'd like to come and join us at the Women's
Institute? Try it, Laura."

Erika Behrens, the wife of Walter, who owned the butcher shop at the top
of the road, was a puzzle to Laura. Slim and vivacious, her frivolity hid
something. Dressed in the latest fashions, the alert blue eyes held
intelligence combined with curiosity. She made Laura feel as if she was
assessing, evaluating all that was said. She liked Erika. There was an
undercurrent about her which might be interesting. Peter had discreetly
hinted that Freddy and Erika were lovers, going back a long time, but had
said no more.

Erika chuckled. "You'll meet our delicious Father Michael. He's
very open minded and approves of most of our madcap schemes to raise
funds for church and the parish. He joins in enthusiastically. We're all in
love with him. Even Annie fantasises about him. Don't you, Annie?" Erika
crossed one slim leg over the other, helped herself to another piece of torte
and looked expectantly at Annie.

Annie, painfully thin, wore voluptuous dresses belted at the waist. Laura
thought there might possibly be more clothes on Annie than there was body

underneath. They all seemed cunningly designed so as to give her the appearance of more weight. Still pretty with her glossy black hair and soft doe-like eyes, she had a nice mouth and teeth. The 'O' coming from the pursed lips shattered the sudden silence in the dining room while the three women waited expectantly.

"Well!" said Annie, slow and deliberate, her brown eyes rolled upwards. "That man gives me shivers up and down my spine."

"I'll bet," mumbled Erika.

"Be quiet, Erika. Every minute that's not taken up with domestic bilge is devoted to that beautiful angel of God. And what I'd like to do to him," Annie moaned and Katrin spluttered, her mouth full of cake.

Erika looked at Laura, who wasn't quite sure what to make of Annie, and said, "Our delectable Father is an improvement on that silent lodger you have living out there. Not much stimulating conversation coming from him. What does he do in the evenings?" winking at Laura, who blushed, and had the distinct feeling that Erika was probing beyond mere curiosity. Three faces looked expectantly at Laura to answer the question.

"Janus works very hard and in return he's got a roof over his head. Peter pays him a wage. There's nothing else." which left her companions smirking at each other. Erika patted her fair hair, a wicked look in her eyes.

"It'll be interesting to see if we can persuade him to talk!" her eyes rested on Laura. "Silent men fascinate me. They have secrets!" Laura again had the impression that she was under scrutiny.

Four days later a letter arrived from Father Michael, in strong masculine handwriting. He welcomed Laura to Dettingen, and said the ladies of the parish had expressed a wish that she was to be invited to their various activities, which pleased him and showed a high degree of community spirit. He had no objections if she wished to attend his church and receive the sacrament, excusing her from the obligatory confessional, in view of her own religious beliefs. He hoped to see her at the service at Whitsun, signed, Father Michael Schiller.

Laura smiled, contemplating his letter. Michael Schiller. The name suited him and the image of his thin face and blue eyes invaded her mind again. Uncomfortable, disturbing. She must not forget to call him 'Father'. Laura intended to go to church at Whitsun, if for no other reason than to show willing to participate. She'd convinced herself the priest had nothing to do with anything.

In the next few days the cherry, apple and pear trees changed their wardrobe. The small fruit trees dotted about the awakening garden, sported a new coat of tender leaves, decorated with fragrant blossoms. The main orchard at the top, bordering onto meadow and stream, formed a canopy of pink and white. Even Janus became more animated and looked duly impressed by this splendour of nature as they walked, wondering what kind of bounty would spring forth in due course.

"What will you do with it all? There's going to be too much for your own use!" Janus asked while he contemplated the huge cherry trees. "They alone could bring in several hundredweight!"

Laura's eyes wandered dreamily into the blossom laden branches, a soft smile on her lips, unaware that Janus was watching her, love and hunger mirrored in his eyes, his mouth curved into a gentle mould, momentarily lost in his own thoughts. "It's so beautiful right now I don't want to think about it. I'll ask what the Schumann's did with it. My neighbours should know!" she said.

"You won't have to go to the market anymore. Come to think of it, you can sell to them instead," Janus remarked.

"What a marvellous idea, Janus. You're going to make a good business man," Laura grinned at him. "And make us both rich."

"Suits me fine!" and Janus looked happy.

As he watched Laura inspect the large strawberry bed, Janus resolved to toil and sweat. He'd make his future here instead of the Party. Laura would love him in time.

Whitsun. The day promised to be warm and sunny. Laura had woken long before the church bells started to ring out for the first service at 8:00 am. A few parishioners left their homes in Annsberg Road, their footsteps forlorn in the stillness of morning.

Laura sat up in the big bed and watched the gentle swaying of the long lace curtains, the sunlight making patterns on the wall. She could see her reflection in the long mirror of the huge wardrobe, and hanging on one of the doors was her new suit. She had fallen in love with the colour. A slim skirt and jacket in leaf green, a cream silk blouse, buttoned to the neck and the pretty matching hat. The dressmaker had sewn a silk cream rose to pin onto the hat. She had tried it on and liked it enough to spend a small fortune, adding new shoes and bag. From what she'd heard, the 10:00 am service was one grand fashion parade and she was not going to look like a frump.

She got out of bed and stood by the window, listening to the bells. Father Michael certainly did not have time to lie in bed on Sundays. Did he like getting up early? When did he make up for lost sleep? By all accounts he was a very busy priest indeed.

As Laura went down to the kitchen she noticed Janus had already had breakfast and left the coffee pot half full on the stove, still hot and smelling delicious. She tucked into rolls and honey, filled with glee at the idea that her friends could not eat until after the service. She really did not think that being a Catholic was at all beneficial to one's health, especially if there was a danger of fainting from hunger in a packed church. What did they do with someone if that happened?

Laura filled a large jug with hot water and took it back to the bedroom, finished her ablutions and sat on the bed to brush her hair. Today it did not want to lie flat and she felt a strange excitement as she dressed in new clothes. It had been a long time since she had made this much of an effort...

As she stared at her reflection, the slim figure in the pale green suit looked more like thirty, not forty one years old, with a son of twenty two. Her face had a healthy colour from hours spent outdoors. She secured the jaunty hat with a pretty pin and was pleased, then filled the new handbag with handkerchief, prayer book and loose change. On her way downstairs she heard Janus tinkering with the motorbike outside on the patio and had a sudden impish desire to see his face. Laura stepped out of the kitchen door.

"Do I look alright, Janus? They're all dressing up today."

Straightening up from bending over the bike, Janus stared, then his eyes travelled from hat to shoes and back to her face. She saw again that strange expression she'd noticed once before.

He only said, "You look fine, Laura," and turned back to the motorbike. She stood still for a moment. It was the first time he'd called her by her name.

Katrin Bulger was with her two children. Eight year old Kurt, a good looking blonde boy, and pretty, dark haired Tonia, who would be the spitting image of her mother in time. Plump, and already plagued with Katrin's passion for cream cakes.

They had just left number 7 across from Laura's. Seeing her friend, Katrin waited, open mouthed.

"Jesus, Maria an' Josef!" she exclaimed. "Laura, you really shouldn't do that to your friends!" Katrin wailed.

Erika Behrens and her daughter Chrissy, who had collected Annie at number 4, also stared at Laura.

Erika muttered, "You sneaky girl. Where did you get that suit and hat?"

Laura was pleased and replied, "In town. You all look wonderful, too!"

The bells began to peal at precisely 9:45. Katrin, pacified, patted her blue linen suit covering her ample figure. Annie's thin figure was draped in a light, cream coat. Despite eating like a horse, she never got fat, and Heini, her tubby husband, was found many times gazing wistfully at the well-endowed Katrin. Being good natured, he endured a great deal of leg-pulling. Erika, dressed in a deep pink suit and hat, knew she looked stunning, but still threw a somewhat envious glance at Laura. The green boater hat was perfect, wisps of curls escaping from under the brim.

Erika and Chrissy led the way to the top of the road and Laura gasped.

"Is everybody going to church?"

Her companions laughed. "Today they are. It'll be packed," Katrin said.

The whole village population seemed to be on the move. The men obligingly stood in the aisles, leaving pews free for the women and children. Erika led them to a row in the middle, Tonia, Chrissy and Kurt joining the children in the front rows.

Unfamiliar with the procedure of a Catholic Mass, Laura needed to concentrate to follow what was happening. The strange odour of incense made her head buzz. She was glad she'd had breakfast. She could see Father Michael, in white and gold surplice, a four cornered hat perched on top of his head and wondered how it stayed there. Surely they didn't use hat pins?

He walked back and forth, slowly, unhurried, performing rituals at the altar. The congregation stood, knelt, sang, prayed and crossed themselves frequently. The young chaplain seemed to be as busy as the priest, and Laura felt alien. She almost wished she hadn't come, the sight of Father Michael sent shock waves through her body. 'Forget it... Concentrate... Don't make a fool of yourself...' echoed around in her head.

Suddenly, children began to move towards the altar rail in an orderly procession, kneeling in a row. The priest placed the sacrament on each tongue exposed in the upturned faces, their eyes closed. The girls curtsied, the boys bowed and left, the next line kneeling down. And Father Michael with his chaplain would start over again. How could he face so many open mouths with their tongues sticking out?

Laura, her knees sore from kneeling for so long, let her eyes wander to the statues and ornaments on each side of the altar. This was splendour she had not encountered in village churches before. And the lavish gold thread in his robe did seem excessive. Perhaps that was why they became priests? Black cassock and white lace surplice.

The row in front of her emptied to take its place behind the kneeling recipients at the altar rail. Erika nudged Laura to follow her up the centre aisle. Laura's head was full of thoughts she ought not to have, but as hard as she tried, they could not be banished. The murmuring of the chaplain and the priest was coming nearer. There was still time to get up and leave, Laura thought in desperation.

Father Michael stood in front of her, said something she did not catch and held up the thin white wafer. Laura lifted her face, looked at him and lifted her two hands palms upwards to receive the offering. Erika watched Father Michael hesitate, unsure of what to do. For an instant he stared at Laura, then gently placed the sacrament into her hands, repeating the words he knew by heart. Erika could not know that today Father Michael said them out of habit, his mind only conscious of the upturned face, grey eyes soft as the early morning mist, the mouth promising something he had no knowledge of, conscious of the beating of his heart and the effort not to betray himself.

Moving on, he was aware that Laura rose, bowed to the altar and left, her place taken by someone else.

He would see her after the service.

Laura knew the service was coming to an end. She tried to listen to Father Michael's sermon, but heard only the voice. A pleasant resonant sound, echoing around the church. The congregation listened in silence. Attentively. Adoringly. 'Oh God... what am I going to do?... I wish I had never come here... I love him... even more than Jack... and what does Michael Schiller feel?... probably nothing... and I can't leave now...

At last, the Lord's Prayer and then a shuffling of feet as the children walked two by two towards the double door to wait for Father Michael, before dispersing onto the village green next to the church.

Laura whispered to Erika that she was not used to the incense and that she didn't feel well. She left the pew and gently pushed through the crowd towards a side entrance, hoping to find her way home without having to go to the front of the church to meet him.

Father Michael Schiller, in plain black cassock, handsome and elegant, exchanged niceties with his flock at the door of the church, hoped no-one was aware of the intense disappointment he felt when Laura was not with her friends. He complimented the ladies on brightening up the day with their new spring wardrobe, but didn't see the pretty green hat with the cream rose anywhere. Father Michael's expectations of a happy Whitsun day took a decisive downward turn and left him strangely uncivil to chaplain Dominik

Stumbling out of the side door, Laura found herself in a garden. She blindly followed its curved lines and stood, horrified, before the stone walled house of Father Michael. She hurried to the gravel path between the two properties across the road that would lead her home. Her head was aching. She met no-one and was grateful.

Almost wrenching the hat and suit from her body, Laura bathed her face in the wash basin and stared at her reflection in the mirror above. The bedroom, the whole house, took on an oppressive silence. For a moment she imagined the priest's face in the mirror, looking at her as he had done earlier when their eyes met, the thin white wafer between them. Was he suffering this torment? Perhaps that fear she had seen the first time they met was real? She hadn't imagined it. He had been afraid and to be afraid he must've made some strange discovery. In the church she knew that he had been disturbed by her presence.

Her mind in turmoil, she lay down on the cool sheet. Her body ached. Two rivulets of tears left their marks on the pillow. Laura tried desperately to find the answer as to why she should have fallen in love with this unattainable man. And why she couldn't feel the same for Janus. Had her love for Jack been as deep as what she felt for Michael Schiller?

She had loved Jack, his impulsive, generous nature and understood his need to leave them alone for months. When he came home, every day was Christmas. She had understood his futile gesture to join the war, thinking he and his friends were indestructible. They didn't live like ordinary mortals, constantly exploring, surrounded by danger.

Had he ever been unfaithful to her? She had never asked that question, although in the last ten years it had crossed her mind sometimes. She couldn't be sure and would never know. They had enjoyed each other like lovers that met now and then, but the intimate details of real life didn't touch them.

Had she really known the husband of thirteen years? Laura felt she knew more about the priest than she had about Jack. He was part of everybody's life here, every day, not just Sundays.

She had stayed alone, untouched, untroubled by feelings until now. The priest had held her hand briefly at their first meeting, but it had been enough, and she knew he too experienced something he didn't understand. Something they would never be able to share. 'Forget him... He'll never be yours...'

Chapter 6

It was the end of June when Peter came home. After a boisterous welcome, they retreated to the kitchen for coffee and she listened to his latest exploits on the dark Continent. He made her laugh and worry about his total disregard for danger. Just like Jack, Laura thought, unconcerned, leading a charmed life and enjoying every minute of it. He was getting more like his father every year. A loveable stranger, stopping for a brief moment at a familiar place to say Hello and move on. She was pleased to hear him say, "I like it here, mum. It's nice to come home," and then he left her to find Janus.

She could hear them talking, heard Janus laughing and wondered what he looked like when he was happy. Peter was the only one that could perform this miracle, although everyone tried to make the quiet, enigmatic man part of the community. With her he was polite, surprisingly eloquent when talking about work and things to be done. Otherwise he kept everyone at a distance. Sometimes she wondered if he was afraid of her. They would work in the garden, but he'd be busy at the other end. She was sure he arranged it deliberately. Many times she'd seen him leaning on the spade or hoe, watching her. She never knew what he was thinking or felt. He was as much of a mystery now, than when she had first met him over two years ago. It was good to hear him laugh, though. A very pleasant sound. She must make more of an effort to make him feel at home here. Home...

Peter filled it with his presence while he was on leave. After that, it would be empty again except for Janus and he never ventured beyond the kitchen. And her thoughts focussed again on Michael Schiller, and last week...

The Women's Guild had made her welcome. They met one afternoon a week and she enjoyed their company. Plans for the festival of St. Quirinus convent and the church were well in hand. Laura contributed some excellent ideas for the exhibition of the sisters work on display and for sale. Father Michael always called in for a cup of coffee and someone's delicious cream cake, but she made sure that she stayed close to Erika and Katrin. Laura had been surprised when the sisters joined them and admired the artistic gifts they contributed to the event in August. She found them as varied and funny as any other group of women. Last week they'd had their coffee and it was her turn to wash up. She'd collected the cups and saucers, stacked the plates on trays and found him next to her.

"I'll take that. It looks heavy," Father Michael said.

She had felt very small as she followed him into the kitchen, where he deposited the tray on the draining board. He had looked at her for some time and she'd seen desperation in his eyes, had heard the softly spoken, "I hope you are well, Laura," before he left through the side door. She had stood trembling, near tears, cursing the futility of her love for this handsome man in the black cassock, which denied him the touch of a woman's hand.

Erika had followed, put her arm about Laura's shoulder and silently led her to a chair in the corner. How much did Erika know?... Why did she come into the kitchen at all?... She was as much of a mystery to Laura as Janus, both of them hiding behind a facade...

"Are you going to fill that pot or stand there all day dreaming, mum?" Peter asked, standing in the doorway. She had not noticed him passing the window. "Janus has settled in very well," he told his mother. "His place looks nice and the garden is coming on. He told me you work hard. Don't over-do it, mum, it's not woman's work." He settled himself on the bench seat, a little boys expression on his handsome face. " Can I have a party on Saturday? Men only. It's the football crowd and my work mates. I'll invite Martin and Father Michael, of course. He'll enjoy that."

Laura stared at him, panic invading her brain, electrifying every nerve in her body and the coffee pot slipped out of her fingers into the sink.

* * *

On Saturday Erika and Katrin helped to prepare the food and the men put up the beer tent on the lawn next to the summerhouse. By late afternoon it was stocked high with crates of beer, wine and whisky. Peter felt generous and left a few bottles for the women in the kitchen. In the summer house, long trestle tables groaned under the weight of food. Peter was pleased and hugged Laura

"There's enough to feed an army, mum. Thanks."

He grinned at her and retreated again to the tent, where Janus was busy stacking glasses on the makeshift bar. She looked at her watch. She'd have an hour to get ready before taking the muslin covers off the food.

"I've got to get dressed, Peter," she called, but heard only a muffled sound from inside the tent. As she stepped out of the shady interior into the evening sun, she saw Janus leaning against the upright of the tent, pipe smoke gently curling upwards towards the clear sky. He looked nice, she noticed, dressed in a new summer shirt and light trousers. He saw her, waved and watched her walk up the path and into the kitchen, love plainly visible in the brown eyes.

* * *

Laura collected hot water from the stove and wished she could go into the wash house and turn on the showerhead. It would cool her down. Instead she sponged face and body in her bedroom, desperately wishing they'd had a bathroom. She still felt hot. Nerves, she told herself...

She could hear the sound of men's voices, loud and cheerful, laughing. Peter's friends were already in high spirits. Was Michael Schiller among them? No, it would be too early for him. Laura slipped the navy dress over her head and arranged the white organza trimming around the 'V' neckline. The cut of the fabric clung to the slender figure, the hemline finished just above the calf. She smiled as she saw her slim legs and remembered the ankle length skirts and dresses she'd worn when she met Jack, so long ago. Times had changed drastically since the war. Hemlines went up, she thought, and the value of money goes down. The papers were filled with doom and gloom and ugly things were happening in Berlin and the South, so Freddy's newspaper kept telling them. It was all so far away...

The pendant of burnished gold Jack had brought from Egypt filled the soft hollow at the low neck line, exposing a tantalizing glimpse of the creamy curves of her breasts. Maybe it was too low? Why had she let Erika persuade her to buy that dress? There had been many outfits more befitting her age, elegant, dignified, but Erika had insisted. Well, she liked it too. Oh, what the hell... Why should she feel guilty? She wasn't in her dotage yet... Although she wondered about that sometimes... Would Michael notice?...

40

Laura defiantly pulled at the unruly curls that framed the soft contour of her face. Stockings, lacquered pumps with the straps crossing over the instep, a dab of cologne on neck and wrists and a last look in the mirror. For a moment she stared at her reflection, a wistful expression in the grey eyes. Of sadness, a longing for love. She picked up the handkerchief, tucked it into her pocket, walked out and firmly closed the door. The sitting room was bathed in the last of the evening sun and the floor length lace curtains on both windows fluttered gently. Laura paused by the window, saw Father Michael as he crossed the road and enter the side gate to the garden. Her heart felt like some foolish young girl's. Damn Michael Schiller... Why did he have to be a Priest?... And why did he have to be here tonight?... Laura wished Erika wasn't with Freddy... She would have to face him...

Before going into the garden Laura paused and watched men at play. The hearty laughter told her that risque stories were being told. Peter and Martin, his Boss, stood with Father Michael. How different he looked in the company of men, at ease and relaxed. His thin face creased as he laughed, the soft breeze ruffling the wavy brown hair. His cassock set him apart and yet he was one of them. Janus too looked happy and laughed at something Jochen said to him.

There was only one way to get to the summer house. She took a deep breath and walked down the slope towards them. All eyes fastened on her and she felt the silence. Then it was shattered by the greetings of men she hadn't seen in a long time. She found herself in Martin's arms, his face alight with pleasure.

"Laura, you look wonderful. Haven't aged one bit," Martin said, as he looked her up and down. "Gardening seems to suit you."

Then Robert and 'Copper' took their turn, Copper's hair sprinkled liberally with grey now. The only three left that had known Jack. Both talking at once as they hugged and kissed her. She shook hands with the younger men that now worked with her son, responded to genial voices, enquiring, complimenting and presently she excused herself, pointing to the summer house. "Food's in there. I'll just take the covers off."

Laura moved away and noticed Janus and Father Michael standing at the entrance of the tent and wondered what they'd been talking about. Both holding a glass of beer, Janus nursing his pipe, Father Michael's slim fingers held a long cigarillo. She knew he smoked, it seemed fitting somehow. She could smell the faint aroma and found it pleasant. Laura smiled, waved and quickly entered the large room, it's windows wide open. She was relieved to hear the men resume their noisy conversation as she removed the covers from the bowls and platters. The voice startled her.

"Good evening, Laura. Can I help?" Father Michael enquired.

"No," she said sharply, then spoke more softly. "No, thank you. I'll manage," trying not to look at him.

He picked up a bottle from behind the door and presented it to her. "A thank you for the party."

His presence made her head buzz, her heartbeat accelerated and her stomach was doing strange things. She took the bottle, heard someone stutter, "Thank you. That's very thoughtful," and realized it was herself.

The noise faded and they stood in a circle of silence. There are eighteen people out there, Laura thought, but we are alone. She stared at him and saw his eyes wander from her face to the curve at the deep neck line, linger there, then travel over her body and back to her face. There was hunger in his eyes.

"You are very beautiful," he said, the clear resonant voice hoarse as if something was choking him. In a moment of defiance, Father Michael raised his hand to touch her face, then let it drop again in a gesture of futility. The desire in his eyes made them appear as dark as the night and told her all he dare not put into words. Not yet. "I'd better go before I make a fool of myself," the Priest said, too abruptly. "Good night, Laura," and left to join the others and the room filled again with the noise of men talking.

Laura pressed the bottle to her, afraid she might drop it. She'd seen desire in his eyes, knew he wanted her and felt hot and uncomfortable with her own longing, shocked at the pleasure it gave to her. So Priests were men after all... She stood and watched him leave the party, turn and lift his hand in a farewell gesture to her, the bottle still clutched to her breast...

Janus had felt a wave of emotion almost choke him when he saw Laura walk down the path. How beautiful she was. He had not seen her in the softly clinging dress before and envied the older men the right to embrace her. When would he have the courage to tell her that he loved her? He glanced at the Priest standing next to him. Deep in thought, a benign smile hovering about the chaste mouth. They'd exchanged greetings and made pleasant remarks. Janus remembered he too was a Catholic, except he had forgotten what God looked like during four years of hell in France. He'd managed without Him and didn't want the Priest to invite him to his church, to listen to sanctimonious sermons. Janus leant against the pole of the tent and watched the other man. Too handsome for a priest. Why wasn't he with the others? But from here he could observe the women at his leisure. He was watching Laura like a doting father might his beloved daughter. Only, this father's eyes told another story. They told of lust and desire, something a Catholic Father had no right to feel or even think about. His eyes strayed to where Laura stood, encircled by her friends. He had not seen her so happy since Peter's last leave. Then she left them, waved to him and the priest on her way to the summer house. Janus took his beer into the tent. He would go and help with the food and maybe they could talk...

He passed the window and saw them. There was no need for him to be inside the room to feel the tension between the woman and the priest. Mesmerized, he watched Father Michael's eyes travel over her face and body. And she let him. Welcomed it. There was so much hunger in the man's eyes that he almost forgot himself in his need to touch her. And she wanted him to, craved for his touch...

Janus silently retreated, shaking with fury he had not experienced for a long time. He found hatred for the Priest reach inside his body, burning his brain. His head was beginning to ache. He wasn't sure what tormented him most. The priest's naked desire or Laura's acceptance of it. How could she even think of this evil...

He slowly walked back to the tent, like someone in a trance. His glass was where he had left it. Janus tucked several bottles of beer under his arm, ducked under the flap at the back and made his way to the orchard. The big cherry tree was laden with ripe, juicy fruit. Yesterday it had given him pleasure to calculate the amount of produce they might take to the market in town. Tonight he felt none of it as he sat on the soft ground below. He was lost in that misery and despair he had known in 1922, when he walked to the river every day and waited on that empty bench for salvation...

The whole country had lain bleeding, waiting for a saviour, while the carcasses rotted and the soul festered. Each day he'd walked past the stately University and wondered what they taught them there. At night the tavern would be full, always the same crowd, noisy, antagonistic about the well-to-do on the south side of the bridge. Then strangers had come to the smoke filled tavern and it became their meeting place.

Lotti, the mousy haired buxom waitress would greet him as he made his way to the table in the corner. 'The usual coming right over, Darling,' she'd shout to him. Shabbily dressed men and strangers engaged in verbal battle.

"We want a free, united Germany!" said one of the strangers, a pin with a swastika on his lapel.

"We've been to the rallies in Munich and Berlin and he was there," said another to the attentive audience.

"He said we need all of you to make Germany free," someone shouted. All of them sporting the same pin. Janus wondered about the man who needed so many disciples. Another Jesus?... They certainly needed somebody... but all the action was so far away...

Then the beautiful Lady walked past him every day and the voices in his head began to fade a little. He was able to pay more attention to the strangers. They promised a shining future, but demanded his commitment. They said, be proud to wear the brown shirt, the black shirt, carry the banner of the new order.. They'd given him a pin to wear, except the French occupied the Rhineland and association with the fascist party was precarious.. They promised to liberate the occupied regions and return them to the Fatherland. Janus was happy about that.

"But what about the Treaty?" he'd asked one of the loud mouthed men.

"Comrade, treaties are just pieces of paper. Tear them up and they blow away in the wind, like smoke. There'll be plenty of that, I promise you, Friend."

And he thought again of his Lady. He wanted a future. To be somebody. Give her wealth, love her, hold her in his arms...

Their numbers grew, and his hopes soared upwards when he knew his Lady had no husband and he'd moved into Rema house awaiting the shining future. THEY had given him a task, trusting in his discretion. He would never be an orator, but had a neat hand. They supplied him with paper, pen and ink. The spies and informers bought information on prominent citizens, Subversives, Communists, Jews... and the files he kept on them grew.

Names...addresses... Freddy, the aristocratic 'Pegleg' who owned the town's newspaper, the priest who wrote inflammatory articles against the new party. His superior in the SA department was pleased with Janus's meticulous work. And then he'd moved to Dettingen, into the viper's nest. He had never handed in any information on the Baron Freddy or the priest. Hubert von Dettingen the Baron's older brother, already a fervent Nazi, was going to do it for him. It would be interesting to see how long the 'pegleg' could hold out. His bet was on Hubert.

It was late into the night. Janus still sat under the cherry tree, empty bottles laying on the ground beside him. He was neither drunk nor sober, trying to think, surrounded by the stillness of a warm summer night. The priest would not be a problem any more. He'd deal with him soon. Hate was instant, love was not so easy. How did one dispose of it? He knew he could never hate Laura, he had watched her go into the house and wanted to follow, ask her to tell him he'd imagined it all. But he'd done none of it and the images kept churning around and around in his head. He wondered what she was doing. Was she dreaming of the treacherous priest?...

There was no-one he could tell, not even Lotti. He hadn't been to see her for months. She'd always asked him a lot of questions when he first went to the tavern, but he didn't want to answer any of them. After that, Lotti never pressed him, just gave him a big smile and brought him the beer. Two was his limit, and Nora, the landlord's wife, said they were on the house.

Her husband, Josh, complained to him once. "Lotti won't let me into her bed. I've got used to creeping up to the attic," and for some reason Janus felt glad. It made Lotti different from the other girls that came over to talk to him. He wasn't that bothered about sex, he had enough trouble with the voices in his head. After a while he could talk to Lotti and she'd make him laugh sometimes when they sat on the steps of the fire escape that led up to her room.

Then he'd fallen in love with Laura, dreamed of her, and when he thought his body would explode with the want of her, he'd gone to see Lotti. He didn't know what to do, his mind was so confused. He wasn't a virgin, but all that was so long ago. She'd asked no questions, just took him to her bed. Janus was comforted by her generous body and wondered what it would be like to hold the slender figure of Laura in his arms. Would he break her? The cheerful waitress had been enthusiastic and noisy as he'd tried to imagine what sounds Laura would make. Soft whispers?... Gentle moans?...And for a time he'd felt better. Lotti never asked why he just came to have sex and never took her out. A few months ago he'd gone up to her. Lying on the bed, she had run her stubby fingers over his body.

"You're getting some flesh on that body of yours," she'd said, giggling. "And muscles. I like a strong man, Janus," feeling his arms and legs. "All that work at the old hag's house is making you fit. Does the Fairy Godmother feed you well?"

He had got off the bed, incensed, and wanted to strike her. His voice was cold as he gathered his clothes together and dressed. "Don't ever call her by any other name than Mrs. Sogar," and left the room. Lotti didn't take umbrage, though. She still talked to him when he went to the Tavern, but never mentioned what had happened. Maybe if he went to see her again, things would be different.

Janus emptied the bottle he was holding and slowly walked through the garden and up to his room.

* * *

Lotti had been rushed off her feet. It was always like this on a Saturday night.

"Four beers and a cognac," shouted Josh, the Landlord.

"Two beers and two glasses of wine for the ladies," said blonde Hans, as she passed. Lotti's ample figure squeezed through the crowd, the tray with drinks held high above her head. She was hot and her head was aching. Her feet hurt and she didn't want those louts in the brown shirts and that stupid armband running their hands over her bottom. Barbarians and thugs, all of them. She may be a barmaid, but she could read and knew what went on. They might think she was dumb; she listened, kept quiet. They were dangerous and she had more sense than to invite trouble.

Not like those two 'Ladies' over there. Dolled up to the nines and having to pay for their drinks later. She missed Janus a lot. He hadn't been back to her room for months and hadn't been in here for weeks. Ever since he moved to the other end of town with that old bag he lived with before. If he didn't turn up soon, she'd pay him a visit...

It was long past midnight when Lotti climbed the fire escape to the attic. The place was always hot in the summer. She took off her damp clothes, poured cold water into the wash basin and sponged her body. The face in the mirror was as round and chubby as her figure, but not displeasingly so. She knew she wasn't a Mona Lisa with her short mousy hair, 'wishy washy' blue eyes and pug nose, but she did have a nice mouth. And she laughed a lot. Could take a joke and give as good as she got. Maybe she was a little brassy, but never vulgar. All she wanted was a nice place to live in, take care of Janus and have his children...

Lotti glanced at the crucifix over her bed and mumbled, "That's not asking for much, is it, God?"

Maybe tomorrow she'd take a tram ride to Dettingen and find Janus...

Chapter 7

The dress hung on its coathanger on the wardrobe door, the white organza frills around the collar outlined in the faint light from the streetlamp below. It seemed alive, the soft fabric moving now and then in the slight breeze from the open window. Reminding her; and the night went on forever, as Laura tossed and turned in her bed. Much later she heard Martin creep into the bedroom next door. Later still, Peter, Robert and Copper came up, and sleep was as far away as ever. The image of Michael Schiller would not leave her. Why him? Why not Janus, who was here and would make a good husband? There could be no solution to a love that was forbidden to a priest. What did he feel? Love or lust? How could he tell the difference?

She wished herself back at Rema House, where life had been lonely, but she had been able to sleep without yearning for a man she could never have, never feel his arms about her or kiss that shapely mouth. Had he ever kissed anybody? Did he know what it felt like to possess a woman? When sleep came, the dream was of Michael and wild desire, the nightmare of a tortuous flight through dark canyons as he fled from her in shame. And she wept in her sleep.

At 7:45 the bells woke her and with them, the thought of a priest at his duties. Laura decided to get up. The face in the mirror was pale, the eyes dark and haunted, afraid of her own passion. She dressed in a pretty yellow frock, sprinkled with tiny daisies and softly closed the door.

The large kitchen was filled with sunlight and she knew Janus had been there. The big coffee pot was nearly full and smelled fresh and welcoming, the stove gave out a gentle heat. She wondered what Janus was doing. Maybe clearing up the beer tent, ready for it to be dismantled. Laura opened the door and window, stepped out onto the patio and looked over the low wall into the garden. It was still and quiet. Of Janus there was no sign.

Martin was the first to emerge. A little bleary eyed but in his usual good mood. "Morning, Laura. My, you look pretty this morning. Hope we didn't keep you awake last night, it was a Hell of a party. That coffee smells good," he grinned, as he sat down at the table, already heaped with food. Laura wasn't sure whether to be pleased with his company, as right now she felt like crawling into a deep hole and disappearing forever. But that would not solve anything. None of it was Martin's fault and she decided to enjoy his brief visit.

"Morning, Martin. Do you want something cooked?"

"This'll do fine," he said, buttering crisp rolls and filling them with slices of cold meat. "Coffee'll be nice, though."

Laura poured. "Will you stay for the rest of the day? I haven't seen you for ages. It'll be nice to talk."

"I'd like to, but I've got to go back this afternoon or my wife'll be complaining. She doesn't see too much of me as it is," he said, a little sadly.

"You're still travelling as much as you used to? When are you going to take it easy?" she asked.

"Can't. The war interrupted my business. I lost a lot of good men and Jack was one of them. It's not easy to pick up the threads again when everybody holds you personally responsible for starting that bloody war. Fortunately, Ryker's had a very good reputation and that helps." Martin sounded proud of that. "This Country is in one hell of a mess. The antics of the Austrian corporal make politics a dangerous game these days."

"But they've put him behind bars in Landsberg, haven't they?" Laura asked. "I thought he and his party had been outlawed."

"Don't you believe it. They'll let him out soon. He's much too useful to a lot of influential people. They need somebody to unite the masses, but in the end he and his thugs will have total control. They'll not tolerate any opposition, no matter where it springs from. The Establishment don't realise that. But enough of politics. Why haven't you married again, Laura? You're a damned fine woman going to waste, if you don't mind me saying so," looking searchingly at her face.

She was startled at his last remark, found heat rising to her cheeks and knew she was blushing. "No, I don't mind, Martin. I take it as a compliment, although it's a bit early in the morning. As to your question, I've been asked a few times, but never fell in love deeply enough to marry any of them," she said, pouring more coffee into their cups.

"What about Janus? He works hard, is a decent man from what Peter tells me. He'll take care of you and isn't bad looking, either. Your son worries about you."

"There's no need. I've taken care of myself even when I was married to his father. You took both of them away, remember? As for Janus..." a shadow crossed over the beautiful face, the grey eyes momentarily touched Martin with their expression of a deep sadness, "...Janus is a good man. I like him as a friend. If I marry again, it will be for love. Nothing less, Martin."

She rose from her chair and started to fill the kettle. The others would soon be down for breakfast. He watched the slim figure and for the first time in his long years of working away from home, he understood the loneliness of the women they left behind. Did wealth make up for their absence? He guessed it might for some, but for women like Laura and his Bella, it didn't compensate.

"Will you stay for lunch, Martin?" Laura asked.

Martin Ryker had already made up his mind. At the station he'd buy the biggest bunch of roses he could find and take Bella somewhere special today, maybe stay at a nice place for a few days. He couldn't remember when he'd done either of those things in the past fifteen years.

"No, Laura. Thanks for the invitation, but I'm going home."

She looked at the large, boisterous man at the table, quiet now, thoughtfully staring into his cup and wondered what had prompted his decision to leave so early. But she did not ask, and smiled. "Bella will be pleased."

Martin got up and folded her into his arms and they stood in affectionate silence, remembering all the years that they had known each other.

* * *

The week had gone so quickly and it was time for Peter to leave again. Laura saw her son at the far end of the orchard, talking to Janus. They had not seen him since Saturday. Then, he'd helped the men put up the tent for the going away party Peter had promised everybody in the village, fetched the table and chairs, but had hardly spoken to her. And at seven in the evening he'd asked Peter if he could borrow the motorbike as he had business in Cologne. They had both gaped at him in surprise, but did not stop him from going. He had not come back until last night and went up to his room. But this morning the stove had been attended to and the coffee pot was full. Laura herself had been up since seven to see to the last minute packing of Peter's luggage. She would not see him again for perhaps three months.

The party had been a great success with Katrin's Tonia and Kurt, and Erika's Chrissy bringing some of their friends early on in the evening. Then most of the villagers called in. Peter's friends arrived, Erika and Freddy stayed, and a noticeable hush settled over the garden when Father Michael arrived. Laura stepped closer to Erika as he greeted her. He handed over a bottle of wine as he thanked her for the invitation. She felt that all eyes were on them. For the rest of the evening they'd only exchanged a few words in passing.

Peter, blissfully unaware, kept the priest occupied, for which his mother was grateful. Father Michael did not stay on to the end, saying he had mass in the morning. Laura noticed Erika's eyes, shrewd, probing, on both of them as he came to say goodnight. And again she felt they were being watched with interest.

Yesterday, Freddy and Erika had collected Peter and herself and they had motored up the Rhine as far as Koblenz and she'd had a very enjoyable day. In an hour, her son would be gone and she wondered how long it would take to get used to the silence in the house. But she would be busy.

The Women's Guild now met twice a week to get everything ready for the Festival on the first Saturday in August. The precious tapestry she and Erika were working on still required hours of stitching. Laura just wished Father Michael wouldn't call in at the meetings. It was getting very difficult to stop herself from blushing when he spoke to her and she imagined everybody was looking at them. If only she could bring the work home. Then she'd have an excuse not to go to the Church hall and suffer the indignity of trying to hide her feelings when they met. He was serenity itself and gave nothing away, except for the time they had been alone. Maybe she had imagined it all...

* * *

The church festival at Dettingen had been well advertised. Freddy's newspaper devoted half a page to the event. The Reverend Mother always insisted on it, reminding him of his duty to the parish. He liked the old girl and they had been friends for years. She had been astonished and pleased by the large tapestry Laura had designed as an offering to the auction. She and

Erika had worked on it and it was a grand piece. Two metres high, one metre wide it would have pride of place.

Even he hadn't realised Erika's talent, or Laura's. The large head of Christ had taken on a spiritual beauty beyond description, but still remained earthly. When he had seen it, the face bore a faint resemblance to Michael and he had not been surprised when Erika mentioned it to him.

What torment they must be going through, hiding their love for each other from other people, hiding from each other. He wished Michael would do something, his face looked drawn and tired lately. Sooner or later one of them would have to leave here and Freddy didn't want to lose either of them. He loved the priest as his brother and was fond of Laura.

* * *

By midday on Saturday the shops closed in Dettingen. The only people in the village that would make money were the church, the convent and the inns. On the green, tea, coffee and soft drinks were allowed, alcohol was off the menu. The village square overflowed with stalls joining the colourful exhibits set out in the courtyard of the convent. At 1:00 p.m. the droves of visitors filled the square and every tram arriving at the terminus was full. The atmosphere in the court yard was as entertaining and lively as on the green, church pennants fluttering in the soft breeze. The sisters looked hot in black habits, contrasting sharply with the crowds, dressed for a summer's day. One or two of the sisters looked nervous at the influx of strangers invading their tranquil existence. Most, however, meant to take the opportunity to let themselves go for this one day of the year, laughing a lot.

The Reverend Mother Agnes was in her element, replacing one wilting sister with another. Sister David, very large and buxom, was in charge of the lottery. She was used to bellowing at pupils on the sports ground and used her full voice to attract customers. Timid Sister Anna, slight and small, allocated to turn the round drum with delicate tiny hands, winced and shut her eyes every time she saw Sister David open her mouth. She constantly thanked God that the good sister had not brought her whistle.

Every year the lottery presented Mother Agnes with a dilemma. She had to part with one of their finest bottles of brandy for cousin Norman, the Bishop, and wheedle permission to use it. After all, it did make a lot of money for the convent.

Freddy's comments were that she could always dress the nuns as French maids, complete with black stockings and garters and that would bring in even more money. Mother Agnes had laughed so much that tears ran down her face. She adored the young Baron as much as Father Michael. Freddy, witty and charming, made her laugh. Michael stimulated her intellect, but lately he seemed distracted, and he looked tired. Something disturbed his serenity. And it had started when Laura Sogar moved into the village. Her sisters picked up a good deal of gossip on their rounds... All she could do was pray for him...

* * *

Erika and Laura had drawn the number for the bric-a-brac stall and Erika wasn't pleased.

"They've fixed it," Erika wailed. "All the stuff nobody wants anymore, including mine. All that unpacking. I wanted the book stall"

Laura managed to pacify her by promising to do the unwrapping. "I've never done this before," she told Erika, kneeling on a pillow, surrounded by mountains of boxes, handing up one item after the other. She looked young, her skin glowed from being outdoors. The yellow dress with the tiny daisies complementing the tan. She had secured the long hair with a slide, a string of white beads hung around her neck.

Erika watched her for a moment and concluded that Laura was definitely getting younger as the months passed, and more desirable, and hoped that Michael was going to do something about their situation soon. He couldn't be that much of a fool to let all this slip through his fingers.

It was almost three by the church clock when Erika spied Freddy and Father Michael two stalls down. "I need a drink. We've done very well. Do we close up or can you manage on your own while I get some coffee?"

"I'll manage. Bring something to eat, this is making me hungry," Laura said cheerfully. "I'm enjoying myself."

Erika patted her fair hair, smoothed her pink dress and walked off in the direction of Freddy. "Hello, Darling! Good afternoon, Father Michael! Have you come to do your bit? We're over there and my friend could do with some assistance while we get some refreshments. Come on, Freddy." She tucked her arm into Freddy's and steered him towards the refreshment tent.

53

Laura saw Michael approach and felt the heat creeping up into her face. Her fingers felt clumsy as she took coins and gave change, and she wanted to run. The small figurine she held in her hand was shaking as she tried to wrap it in tissue paper. Father Michael stepped behind the stall and took it out of her hand to give to the woman who had purchased it.

"Thank you, Father," she beamed at him.

"I have orders to assist you until Erika gets back with coffee and food," he said to no-one in particular. They were both relieved to be busy and engaged in inconsequential chatter with the never ending stream of visitors and residents.

Erika and Freddy, on their way back with coffee and cakes, watched the two people, so ill at ease with each other. "He should leave the church and marry her. So much passion going to waste," she whispered to the man at her side.

"Give him time," Freddy whispered back. "Something like that can't be decided in a hurry."

"Coffee time!" Erika called out. "To the back of the stall. You deserve a rest. And thanks for helping out, Father," she said, mischief in her eyes as she handed him the tray.

"You are a terrible bully, Erika. Come, Laura." He led the way to the small strip of grass. They sat down and he handed her a cup. She felt nervous and concentrated on drinking, conscious of the man so close at her side.

"Are you enjoying yourself," he asked. She nodded.

"Yes. It's fun. I like to be part of it."

"The tapestry is a magnificent piece. Mother Agnes is very pleased with it. I only saw the finished work today. It's very beautiful. Like you."

She knew he had been watching her all the time and she felt her heart thumping. Laura lifted her eyes from her cup and met his, dark with longing.

"You shouldn't say things like that, Michael. It's not right," and was shocked when she realised she had simply called him Michael. He had noticed and smiled at her.

"I know, Laura," and looked at his watch. "I have to go and fulfil my duty," Father Michael's tone was serious, his voice firm. "Please come to my study on Monday. There are matters we have to discuss."

Laura stared at him in surprise. "What do we have to discuss that warrants a visit to your house? I can't come there. Not alone. I'll bring Erika," she said, her voice small and frightened. Michael Schiller got up, as graceful as a jungle cat. He extended his hand to her and as they joined they both felt again the spark that had touched them at their first meeting. This time he held the small hand in his, strong and firm and she heard the authority in his voice.

"I wish to talk to you alone. About us. If you will not come to my house then I must come to yours. Please, Laura. It's not easy for me either. Monday, at two o'clock. Be there."

Before she could think of an excuse for not going, he walked to the front of the stall to say goodbye to Erika and Freddy, and quickly crossed the Green to the church and his house.

Laura gathered the cups and untouched cakes. She did not see Janus leaning against the back of one of the stalls. There was hatred in his eyes as he watched the Priest leave her.

The people were still thronging about the Green in droves. Laura handed the cakes to Freddy.

"Will our gorgeous Father come back later?" Erika asked casually. Laura shrugged her shoulders.

"I don't know. Are you buying something, Freddy?" she asked, changing the subject.

Freddy grinned, licking the cream off his hand where it had squirted out of the pastry case. At thirty, deeply tanned, his fair hair falling over his forehead, Freddy still looked like a twenty year old. Laughing brown eyes wrinkled up at the corner, showing tiny crows feet. He picked up a pair of Dutch dolls. The girl doll he kept, but handed the boy doll and some paper money to Laura. "He's for you. To keep you company. Take my advice, find yourself a real man to play with, Laura. It's a shame to waste all that beauty," which made her blush.

"Stop it, Freddy. I'm fine as I am, thank you." She hugged the doll and replaced more items to fill the empty spaces. On impulse she asked Erika. "Can you come to my house tonight?"

Erika shook her head. "Can't tonight. We're going to see some friends when we've finished here. Will tomorrow do?"

Laura looked at both of them and felt a sense of isolation. "Tomorrow'll do. Come in the evening. Janus'll be out then."

* * *

Janus mingled with the people, hoping to find Laura. He had not seen her all day. When she worked in the garden he could at least watch her. He didn't know what to say to her these days, it was as if the priest always stood between them. She had made him feel tongue tied and shy at Rema House. Then they moved here and at least he could talk to her about the garden and what they planned to do. Since Peter's party they didn't have much to say to each other. Maybe it had all been a mistake, maybe it was all the priest's fault and she had been embarrassed, or flattered.

He saw Erika and the Pegleg, but Laura wasn't there. Janus walked past three stalls, avoiding the bric-a-brac stand, then turned to the grass verge and saw them, sitting close to each other, and the look in the priest's eyes was enough to fuel his hatred. The image of the two of them in the summer house haunted him again and he walked away.

Janus followed the path between the houses. He'd find enough on the lecherous Priest to hang him. It wouldn't be long now...

Chapter 8

The kitchen didn't feel right when Laura came down for breakfast. There was no gentle warmth from the stove, the coffee pot stood on the shelf. Clean and cold. She raked the faint embers, placed slivers of wood through the door in the front and pulled the lever to gain enough draught for the strips to light. She filled the copper kettle, removed the rings on the hot plate and hoped the logs she had added to the thin wood were going to burn. She hadn't had to do this before... Where was he?...

The piece of writing paper lay on the table. She frowned slightly as she read, 'Have gone on the bike to Cologne. Will be back tomorrow night. Janus...'

Cologne?.. she mumbled. He must've gone before she got back from the festival for the stove to be nearly out. She noticed the square box was filled with briquettes, the copper bucket with dry wood. Oh, well. He was entitled to go off and didn't have to account to anybody as to where he went. It was her fault she hadn't seen the note last night. She had spent what was left of the evening with Katrin and then gone to bed.

It was long past eleven o clock when Laura finished her leisurely breakfast. There was blissful silence after the last peal of bells for the morning Mass. With the doors and windows wide open she'd heard the tinkle of the little communion bell, sweet and pure. As she watched wispy clouds high on the horizon she imagined Father Michael and the young Chaplain going along the altar rail, back and forth... back and forth... holding up the thin white wafer in front of the faces... placing it on outstretched tongues. She remembered Peter's party... and yesterday afternoon... What did he feel?... And what was he going to tell her tomorrow?... That there was no hope for them, but he desired her body?... No, he wouldn't tell her that...Would she have the audacity to ask him?... No, she couldn't, she would just have to wait... sitting here wondering was just a waste of time...

Laura shook her head, got up and resolutely cleared the table. A cardboard tube lay on the bench. Ed's plans for the bathroom. Peter had some discussions with the local builder and they might get a bathroom soon. They even talked about central heating for the whole house. She'd believe that when she saw it. The loft above the kitchen was the most sensible place, Ed had remarked. She spread the drawings on the kitchen table and immersed herself in the strange, unfamiliar language of building plans. The first ring of the bell went un-noticed. The second was more insistent and Laura hurried to the front door, wondering who was calling on her on a Sunday morning. Erika, in skirt and floppy shirt, bare legged, seemed agitated.

"Erika." Laura looked foolishly surprised. "You were coming tonight."

"Is Janus in, Laura?" Erika asked, as she stepped into the hall and opened the door to the sitting room. They rarely spent time in there, the kitchen and the dining room were less formal for their every day needs.

"No, why?" Laura queried. "Coffee?"

"No thanks, Pet." Erika sounded distracted as she made herself comfortable on the settee.

"You look pale. Are you ill?" Laura scanned the face of her friend. She watched Erika take a packet of cigarettes out of her pocket, put one into a black holder and light it. Laura shook her head. "Why do you smoke, Erika?"

"It soothes my wounded spirit, friend."

"I didn't know you had one," Laura remarked, grinning.

"There's much you don't know about me, Laura," Erika said softly. "Any more than I know what goes on in that pretty head of yours. You are like a lily. Beautiful, mystical, untouchable. What is under that desirable facade I often ask myself. A flesh and blood woman?"

Laura stared at her friend, composed again, nonchalantly smoking.

"Erika. Have you been drinking?" she asked, concerned, but received only a smile. "For your information, I am flesh and blood and suffer just like everyone else. I just hide it better. Why did you ask whether Janus was home? He doesn't normally come into the house anyway, only the kitchen."

Erika inhaled deeply and asked. "Do you know where he is?"

"In Cologne. He left a note yesterday saying he wouldn't be back 'till tonight." She paused, a puzzled frown on her brow. "It's strange. He comes and goes but never stayed away overnight. Since Peter's party he's been to Cologne twice. Why do you want to know?" and sat down in the other corner of the large settee, tucking her legs under her.

"Walter saw him last night in some dive in the City. You can't mistake Janus. He just doesn't blend in with the crowd. Your man was in very

58

unsavoury company, Laura. Dangerous company," Erika said, looking serious. Laura was still confused about her friends interest in Janus.

"What do you mean by dangerous? Women? He's old enough to go with who he wants.."

"No, not women," Erika said slowly. "Men, Dear. He shouldn't be associating with that fraternity. They are the scum that follow the Austrian corporal."

"That's odd," and Laura remembered her conversation with Martin Ryker. "Peter's Boss called him that as well. Didn't think much of his tactics, politically. Surely they can't be gaining that much ground with him in prison?"

"They are gathering the thugs and thieves, the ignorant who believe anything they tell them as long as they do it often enough. There's a cauldron simmering and it's a stinking brew, Sweetie. And Janus seemed to be very friendly with them," Erika said, the usual mischievous expression absent from her eyes.

"I can't believe that Janus is mixed up with them, although..." Laura paused, trying to remember something, "He asked me to come to the pigeon loft after he'd finished doing it up. Made it very nice and comfortable. He's divided it into a living room and a bedroom, and behind the stove hung a wide belt with a gun. I asked him what he needed it for and he said it was to protect me. Got very upset when I reminded him he needed a permit. I'd forgotten all about it as I haven't been up there since."

"Maybe he's got the uniform to go with it. Our Janus is a very dark horse. Secretive. It'd be interesting to find out what he's up to. Wouldn't it, Pet?"

Laura stared at Erika, horrified. "I hope you're not expecting me to ask him. He nearly bit my head off the last time I mentioned the gun. It's not for me to interfere in his private life."

"Oh, but he'd like nothing better than for you to interfere with him, believe me," Erika grinned, but found no response to her remark. Instead, Laura's voice was cool and precise.

"What was your Walter doing in a place like that, Erika?"

"That was very clever, Darling." Erika gazed at her friend, taken aback by the question. She fitted another cigarette into the holder and lit it, blowing smoke puffs towards the ceiling. "My dear Laura, you don't concern yourself much with gossip. Village life is like a still, deep pond. All is calm on the surface, until you cast a fishing line and bring up the murky things lying at the bottom. Everyone knows they're there, so they don't stir the water. Only strangers go fishing."

"Like me?" asked Laura.

"You would've got to know sometime. Walter goes to Cologne every Saturday. Ever since Chrissy was born. My husband, who's not been a husband in the literal sense for most of our married life, needs something I can't give him. Sasha in Cologne does," and a strain of sadness crept into the soft voice of the attractive woman.

"How do you know about this woman?" Laura expressed surprise. Erika leant back, crossed one slim leg over the other and grinned at her.

"Known for years. Freddy found out for me. Sasha's not a woman, Pet. His name is Leon. Looks very pretty all dressed up. He operates from a fashionable apartment and is very particular about his clients."

Laura, incredulity and shock written all over her face, stared at Erika. "But... but what about you?"

"Me? I've got Freddy. We've loved each other since we were children," and laughed at Laura's open mouth and wide eyes. "Freddy's mother was a bitch. Sons of Barons don't marry shop-keeper's daughters, even when daddy's a pharmacist. According to her it was still a shop, and Freddy was bundled off to the Military Academy. I married Walter and didn't know what I was letting myself in for. When Freddy came back we just comforted each other. I needed him and he had to prove to himself that he was still a man, even with one leg missing. Everybody's happy."

"And the people here. Do they know?" Erika laughed again.

"Everybody knows. There isn't a thing you can hide in this place. Or any other village, come to that. It's life and we make the best of a bad situation. They do approve." She looked at Laura. "Are you shocked?"

The beautiful face held no indication of what went on in her head. Laura contemplated the lovely woman, elegantly holding a cigarette holder, a line of grey smoke wavering in the breeze from the open window. Was that the secret she felt Erika had been hiding from her when they first met? How much more lay beneath the frivolous facade? She smiled at Erika.

"I'm surprised at myself, but I'm not shocked. Maybe I'm becoming part of this place, learning to accept its ways," and carefully added. "Does...does Father Michael know?"

Erika broke into peals of laughter, choking on the smoke she'd inhaled a moment ago. "Of course he knows. And everybody knows he's in love with

60

you. You two are trying so hard to avoid each other, we're having bets on how long it's going to be before something happens." Laughing again at Laura's shocked crimson face. "God, I wish you had enough courage to end all that agony. It's bad for your health, Pet." Erika paused, and placed a hand on Laura's. "I do know what it's like. It can destroy you. We all love Michael and feel his distress. He's part of us. Until you came, his life belonged to God. Now he's confronted with something he never thought he would experience. Michael's found out he's also a man and is struggling, trying to make a decision. What about you, Laura?" she asked, gently, compassionately, watching pain cloud the eyes of her friend.

Laura felt the tears spill over as she whispered. "I loved him from the moment we met and I don't know what to do. He's a priest."

Erika pulled the shaking body to her, stroked the golden hair, handing over a handkerchief. "Be patient, Sweetie. Blow your nose. We need a drink."

Laura jumped from the settee, a determined look on her face. She opened the lower door of Mara's elegant wall unit and brought out a bottle, still wrapped in tissue paper. She stood it in front of Erika and handed her the cork screw.

"Open that. And if it's not up to scratch I'll tell him so tomorrow. I've been summoned to his study at 2:00 p.m. with strict instructions to come alone. He wants to talk about us. Maybe..." her voice faded away. She fetched two glasses and Erika filed them to the brim. As they toasted each other Erika grinned, a wicked gleam in her eyes.

"I hope you'll stay the distance, Laura. Make it happen."

"I will, Erika. To friendship and love," and raised her glass.

"I'll drink to that," Erika said, then looked thoughtful. "Be careful of Janus."

"Why? He's harmless enough."

"A man who's on intimate terms with some of the well known radicals of the National Socialist Party isn't harmless any more. Besides, he loves you and that makes him doubly dangerous. To Michael, Freddy and you."

Laura knew with certainty that they were all bound together by a quirk of fate, in this place she now called home.

* * *

61

She woke early, remembered her appointment and knew that this Monday would change her life. Should she go ahead with the bathroom? Perhaps it would be better if she moved away from this place, away from whatever would be decided between them this afternoon. She had promised Erika to tell Michael that she loved him. That was after the third glass of his excellent wine. They'd taken food and another bottle to the summer house, feeling happy and relaxed without the presence of Janus.

Like two silly school girls, giggling and making pie in the sky plans about weddings and a wonderful future. Except, that this morning there was no rosy haze out of a bottle, no pretending...

She'd take the plans back to Ed on her way to see Michael. But first she'd show them to Janus, just in case...

He had been to in stoke the fire and coffee was waiting. It smelled good. The fresh rolls tasted good, too. And it was going to be another beautiful day. Laura looked fresh and cool in a white linen blouse and navy skirt as she stepped out onto the patio and leant over the wall, but couldn't see Janus anywhere. The door to the tool room was open. She walked in and stopped at the bottom of the stairs contemplating the closed door above. It seemed strange. He usually left it ajar when they were both at home.

"Janus!" she called.

The man that opened the door seemed like a stranger. It looked as if he'd pulled on his clothes in a hurry, his usually well brushed hair in disarray and there was a suggestion of dark stubble on his face. Laura stared up in surprise. She had never seen him other than neat and well groomed since the days when he sat on the bench by the river.

Taken aback, she stuttered, "I... I'm sorry. Didn't mean to disturb you. I... I wanted you to have a look at the plans Ed left on Friday."

The face that looked down on her made her shiver. His lips, tightly pressed together, made the mouth a disagreeable shape and the nose appeared hawk-like. Brown eyes burned into hers with an intensity that frightened her, but his expression softened a little as he spoke.

"Give me ten minutes and I'll have a look at them." He disappeared back into his room.

Laura walked slowly to the garden wall and stared at the neat plots, ready to receive mountains of straw before the frost. Why had it become so difficult to talk to him? They had managed to live amicably together before Peter's party. Since then, Janus seemed to be withdrawn and there was an undercurrent of something she couldn't put her finger on...Sometimes he broke off in the middle of a sentence and looked at her. As if he wanted to say something important and then changed his mind. He rode off on his bicycle most evenings now. She would hear the gate click, hear the tyres on the gravel path fading in the direction of Annsberg. Maybe he turned into the path by the stream and went to the river...Or the tavern. About midnight the gate would click shut again. Why couldn't they talk anymore?

Last night she'd heard the motorbike and wondered what he had been doing in Cologne all weekend...She hoped he was going to be in a better mood, the visit to Michael after lunch was ordeal enough for one day...She had to keep calm if she wasn't going to make a fool of herself.

Laura returned to the kitchen, the kettle sprouted steam and she made fresh coffee. The knock on the open door made her jump. Janus entered, shaved and looking clean and tidy in his work clothes and she was relieved.

"Let's have a look," he said, unrolling Ed's plans onto the table.

"Would you like some coffee, Janus?" she asked the broad back bent over the drawings.

"Please," he answered, his mind elsewhere.

Laura placed the cup and saucer on the edge of the table and ventured, "Did you have a nice time in Cologne?"

He looked at her for a moment, intently, and again she saw the strange expression, disturbing her, but his voice was calm.

"I had business to attend to," and turned his attention back to the drawings. "This looks fine to me. The loft isn't the height of your other rooms, but it should be enough for a bathroom. Did you enjoy yourself on Saturday?"

She was taken aback momentarily. "Yes. It was more fun than I thought it would be," then added softly. "Did you go?"

Janus drank his coffee. He hesitated, as if he wasn't sure whether to say yes or no, then answered simply. "Yes, I did go," his eyes resting on her face.

She looked surprised. "I didn't see you," and noticed his expression change, become hard and distant.

"You were..." he paused, "busy." He placed the cup on the table, saying, "I've work to do," and walked out of the kitchen.

Laura watched him go past the window, into the garden, a thoughtful look on her face. What kind of business did he have in Cologne and why hadn't she seen him at the festival? It was all very curious. She prepared a cold lunch for him and left it, covered with muslin, on the table.

She was going to get dressed and reminded herself to eat before going to Ed's and then on to meet Michael at his house.

* * *

What to wear?... Laura was undecided. The green suit or the navy blue? The cream blouse would go with either... No! not the green, too festive... She wasn't going to a party... The dark one.

Then another momentous decision. Hair up or down?... A chignon made her look severe, the curls always sprung away at the side. A slide would hold it neatly at the back and to hell with the rest... She must eat something, but her stomach felt queasy... and she wondered if Janus was in the kitchen... she didn't want to sit with him today... he was making her nervous... everything was making her nervous... The stockings wrinkled and she pulled them up, vowing that she'd get some suspenders to hold them up... Skirts were getting shorter and garters were going out of fashion... Her shoes felt tight... Wriggling her toes, she wished she could've gone bare legged in sandals... but that wouldn't do... One last look and she was satisfied...

The kitchen was empty and the table cleared. Laura buttered bread, filled it with her favourite cheese, but tasted nothing... A piece of cake?... That too had lost it's attraction... Give it up, she thought...

Collecting her bag and the plans, she walked out of the house.

Laura's stomach gave a lurch as she glanced at the church clock. It was almost 1:30. Only three people had passed her, commenting on how nice she looked, asking if she was going into town. She laughed and said, 'no, not today' and the laughter had sounded feeble. Ed was out and she left the plans in his office, then slowly walked back to where the four paths crossed and turned right. She could see the school at the end and the walled garden of the presbytery. Laura crossed the road, resolutely walked up the steps and rang the doorbell.

Janus was still thinking about the plans for the bathroom and couldn't recall where the downpipe for the drainage was located. It was not on the patio, where he would have noticed it, and he needed to look at the drawings

64

again. The kitchen door was locked. 'She must've gone out,' he thought and fetched his own key.

The kitchen table was cleared and the roll containing the plans had gone. Janus went into the dining room, opened the door of the sitting room, walked through and came out into the hall. There was no sign of the tube. He passed the telephone and wondered about calling Ed. He didn't like telephones. He returned to the kitchen, locked up and wheeled his bicycle out of the tool room.

He rode past Walter's, into Wendel Road, turned into the path that led him to Ed's. It was as straight as an arrow and he could see the yard in the distance. He also recognised the small figure in blue, who turned off to the right as she reached the centre point of the four paths. Janus pedalled faster, stopped and watched Laura cross the road at the far end and enter the gate of the Presbytery, go up the steps and ring the bell. In a rage, he reversed the bike and returned home.

* * *

Father Michael sat behind his desk, staring at the green leather bound writing pad. Slender hands laced together, his head full of images and words he wasn't sure he'd be able to say to her. He had been grateful to Erika on Saturday... she and Freddy would have guessed by now... Just for a short while he had been allowed to look at Laura without having to hide his feelings. He'd wanted to kiss her... take away the slide and feel the softness of her hair... the silky smoothness of her skin.

Later, he'd found it difficult to concentrate on the confessions... he had no right to be here anymore... The Bishop would send him off to the Retreat... after that, another parish... the situation was not uncommon... Even Bishops had been removed from the seat of temptation before.

Father Michael was very confused and deeply troubled when the sound of the door bell made him jump. He opened the door, his heart pounding like a noisy sledge hammer in his chest.

"Come in, Laura," and held out his hand. She placed her own into his for a fleeting moment and withdrew it after the merest touch.

"Good day, Michael." She fully intended to carry out her resolution to remain cool and calm. He led her to the study, pointed to a wide chair which

65

almost swallowed her as she sat down. She would've preferred one of the hard, plain wooden ones.

Michael Schiller retreated behind his desk and had the advantage of observing the woman he loved, slim legs and neat feet resting on tip-toe on the carpet.

"EHM... Have you recovered from all that work on Saturday? We made a lot of money. Mother Agnes was very pleased with her gains," he said, his eyes resting on her face. He felt again the sinful desire, and forced himself to pay attention to what she was saying.

"I'm glad. Everyone's worked so hard."

Michael opened a silver box on his desk, extracted a cigarillo and tried to light it, but had difficulty in controlling his shaking hand. He leant back in his chair, inhaling deeply, only his eyes betraying his torment.

"Thank you for coming, Laura. It's good to see you. We need to talk."

"Yes, I know," she acknowledged, and let her eyes wander about the room, waiting. It was a peaceful place, books everywhere. Was this his chair?... The house was quiet and serene, the furniture elegant, a restful room, except now the tension was swirling about them like an early morning mist... There was a more than the distance of the desk between them; and yet, if he chose, he could breach it in two strides.

Michael's voice reached her, full of sadness and resignation. "I should not believe in fate, only God. But that is no longer true. Love for you has made me question my life. My very existence." It was the first time he had spoken of love.

"How do you know it's love and not just infatuation?" she asked softly. He looked into grey eyes full of uncertainty, full of questions, but countered hers with his own.

"Doesn't that apply to you too? What will you answer me if I ask 'do you love me?' Will you know the difference?"

They both fell silent. She realised he had neatly turned the table on her. How very clever, but then, he would be. And he was waiting, patiently; the long fingers interlaced tightly together, the very blue eyes watching her. Laura returned his gaze, remembering Erika's words and her own boast that she was going to tell him of her love. At this moment there could be nothing else between them but the truth. She took a deep breath, sat up as straight as the deep chair allowed her to, her voice firm and clear.

"I know the difference, Michael. I love you and will never love anyone else, or marry again."

For a moment she saw the hint of fear she'd imagined at their first meeting. Then he bowed his head as if she had placed some heavy burden on his shoulders. Michael lifted his eyes and stared at the large crucifix on the wall. She noticed the faint lines on his brow, the vertical indentations along the slender nose seemed deeper than on Saturday, making his face look thinner still.

A crucified Christ, Laura thought and involuntarily glanced at the bronze Jesus in the posture of agony. She wanted desperately to cross the space between them, comfort him, but they had never touched except for a handshake. It was not her place. As if by some great effort he took his eyes off the cross, straightened his body and rose to go over to a small cabinet in the corner of the study.

"I'm not in the habit of drinking during the day, but I think we both need this," and poured a large measure of brandy into two glasses and handed one to her. Michael did not return to his chair but stood by the open window. Laura could hear the chattering voices of the sisters in the convent garden, their laughter echoing below the hills. She took her glass and joined him, heard his voice from above her, a little sad, but strong.

"It was unfair of me to ask if you loved me, but I needed you to tell me." He looked down at her with a wry smile and she saw only love. He spoke again. "I've asked myself a thousand times if what I feel for you is just infatuation. My love for God would've ended that long ago. What I feel is so incredibly beautiful, it terrifies me. It's the very essence of life and the Church has no right to deny this to any man. I love you and I love God, who's been all I ever wanted, 'till now."

"Have you ever loved anyone else?" Her voice sounded small and Michael turned towards her, saw the moisture in her eyes and felt an overwhelming desire to hold her close to him. Instead he stepped back and casually sat on the edge of the desk, reached over to the box and took out another cigarillo, the remains of the brandy beside him. He watched the tendrils of wispy smoke drift towards the window before he answered.

"No, Laura. I've only loved God. I'm happy in the company of men, but never desired any of them."

"And women?..." Laura ventured.

"I like to be with them when the occasion demands it. No-one disturbed my life before. Only you," and she remembered that first morning again and knew why this man, approaching middle age, had an aura of childish innocence. She sipped her brandy and found it settled her nerves, felt vaguely disturbed by his presence so close to her. He had been remote behind the desk. Safe. She turned her back to him and stared out into the garden to escape the longing in his eyes.

"What are we going to do, Michael? Do you want me to leave Dettingen? I will go out of your life if that's what you want."

There was a deep silence in the room, unnerving her. She faced him. Michael swirled the last of the brandy round and round in the glass. Absent-mindedly. As if he was struggling with some terrible conflict within himself. His voice was firm when he spoke at last. "It means everything to me to hear you say that. I know I love you and will do so always, but I am a priest and must decide with whom I'm going to spend the rest of my life. You or God. On Friday I'm leaving for Thuringen. I have a house there. The mountains will be good for me. I'll be back when I've reached my decision," and he finally looked at her. "Come with me."

Laura, taken aback, could feel the tension trying to drown them. She lifted her head, her gaze steady. "No, Michael. If you wore anything else but that... that frock, I wouldn't hesitate for a moment. I'll not influence your decision one way or another. When you get back and tell me you wish to remain..." the pause was almost imperceptible, "...whatever you are, then I'll accept that and move elsewhere," knowing she had thrown down the gauntlet.

Michael Schiller stared at her. The narrowing of the eyes betrayed anger at the applied insinuation. "A strange choice of words to describe a cassock. Women wear frocks, do they not?" he asked, too quietly. She shrugged her shoulders, at a loss on how to answer his question.

He emptied his glass, placed it gently on the desk. For a moment his eyes travelled over the small proud figure standing by the window. Resolution replaced anger and a half smile appeared on the soft full lips. He left the desk, took two strides and stood towering over her. Laura saw the blue of the irises glitter like sapphires, lit by a fire he couldn't control.

"So you think the 'cloth' is a frock. Do you also wonder whether I'm a woman?" the soft voice asked from somewhere above her. He lifted her chin and she saw determination and a hint of amusement in his eyes. Before she could move, he pulled her to him and his kiss was not gentle, but that of a man new to passion. Hungry. The long sensitive fingers she'd watched holding the thin wafer above the faces of his parishioners were hesitant at first, exploring unfamiliar terrain, unknown territory. As he pressed her body to him, there was no doubt as to who he was, and Laura felt herself drowning, spinning, responding to the man who held her in his strong arms. "Come with me, Laura. I need you."

Laura, trembling and dismayed at her own ferocious response to his touch, disentangled himself from his embrace. Her voice trembled. "No, Michael, you must decide on your own," then picked up her bag, rushed out of the house and hoped she'd not meet anyone on the way home.

* * *

Erika rang Laura's front door bell. She had seen her half an hour earlier running down the road as if the devil was after her. Katrin too had no response as she called to her from the window. Erika was worried, wondering what had happened in Michael's study. She rang the bell again, determined not to go through the garden in case she met Janus. He was the last person she wanted to see just now.

The door opened. Laura was still in her suit, which looked as if she'd slept in it. Erika took in the tangled hair, feet without shoes, red swollen eyes and stepped inside. She guided the silent woman by the shoulder into the sitting room and to the settee, closing both doors.

"Sit, Pet. You look a mess," she commanded. "What happened?"

Laura sat hunched in the corner, near to tears again. "It's all so terrible," she wailed, while Erika looked in the wall unit for the bottle of whisky Peter had left in the kitchen on the day of the party. She knew Laura wouldn't touch it, but this was an emergency. She found the bottle and poured a generous amount into two tumblers.

"Drink this," she ordered, and settled herself into the other corner. "Now, you're not the crying type, Pet. What happened over there?"

Laura took a long swallow, and sniffed. "I've ruined his life by coming here. He's not sure if he wants to be a Priest anymore. And I'm responsible. Why, Erika? Why me?"

"If you can accept that some things are meant to be, you're halfway to answering your own questions. I believe in destiny, Laura. Maybe it's foolish, but it hasn't been too unkind to me," and a big grin appeared on her face, the eyes full of mischief. "As for our beloved Michael, he's up a gum tree and has to decide whether to stay up there or jump off," she chuckled at the thought. "Just imagine our elegant father up a gum tree, Laura," and saw a suspicion of a smile appear. "You must admit he's one hell of a man. Love has no boundaries and doesn't ask permission. It just hits you and he's found that out."

Erika watched, fascinated, as a pink blush spread over her friend's face.

"I know," Laura said, furious with herself for blushing. "He loves God and me and he wants..." she stopped in mid-sentence and felt her face go hot at the memory of what had taken place in Michael's study.

"Oh, dear," Erika said, trying hard to keep a straight face. "He wants your body? How do you know that, Pet? Did he say so?"

"No, he didn't say, he just..." and she took another drink. "I think I insulted him, and he got annoyed."

"What? Our saintly Michael annoyed? Tell me more, please," begged Erika.

"Well... I told him that the cassock was a frock... and... and he said women wore frocks... and did I think he was a woman... and he..." Laura shifted uncomfortably in the corner of the settee, her face crimson. Erika could not stop herself from shrieking, hardly able to talk.

"Did our pretty boy show you that inside that frock was a man?" ignoring the pleading look of the embarrassed woman opposite her. "Hallelujah," she said with feeling. "So he finally found out his equipment has other uses. And you ran out on him?" she asked, giggling, then remembered how dishevelled Laura had looked when she opened the door to her, the swollen eyes of her friend and spoke gently. "How long has it been, Laura," she asked, and saw that the question touched on long forgotten memories, as the grey eyes filled with sadness.

"Ten years. Lonely, empty years, Erika. There's been no-one since Jack. Not in that way. A few asked me to marry them, but I didn't love them. What if Michael can't leave the church?" Eyes dark and fearful implored Erika to know the answer.

Practical, sensible Erika didn't know and felt helpless. She took Laura's hand into her own and found her words empty, feeble. "Love is a gamble. He'll decide and you're left with the options. Wait till they're presented to you." She knew that whatever Michael's decision was going to be, it would be final. Erika forced herself to pronounce, "There'll be a wedding in the not too distant future, Sweetie. Walter will give me lots of money to buy a dress fit to be my best friend's Matron of Honour. Let's drink to that!"

Chapter 9

Every Thursday evening, the man from the bureau came to the tavern to collect whatever he had prepared. Janus glanced at the large clock face on the tower of the University and decided to make him wait. He did not particularly like him anyway. Since Monday, when he'd watched Laura go into the priest's house, he had worked like someone possessed and needed to think.

The bench by the river was empty. Janus dismounted from the bicycle, leant it against the railings and sat on the seat he had occupied day after day when he first came to this town. The evening sun touched the tips of the swell on the river as it had done then. He stared at the green water but saw nothing. Conscious only of the need to make a decision. The long list had been completed. Neatly filed, names of known agitators, important people to be cultivated, influential people to be wooed and charmed.

Everyone was listed, except three. The pegleg, the arrogant priest and Erika Behrens. The Baron's newspaper still published inflammatory articles against the New Order that grew stronger every day. But he did not write them himself, the priest did, and they were not printed by the newspaper presses. There was another highly efficient press somewhere and he intended to find it. Mrs. Behrens was involved, possibly with the printing, most certainly with the distribution of leaflets, posters and newsletters. The convent was a convenient place and the nuns did print books. They, like priests, were a devious lot when it suited them. The Reverend Mother looked shrewd and fly, in spite of her oh-so-Holy appearance.

At the moment they had to tread softly here. Until the Rhineland was free from French occupation, they must be patient. When the Leader was pardoned it would drive the fanatics to even greater aspirations to cleanse and unify Germany. Why the removal of the Jews was such an obsession with the Leader he couldn't quite understand. Unlike the gipsies, they lived and worked here, were born here. He had fought with some on the front and they shot the enemy as he had. They had died, like his brother. Bled like him. And when all was said and done, Adolf Hitler was born in Austria, but he shouldn't be thinking about that...

The pegleg and the priest were his personal quarries. Without them Erika Behrens was useless. For now, they had to be careful, though. The French didn't allow the brown shirts too many liberties. In Berlin and the South they could defy the feeble authorities and hold their rallies. Here they had to wait for Liberation Day...

Janus collected his bike and rode along the promenade towards the tavern. At the water front people sat on rough benches outside the Tavern. Lotti had not lost weight, in spite of rivers of sweat that poured off her every day. Each summer seemed to be hotter than the last one. Going back and forth, now she had to serve the rowdy crowd in the back room as well. Nell did her best, but Josh seemed to spend a lot of his time with the men in their brown shirts. She didn't like to hang around in there too long or get too close to the thugs. Janus was with them whenever he came in, carrying that leather satchel stuffed full of papers. He was still nice and talked to her as he used to, but somehow he seemed harder. He had never been back to the attic and she still missed him.

Lotti saw Janus as she held another heavy tray above her head. The heart inside her ample bosom gave an extra lurch at the sight of him. She wanted him so much. He looked brown and fit, so different from the shabby men that came here, so nice in his white shirt and pressed trousers.

"Evening, Janus. Nice to see you," hoping his eyes would show pleasure at the sight of her, but they remained just friendly.

"Evening, Lotti. It's hot again tonight. I'll be glad of a beer!" He took the satchel off the carrier seat at the back of the cycle and walked into the tavern, through the bar and into the room at the back.

* * *

Next morning, Laura looked for the post. She felt disappointed. He had not even sent her a note, but she consoled herself with the thought, 'perhaps tomorrow,' although he had not promised to write. Michael was leaving today.

Ed, the builder, was due at 11:00 a.m. to discuss the last minute details for the bathroom before starting work. Laura decided that she needed Janus there. Boilers, pipes and all the other complicated measurements this addition entailed did not mean much to her. She walked the length of the

73

garden and saw him pruning the raspberry canes, shirt-less, his brown back bent over the neat row.

"Janus?" she called softly. He stood up, looking surprised and smiled. Then it was gone, as if he'd remembered something and the brown eyes drew a curtain over what had been there a moment ago.

"Yes?" he said curtly. "Did you want me?" and waited in silence.

"Ed's coming at eleven. Can you spare an hour? I don't know what he's talking about. Please?"

As if to make her wait deliberately, he took his time, then nodded. "Alright, I'll be there," and turned away to resume his work. Dismissed, Laura walked back to the house, wondering again what was upsetting him.

Big Ed arrived on time, so did Janus, having put on a shirt. She listened to the two men, deep in conversation, bend over the plans spread on the kitchen table, supplied coffee and cakes, marvelling at the eloquence of Janus as he pointed to this and that on the drawings, asking numerous questions. When Ed left, Janus was still poised over the plans.

"This'll take some time to explain. Can I see you about it tonight? I've got to finish the raspberries."

"Alright. Will you come to dinner?" she asked.

"That'll be nice. We can talk then," and left.

* * *

Laura had changed into a pale grey cotton dress. The dinner was ready. It was still warm outside, the rays of the sun reflecting on the cutlery on the kitchen table, the pretty cloth matching the cushions on chairs and bench seat. She placed two wine glasses next to their plates and was startled to find Janus standing in the doorway. She had not noticed him passing the window. How long had he been there?

"It smells good," Janus said, handing over a bottle of wine.

"Thank you." Laura took the bottle. "It's very kind of you, but there was no need. We'll have it with our meal. Will you open it? Corkscrew's in there," pointing to the drawer of the large dresser. She felt awkward, not quite knowing what to say to him. He looked nice, had changed into clean shirt and trousers, his hair soft and shiny, his manner wary, but affable, as if he had made up his mind about something.

The meal was pleasant and the conversation centred mainly on the work in the garden.

"Tell me about this wonderful idea of Ed's," Laura invited. And in between eating, which Janus did with surprising grace, he explained the complexities of central heating, while she listened attentively. Sometimes, when he became too technical and realised she hadn't followed what he'd said, he explained it more simply. "It all sounds quite wonderful. No more stoves. I dreaded the winter, to be honest. You always kept Rema House so beautifully warm," she said and got up. "I'll make coffee."

He too got up and collected the plates and dishes from the table. "I've enjoyed the meal, Laura. Thank you," as he stacked the crockery into the sink. Laura cleared the food away and found him washing up. What a strange man he was. Someone had taught him well.

Until this evening he'd hardly spoken to her, but over dinner he had been as pleasant as he'd been before Peter's party. Then, he'd taught her about plants and seeds, soil and seasons of which she had been so ignorant. She had enjoyed his company this evening and wished it could go on like this. She liked him as a friend and perhaps, if there had been no Michael, they might've grown closer in time, but that would not happen now.

"Shall we take our coffee into the summer house?" she asked. "It's a lovely evening and I like the smell of the garden."

He hesitated as he wiped his hands, his face blank for a moment. "Let's sit on the bench outside. I'll take the cushions," and collected them off the seats and took them outside. Laura frowned, but followed with the tray onto the patio. Janus expanded further on the installation of central heating, while she poured hot steaming coffee into serviceable but pretty china.

"What about the wash house? I'll have a radiator in there too. It'll make it nice and warm for you to have your showers in the winter," she said happily.

Janus did not reply immediately, intent on lighting his pipe. He had pushed all thoughts of the treacherous priest and the party out of his mind since midday. The Father had not been seen in the village since Wednesday. Maybe he'd gone for good? Laura didn't seem too upset about it. He could've been mistaken when he thought she'd wanted him too. To be fair, they were men after all and it was so easy to fall in love with this gentle, beautiful woman. He should know. He had loved her for more than two years, so why shouldn't the priest? They weren't infallible... Maybe he had removed himself from temptation?...

His eyes fixed themselves on the summer house, which suddenly seemed a lot friendlier. He removed the now gently smoking pipe and said quietly, "I might not be here in the winter to take showers."

"What?" She had watched him filling and lighting the small pipe and thought how relaxed and comfortable he looked, contented, smoke curling lazily up into the air. Then the image of Michael floated into her mind. As he had sat at the edge of his desk, holding the slim cigarillo between slender fingers, smoke curling up and out of the study window before he had kissed her. He had not telephoned or written to her. Would he ever come back? Don't think about it... "What did you say, Janus? You might not be here? Why?" and almost said 'But you can't,' then remembered she had no right to keep him here.

With an effort, Janus took his eyes off the white building and looked at her. She could see a smile hovering above the nicely shaped mouth. The sunburned face had lost its angularity with good food and fresh air, the chin was round and the nose appeared slender rather than thin and pointed. If he did not slick his hair back and left it alone, as he had tonight, it fell in a natural wave across his forehead, and made him look younger than his thirty two years. Brown eyes, soft and full of love, gazed at her for some time before he asked, "Don't you know, Laura?"

She stared at him, then lowered her head, closing her eyes for an instant. Laura knew she was going to hurt this man and whispered a barely audible, "Yes, I know."

Janus placed the pipe on the table and took both her hands into his own. They were brown and strong and she noticed again how clean the square cut finger nails were.

"Look at me, Laura," Janus said gently. She lifted her face, not wanting to see his love so openly displayed. Deep down she had always known it, but as long as the subject had not been broached, it hadn't mattered too much. Laura heard the strain in the quiet, low voice.

"I've loved you from the very first day I saw you on that empty embankment back in 1922. Always I hoped you might come to love me in time. That's why I came with you, to build a future here, as man and wife, as equals. But things have changed. I'm asking you to marry me, Laura. I'll wait and give you time, but I've got to know if you'll have me, otherwise I can't stay here. Will you marry me?"

Laura, her head in a turmoil, withdrew her hands from his grasp, folded them in her lap to stop them from trembling, as she whispered a painful, "Please Janus, don't ask me," and at last, grey eyes, dark with sorrow, looked into his.

"Why not, Laura? I love you and take care of you. Am I that repulsive to you?" he asked.

"No. You could never be that. I value your friendship and all you've done for me, but I can't marry you," she said, hopelessly.

The face of the man sitting next to her had lost its gentleness. Janus picked up his pipe and matches, then left the bench to lean on the garden wall, staring out over the vast expanse of prepared plots, towards the far orchard and she knew that his dream was tumbling into nothingness. She could see it in the stoop of his broad back, the shaking of his hands as he tried to light the pipe and match after match failed to make contact with the bowl and its contents. Laura did not know how to console him in his misery.

Janus finally succeeded and billows of smoke curled away into the garden. His voice was cool and distant when he turned to face her. "It's been too long for you to be grieving for a husband that died ten years ago. Do you love someone else?"

Laura stared at him, his face implacable, the eyes that had held so much love a little while ago were shrouded in nothingness, keeping what he felt a secret. Should she lie?... No! Whether Michael left the church or stayed would make no difference. She still couldn't marry Janus. "Yes," she said firmly, looking into blank eyes.

"So I wasn't mistaken," he said slowly and she felt a chill as she saw a flicker of fury reflected in the brown orbs staring at her.

"Mistaken about what, Janus?" she asked with enforced calm.

He hesitated, then stood tall, almost menacing, before he answered, "I saw you and the priest in the summer house at Peter's party and again at the back of the stalls on the day of the church festival. I'd hoped it was nothing more than a passing infatuation. It isn't unknown for holy Fathers to pursue carnal pleasures forbidden to them. Where is he, by the way? Left you already?" his voice filled with contempt.

Laura felt anger rising in her at the insinuation. She stood up and left the bench, walked towards the man she had hurt so much, had shattered his dreams. And his strange behaviour lately suddenly became clear. She lightly touched his arm, looked up into the stony face, pleading. "Please, Janus. I'm sorry," and flinched from the sudden explosion of hate and anger expressed in the contorted features, from the tormented sound that left the shapely mouth.

"So where is your lecherous holy man? I hope he rots in hell."

She replied quietly. "That's where we have been for the last few months. Not indulging in carnal pleasure. He has gone to..." Laura stopped, the enormity of what Michael's decision might mean for both of them hitting her with the force of a physical blow. "...he has gone to make his decision. And whatever that is I must accept it. Maybe you and I'll both lose what we want most, but so will he. Love crosses boundaries and doesn't ask permission to enter. You, more than anyone else should know that, as I've never encouraged you. It just happens, Janus," and she looked into eyes full of torment, squared her shoulder and knew she would deliver the last drop of poison. "Whatever Michael chooses to do with his life, if I can't marry him, I'll never marry again."

Janus lifted his hands and for a moment she was afraid that he was going to strangle the life out of her. He gripped her shoulders so hard that his fingers felt like clamps. He stared at her, his breath hot on her face as he hissed. "He had no right, and I'll destroy him." Laura could not move and then she felt the pressure easing, but instead of releasing her he drew her to him and she was shocked by the unexpected exploration of lips, tongue and hands by this man she had only thought of as a friend.

And just as suddenly, he thrust her away from him and walked to his rooms, banging the door shut.

Chapter 10

It was late on Friday afternoon when Freddy dropped Michael Schiller off at the small two storey house in Gelden. They brought in his luggage and several boxes full of his personal possessions. Freddy was going to stay the night and leave early morning. This evening they would have dinner at the only hotel in the village. Michael had invited Doctor Manfred Harber and Niels Knudsen, the headmaster, his friends from childhood, but did not reveal the reason for his unexpected arrival. He usually picked a more convenient time so that the three men could climb the mountains they loved so much.

Except for their time at University, Michael was the only one that had left the place where he was born. When his father had died on the mountain, his mother had insisted that he continue with his studies and watched his ordination with pride. The severe influenza epidemic hit the quiet village just before the outbreak of the Great War. His mother nursed most of the younger children back to health, and became another victim of the virulent virus.

God had been Michael's comfort in his grief and then, the dying and the wounded at the Front left no time for personal sorrow. He had kept on the house and came back to it at every opportunity, changed nothing, content to be surrounded by familiar things his parents had loved.

Since last Saturday he had lived with the silence of the mountains, leaving his house early in the morning with enough provisions for the day and returning just before dusk. His friends did not intrude on his solitude, as both of them realised that Michael was fighting a momentous battle within himself. He would tell them when he was ready. The conflict raged for what seemed an eternity, instead of a paltry seven days. Every day he expected to receive a sign from the God he had served faithfully since he was sixteen years old. But there was no sign and he knew he must make his own decision. Despite the absence of an answer to his prayers, he did not lose faith in the Almighty.

On Sunday morning Michael wrote three letters, and posted them. Already he felt free and relieved and accepted Doctor Harber's invitation to dine with them that evening. Michael unburdened his soul to his friend who applauded his decision and hoped he wasn't going to let the Bishop persuade him otherwise.

"Don't let him bully you, Michael," Manfred Harber said.

The Baron Cornelius von Dettingen-Annsberg read Michael's letter and felt happy and sad at the same time. So the rumours had foundation after all. He should miss the man as a priest but had every intention of keeping him as a friend, and would welcome his wife to be. Cornelius was curious, never having met the much talked about Mrs. Sogar. He intended to rectify that state of affairs at the earliest opportunity and put gentle pressure on Norbert, The Bishop, to go easy on the 'fallen' father.

The Reverend Mother Agnes had looked for a long time at the familiar hand writing and the post mark of Gelden. Usually it would be just a post card when Father Michael went on location to his beloved mountains. She placed the long white envelope on one side and dealt with the other correspondence. She felt uneasy, perturbed about the letter and rang the small bell on her desk. Sister Anna knocked timidly on the door to the Reverend Mother's study and entered.

"May I have some coffee and a piece of sister Gudrun's fruit cake, please. After that I don't wish to be disturbed until I ring you, Sister Anna."

The sister hurried to the kitchen and prepared coffee and cake, then hurried back to the study, wondering what terrible calamity had befallen the convent, but equally determined not to let her worry become apparent to the other nuns. For the Reverend Mother to ask for coffee and cake was the equivalent of an earthquake, a flood or the total failure of the harvest. Mother Agnes did not even ask for coffee before the bishop arrived, only after she had wheedled whatever she wanted from her cousin Norbert. Again she knocked gently and deposited the tray on the desk and found Mother Agnes staring out of the window. She held two sheets of writing paper in her hand. Sister Anna withdrew hastily, awaiting the impending disaster.

It was fifteen minutes later when the silver bell rang again and the sister hurried to the study. The Reverend Mother sat behind her desk, writing, then handed the sheet of paper to the sister, her face had the determined look they all knew so well.

80

"Take this to the post office and send what I have written on there by telegram, sister. Immediately," handing over some coins.

The telegram to the Bishop was on it's way within half an hour. By late afternoon came the reply from the Bishop's residence.

'Expect you at the suggested time tomorrow, Tuesday. Norbert.'

And a smile made Mother Agnes's round face even more pleasant to look at.

She left early next morning, caught the tram into town and boarded a train for Cologne. On arrival, she took another tram ride to the bishop's residence, a mere stone's throw from the twin spires of the City's Cathedral. At 10:30 she knocked resolutely on the door of the study. His Grace, the Bishop Norbert Hessler, son of her mother's sister, called 'Enter.'

The Reverend Mother Agnes did do her cousin the courtesy of bowing to him as an acknowledgement of his office, but did not kneel. In the privacy of his study, Agnes disregarded the obligatory duties towards her spiritual father and came straight to the point, after sitting down in the most comfortable chair.

"What are you going to do about Father Michael, Bertie?"

"So that's what your urgent visit is about? You've always had a soft spot for that renegade Priest. I'll do what I consider fit under the circumstances," he answered, irked at her impudence and knowing full well that he had never been able to get the better of his wilful cousin.

"And what punishment do you think fits his crime?" Mother Agnes asked sweetly.

"Banishment, of course. Six months at the retreat is the prescribed remedy. For reflection and repentance. I will not let him go easily; he's far too valuable to us as a priest," the bishop replied firmly. "Do you know of this woman he wishes to marry after almost half a life time in the priesthood?"

"Yes, I know her. In his letter to me Father Michael makes no apology for loving Laura Sogar. They are both going through purgatory, but have behaved with the utmost decorum. You may banish him for as long as you like, but he'll not give her up now he's made his choice. They will wait. He'll not run like a skunk with his tail between his legs, Bertie."

The bishop's eyes met hers, and he saw the faintest glimmer of contempt in her gaze and felt uncomfortable, sliding his finger between the inside of the clerical collar and his neck, felt the moisture as he withdrew it. He spoke hesitantly now. "And what would you suggest I do with him, cousin?"

"The minimum time at the retreat. One month, then let him go. He's served us faithfully and deserves what he now desires," Mother Agnes said forcefully.

"What is this woman like? Is she of our faith?" He sounded curious.

"No, she's not a Catholic, but may become one in time, if she marries Michael. What is she like? Beautiful, gentle, and she reminds me of someone we used to know," and again her gaze held his, steady, uncompromising.

The bishop dropped his eyes and remained silent for some time. Then he spoke, subdued, and thoughtfully addressed his cousin. "Will you..." he paused, "...will you take tea with me, Agnes?" and she knew she had won. A large smile bathed her face.

"Of course, Bertie. I'd be delighted. May I have some cake, please?"

And for the second time in as many days, the Reverend Mother Agnes broke her vow not to eat between meals. She was getting much too fat for her Habit.

As she took her leave of the bishop she reminded him, gently this time. "One month only, Bertie."

The Reverend Mother made one more visit while in Cologne. After each visit to Bertie, the lofty twin spires of the ancient cathedral beckoned to her to do penance for holding the Sword of Damaclese over his head once again. She entered the side door and waited with other sinners in the long pew before the confessional. Presently she asked the unknown father for absolution of impure and vengeful thoughts. Only then could she step out lightly towards the station.

The train to Bonn was waiting and she settled herself into a corner, intent on enjoying this rare occasion of liberty from the constant demands the convent and her sisters made on her every day. Just for the duration of this journey she could be happy for Michael and Laura. She knew only too well what it felt like to be desperately in love, still remembering the agony she had endured before taking the veil, embracing God instead of a lover.

Had she been as much of a coward as Bertie? Perhaps? But her choice had been one of many and the one she loved had not deserted or seduced her. He behaved impeccably, discharged the obligation his friend had imposed on him and been the most wonderful escort any school girl could ever imagine.

It was not his fault she had fallen in love with him. Time lessened the pain, but never her love. Dear, dear Cornelius...

The train moved slowly out of the platform, the wind blowing white clouds of steam to fill the enclosed platform. A gentle rocking motion of the carriage and the percussive rhythm of the engine contributed further to the well-satisfied feeling of the Reverend Mother. She closed her eyes, the chatter of the other passengers receding into the distance. Images crowded into her head, suppressed and forbidden, and a small voice in her head cried... 'Just once, Lord. Let me dream...' and the images transported her to another time, another place...

Koblenz, 1890, a garrison town full of young officers and soldiers. She was sixteen when she had met Cornelius...

The College for young ladies of good families was noted for teaching its students more than good manners and social grace. The Principal, a formidable lady, convinced them that women should be of more use to the world than just being wives and mothers.

Ira von Sarfeld didn't particularly want to be anything else, but played the game. Baronesses didn't have to go to work. She'd marry a baron, a count or even a minor prince if she was lucky. She was, however, determined not to be an ignorant wife.

Felicia Goodell's intentions were only slightly more ambitious. Dainty, doll-like, pale blonde hair framing an elfin face with eyes of the deepest violet-blue gazing serenely at the world around her. She would be a teacher until Bertie asked her to marry him. Felicia earnestly hoped that his desire to be a Priest was just a passing phase. She, Agnes and Ira had grown up together, sworn eternal friendship on their confirmation day and it would be comforting to be close to her friend.

Agnes, the oldest of three daughters of wealthy Alfred Zimmermann, furniture manufacturer, Jewish and married to the head-strong catholic Emmeline, intended only to get the best possible grades just to please her doting parents. She was happy in the company of her two beloved friends. Bertie, tolerable as a cousin, could be a pompous ass when he felt like it. If he went through with the notion of becoming a priest, Felicia would be heart-broken. What that lovely creature saw in him she couldn't understand, although, Agnes supposed, he wasn't bad looking in a timid sort of way. She liked Paul, Ira's brother, because he always made her laugh.

At sixteen, she and Ira were as tall as the boys, now twenty. Paul, an officer in the Prussian Army, stationed at the old Roman Fort in Koblenz, had in a moment of pure generosity promised his sister to take her to the garrison ball for her sixteenth birthday. Ira refused to go without Agnes and Felicia, and escorts had to be found. Paul did not intend to play nursemaid to three school girls all night.

There had been magic in that evening. The opulence of massive rooms, the banquet, music and the glittering jewellery on shimmering ball gowns took their breath away. The three schoolgirls, in plain white dresses, relieved only by broad colourful sashes, a simple cross around their necks and flowers instead of feathers in their hair, felt like three sisters transported to fairyland meeting their princes.

Ira was claimed by the tall thin Count Alexander von Riesenheim. Shy Felicia was placed in the care of a stocky lieutenant. When they rested between dancing both were engaged in earnest discussion on the merits of educating women, of which the serious minded young man whole-heartedly approved.

Agnes discovered a new world when twenty four year old Baron Cornelius von Dettingen-Annsberg led her to the ballroom, where officers in scarlet and blue whirled with their partners to the polka. Agnes felt her feet leave the ground, float on imaginary clouds in the arms of the handsomest man she had met so far, with unruly brown hair, roguish, flirty eyes and charming manner. Cornelius took her into supper, made her laugh so much she nearly dropped her cup of punch. All night they danced, made trivial unimportant conversation and she fell in love.

It was after two o'clock in the morning when he took her home. He draped his coat courteously over her shoulder, thinking she was cold. He couldn't know that her body was lit by a fire inside and had there been a blizzard, she still would've been warm. She had stood at the door of her parents house, waiting for him to ask the one important question. "Goodnight, Miss Agnes," Cornelius said and gallantly kissed her hand. "It has been a most pleasant evening. Thank you for your charming company," and stepped back to wait until she entered the house. He had not asked to see her again and Agnes felt deeply disappointed.

After Mass the following morning the girls walked to their favourite place where the Mosel and the Rhine met. The grass was soft and a gentle breeze ruffled the smoothness of the water.

Ira mentioned casually. "Alexander wants to see me again. I think I'll marry him. Will I make a presentable Countess?"

Her companions looked at Ira, speechless. Then Felicia smiled, placed a hand on the arm of her friend and said gently. "You'll make a splendid Countess," and Agnes, thinking of Cornelius, recovered sufficiently and agreed.

Ira was reassured and pleased. "Your escort didn't ask to see you again, did he, Agnes?"

"No," came the answer, expressing all the regret she felt.

"I'm glad," Ira sounded relieved. "He's engaged. To the Baroness Gertrud von Ahlen. Alexander said she was rich and beautiful, but cold and arrogant. Not at all the kind of woman he expected Cornelius to marry. His parents picked her as a suitable wife." Agnes felt light headed and the river suddenly swirled and heaved before her eyes. She opened them and wondered why Ira and Felicia seemed distressed. "Are you alright, Agnes?" Ira wailed. "You've fainted."

"Shall I get a doctor?" Felicia asked, at a loss at what to do. The river was calm again, Agnes noticed, but her soul had fragmented into a thousand pieces. So that was why he had not asked to see her again. This was what it felt like to love someone, knowing you could never have them.

"I'm fine now," Agnes said bravely. "I don't need a doctor, just breakfast." She never again mentioned Cornelius. It would be thirteen years before they met again in Dettingen and it was the only time in her life that Agnes fainted.

The Baroness Ira did not complete her education. She married Alexander and was a mother at eighteen, adoring and adored by her husband and his heir, Oliver. The bond of friendship was not broken, Felicia and Agnes travelled south to spend the summer holidays with Ira and the baby.

It was Easter 1892 when Felicia and Agnes graduated. Agnes, slim as a willow, could not forget. The church and God seemed to be a reasonable substitute for Cornelius, and the Convent at Oberursel, some sixty-five miles from Koblenz appealed to her lively, no nonsense temperament. The liberal attitude of the Mother Superior encouraged the sisters to study and follow a chosen profession. There was only one other Convent in the Region that shared the same principles. The Order of St. Quirinus in Dettingen. One day, Agnes vowed, she would go there.

Just two weeks before Agnes was to enter the Convent as a novice, she travelled the ten miles to say goodbye to Bertie. Felicia came too and they spent a pleasant day together. It would be a long time until Agnes saw her cousin again.

The gentle Felicia felt at a loss without her close companions. It became a ritual to visit Bertie and their love affair blossomed until Spring, when the inevitable faced them both. The afternoon was warm as they walked by the stream. Felicia seemed pre-occupied, reluctant to engage in their usual frivolous antics when away from prying eyes.

"Bertie?" her voice was hesitant, subdued.

"Yes, Darling?" he asked, pulling her down onto a patch of grass under the weeping willow tree, cocooned by overhanging branches dipping into the water.

"We'll have to get married. Soon. I'm having your child," the quiet voice said, at the same time aware that he had loosened his hold on her. There was no sound from him and the face that had been pleasant and cheerful moments earlier was chalk white, frozen in terrified disbelief. When words finally left to form sounds, she heard the finality, but hoped she was mistaken.

"I can't marry you, Felicia. The church is my life, you knew that."

She stared at him, the horror of what he had said creeping into every fibre of her soul.

"But..." Felicia stuttered. "But... you said you loved me..." the sound torn from trembling lips. She saw anger and rejection in his eyes as the cold voice sealed her fate.

"I do love you, but priests don't marry," and somehow he seemed to have shrunk.

"What about me and the child? Your child, Bertie? What about us?" the girl asked pitifully. "What am I going to do?" finally grasping the terrifying enormity of her plight, tears welling up in never ceasing waves.

Bertie Hessler drew her close to him, torn between his love for her and the incomprehensible prospect of facing life as husband and father. The only words he could find in answer to her question sounded hollow and as pathetic as he felt.

"I don't know, Felicia. I don't know," and she knew that love had lost it's meaning, that she must acknowledge that his fear to be like other men far outweighed the sweet words of love he had murmured during their hours of passion. The church would be his refuge and he had abandoned her and the child, but she would not demean herself by begging to be relieved of the burden she would have to face alone, begging to be spared the shame and horror that was already assaulting her sanity. Felicia gently extracted herself from his embrace and looked into the face she had loved for so long. It was the face of a stranger, someone she didn't know. Perhaps she had never known him. She had given herself to this man, believed the lies he had whispered to her.

"I must go home, Bertie," she said, and rose to her feet, the violet-blue eyes looking down at the stranger and there was pity for him in her soul. "Mama will know what to do."

Felicia turned to walk back the way they had come, a life-time ago.

* * *

The Mother Superior at the convent of Oberursel studied the quarterly accounts sister Margaret had placed onto her desk.

"Last year was most profitable. The father of sister Agnes was very generous. Let's hope this year will be even better. The number of wayward girls shows no sign of abating," referring to the astronomical fees extracted from wealthy parents to care for their unfortunate daughters until the unwanted child was born. The babies, of good stock, were as valuable to the Mother Superior as the mothers, the donation to the convent from adoptive parents was also very handsome. It compensated for the inadequate renumeration the church itself contributed to the upkeep of the young nuns and novices seduced by lecherous priests.

Sister Margaret nodded in agreement and said. "The child Felicia needs a little more attention than the others. She's so pretty, but not very strong."

Mother Superior did not answer immediately. She too was pondering on the tragedy of the girl with the pale hair and violet-blue eyes. "What do you suggest we do? She cannot be confined to the sick bay for six months."

"Sister Agnes was her friend. Absolve her from domestic duties for the time being and make her responsible for the girl," the plump sister replied.

"Excellent. I don't know what I'll do without you. Sister Agnes is a puzzle to me. She's strong willed, devout, but not pious. I wonder what made her come here?" the Mother Superior asked.

"It is only the pious ones that are without secrets, Mother," sister Margaret said softly. "The rest of us have reasons only God is aware of."

"Will she make a good nun, though?" asked Mother Superior.

"Oh, yes. And in time she'll be ready to take my place, or yours," smiled sister Margaret.

* * *

It was the day after Christmas when sister Agnes held Felicia's child in her arms. The baby was smooth and round, unlike some wizened newborn infants she had seen here.

"You have a beautiful son, Felicia. Will you hold him?" but the mother turned her face away, closed her eyes, tired, weary of life itself. Sister Agnes gazed at the face of the child, willing it to open it's eyes. What colour were they? Violet, like Felicia's or pale, non-descript, like his father's. She held the infant close to her, for this one moment in time he was part of her.

The rope of Felicia's dressing gown did not break when she jumped off the cross beam in the bell tower. They found her when it was time to ring for vespers. Sister Agnes was given leave to take the coffin back to the family. Felicia's absence had been explained long ago. The scourge of the century, they had said. Consumption. Of a child there was no mention and Agnes understood.

Ira von Riesenheim travelled from her estate near the Austrian border in the depth of winter to be with her friend on her last journey, ignorant of the tragedy that was to touch them always.

The countess and the novice, in warm winter coats and boots, walked down to the river, to the place where they had sat in spring and summer at the water's edge. They stood in silence, their arms about each other, crying for the gentle, beautiful girl they had lowered into the cold, frozen earth this morning.

Agnes spoke and there was an urgency in her voice. "I want you to come back to the Convent with me. You can stay overnight."

The countess, not yet nineteen, seemed older. She looked surprised, then worried.

"Is something wrong? You're not ill, are you, Agnes?" she asked, concerned.

"No, Ira. I'm not ill. There's someone I want you to meet there."

The Countess von Riesenheim looked into violet-blue eyes and Felix seemed to smile as he curled a tiny finger around Ira's long one. The baby behaved beautifully on the journey to Ira's home, where Oliver gurgled at his new brother.

* * *

It was to be thirteen years before Sister Agnes got her wish. Father Norbert Hessler, private counsellor to the ailing bishop of Cologne and Koblenz had agreed to receive her. His reply to her letter had been courteous, if somewhat distant. She was well aware of her cousin's steady rise up the ecumenical ladder. They met in the foyer of the bishop's residence in Koblenz.

"Agnes. How wonderful to see you again after so many years," father Norbert said, his hand extended in greeting. He had gained some weight, put flesh onto that skinny body she remembered, but otherwise he looked much the same.

"Hello, Bertie. It's been a long time. You're looking well. Quite a place, this," Agnes remarked, looking at the opulent reception room dotted liberally with gold painted chairs, seats and backs covered in scarlet velvet. Father Norbert led her to a secluded alcove and pointed to the two seater couch.

"You've come a long way, Bertie. What's next? Bishop? Cardinal? Pope, maybe?"

He did not miss the slight edge of contempt in her questions. For the first time since his return he felt the confidence he had acquired over the years ebbing away. He dreaded looking into Agnes's eyes, wondering what he would find there. She had lost none of her candour and could still make him feel gauche and timid. Only Felicia had made him feel like a man, but he had deserted her. And Agnes knew.

"The bishop is frail, but very alert and will go on for many years yet," and changed the subject. "I have given your request a lot of consideration. Why Dettingen in particular?" he asked.

"I've been at Oberursel for thirteen years, learning how to be a good sister. At Dettingen, I want to learn how to be a good Reverend Mother, Bertie. And if one has the right connections, they should be made use of. After all, we both come from hard-headed business stock and ambition sits well on us. Dettingen will suit me nicely." Sister Agnes's tone left him no room to persuade her to go and open a convent in Africa or any of the other Dominions. They made small talk about their respective places of residence and then Bertie rose, an indication that the visit had come to an end.

"I will talk to the bishop about moving you to the place you wish to be, Agnes. And write to the Mother Superior at Oberursel. She will tell you when the time comes," he said.

Sister Agnes rose too and smiled at him graciously. "Thank you, Bertie, for your time and your recommendation." She felt that it was settled already. Father Norbert knew it was. They served the same God and should have been closer to each other, but his brutal desertion had condemned Felicia to death and nothing would ever be as it had been before that time. "I hope the letter to Oberursel won't take too long," Sister Agnes said softly. "Goodbye, Bertie."

"Goodbye, Agnes," he said as they shook hands. She gave him a searching look, walked to the wide doors and stepped outside.

Three months later Sister Agnes was given permission to enter the Convent at Dettingen where she learnt the art of printing and book-binding. Cornelius rode in on the black stallion to see the Reverend Mother on business sometimes and showed great interest in the printing presses, and he recognised the new Sister as the girl he escorted to the garrison Ball. Sister Agnes's heart did a strange dance whenever he came. In her most sinful moments she knew that somewhere in the depth of her soul the love she had felt once, so long ago, was still there. She disliked his baroness intensely, as she did his oldest son, Hubert. Eleven year old Freddy, destined to take over his father's newspaper one day, would always have a special place in her heart. He was already the image of Cornelius.

* * *

It was two days after the bells had proclaimed the new year of 1910. In the study at the convent of Dettingen the Reverend Mother Philippa sanctioned leave for her capable assistant to go home and attend the wedding of her sister. The town of Koblenz lay under a blanket of snow. The wedding had been elaborate and beautiful and sister Agnes had met old friends again. Father Norbert had reluctantly agreed to officiate at his cousin's marriage ceremony.

Sixteen years ago, Felicia had died and Agnes needed to visit the grave before returning to Dettingen. In her long woollen cloak and hood and stout boots, she walked to the cemetery, thinking of Felix. How proud they were of him. Ira kept her up to date with even the smallest detail.

Soft, fresh snow deadened the sound of her boots on the wide path. The black robed priest, his hat held in his hand, stood with bowed head at the foot of the grave, the white marbled head stone with it's black lettering a reminder of the girl they had known, but the grave itself was undisturbed, the snow lay virginal and not even the feet of robins or sparrows had made any imprint. He did not turn as she joined him.

"I'm glad you remembered the day, Bertie."

The priest and the nun stood in silence, then she heard his voice, trembling, as if he had to suppress tears and regret. "I did love her, Agnes. I still do and pray every day to be forgiven for my sin."

There were many recriminations Agnes wanted to fling at her cousin, but did not. The man standing next to her seemed empty, as if Felicia had dimmed the flame of life, taken it with her. She should pity him, but could not do that either, remembering the suffering of her friend. The church was his sanctuary and it was rumoured that he would take the bishop's place.

"I still miss her and pray constantly for her soul to be received by the Holy Father," she said.

Father Norbert looked puzzled. "Why shouldn't she? I seduced her with meaningless words. The sin is mine," he said.

"Felicia killed herself, Bertie. That's a mortal sin."

The pale features of Father Norbert grew chalky and Agnes saw him sway a little, his voice hoarse. "They said she died of consumption."

"The girls that come to Oberursel don't kill themselves. They leave their infants behind and return to their families. Felicia withdrew from life long before the baby was born," Agnes said quietly.

"What about the child?" he asked.

"It was a boy," she spoke softly. "A beautiful healthy child, with his mother's eyes. I saw him born, held him and couldn't let go of him."

"Do you know where he is?" and she saw a glimmer of light return to his eyes.

"Yes. But I will never tell you," Agnes said firmly. "You have a son to be proud of, Bertie. Take whatever comfort you can from that."

"Tell me where he is, please. I must know."

"I swore never to reveal his whereabouts. Nor will I. You of all people have no right to him."

He knew she was right. Desolation came over him again, as it had done for years, his only consolation his service to God. Now, the burden was heavier still. "I am grateful for your silence and shall be forever in your debt, Agnes."

"When you become Bishop, as is rumoured, remember that, Bertie. St. Quirinus will need a new Reverend Mother in time and I'm eminently suitable."

"I'll remember, cousin Agnes, although it is by no means certain that I shall be Bishop," Father Norbert said, somewhat taken aback. "Will you walk with me?"

"Of course," Sister Agnes replied sweetly. "You will be the new Bishop, Bertie."

* * *

Four years passed and war was imminent. Agnes, Reverend Mother of St. Quirinus at Dettingen said goodbye to Freddy, handsome in his uniform and looking exactly like his father had done so long ago. She wrote to Oliver and Felix before they too left for France. Ira wrote volumes about her two younger sons, Christian and Walmar and then of the new arrival of a longed for daughter, Bettina.

It took a tragedy for Mother Agnes to travel South to be with Ira and Alexander. Oliver was brought home in a plain wooden coffin. Two bullets had ripped his chest open as he led his men over the trench at the Somme. They removed the heavy gold ring, embossed with the crest of the house of Riesenheim, to be passed onto Jurgen Alexander on his twenty-first birthday.

When it was over, Freddy came home, without his right leg and brought Michael to be the new parish priest. Felix returned safe and sound.

The Reverend Mother felt concern for the political upheaval in the country, sympathy for the misery of a defeated people and worried about the growing numbers of the Nazi Party. She firmly allied herself to the cause of Freddy and Michael. The ancient printing presses had been up-dated by Cornelius and proved to be the inspirational source to uphold wavering democratic ideals.

In 1923 she again boarded the train to be with Ira when they brought Jurgen Alexander home, his mutilated, mangled body resting in the oak coffin. He had taken part in the massacre with his fellow students in Munich, wearing the brown shirt of the Nazi's, the armband still fixed to his sleeve. They had fought the Communists in a bloody battle, the men accompanying the coffin said, all wearing the hated brown shirts and kepis, flaunting their badges.

Alexander and Ira wept again, looking at the unrecognisable features of Jurgen, but his mother knew that this man was not her son. They had his papers, but the finger that should have worn the ring they had given to him two years ago, was bare and showed no sign of ever having worn an ornament. If someone had removed it, it would have left a mark on Jurgen's hand. And all of them waited for him to come home.

They buried the unknown man in the vault and Ira placed flowers on the stone slab bearing Jurgen's name, remembering that somewhere there could be another woman, waiting, praying, wondering...

The train jolted to a halt at the station in Bonn and Agnes, the Reverend Mother, was startled. She had dozed off on the journey and dreamt of so many things that happened so long ago. She left her seat and alighted from the carriage, helped by a courteous gentleman and thanked him graciously, remembering Ira. Soon she must try and make time for a visit.

But first, she must wait and see what was happening to Michael. She felt sure he would come back and see Laura before being banished for a month at the Retreat.

Chapter 11

Father Michael received the telegram on Wednesday morning. He tore it open, wondering what was so urgent. Cornelius?... Laura?... But the contents instructed him to be at the Bishop's residence on the following day at 2:00 pm. On no account was he to return to his parish. Father Michael seemed perplexed. Why the telegram? A letter would have done just as well. Doctor Manfred drove him to the station on Thursday morning to catch the 9:24 to Cologne and the meeting with his Bishop.

The Bishop's study was at the end of a long, highly polished corridor. It reminded him of Mother Agnes's private office. Why did they have to make everybody walk for miles? Intimidation, he thought. Well, it wasn't going to work. Not Bishop, Cardinal or Pope were going to dissuade him. He took a deep breath as he stood before the wide oak door, then knocked. The voice of Bishop Norbert Hessler called. "Enter!"

The study was large, the space between door and desk a yawning void of parquet flooring. Father Michael stood, waiting. The rotund figure seated in a high, ornately carved chair remained silent, staring at the tall figure by the door. So erect, so proud when he should be humble. He had always liked and admired the priest, even more so after listening to Freddy's account of his war time bravery. Listened with envy, wishing he could be like this man and knowing that he was not. On the few social occasions when they had met at the Baron's mansion he had enjoyed the Father's company and could relax, talk about church business in front of him and rely on his absolute discretion.

"Come. We will sit by the window." The Bishop rose and led the way to two large chairs in the alcove, where the row of four high windows gave superb views over immaculate lawns at the back of the building.

"Thank you, your Grace," Father Michael said and noticed his superior did not stretch out his hand for his priest to kiss the ring of office. The ample bulk of the Bishop settled into one of the deep red plush covered chairs, motioning to Father Michael to sit in the other.

94

"Now, will you explain the real reason why you wish to leave the Priesthood and the church you have served with such devotion for all these years?"

Father Michael answered simply, "I wish to marry the woman I love and live like other men."

"Is there no easier solution to your problem, my son?" The Bishop's voice was gentle, knowing already that nothing was going to persuade this man to stay.

"No, your Grace. There is not," Father Michael said firmly.

"What about your allegiance to God? Your vows of obedience?" asked the Bishop, fully aware of the futility of his questions. For this Father, matters were settled. Michael Schiller did not hesitate.

"My allegiance to the Lord will not diminish by my marriage. The vows of obedience and chastity do not have the same value in the outside world. Chastity will be meaningless and obedience becomes a matter of choice."

The Bishop pondered the priest's reply for a moment, looking out over the expanse of lawn. "Very well put, Michael. You state your case most eloquently. But then, you are a remarkable man. The Lady is not of our faith?"

"No," Michael said. "Conversion from Protestant to Catholic must be a choice for her own conscience, it will not be a condition of our marriage."

The Bishop was silent for a moment, then asked. "You will of course abide by my order not to return to your parish and present yourself at the Retreat on Sunday as instructed?" He watched Michael, saw the determination and felt envious of this man, approaching middle age and wanting something the church could not allow him to have.

"I will be at the Retreat on Sunday. For the required minimum period of one month, your Grace. After that I shall leave, with or without your permission," deliberately refraining from answering the first part of the question. Norbert Hessler noted the abstention and let it pass. His mind was already made up, but rules had to be observed. He must find a replacement quickly, and one that would be acceptable to Cornelius.

"What will you do when you leave the priesthood?" he asked.

Michael's face relaxed a little. He was surprised at the ease of this interview. What he had expected had not happened. There had been no pressure, no anger, no threats and he felt a curios affection for the older man. Balding, folds of fat showed his fondness for good foods and wine.

Whenever they had met at Cornelius's or on church business, he had found him genial and good humoured. The Bishop was a large man and could absorb the excess weight without losing any of his presence, the pale blue eyes, hooded, appeared to look into a man's soul.

"I shall find work to support my wife," Michael said with conviction.

"Very well, my son. I will inform you of our decision at the Retreat," and rose without the slightest effort. Michael stood too and as the two men faced each other again the Bishop did not hold out his hand for the ring to be kissed. Instead he grasped the hand of the younger man and held it. "Goodbye, Father. May God be with you always," and Michael, strangely moved, reverently kissed the symbol of the Emissary of God, the ring of Office.

"Thank you, your Grace. Goodbye," he said and bowed deeply.

Michael Schiller strode lightly across the space as big as a ballroom, and somewhere in that void he heard the Bishop's voice. It sounded stronger than he had heard it before.

"Michael!" and as the priest turned and waited, Norbert Hessler said clearly and distinctly. "I wish I had had your courage thirty one years ago, but I was afraid to face the world outside. Afraid to take the love that was offered to me!" and across the empty space Michael saw deep sadness in the other man's eyes and understood at last why he hadn't been crucified here. The Bishop continued. "I'll inform you when I shall be at the Baron's place. I'd like to see both of you there, to satisfy my curiosity as to who could have so much power to take you away from your vocation. Please come!"

The two men looked at each other for a long moment. Michael bowed and said. "Thank you, we'll be honoured," then walked to the door, a smile on his face.

* * *

His grace, the Bishop of Cologne and Koblenz, sat down, suddenly weary. He hoped his clerk would heed his instructions not to be disturbed for an hour. As he gazed out over the well manicured grounds, jumbled thoughts raced through his mind. Had he been foolish? Too lenient with Michael Schiller? Norbert Hessler could not bring himself to condemn anyone to feel the desperate loneliness he had experienced for more years than he cared to remember. What Agnes had touched on last Tuesday had not left him for one moment. He'd dreamt again of Felicia, the frozen pond where they had skated and laughed, had been in the room where he committed the sin that led to her destruction...

They had placed him with the Priest in the small village not far from his hometown, Koblenz. Agnes had come to say goodbye before entering the convent as a Novice. Big and boisterous, she had brought Felicia, so dainty, golden haired and still so shy. They had known each other since childhood, but suddenly, she began to occupy his thoughts day and night and he was tormented by doubts about his vocation. He wanted what was forbidden...

All through the summer they met, talked and walked, happy in each other's company. And her visits continued into the winter.

For a fleeting moment the pleasant lawn outside became a frozen pond and he imagined the girl with the pale blonde hair and violet-blue eyes in the velvet coat of the same colour, the white fur hood and muff. They had skated all afternoon. When the tip of her delicate nose shone red, he suggested they should return to his room, to sit by the fire, toast muffins and chestnuts. The stillness of the house drew them together, inviting closeness for warmth. He had calmed her fear with sweet words of love he'd practised for a month, took her with tenderness and passion until they'd both cried and laughed and all vows of chastity forgotten. They had made love again and again. And so many times after that, until the spring, when she'd told him that she was carrying his child and that they must marry, soon. Except he couldn't face the thought of leaving his safe, protected world, his sanctuary.

Whenever he and Agnes met he looked into her eyes and felt diminished by the contempt displayed there. She had kept his secret, but never forgave him for Felicia's death. Sometimes when his despair was greater than his cowardice, he wanted to go and beg Agnes to tell him what had happened to the child. But he never did. Sixteen years had passed before she told him that he had a son to be proud of, at the same time steadfastly refusing to give him any more information. Sometimes he felt like shaking her, beating the truth out of her, then realised he forfeited that right years ago.

The sweet face of Felicia haunted him today and every day. How could he deny Michael Schiller his request to be like other men? Or punish him for having the courage to grasp his happiness outside the church, while he himself must live with the shame of his cowardice, the denial of two people. The gentle, loving girl and the child, his flesh and blood. The absolution he received before his ordination had done nothing to still his conscience. It would remind him every day until he died. Oh, dear God. Forgive me!... and his Grace, the Bishop, buried his face in his hands and wept. For the girl, for the son he would never know and a love that had not faded with the passing years.

'Felicia...' the man whispered softly.

Chapter 12

On the same day as Michael Schiller took his first step to freedom, Laura was commanded by Erika to attend a small dinner party at Freddy's place. It was unusual, as Erika very seldom went up there during the week. She and Freddy would go into town, to the theatre or the cinema, but not to his place. That was exclusively reserved for Saturday nights, when both pretended to be man and wife. This dinner was to be special, but Laura was reluctant, remarking she would not be very good company. Erika insisted the fourth guest would keep her amused. For one hopeful moment Laura prayed it might be Michael. He had neither telephoned nor written and she missed him more each day, wondering what he had decided. Maybe Freddy and the other guest would take her mind off the agony of waiting.

Laura had taken care with her appearance, the green suit and the cream blouse looked elegant. She had taken the silk rose off the hat and pinned it to the lapel of the jacket. Freddy picked both of them up at 7:00 p.m. but Erika refused to say who else was coming. The Lodge, snug in it's own garden, lay between the high gates of the long drive and the Mansion itself. Freddy had moved into the two storey building when he returned from the war. It provided him with the solitude he needed and gave him the freedom to invite his own kind of people to stay. Laura was amazed at the spaciousness of the Lodge and Freddy's taste in furniture. He never ceased to surprise her. She had expected a kind of chaotic throwing together of old and new, but Freddy's home had a quiet elegance and a feeling of tranquillity. How much was due to Erika's influence Laura could only guess. Here, they both complemented each other and were in harmony with their surroundings, in stark contrast to their frivolous behaviour in the world outside. This was their home, if only for one night of the week.

The other dinner guest strolled through the front door as if he too was at home here. Cornelius, Freddy's father, greeted Laura, took her hand and gallantly placed a kiss on the back while she could only stammer a cordial response to the older version of Freddy. Still slim, white haired, the neatly trimmed moustache hid a gleeful smile. Eyes full of mischief, exuding charm in great volumes, he said, "Enchanted to meet such a beautiful lady.

May I call you Laura? It would give me great pleasure," and she felt like a queen bestowing a favour to her favourite courtier.

Cornelius told hilarious stories all evening and was very attentive. Laura felt beautiful because he said she was and she did not think about Michael. No-one mentioned his name and she didn't like to ask. Erika revelled at playing hostess, with an adoring Freddy at her side, and Laura felt a brief moment of envy seeing their happiness.

It was almost midnight when Cornelius stopped the car outside her house. "Thank you for a most pleasant evening, Laura. I have enjoyed your company."

"Me, too. It was so different seeing Erika and Freddy at home. Don't you mind about them?" she asked. For a moment the joviality left his face, he looked sad.

"I should've opposed my wife's objection and let them marry. I'm as much to blame for the situation as my wife was. Freddy has always been my favourite son and I'm vain enough to glory in watching my own image all over again. Something I can't expect of Hubert. I love Erika because she restored Freddy and made him feel a man again and I won't begrudge them what happiness they can salvage out of a delicate situation."

"Can anything be done?" Laura asked.

The old man went silent, staring out into the glow of the street lamp outside the house, then said quietly, "You and Michael have a choice. They have not. Unless they wish to leave the church and that is out of the question for both of them."

He noticed Laura start at the mention of Michael's name, saw her hands tightly clenched together, heard the soft voice. "How much do you know about Michael and me?"

Cornelius felt the greatest temptation to tell her of the telegram Freddy had received late afternoon, but they had agreed to keep the secret as Michael had requested. He wanted to tell Laura face to face and tomorrow night there would be another dinner party at the Mansion. All he had to do was persuade this woman to come as his guest. Thankfully Hubert and his family were still on holiday in Switzerland. Cornelius turned towards her, sitting stiff and erect in the passenger seat. How lovely she was, even in this unyielding posture. There was a tenderness in his voice which made her feel a great affection for Freddy's father.

"I'm well informed, Laura. Michael's like another son to me and I'm concerned that he'll make the right choice. I wanted to meet you." There was a small pause. "He's a lucky man." Cornelius reached over and gently prised the clenched hands apart, took them into his own and held them. "I wish I had met you during the last ten years."

Laura felt the tension draining away. She looked at the face so like Freddy's, the roguish smile, mischievous brown eyes and knew she would adore this man always and rewarded him with a dazzling smile.

"Thank you, Cornelius. For a wonderful evening and making me laugh. I've not had so much fun for a long time."

Cornelius knew that this was the right time for an invitation, and exerted all his charm. "I have to give a dinner party for an unexpected guest tomorrow night. Can you make an old man very happy and be my Lady for the evening? Erika has Freddy and you would make a splendid addition to the company I'm entertaining. Please?" and he lifted her hand to place a fleeting kiss on the back of it.

"I think I can force myself if it will please you, I am in dire need of cheerful company at present. Yes, I'll come and thank you for inviting me."

"It will be a special evening for us all, I promise," he said, laughing, and leaping out of the car he walked round to open the door for Laura, bowing with a flourish. "Madam," he said, "I wish you goodnight. Until tomorrow."

Laura stood under the lamp and extracted her house key from her bag. On an impulse she stood on tip-toe and kissed him on the cheek. "You are as much of a clown as Freddy. Goodnight, Cornelius," and he waited as she unlocked the door and entered the silent house.

* * *

By 8:00 a.m. on Friday morning Michael Schiller had packed and was ready to leave Gelden. Freddy would be here at midday and by 5:00 p.m. they'd be at his place in Dettingen. There he would stay until Sunday. Before his departure to the Retreat in the Black Forest he was determined to inform his parishioners at the 10:00 am Mass of his decision. He was not going to slink off like a coward. But somehow he must see Laura and Freddy would have to fetch her. To Michael it did not seem strange to disobey his Bishop's orders not to return to Dettingen. He was not going to stay in the village or the presbytery and he had promised to be at the Retreat on Sunday. That he would do. No specific time had had been mentioned when he must present himself.

The house was in order and could be left for a month. Manfred's wife would keep it fresh and aired. He again read the letter from Cornelius. Tonight they would have dinner at the mansion to celebrate his freedom. Michael could feel the moisture welling up in his eyes. The old man had been like a father to him and he was grateful that Cornelius had not rejected him. But when was he going to see Laura?

He took one last walk to the school to say goodbye to Niels, called at the surgery where Manfred embraced him tightly and said, "Good luck, old friend. Bring her to us when you come out," making it sound as if he was leaving to serve a prison sentence, which Michael supposed it was in a sense. But he would leave his prison in a month. He called at each of the small shops he had known since childhood and said goodbye to his friends. If all else failed he would bring Laura here and they could plan a future. He was not without means and they would have a roof over their heads...

Michael placed the two suitcases by the front door. One held his cassock and collars, which he would need on Sunday. The other the well tailored clothes he always wore on vacation. He had packed his riding breeches, boots and jacket, looking forward to mounting the grey stallion in Cornelius's stable. The kettle was singing and the sandwiches he'd prepared looked inviting, but he would wait for Freddy. Michael stepped out into the neat garden and looked up at the mountains rising high behind the house. There he had sat for seven days, the time it had taken God to create the world, praying for guidance. But neither God nor the mountain had given him the answer to his prayers. Or perhaps they had and he had failed to notice. Now it was done...

Freddy arrived and was in high spirits, ravenous and thirsty. Michael felt the weight lifting from his shoulders as he listened to Freddy's cheerful voice. After an hour they left for Dettingen.

"The old man is having guests tonight," Freddy remarked. "His last fling before Hubert and his family get back. He's invited a suitable partner for you. Thinks you ought to have some practice on how to conduct yourself in society. Particularly where the ladies are concerned."

"I don't need practice with ladies. All I want is Laura," Michael said gloomily, glancing at Freddy's laughing face.

"You'd better tell him that tonight. He thinks highly of this one. Reckons she's a tasty morsel and wouldn't mind making the running for her affections himself. The old rascal never gives up, bless him," Freddy joked.

"I'll be nice to his guest, but that's all. He can have her as far as I'm concerned," and couldn't understand what Freddy found so funny.

"You may have to eat your words, friend. Wait 'till you see her. Now that you're on the loose, so to speak, inflicting your imposing presence on the fairer sex, Pa thinks you should taste the thousand and one delights of womanhood."

Michael looked worried. "When are you going to fetch Laura for me?" he asked.

"Erika is organising that and will tell us tonight. You're not supposed to be here, remember? She'll think of something."

"I can't wait to tell her," he said wistfully. "What is Hubert doing these days?"

"He's getting a highly political slant on things." Freddy's face lost its cheerful expression and Michael saw the other man. Committed to their cause, not afraid to speak out against the tide that threatened to engulf them all. One of the few with the power to influence a dispirited nation with the words of freedom and democracy.

"Is he interfering with the paper?" Michael asked.

"He can't do that. The paper belongs to me. He's got the title and the Estate when the old man snuffs it. With his brats he's made sure of the Baronial dynasty. No, it's his admiration for the Austrian painter that worries me. It's upsetting Pa. The boys are getting the same ideas," Freddy said, concern in his voice as he spoke of his father.

Michael hoped to play down the seriousness of their conversation. "Will anyone else be there tonight?"

"No. Just my old lady. Pa likes her. Always did. He's hoping Walter will get murdered in one of those dives he hangs out in Cologne. Then we'll get married. Pa often comes to dinner on Saturdays. He enjoys Erika's cooking and we have a good time while Walter is safely tucked up with his whore."

"Freddy?" Michael sounded utterly miserable. "Couldn't I see Laura before we go to your father?"

Freddy had driven over the bridge that divided Cologne East from the City proper and turned into the highway to Bonn. They both felt excited now that they were on home territory. As they sped along the familiar road,

Freddy glanced at his friend and felt a twinge of conscience about putting him through the suspense, but Cornelius had forbidden him to mention who the other dinner guest was. It was just like the old man to play games. A mischievous smile played around Freddy's mouth. "You'll see Laura soon enough, Brother. I'll think of something to get you out of the clutches of Pa and the lady. That's depending whether you want to be rescued."

"I just want to see Laura," the tall man said with a hint of despair.

"You will, Michael. Be patient."

Freddy stepped on the gas to get up the hill to the Dettingen estate.

* * *

Laura was in a panic. Erika was going to be here soon. Freddy was going to be here soon. She was a nervous wreck and she couldn't understand why. Nothing was going as she had planned it. Hopefully Janus was in his room getting ready to go wherever he went to every evening. She didn't want him to see her being picked up. He was aloof and he hardly spoke to her. There had to be a solution to this stalemate. Perhaps Erika was right. She would ask him to leave but not before Michael told her what he intended to do with his life. Right now, she was glad Janus kept out of the way. She wished Michael would write, but he had not promised to do so. It was over a fortnight since she had fled from his study.

Since Cornelius's invitation last night there had been no time to go shopping for a new dress. For once she had slept late and felt better, actually looking forward to tonight. She had ironed the frills on the navy silk dress she hadn't worn since Peter's party and Jack's pendant gleamed on her tanned skin. She found a pair of gold drop earrings and smoothed the dress over her slender body. At least her stockings would stay up, even if she felt strange in the narrow suspender belt. Laura couldn't make up her mind whether she liked garters after all. The tooting of a car horn told her Freddy was waiting.

She collected her bag and the silk shawl Peter had brought her from Persia once and took a last look in the mirror, never realising how stunning she looked or how the folds of the dress clung so tantalisingly to her body, unaware of her beauty or the impact she had on men. She quietly let herself out of the house, feeling like a girl trying to evade her capturer.

Freddy let out a long wolf whistle and Erika grinned at her with pleasure. Laura took a seat in the back of the car and tried to look as if tonight was an everyday occurrence.

"Good Lord," Freddy drooled. "You take my breath away."

Laura replied with mock dignity. "If your father does me the honour of asking me to be his guest, then I shall not disgrace him. It's not everyday that I'm asked to dinner by a real Baron," looking smug.

"Wait a minute. I asked you to dinner last night," said Freddy with equal mock indignation. "I'm a Baron."

"Ah..." Laura laughed out loud. "You don't count, you're my friend."

Erika started giggling. "You look absolutely wonderful. It's going to be a very good evening. Somebody will be proud of you, Sweetie."

Freddy chuckled and remarked, "Somebody will, that's for sure," as he drove off towards Annsberg and then up the hill to the Mansion. "Here we are, Ladies," Freddy said as they drew up at the wide doors of the Mansion. "Let's go and have some fun."

Erika opened the door and got out. She had long ago learnt that Freddy didn't need anybody's help to get out, but neither did he open doors for her. She joined Laura, who looked puzzled, staring at one of the downstairs windows. The evening sun threw its last golden rays to reflect in the many glass panes.

"What is it, Darling?" Erika asked. Laura blinked, a frown between the black eyebrows.

"I thought I saw..." she broke off in mid-sentence, shook her head, murmuring, "No. It couldn't be."

Erika asked softly. "It couldn't be what, Pet?"

"Who else is here tonight, Erika?" who shrugged her shoulder.

"Oh, just some man we know. He's very nice. Cornelius likes him a lot."

Laura had seen Cornelius walk past the high window in the company of another man. A little taller than the Baron. His hair was neatly trimmed to meet the white shirt collar at the back of the neck. He wore a grey suit. She'd only had a fleeting glimpse of him before Cornelius obscured her vision. For one dizzy moment she imagined it was Michael, but he would be all in black, if he was going to be here at all. She closed her eyes for an instant, waiting for her heart to stop racing.

Freddy seemed to take an unusually long time to get out of the car. Erika muttered. "I'd better go and see if my Love's got stuck. Go on in. Cornelius is waiting. First door on the left, Darling."

Laura walked to the steps and entered the large hall. The door on the left was wide open and she hesitated. The Baron was nowhere to be seen, but the man standing by the fire place turned as if he had sensed her presence. He looked fit and brown, slimmer than she had imagined him to be. The world disappeared as they stared at each other. Laura heard someone shout 'Michael' without realising the sound had come from her own mouth.

Michael Schiller took two long strides, his arms outstretched and she ran, to be held against a chest who's heart was beating as furiously as her own. Tears made a wet stain on the suit, while Michael stroked her hair, saying over and over. "I'm free, Laura. I'm free. Will you marry me?"

The three people standing in the doorway watched them affectionately, then moved off to the dining room and opened the champagne, congratulating themselves on the success of their charade. Cornelius lifted his glass to Erika and Freddy, his voice a little wistful. "Pity. She would have made a fine Baroness!" and all three broke into loud laughter.

* * *

Young Rudi, stable boy and in charge of cleaning the cars at the estate, saw Freddy deliver his woman and the pretty Mrs. Sogar to the front door at the big house. He intended to give Freddy's Mercedes a quick spit and polish, hoping to be let off for the evening after that.

Rudi was puzzled as to what Father Michael was doing here in 'civvies.' He'd never seen the priest in a suit before. When he came up to ride the Grey, he'd change into riding clothes, but always left, wearing his cassock. Rudi had wanted to clean the car as soon as they had arrived, but Freddy told him to leave it. He was going out again. That car had travelled some distance, Rudi guessed. It was in a right state and Father Michael had carried two suitcases into the house. The old Baron had been like a dog with two tails all day. It was all very strange. Delia only knew that somebody was staying here for the weekend and tonight there was going to be a special dinner party for five.

When Freddy had come back the second time with the women Rudi waited long enough for him to get out and go inside with Mrs. Behrens, then got into the car, ready to give it a quick clean up in the garage. He saw somebody in the drawing room, heard a shout and curiosity got the better of him.

He looked again and again to make quite sure of what he saw. Father Michael was holding Mrs. Sogar as if he didn't want to let go of her, ever. He was stroking her hair and for a minute Rudi thought that both of them were crying, but that must've been his imagination. The woman, maybe? But a priest? Never! And what was he doing holding her so tight?

Rudi looked again. That was some tale to tell the boys tonight.

* * *

Delia, the parlour maid, had laid the table in the dining room, put fresh flowers everywhere on the instructions of Fritz, the butler. She'd asked who was coming because of all the fuss that had been going on all day but he'd said to get on with her work. He knew everything, but never told. The old Baron had had him as a batman in one of his wars before the last one and they were as thick as thieves. Fritz married Hanna, the cook and she never let on about anything, either. All Fritz would say was that there was a house guest until Sunday.

She had nearly dropped the bowl of roses when Father Michael walked in this afternoon. Hadn't recognised him at first. He looked so different in a suit, shirt and tie. Almost like a Baron himself. He wasn't at all embarrassed when she'd stared at him. Just said, 'good afternoon, Delia. How are you?' and she didn't know whether to say, 'very well, Father,' or address him as 'Mister.' Something was going on here. The old man had almost thrown his arms about the Father and then they'd disappeared into the study.

Freddy had gone off again and brought Erika and the pretty Mrs. Sogar back. That was funny. Erika didn't usually come up to Freddy's 'till Saturday and very seldom to the big house.

Fritz always waited at the table, but she had to bring in more fruit and noticed that Father Michael and Mrs. Sogar sat close together. She'd mentioned it to Fritz and Hanna but they told her they would be obliged if she'd mind her own business. She had tried to sneak over to Rudi but he'd already gone off into the village. Then they'd finished for the night in the kitchen and Hanna told her to go to bed. Tomorrow was going to be a busy day.

Her room was in the attic. Nice and big, at the end of the house. It had two windows. One facing the front drive, the other at the gable end looking out over the stables. She and Rudi had worked out their own system of communication by switching lights on and off before they met in the old barn.

Delia didn't feel tired and decided to wait for him to come back. The dormer window at the front allowed her to see whoever came along the drive and that was where she was standing, when she noticed two figures crossing the drive to go into the vinery on the right side of the house. The lights from the drawing room windows and the hall illuminated the arbour just enough for Delia to distinguish the tall man and the dainty woman, walking hand in hand.

"God Almighty," Delia whispered to herself, leaning further out of the window. Mesmerised, she watched Father Michael take Mrs. Sogar into his arms and kiss her. Just like Rudi did when they got together. Delia stared in wonder at the couple below. She never knew priests could kiss like that and his hands seemed to wander all over Mrs. Sogar. Maybe he was familiarising himself with a woman's body. He wouldn't know too much about things like that. He wasn't as rough as Rudi, though. Gentle and refined, as if he were afraid she might break. Mrs. Sogar seemed to enjoy it too. Then they stopped and she tidied her hair and they walked back into the house, hand in hand. Well! What a carry on...

Delia remembered Father Michael telling the Baron that he was going to give the sermon on Sunday and say goodbye to his friends. She'd taken coffee and cakes into the study, but didn't dare stay to hear more. Where was he going? She'd have to get word to Ma and Pa to get everybody to the church for the ten o'clock service. That was when Father Michael was going to tell them whatever it was. Delia didn't think that dumb priest they had as a stand-in would stop him. She was going to be at the church as well and Hanna could lump it. No early service for her this Sunday. And she wasn't going to stay with Rudi all night, either. This was far more exciting...

Delia sat in the high rocking chair by the window. She had dozed off and looked at the clock. Nearly midnight. Downstairs the lights were still blazing onto the drive. She stretched herself and walked over to the side window. Rudi was not home yet. Delia made up her mind. She had no intention of going to bed, crept down the backstairs in her stocking feet and slid back the bolt on the stout back door. Rudi will have to put some grease on that, it was squeaking again.

Outside, she put on her shoes and locked the door, hoping Fritz wasn't going to get out of his bed and check the bolt. She glanced once more towards Rudi's quarters, then kept to the edge of the drive and hurried to the plateau and the bench where she sometimes waited for him. On a fine summer night they would go to their place in the wood. She liked to feel the pine needles under her body, soft, dry and sweet smelling. Delia wound the thin woollen shawl around her and lay on the bench. She hoped Rudi wasn't going to be that long or she might fall asleep. It wasn't long before she heard footsteps on the gravel lane.

"Rudi?" she called softly into the night. And he quickened his step, eager to have some fun, which he hadn't expected tonight.

"Couldn't you sleep without kissing me goodnight, Dilly?" he said, using his pet-name for her. The local dialect they spoke when away from the house was pleasing and musical. He sat down on the bench and snuggled up to the well-endowed young woman, but she gently pushed him away.

"Don't want any kisses tonight. You'll have to go down again and see my Ma, Rudi. Now!"

Rudi opened his mouth in astonishment. "You've gone daft, girl? It's long past midnight and I've just come up. What's wrong with you? Are you sick?" he asked, a note of concern in his voice, which did please her.

"There's nothing wrong with me, but plenty with them at the house," Delia said, pointing her thumb in the direction of the Mansion. "I think Father Michael's going to marry Mrs. Sogar from Annsberg Road, and he's going away, but before that, he'll say his piece on Sunday in church. And I want you to go tell Ma she's to tell everybody to get there."

"Now I know you've gone daft. He couldn't. He's a Father, and they're not allowed to marry anybody!" Rudi said, indignantly, but Delia was adamant.

"I know what I've heard and I know what I've seen," she said, "and just listen to this," and Delia got more and more excited as she related to him what she had seen. Rudi forgot all about having sex and when Delia had finished, he ran all the way down the hill, through the path to Wendel Road and hammered at the door of Delia's Ma and Pa's house.

After delivering his message and instructions he saw Jochen clearing up the bar, with Andreas, the football coach and Heini, the shoe repairer from next door, helping while finishing one last beer. They all needed something stronger after Rudi dropped his bombshell, a smug expression on his face.

* * *

Instead of a few old parishioners attending confession early Saturday morning, Father Bernhard was confronted by a very large number to his flock. They did not confess anything out of the ordinary but he had the impression that something was not as it should be. A peculiar undercurrent seemed to have invaded the church. As if they all wanted to get the obligatory duty over and done with as soon as possible, because today they had more urgent business to attend to. He couldn't think what it could be. Even the sisters from the convent across the road were not as penitent as usual. As if they too wanted to get back in a hurry.

Father Bernhard was perplexed. No festivities were scheduled in the parish and he dismissed it as imagination. The simple Father was blissfully ignorant of the news Delia's Ma had imparted to a few trusted friends and it was spreading like wildfire. To add to his confusion, a note on Baron Cornelius's heavy embossed writing paper awaited him when he returned about 11:00 a.m. to the presbytery. Rudi had delivered it promptly. The short note requested his presence for lunch with the Baron and left no margin for refusal.

The bewildered Father had just time to change into a fresh cassock.

* * *

The middle aged priest plodded laboriously up the hill, following the wide gravel lane which he had been told by Clara would lead him to the gates of the ansion. Why did the rich always have to live on top of a hill? he thought, already sweating profusely. He envied the young people in their shorts and walking boots, bare chested and brown. All the priests he knew had pale bodies like his own and he must be in bad shape, his heart was beating like a hammer. If he had the good fortune to be assigned to this relatively quiet parish, exercise had to be included in his timetable. By the time he arrived at the Baron's door, his clothes were damp from the un-

110

accustomed climb and the apprehension he felt at the meeting. Perhaps he would be told why he had been assigned here at such short notice. His superior only explained that the incumbent priest needed a rest. He'd heard of Father Michael and he did not sound like a man that would be sent off to the retreat for a rest. Maybe he had been taken ill?...

Cornelius was inspecting the arches of vines, prolific with fat, blue grapes. He had watched Father Bernhard lumbering along the drive, visibly wilting from the effort of his climb. Cornelius looked at his watch and felt a twang of conscience. He should've sent Rudi with the car. On the other hand, it looked as if the portly Father could do with some exercise. After all, he himself was coming up to sixty and still walked up the hill without getting out of breath, which was more than could be said for Hubert, who at thirty-three was already going to seed.

He remembered with sadness that he had never liked his first-born son. Always considered him to be a carbon copy of his mother, both of them devoid of warmth and love of people. At least Gertrud had been beautiful, whereas Hubert had not one endearing feature to make him likeable. Ugly of face and body, perhaps that was what had made him sadistic and cruel to his brother, servants and animals alike. Hubert had not outgrown any of these tendencies, passing them on to his own boys. Only fifteen year old Jon had a spark of humanity in him when he was with his Uncle Freddy or himself.

Cornelious stepped out from behind the vines to greet the priest.

"Good morning, Father Bernhard. Bit of a climb, isn't it? Come in and have a cool drink. There's someone I'd like you to meet," and led the way to the splendid dining room with it's array of drinks on top of the long side board. "A long drink or something stronger?"

"Something stronger, please, Baron," said Father Bernhard with enthusiasm.

"A man after my own heart," laughed Cornelius, and poured a good measure of whisky into two tumblers. "How do you like our parish, Father?"

"Very much. The people here are friendly and not unduly troublesome," the priest said, pleased to be able to feel at ease with the old man and hoped the rest of the family were like him.

Cornelius smiled, "We have our share of black sheep, of course, but no more than anywhere else, perhaps less. Come and meet Father Michael before we have lunch."

The Father followed the Baron into the drawing room where Michael Schiller sat, reading the morning paper. Gleefully, Cornelius saw the priest look round for someone dressed like himself. Michael rose from the deep settee and also smiled at the puzzled expression of the Father, as Cornelius introduced the two men to each other. It took all Father Bernhard's limited resources of intellect not to stare at the tall man facing him, dressed in check shirt, jodhpurs and riding boots. His hair tousled from the wind, face and neck a healthy tan, he seemed to be completely at ease in his surroundings. The extra-ordinary blue eyes revealed a sense of fun, when surely he should have been sombre, Father Bernhard thought. He did not think this priest was ill and envied him his ruddy good looks. He was a most handsome man and Father Bernhard envied him that too, and hoped God would forgive him for such feelings. Cornelius sensed the confusion of the priest and motioned him to sit down.

"Father Michael is my guest until tomorrow, when he'll depart for the retreat," and smiled pleasantly. "He has a request to make. Tell him, Michael."

The older priest noted the familiarity expressed by the Baron towards the younger man. Perhaps, if he stayed here, he himself would be so honoured. That would really be a feather in his cap, something to boast about to his fellow priests.

Michael Schiller chose his words carefully. He was not sure how much his replacement knew of his orders not to return to his parish. The last thing he wanted to do was embarrass the amiable Father. "May I ask your permission to deliver the sermon in the morning? I should like to say goodbye to my friends before my departure," Michael smiled and Father Bernhard's spirit lifted. Such a simple request. Such a beautiful smile. Even, white teeth looked whiter still in the tanned face. Why was he not wearing his cassock? He still didn't understand why he had replaced Father Michael in such a hurry. Unless he wasn't coming back here. He had the timid thought of asking these questions, but changed his mind. He himself might be fortunate enough to take this man's place and the less he knew about the affairs of the departing priest, the less trouble he'd be in. He could always plead ignorance and say he'd acted in good faith.

Father Bernhard graciously expressed his delight and said he would expect Father Michael for the 10:00 a.m. service.

"Thank you, Father. I shall wear my cassock, of course," said Michael gravely. The good Father had the uncomfortable feeling that the Baron and the younger man were laughing at him, but their faces remained genial and friendly.

* * *

Cornelius studied the new Priest. Almost bald, too heavy for his age, the watery blue eyes conveyed little personality, the pale lashes did nothing to enhance their non-committal expression. The round face with its fleshy nose looked florid already. The father was too fond of the whisky. If his people did not like their priest, they could be mighty troublesome. On the other hand, if the villagers decided after tomorrow morning that Michael and Laura should make their home in Dettingen after their marriage, then it didn't matter too much who the next incumbent at the presbytery was. Michael would be surrogate priest, leader of the community and remain what he had always been, the best friend anyone could ever hope for, with or without the cassock.' And the lazy Father would be quite content to let Michael take the load off him and keep the parishioners in order.

"Gentlemen, let's go in to lunch," Cornelius said and hoped Father Bernhard had a busy afternoon in front of him and would depart as soon as the meal was over. He'd even drive him down himself. He wanted to talk to Michael, do some riding and look forward to tonight. Dinner at Freddy's with Erika, Michael and the beautiful Laura.

What more could a man ask for?

Chapter 13

The bells rang out as they did every Sunday. Perhaps a little more stridently today, or so it seemed to Laura, waking from a pleasant dream. She stretched, still engulfed in euphoria. Michael had driven her home just before 2:00 a.m. but had not got out of Freddy's car, so as not to give anyone that might still be about at that hour more reasons for gossip. They had said their goodbye's at the lodge, walking in the secluded garden. She would not see him again for one whole month, but he had promised to write this time, although he was not permitted to receive mail or telephone calls. Only a matter of life and death waived that rule and neither of them could foresee such a calamity. Their life would begin when he left the retreat, and where that might be would be decided by the parishioners this morning.

Laura looked round the bedroom and felt a small wave of apprehension wash over her. If they could not be accepted as man and wife in this place, then they would go to Michael's house. To leave here was going to be a wrench, but she would follow him to the ends of the earth, if necessary. They had felt like sixteen year olds last night, embarking on a strange and exciting journey. She closed her eyes again, recapturing the magical feeling when he had kissed her, held her close to him, both lost in the heat of passion neither of them had thought to experience. And what would it be like on their wedding night? Would he still think that it had all been worth it? What if he wanted children and she couldn't give them to him? She had never conceived again after Peter was born. It hadn't mattered with Jack away for most of the year. Peter had been enough.

The faint sound of the eucharist bell sounded through the window. After that, Michael would tell the people of this village of his decision to leave. Maybe tomorrow they would all come and denounce her as a jezebel, or worse, as a witch? And maybe nobody was going to speak to her ever again and she would have to leave anyway. Was Ed going to put in the bathroom? Suddenly, a thousand terrible questions raced through her mind. Erika had promised to drop in later and tell her what was happening out there. She remembered Janus and her spirit dived even further. She had forgotten about him. The thought of having to tell him that she was going to marry Michael filled her with dread. His last words on that awful evening had been 'I'll destroy him.' What had Michael done except fall in love with a woman? But jealousy did strange things to people, made them dangerous. In spite of her misgivings, she felt pity for the man she had rescued on the embankment by the river and knew he would not stay.

* * *

Michael, in plain black robes, waited in the sacristy. He had declined Father Bernhard's offer of officiating at Mass instead of the chaplain. This was worse than war. Listening to the muted strains of the organ, he knew it would not be long now. He felt like Judas, on the point of betraying his people. His glance fell on the large bronze cross on the wall and he silently asked for the strength to go through the ordeal awaiting him. Then he walked to the door.

All eyes were on the tall, erect figure as he climbed the short wooden steps to the pulpit. Elaborately carved, half round, it seemed as if the priest was suspended in mid-air, looking down at his parishioners for the last time.

Michael Schiller did not need notes. As he looked at the familiar faces below, he remembered the past five years. He had grown to love every one of them, gained their respect as a priest and as a man, and wondered for a moment what life was going to be like after this, his last sermon. And he spoke into the silence. His familiar voice cast it's charismatic spell as he told them of his love for God, his affection for the many friends he had made in this place, which he may have to leave forever. He spoke of duty, to God and himself and then delivered his bombshell.

"I have deliberated long and deeply about duty and finally realised I also have a duty to myself. It is my decision to leave the priesthood and live like other men. I shall never forsake God or my religion, but I will marry the woman I love. I can no longer fulfil my vows and obligations imposed on me as a priest. It saddens me deeply even to contemplate that I may not be in your midst and it must be your choice whether you'll accept me here as a man. If that is so, we will remain in this place we love. Forgive me. May the blessings of the Lord be with all of us."

He looked for a moment at the stunned faces below him, made the sign of the cross and lightly ran down the steps, knelt in front of the altar and vanished through the door to the sacristy, aware of the shocked faces of Father Bernhard and the young chaplain. Soft murmurings followed him and he was glad to step out into the rose garden, following the path he had taken so many times when church duty required him to be at the Convent. The Reverend Mother Agnes was expecting him. The note the young novice had delivered yesterday at the mansion ordered him to be at her study after the service. She wanted him to join her for coffee and cakes before he left for the retreat.

Michael smiled. At least she would remain his friend. He would not receive thirty pieces of silver, but something much more precious. The love of Laura, who was to be his beloved wife as long as they should live.

No-one noticed Janus at the back of the church, listening attentively to the priest's voice echoing around, firm and clear. He had slipped in through the side door while the congregation filed to the altar rail and had waited behind one of the round marble pillars. When Michael Schiller finished speaking, he walked slowly out of the same door, an ugly expression on his face, mounted the motorbike he'd left at the curb and pointed it in the direction of the town.

There was murder in the heart of Janus.

* * *

Laura had dressed and found the kitchen stove had not been attended to. So Janus had not come home and she felt somewhat relieved, as on this morning she did not want to see him. It took some time to get the fire going and for the water to heat. She tried the rolls, but they had lost their freshness. A boiled egg did nothing for her taste-buds, either. At last, the water bubbled and the aroma of freshly brewed coffee brought back a sense of normality.

She wished she hadn't slept so late. The day was bright and sunny and warm. After the second cup of coffee, Laura saw the world in a different light, even tackled another of yesterday's bread rolls. Now that matters between her and Michael were settled she would have to attend to the things that had been left in the last two weeks. Janus wasn't going to be with her. Maybe he had left already, a small guilty thought whispered hopefully. Laura had the uncomfortable feeling that he would not make his departure that easy for her.

She walked out of the kitchen and into the garden, where he had toiled so hard, day after day. It all looked so well planned, so comfortably tidy. Perhaps they would all have to leave soon. She would miss the summer house and the smell of the flowers, miss the orchard when it was in blossom and the sweet smelling meadow going down to the stream, miss the house she had looked on as her permanent home. She would regret leaving this village and it's people...

The sound of a persistent ring on the doorbell brought her back to reality and she ran back into the house to find Erika waiting at the door, a big grin on her lovely face and holding a bottle of Laura's favourite wine in front of her.

"To help us celebrate, Pet. He did it! It was a marvellous performance by your Beloved. The church was packed and as quiet as a tomb when he told them. I've spent the last two hours in Jochen's bar with the boys, Annie and the rest of our neighbours. Rudi's been sounding out the other four pups. I don't think anyone's going to get any lunch at home today. They're too busy debating what to do about you two."

Erika led the way to the dining room, collected glasses and the corkscrew, withdrew the cork with expertise and poured. She settled herself in a corner of the old comfortable settee Laura had thought of replacing with something less bulky.

"Oh, Dear," Laura moaned. "Is anyone ever going to talk to us again? Will Ed still want to do my bathroom? And dare I go shopping without getting lynched?"

Erika laughed and Laura's spirits lifted at the sound. "That's why I'm so late. Jochen sent the bottle round with his best wishes, by the way."

They both drank and Laura laughed. "So what has been going on? I'm dying to know."

"Well, Michael left after his sermon, Freddy took Cornelius back home as they didn't want to influence any debates they knew would be going on. And I stayed with our crowd at Jochen's. The majority in this place want you to stay here and get married. You'll have the biggest wedding there's ever been around here. They've all invited themselves. Only some of the old ones think it is quite shocking. They've forgotten what it's like to be in love, but will come round in the end. Here's to you and Michael!" Erika toasted her friend, glad to bring the good news.

"Does Walter know?" Laura ventured.

"Of course. I told him on Friday evening. He was getting worried, wondering what was going on, with me going up the hill two nights running. But he promised not to let the cat out of the bag until Michael had told everybody. He will have told Leon, but that doesn't count. He's pleased for you both, said it was about time you two got together. Have you told your lodger yet?" Laura shook her head. "Well, he knows already, Sweetie. Somebody thought they saw him in church this morning. Where is he?"

Laura shrugged her shoulder. "Don't know. The bike's not there and I don't think he was home last night. The stove was out. I'll have to tell him when he gets back tonight. Get it over with," and then added, "And tell my son that his middle-aged mother is getting married. What do you think he'll say when I tell him who his stepfather is going to be?"

"Well, Pet. Your son leads his own life away from you. So did your husband. I'm sure he'll be delighted. Let's have a pleasant afternoon and talk about weddings and love," and they toasted each other again.

* * *

Laura sat at the dining table and wrote to her son. It had been easier than she imagined. She did not apologize for falling in love and felt sure Peter would accept Michael as his step-father. The only regret was that Janus would loose his home. She promised her son that there would always be a place for him here and he would always have her love, and Michael's.

Laura debated with her conscience whether to elaborate further on the situation and tell her son that nothing improper had taken place, but decided that was a matter between her and Michael. She did not pry into Peter's love life. Like all young, healthy males he was not adverse to the attentions of the opposite sex and again she wondered if Jack too had indulged in affairs when away from home. But that she would never know. She pasted down the envelope, ready to post in the morning. The light meal she prepared for herself did not taste as it should've done. Sometime tonight she would have to deal with Janus and it was making her nervous. For the rest of the evening, Laura retreated to the sitting room, stretched out on the wide settee and tried to read, while listening for the motorbike.

It was 10:45 when she heard the bike stop outside the door. It would take him a few minutes to push it up the path and into the room below his own. He never left it outside. Laura went into the hall and flicked on the

118

light, glancing at her reflection in the mirror. She had dressed in a navy pleated skirt, a long sleeved cream blouse and navy waist coat. She'd considered it sober enough for the delicate mission she intended to get over with tonight. There was no vain conception in her eyes of the attractive picture she presented, plain gold earrings, hair neatly tied back in a large slide and slim legs in stockings and navy shoes. Grey eyes dark with apprehension, she switched on the outside light and opened the door to the patio as Janus was coming through the gate, pushing the machine towards the store room.

She called his name and saw him start in surprise.

The face that turned towards her was inscrutable, the dark eyes neither angry nor kind, devoid of emotion. Laura felt at a loss, remembering the evening when he had walked away from her. She had seen him come alive when he talked about their future and then she'd shattered his dreams. Tonight, his face was as empty as it had been two years ago when he'd sat on the bench, alone in the world.

He spoke listlessly, "Yes, Laura?" and pity gripped her soul.

"I have to talk to you. Please, come into the sitting room," and before he could answer, she retraced her steps, leaving the door to the hall open.

She sat down in the corner and waited, her gaze wandering about the high and spacious room, the octagonal glass topped table with it's bottle of wine and two glasses, sweet and savoury biscuits in shallow dishes, the elegant brocade covered three piece suite flanking the table. She loved this room, but felt lost in it, much preferring the smaller dining room. The knock on the door startled her and she stared at the man entering the room. Only the hair seemed familiar. He stood, waiting, the long black leather coat still buckled about his slim frame. Why the coat should frighten her she did not know. A lot of motorcyclists wore them, but somehow on Janus it looked sinister. It was the implacable face of a stranger more than the coat, Laura surmised, as she looked into blank eyes.

"Sit down, Janus. Please," she motioned to one of the chairs. He started to undo the belt, discarded the coat and Laura stopped in horror, foolishly holding the glass she was going to fill in her hand. The brown shirt, black breeches, glossy black riding boots and the holster with it's revolver tucked inside jolted her, but it was the obscene armband, red, white and black, the swastika glaring at her, which turned shock into anger. "Why are you wearing that clown's uniform, Janus? It doesn't suit you!"

Janus stood in the large empty space between door and chair, tall and erect. The faint sardonic smile and the strange light that suddenly appeared in his eyes made her aware of the faint horizontal lines across his brow. When he spoke, softly and quietly, the very softness of his voice carried menace.

"I went to the church this morning, Laura. To hear your priest announce my death sentence, metaphorically speaking, of course. I knew of the rumours yesterday when I went to the barber's, but hoped that he'd change his mind and tell the congregation he wouldn't leave. But maybe that was too much to expect. One must give him credit for guts, though. This clown's uniform will be my future. We'll win, Laura. Unite Germany again and take care of the people that stood against us!"

Laura became aware that her mouth was wide open, closed it and composed herself with all the self control she possessed, the small tremble in her voice the only indication of her distress. She had learnt years ago to hide the unbearable loneliness from her young son and present a serene facade to the world.

"Please sit down. Just be careful that revolver doesn't go off and damage my furniture," and watched him unbuckle the wide leather belt she had seen months ago hanging from the hook behind his stove. Janus had the grace to look faintly embarrassed as he placed the belt on the floor, where he had left the leather coat. He settled in the chair and she noticed the boots. Made of fine leather and she presumed them to be expensive. Several badges were pinned or sewn on the shirt and she wondered what rank he held in this new party people either joined with enthusiasm or were afraid of. She poured some wine into the glass and handed it to him without asking if he wanted it. Janus watched her in silence, his face withdrawn, empty.

Laura spoke gently, "Politics have never been my strong point, Janus, but I think it's is time I concerned myself. I read of the rallies and riots that go on in Berlin and the South, Munich in particular. It's been relatively quiet since the imprisonment of your so-called Leader. The Rhineland is a neutral zone and the French are not likely to give it up to a little nobody like your Austrian Corporal."

She saw a spark of anger in his eyes at the mention of the Corporal. He considered for a moment before answering, ignoring the reference to his Leader, his voice cool and crisp.

"You're not as ignorant as you pretend to be. We'll take our time, hold democratic elections. The people need a new direction. They know Chancellor Hindenburg is an old man. He can't lead them to the promised land and Adolf Hitler has too many followers to be ignored. They'll have to let him out, and soon. Then the real task of rebuilding this Nation will begin."

"What about the Christian Democrats, Communists and Conservatives? Most of the influential people are Conservatives," Laura remarked, curious to find out how committed Janus really was and what part he played in this new order they talked about so much. He looked at her, searching her face as if he too was curious as to how much she knew.

"The Democrats are weak and unstable," he said cautiously. "The Communists will be purged or eliminated and the old Conservatives are wavering, except for the hard core, who'll oppose us. A great many have already joined us or sympathise with our cause, because it'll bring them the greatest benefits, if Hitler wins an overall election some time in the future."

"And what will happen to that hard core that has and will oppose you?" she asked.

"We have plenty of time to persuade them," Janus replied.

"What if they don't wish to be persuaded, Janus? What'll you do then?"

"They'll have one chance, to be with or against us. Or..." his voice petered out, he reached for the glass and finished his wine.

"And how do you know all this?" Laura asked, and she saw his face tightening and the lips compress. She refilled his glass as he looked at her, not certain where she was leading him with her questions, so he countered with his own.

"Do you mean the Party, or me?"

"You. I should like to know what position you have in that new world you are promising the people and if I have to be careful what I say to you."

Janus studied her for an instant before replying. "You'll be in no danger from me, you've got to believe that," he said with the utmost conviction. "But you should choose your friends more carefully, Laura. They'll put you in danger. Particularly if you marry the priest."

Laura felt a chill, although the room was pleasantly warm. It was the hint of menace in his voice again, but she was determined to remain calm. "Which friends are you referring to? And what has my marriage to do with danger?" she asked, taking a long drink of wine.

121

"You asked me what position I hold. I'll tell you. Every organisation, big or small must have order and co-ordination if it's to succeed and achieve it's objective. This one is already very big. That means there have to be people that are able to sift through the information received from the informers, spies and every crawler that betrays his friends and neighbours for a few measly marks, so that we can be sure who our friends are. It's been my job to do that for the past two years in this Region and I'm very good at it. I've learnt much about human nature in that time and I don't find it too uplifting."

"I never realized before how little I know about you. What kind of a man are you? Do you spy on your friends too?" her voice held a note of contempt.

There was a strange silence as Janus stared at the light reflecting on the glass of the table, as if he was formulating a suitable reply. He sounded faintly apologetic.

"My business is to find the enemies of the party and keep the files for future use, linking this Region with all the others. I've no friends, Laura. Can't afford them in my kind of work, but the information on certain people I've kept to myself, so far. They were Peter's friends at Rema House and became yours when we moved here. I've known of the activities of the priest and 'Pegleg Freddy' for a long time. They and Erika Behrens, and some of the nuns at the convent, have been waging an anti-Nazi campaign for years. Did you know that?" He sounded agitated. Laura shook her head, another chilly wave filling her body, she felt her hands shaking and laced them together so he would not see, her own voice rang strange in her ears.

"No. We don't discuss politics. And don't call Freddy a pegleg. He lost it in the same war you fought in, remember?"

For an instant there was a flicker of anger in his eyes and his voice took on the coolness of before. "Times have changed since then. I've been lucky, but millions are still in the gutter and nobody's getting them out."

"What is going to happen if you add their names to the files?" she asked.

He shrugged his shoulders. "It depends on what I'll put in there."

"Are you that powerful already? What'll happen to the others on the list, Janus? Will you shoot them with the revolvers you're so proud of parading around in?" and again she saw a faint anger.

"I'm not going to shoot anybody. It's not my job," he retorted sharply.

Had she touched a raw nerve, Laura wondered, as she watched him grab his glass and gulp down the remaining wine.

"You're like Pontius Pilate," she said softly. "You write names in your files and then wash your hands of them. What will you do about my friends, Janus? And about Michael in particular?"

He almost winced at the mention of the name, she wasn't sure if it was pain or revulsion. "I'm not sure yet. It depends. He's taken you from me and without you, all I've got is the Party," he said, leaning forward, staring at the pale grey carpet. He appeared the personification of utter misery, but Laura could not help feeling threatened. She knew that he had not finished with her yet.

"Janus." He looked up as her voice seemed to reach him from wherever he had been and she found in his eyes an expression which scared her, as if he had decided some important matter. "You haven't answered my question. You told me you loved me, but I love Michael and my friends. Their safety is important to me. I'll give you anything I possess to keep them that way," and as the words left her mouth she knew she had blundered, watching a sardonic smile hovering around the well-defined lips.

"Anything?" Janus asked, the smile deepening. "You want to be careful with that word, Laura."

Laura shifted herself from her comfortable position in the corner and sat up, her feet neatly placed side by side on the carpet. Janus watched the soft grey eyes take on a flinty edge he had never seen before, her voice too had a resonance with which he was not familiar. This was not the soft gentle woman he worshipped. He realised there was another Laura somewhere deep down and he wanted her. Wanted this cool mysterious creature with a fierceness that shocked him. To possess this stranger would diminish any guilt he might feel later.

"What will it take, Janus? The garden? My house? You can have it all and start a new life away from the Party. Go anywhere, but don't betray them, I beg you."

"I dreamed of all that once, but it has no meaning now," he said sadly.

"Then what will it take for you to promise me their safety?" she asked and already knew the answer as she watched the smile deepening to a leer. His eyes, bright now, too bright, travelled over her body and she waited for what was to come. If he proposed what she thought he would, then the association with the lowest of the low had already brutalized him. It would not be the gentle man she had known all these years. Or maybe she didn't know him at all?

He spoke then, softly but clearly. "I want to stay with you tonight. I'm leaving at 6.00 am and shall be out of your life forever, but tonight is mine."

When the words became a real sound, Laura was not as shocked as she expected to be. There was a hard core within her that had never been tested. She had imagined that loneliness and the suppression of the need for a man's touch had been the ultimate in endurance. She had never experienced hardship, poverty or needed to make a choice such as was presented to her just now, but he held the lives of Michael, Erika and Freddy in his hands, maybe the lives of the Reverend Mother and Cornelius, too. As she stared at the man sitting in the large chair opposite her she could not imagine him taking her by force, unless... Well, she would call his bluff...

"I'm not sure whether I ought to be flattered, insulted or regard what you've just proposed as a bad joke. I did hear you correctly, didn't I, Janus?"

He sat very still, returning her steady gaze. "You did hear me and it is no joke. Give me this, to remember for the rest of my days. To remind me of a time when I still had dreams," he said, neither begging nor forcing the issue. "The choice is yours, Laura."

"And if I don't accept your proposition?" and again he shrugged his shoulder.

"Make no mistake. I have the power to divert attention away from their activities, and I will do so if I get what I want. If not, there are no guaranties your precious priest and company will not be found in some alley or other, dead or as near as makes no difference. Read the papers, Laura. They're doing it all the time and it'll get worse, believe me. I can save them, but I want my reward."

The images of Michael and Freddy, dead or beaten beyond recognition, shocked her to the depth of her being and a night of submission became less terrifying. She saw Janus get up, collect the gun belt and his coat and for a moment he stood, towering over her, his face set, empty of emotion. Then he turned towards the door to the hall.

Her voice, trembling, but clear, reached him. "Janus. I'll be waiting in the guest room. Don't come up wearing THAT," her contemptuous tone piercing his conscience like arrows. He nodded and left her.

Laura had found the pale grey lace trimmed night gown and matching house coat she had never worn yet and would not wear again after tonight. The large bed looked unfamiliar with the cover turned back. Only Martin had slept in it since she had moved in. She sat in the small wicker chair, numb and cold. Another sip of whisky warmed her a little and she marvelled at the effect of the amber liquid in the glass. Should she have screamed and shouted? She didn't know how to do that. Should she have begged and cried? She didn't know how to do that either. The debate within herself was full of conflicting advice.

'You're not a virgin, one half had said... 'But I feel like one, it's been so long, the other countered... 'It's only for a few hours and he'll be gone and no-one will ever know... But I shall and I must live with that, keep it from Michael, when we shouldn't have any secrets from each other... Common sense gained the upper hand and commanded: Michael and the others will be alive and safe, just remember that...

As she waited, hoping that Janus had not really meant to carry out his intentions, she heard soft footsteps on the stairs. He knocked gently on the half open door and stood in the doorway, bathed in the warm light from the bedside lamp. She noticed he had changed into shirt and trousers, the leather slippers she had given him last Christmas on his feet. Janus looked like the man she remembered from before Peter's party, before he knew about Michael and she felt a strange compassion for him. In a few hours it would all be over, she told herself, as he came towards her and stretched out his hand.

"Come," he said softly, and she knew that he had drunk whisky, too. Had he needed it to give him courage? Laura stood up and with a swift motion he lifted her up into his arms and placed her onto the bed. There was nothing more she could or would say to him. Janus did not undress, but lay down beside her, looking at the beautiful woman he desired so much. But this was the gentle Laura he had fallen in love with, who had given him back his life and he tenderly wiped away warm tears sliding slowly down her cheeks. His voice had changed too and she saw in his eyes only a deep love and the pain of rejection.

"I could never hurt you, Laura," he whispered, stroking back loose strands of her hair. "You're the only woman I've loved and will love as long as there's breath in my body. So beautiful, so courageous. It makes me afraid because I won't be here to protect you."

He held her for a long time, not moving, his face buried in her hair, as if he wanted to absorb the very essence of the woman prepared to lose her honour to save the man she loved and her friends. To possess her completely had become irrelevant.

He let her go and sat on the edge of the bed, his eyes gazing at her face and the body he was aching for, but could not violate.

"Forgive me," his voice was barely audible, as he stood up and gently tucked the cover around her. Then he spoke more forcefully, "You must promise me to tell your..." hesitating a fraction, "...tell your friends to stop this senseless campaign. I'll do all I can, but I'm leaving for Munich. What Hubert will do to his brother I have no control over. He's already well on the way to the top. But the others should be safe enough if they don't meddle in politics. Promise me you'll do that?" He bent down and kissed her, a fleeting, tender kiss, which brought more tears. "Goodbye, Laura. Be happy."

And all she could do was whisper, "Goodbye, Janus," as she watched him leave the room. She wept for him, and Michael, for their life together, and finally fell asleep.

Laura did not wake when the Mercedes drew up at the door. Did not see Janus glance one more time up to the window on the first floor after he had stowed his few belongings into the big shiny car, which would take him out of her life.

She rose about 7:30 a.m. and didn't quite know what she felt like. Glad that she had been spared the ordeal, sad that Janus had to leave and joyful at the future with Michael. The stove in the kitchen was warm and welcoming, the kettle gently steaming but the coffee pot was empty, ready to receive ground coffee beans.

In the dining room, by the black tiled stove, stood Janus's rocking chair. The note left on the cushion just said, 'For you, with my love. When you sit here, think of me sometime. One favour I need from you. Go to the Mission and give Daniel a home. He'll help you with the garden. Take care of him as you did of me. If you need me, go to the tavern and see Nell. Daniel will take you. Janus.'

Laura sat in the rocking chair and remembered the kind, softly spoken man she had found by the river and vowed whoever Daniel was, she would look after him too and wondered who Nell was...

Chapter 14

A telegram arrived for Laura. It said, 'Congratulations. Stop. Arrange wedding for December. Stop. I love you both. Stop. Peter,' and for some unfathomable reason she burst into tears. Everything would be alright, her son was going to be there to give her away and life with Michael could really begin. They would have six weeks to arrange everything after he left the Retreat. It would be cold and she must find a suitable outfit in town. First the Registry Office in the morning, then lunch with her closest friends at Jochen's. The church ceremony was in the afternoon and after that Jochen would put the ballroom at their disposal for the rest of the day. They expected everybody and she knew he was going to provide the musicians to keep things lively. It would be wonderful to dance with Michael, and everybody else and then go home...

* * *

On the last Saturday in October Father Michael became Mr Schiller. Freddy had collected him from the Retreat. He looked fit and brown. Tonight there would be dinner at Freddy's place, but now Michael wanted to see Laura.

It was almost midday when he rang the doorbell. Laura threw herself into his arms and they stood, just holding each other, overcome with the joy of his freedom. Then he put her away from him. "Let me look at you," Michael said. "You're more beautiful than I remember, Laura. I love you."

He heard the tender, "I love you too, Michael," before drawing her to him again to kiss her, his mouth strong and purposeful on her lips. They hardly noticed Erika and Freddy entering the hall.

"Sorry to break up this touching reunion, old friend," Freddy said, tapping Michael on the shoulder, "Your presence is required at Jochen's. There's a welcoming committee waiting at his place. You too, Laura."

"But I want to talk to Michael," Laura wailed.

"You can talk to him tonight, Pet," Erika grinned at her. "Jochen's got champagne on ice. Come on."

Michael placed his arm around Laura's waist and together they walked up the road, turned the corner of Wendel Road and a great cheer went up from the crowd in the bar as they entered.

"Welcome home, Michael," they said as they shook his hand, embraced both of them with affection.

"Here's to love and a long married life," said Jochen, beaming from ear to ear, placing the bubbling champagne in front of them. "Drinks are on the house."

It was three hours later when the four of them returned to Laura's house. Warmed by the welcome, whisky and champagne, Michael looked happy and Laura was radiant. He stood in the middle of the sitting room, looking about him.

"It's still the same as the last time I was here. Then, I said goodbye to Mara and Josef Schumann."

"I hope you like living here, Michael," Laura said. "It'll be your home soon."

"I always liked this house, Laura. There was peace and love here and I still feel it. We'll add more love," he said tenderly, and placed a gentle kiss on her lips.

"Freddy's got some things to do before he comes to fetch you and Erika for dinner. I'll see you tonight, my Love."

On Sunday morning Michael and Laura met outside the church and walked in side by side. A sea of smiling faces nodded their heads as they passed along the middle isle, to part just behind the children's row. Laura joined Erika and Chrissy, Michael went to sit with Cornelius and Freddy. To listen to a Mass, not conduct it, felt alien to him and for a moment he placed a finger between the stiff collar of his shirt and neck. Cornelius saw the gesture and patted Michael's arm reassuringly.

Father Bernhard was a bore, he thought, perhaps he could persuade him to let Michael read the lessons, if only to break the monotony. Or get a new priest...

They had agreed that Michael was not going to spent his evenings at Laura's house. It would be improper for him to do so. Today, Monday, he was going to collect her at three o'clock to go into town, and later have dinner at the Hotel Kurfurst.

Laura was waiting, dressed in her dark suit, a perky navy blue wool hat on the blonde hair. She had not fastened it with the pretty hatpin when she opened the door to Michael. Lost in his embrace and ardent kiss, the hat went flying.

"I think we'd better go, Michael," Laura said, after she got her breath back.

He grinned at her, looking her over. "Maybe you're right, my Love. You're too dangerous to be alone with. It's going to be hell until the wedding."

"You could always go to your house and wait there," Laura teased.

"I'm not letting you out of my sight, Woman. Cornelius might persuade you to be his baroness when my back is turned. He's very fond of you."

"I know," she said, laughing. "I like him too," and Michael enfolded her in his arms again, and murmured,

"I'll never let you go, Laura. Never."

They walked through the village, hand in hand, greeted people they met, their faces beaming and boarded the tram, where they talked to Mr and Mrs Rademacher also on their way to town.

"What's it like, Fath... er... Michael? To be one of us instead of one of THEM?" asked Carl Rademacher, grinning.

Michael contemplated the question for a moment, squeezing Laura's hand. "I never thought it was so wonderful to be in love. This woman...," he looked lovingly at Laura, "..has turned my life upside down. I like it."

"Yes, Love does strange things to people," Therese Rademacher remarked, smiling. "What does Peter think about you getting married, Laura?"

"He's very happy for us both and is going to be home the first week in December to give me away. Get rid of me to some other man who'll be responsible for me, he said in his letter. Anybody would think coming home every three or four months was being responsible. But he's pleased," Laura said.

"What'll you do now, Michael?" Carl asked.

"Freddy has offered me a job on the newspaper as a reporter. I've got to learn the ropes and see how it goes. There's a lot going on. The whole Country's in a mess," Michael replied, carefully. Therese was well known for her lack of discretion. Living among his former parishioners he had the

129

advantage of knowing them all, their weaknesses, their strengths and whom to trust.

They parted from the Rademacher's at the station and he led Laura up the wide Remigius Avenue to a small but elegant jewellery shop. The dark suited man behind the counter kept a discreet distance while Michael and Laura inspected a tray of wedding rings. She pointed to a pair of broad gold circles. Later they would have dinner and place the rings on their left hand to tell the world of their betrothal. At the wedding, the rings would be blessed and worn on the right hand forever.

"Would you bring some diamond rings for my fiance to look at, please?" Michael asked the dapper man in the dark suit.

"Certainly," he replied courteously.

Laura's voice was firm. "No diamonds, please. I don't like them," she said to the man, who smiled, lifting one eyebrow, surprised to find a woman who did not like diamonds. Most of them grabbed the biggest he could offer, their avarice clearly visible in their eyes. He was pleased. The hard, cold stones would not enhance the beauty of this woman. He looked at Michael, then at Laura.

"As you wish, Madam. May I show the Lady something else? Perhaps this?" and opened a glass case behind the counter, removed a tray of rings and placed it in front of them. "May I suggest this one?" pointing to a square cut sapphire stone set in a slim band of gold.

Laura looked at it and Michael took it out of the tray and placed it on her left ring finger. "I like this one, Michael. It's so beautiful," Laura said softly.

"Yes," Michael agreed, holding onto the small hand. "I like it too. It's perfect."

Mr. Rosenstein looked very happy. This ring had been one of his favourites. Instead of the usual plain gold brackets, the intricate claws holding the stone at each corner gave it a look of classic distinction. Michael followed Mr. Rosenstein to the small desk at the end of the counter, while Laura gazed at the array of sparkling diamonds and wondered who would wear such opulent things.

"Will there be a wedding soon?" Mr. Rosenstein asked. He felt an extraordinary affinity towards the tall man. A handsome man. Perhaps he was a diplomat? And obviously very much in love with the woman. Were they both widowed? He wished them well, with all the love he could summon for any other race but his own.

"Yes," Michael answered. "In about six weeks."

"Should you contemplate a wedding present, why not match the ring with a necklace and earrings?"

"I'll come in on my own and we'll discuss it," Michael said, handing over his cheque.

Rosenstein looked at the signature. "I'll look forward to that, Mr. Schiller," he said, wrapping the boxes, then bowed and escorted them to the door. He watched them walk hand in hand up the Avenue, somewhat curious as to who they were.

The dinner at the Kurfurst was in place of an engagement party. The wedding, only six short weeks away, would make up for it. As Michael had requested, the waiter led them to a table for two in a secluded corner. The dining room was already filling up with a clientele dressed to go on to somewhere else after the meal. Laura wondered where they were going. The Opera? The Theatre? Since moving to Dettingen she had not been anywhere except shopping. Erika and Freddy had asked her many times but it didn't feel right to impose her presence without a partner.

"Michael?" she asked, after they had settled themselves. "Are we going to the Theatre after we're married? I do miss it, you know."

"We shall go wherever you like. And we don't have to wait until we're married, my Love. I have a lot of catching up to do myself."

"Do you like opera? And music?" Laura ventured, realising how little they knew about each other, their likes and dislikes. Michael considered the question for a moment.

"I went to the opera quite often during my years at the college, but haven't been since then. Somehow I never found the time. I'll enjoy going with you. And yes, I like music."

The waiter brought the bottle of wine Michael had ordered and poured. The subdued conversation and faint clattering of cutlery on gold rimmed plates receded a little as the burly figure of the waiter hovered over them, taking down the order for their meal. Laura felt like a foolish young girl on her first date and wondered whether Michael felt the same.

As soon as they were alone, Michael opened the jewellery boxes, took out the wedding rings and slipped the smaller one onto Laura's left hand. "I love you," he said, as she placed the larger wedding ring onto his finger.

"I love you too, Michael."

He lifted his glass and they toasted each other. "To Mr. and Mrs. Schiller," he said, grinning like a boy, then opened the third box and slid the ring Laura had chosen onto her finger. "My engagement present to my beautiful wife to be," watching her admiring the light of the chandeliers reflecting in the stone.

Anton, the waiter, knew their meal was ready, but the two middle aged people had more important business to attend to, which had nothing to do with eating, but everything with love. Dinner could wait a little longer.

* * *

Katrin from across the road called on Laura the following morning and immediately noticed the gold band, half hidden by the square sapphire stone. "Congratulations, Laura. I'm so happy for you. Is Michael here?" she asked, hugging her friend affectionately. Laura smiled, aware of the underlying meaning of Katrin's question.

"Thank you, Katrin. No, Michael is not here, as you very well know. He's staying with Freddy until the wedding and today has started work at the paper. Freddy thinks he'll be very good at the job of reporting," leading the way to the kitchen to brew fresh coffee. Katrin settled herself at the table, bursting with curiosity.

"Now that you're engaged, are you going to try him out?" she asked, a wicked grin on her face. "He's as pure as the driven snow. You'll have to teach him."

"Katrin," Laura remonstrated, amused by her friend's impertinence, "Nobody's going to try anything out until we're married. It's been so long since I've made love to Peter's father I've almost forgotten what it's like," she lied. "We'll manage."

Katrin took the hint and knew as far as Laura was concerned, that that particular subject was closed. "What'll happen to the garden now Janus isn't here anymore?" she asked.

"We're going to the Mission on Saturday to ask the boy Daniel if he'd like to come and live here after we're married. That's why we're not going away. We'll have a few days on our own and Daniel will be with us for Christmas. It'll be nice. He does the gardening at the Mission. Between us we should be able to cope with the work," Laura said, sounding optimistic, when the doorbell rang. "Make the coffee, Katrin," she said and hurried out.

Erika too wanted to know whether to congratulate Laura, who held up he left hand and was enfolded in loving arms. "Congratulations, Pet. It's been worth it, hasn't it?" Erika whispered into her ear, a suspicion of moisture clouding her eyes. Laura nodded her head.

Over coffee and cakes, the ring was very much admired and Laura smiled as Katrin remarked, "You should've had a diamond as big as this. They'll always keep their value. A girl has to think about these things in case of hard times."

"I don't need diamonds, just Michael. I wonder how he's getting on?" Laura said.

"Freddy's teamed him with Franz Stahl. He's the best. Michael will be fine with him. What he doesn't know about reporting isn't worth knowing," Erika stated with conviction.

Katrin remarked dryly, "He'll have to learn what it's like in that nasty world out there. Michael's got a living to earn, like everybody else."

Laura frowned a little, remembering Janus's warning. "I just can't see him spending the rest of his life flitting about the Country as Freddy's political correspondent. It's too dangerous."

"Stop worrying. He'll be fine with Franz," Erika's voice was soothing. "Maybe Freddy will give him a desk job after he's learnt the ropes," she said, recalling the many scathing articles Michael had written for the paper in the past, of which Laura had no knowledge and she couldn't tell her.

* * *

Franz Stahl had been briefed by Freddy to take Michael Schiller under his wing. He was waiting in the outer office for his junior to appear.

"Freddy's taking his time with the new kid," he said, somewhat disgruntled, to the stern looking woman behind the desk. Mirna was still unmarried, in her late twenties and not at all bad looking when she decided to smile, which was not very often, Franz thought, watching the busy fingers flying over the keys of her typewriter. "Come and have dinner with me sometime, Mirna. I'd like to take you somewhere special."

How many times had he asked her that? He knew what the answer would be. Always the same. "No, thank you, Franz. When you settle down behind a desk, keep civilised hours like normal people, I'll come out with you. I can wait," Mirna said, giving him one of her rare smiles which made her look much younger and very soft. "And that's no kid in there," pointing to the closed door of Freddy's office. "He's very special, a friend of Freddy's and you'd better take good care of him. Just don't teach him any of your bad habits, Darling."

Franz chewed on his cigar, which he knew he shouldn't smoke, drew himself up to his full height of five foot ten and tried to tighten his stomach, without much success. He felt good when she called him 'darling' in that tone of voice. And as always, he promised himself to lose some weight. He was not as agile as he used to be, too much fatty food eaten at the wrong time, too many bars and he wondered which rich papa had sent his son to Freddy to learn reporting. Most likely one of the graduates from the University, full of ideals and not one ounce of common-sense in his head.

The door of the inner sanctum opened and Franz stared at the tall, slim figure of Michael, in a grey suit with faint pin stripes. He looked at Mirna and she nodded her head. "Michael," she addressed the man, as if they had known each other for a long time. "This is Franz Stahl. He'll take care of you, won't you, Franz?"

Freddy's political correspondent stood open-mouthed, holding his cigar in mid air, looking into the intense blue eyes and tried to remember where he had seen that thin, Jesus-like face before. A long time ago.

Michael extended his hand in greeting and Franz grasped it, surprised at the strength in those slender fingers. "Nice to meet you," Michael said, smiling. "Freddy said you're the best. I hope I won't be too much of a nuisance to you."

Franz beamed at his new partner. He liked a man who knew his limitations. This was no green kid and he wondered what he had been doing up to now. The face still bothered him. "Come-on. I've got some leads to follow up. You might as well tag along," and leaning over the desk he whispered to Mirna, "I'll see you later."

She watched both men go out and knew Michael was in good hands. Franz liked him. His chubby face had looked a little perplexed at first but it did not take long for Franz to assess a man's character. She admired his keen intelligence and wished he'd take that office job Freddy had offered him. Then she'd marry him.

They had been to several addresses, caught trams and walked for miles to meet a strange character in the park. Michael had listened carefully and felt

134

an immediate respect for the patience and subtlety of Franz Stahl. He had a lot to learn if this was to be his life from now on. At 1:20 pm Franz announced that it was time to eat and led him to a small restaurant, plainly furnished, but friendly, just off the market place. The Landlord pulled two beers and slid them across the counter.

"Thanks, Erik," Franz said. "Bring us the usual," and collecting the two beers he preceded Michael to a small table in the corner. "Do you drink beer?" he asked, as an afterthought.

Michael nodded. "Yes, I'm ready for one. I never thought you had to do so much legwork."

Franz grinned, sprawling in the chair, his legs stretched out into the room. "Some days are worse than others. Information doesn't fall out of the sky. Do you think you'll like it?"

"It's hard to tell. I'm used to people and being busy, but this is different. No fixed base to work from. I'll let you know at the end of the week," Michael grinned, taking a long swallow of the cold beer.

"Have you been involved in writing for a paper before? You look like a society reporter. You know, going to fancy places with the rich and famous. Gossip column?" Franz asked, waving to Erik for more beer.

"I've done some work for Freddy. Political, mostly. Wrote under FM," said Michael.

"That was you?" Franz gasped, taken by surprise. "That stuff was dynamite." He looked at his apprentice and knew there wasn't much he could teach this man, except to survive. "I liked the column. Sorry to put you in the trivia bracket." He sounded apologetic, then looked puzzled. "Have we met somewhere before? I've a good memory. You need that in this kind of work. Your face seems familiar. Maybe you've got a brother?" Franz could not shake off the faint image which had floated in and out of his mind since this morning, so fleeting that it could not be fixed, but it was there just the same.

"No, I don't have a brother, and I don't think we've met," Michael answered, searching his own memory for some recollection. It was a round face, with a wide mouth and pug nose and eyes that expressed a quick intelligence. They were a warm shade of brown, like his straight hair, but missed nothing. Franz had a pleasant voice, persuasive when he wanted something and firm when talking business. It would be interesting to work with him.

"It's a long time ago. Were you in the war?" Franz knitted his eyebrows together. He couldn't stand things going round his mind with no purpose.

"Yes," Michael answered. "Four years. It was hell."

"I've worked for Freddy since I left school and joined up as a war correspondent. Sent a lot of stuff back to the paper. Got myself a bit of a reputation. There were soldiers talking about this crazy catholic priest who dragged the dead and wounded back into the trenches. I went to find him but couldn't pin him down. He seemed to be every place I wasn't. As I got close to Freddy's lot, they shot my left arm to pieces and then I met him. He just bound it up to stop the bleeding and called for the medic. They followed him like sheep. In spite of the pain, I remember his eyes and how clean his uniform was. He looked just like you." Franz searched Michael's face but found nothing in the quiet, still features that would help him.

"Ypres. 1917. That was the worst," Michael said quietly. "I lost count of the dead and wounded."

"That's the place and it was you, wasn't it?" Franz asked.

Michael nodded. He liked this man and sooner or later there would be the inevitable question of what he had done before this. "Yes, I was there, but I can't remember all the faces. There were too many of them. It never stopped. And all of them so young. I came back with Freddy and was the parish priest of Dettingen until a month ago."

"Why are you doing this?" Franz looked puzzled.

Michael smiled at him. "Last February I looked into a woman's eyes and fell in love for the first time in my life. It's been a long hard struggle for me. For both of us. The church lost and the wedding's in six weeks."

"You don't waste much time, do you? Congratulations to you both. She must be something very special to get you away from your God," Franz laughed.

"She is. Special and very beautiful," Michael said softly.

"Then my advice to you, my Friend, is not to get involved in this business. That's why I never married. It puts too much of a strain on any relationship. I like you, Michael. Find some other job and stay home with your new wife.

Chapter 15

They were waiting at the station in Bonn for the express from Hamburg. Peter was home for his mother's wedding. Freddy had offered to take Michael and Laura in the car, while Erika put the finishing touches to the evening meal. The train was on time and Laura ran to her son, to be embraced in a fierce hug, then kissed soundly.

"Hello, mum. You look wonderful. Being in love suits you," Peter grinned at her. "Where is the happy bridegroom?"

"Over there," Laura pointed to where the two men were standing. "Oh, it is good to see you, Peter. You look marvellous." Suntanned, he stood out like a bronze God among the travellers in their warm furs and heavy coats. Michael walked towards them, stretched out his hand in greeting but instead was also embraced heartily.

"You're a courageous man, Michael. Giving up a peaceful life to marry my mother. I'm very happy for you both," Peter said, and waved to Freddy.

Michael took the large suitcase. "How long are you going to be with us? Until Christmas, I hope. We'll have Daniel as well. It'll be nice," he remarked.

"Change of plan, I'm afraid. I'm off after the wedding. Going South with friends," Peter replied casually. "Hello, Freddy. Good to see you, old Friend," a huge grin on his face as they too embraced. "How's Erika and your Pa? You're the best man at this very sudden wedding, I hear. Well, between the two of us we'll make quite sure these two get hitched," he laughed, putting his arm about his mother. "You'll be so happy with your new husband you won't miss me one little bit."

"I always miss you, Son. You just don't come home often enough for me to get used to you," Laura reminded him.

"But as from next Saturday, you'll have Michael to keep you company," was the cheerful reply.

Ten minutes later they arrived in Dettingen just as the Sunday evening service had finished. The parishioners attending had dwindled since Father Bernhard had taken over. Freddy's car horn honked and they waved as he passed. "Not too many tonight," Freddy said. "The old boy hasn't got what it takes."

"Well, they can't have Michael back. He's mine," Laura announced and snuggled closer to Michael.

"That's right, my Love," he agreed, holding her tight to him.

In the dark interior of the car, Laura's delicate perfume filled Michael's senses and he could not resist kissing the soft mouth in the upturned face, oblivious of Freddy and Peter in the front.

"They're like young kids," Peter remarked in low tones.

"That's what love does for you. Just wait. Your turn will come," Freddy replied.

"I'm doing quite nicely without love. Playing the field is much more exciting," Peter commented.

Erika was waiting for them and suffered the same exuberant embrace from Peter as had the others. "Hello, Erika, it's nice to be home. I'll have a beer, it's been a long journey."

"Don't bother to tell me I look beautiful, you monster. I'll get your beer," she grumbled, pretending to be upset. "Food's ready."

Most of the evening Peter entertained them with his usual flair, relating all the comic and near tragic events that had happened to them on the other side of the world. Laura watched her son and marvelled again at seeing a replica of Jack before her very eyes. It would be so different with Michael. She'd have him home every day. To love and care for. Not just once every three or four months.

"I've got presents upstairs," Peter announced when the meal was over. "Michael, come and help me get that 'enormous' wedding present down."

As both men had left the room, Laura looked puzzled. "He only had one big suitcase and his travelling bag. The present can't be that big?"

Erika and Freddy looked at each other. "I think they're having a man to man talk, Laura. The last time Peter was home Michael was still a priest and there was no mention of love or marriage between you. It must be strange to your son for his mother to acquire a husband and he a new father all in the space of less than three months," Freddy said.

"I suppose so," Laura's voice was subdued.

"Cheer up, Pet," Erika cajoled. "They'll be fine.

Michael had followed Peter to his room and stood, wondering if he was going to get a lecture.

"Sit down, Michael. It's strange to see you in a suit. I hadn't really taken it all in until I saw you at the station. And kissing my mother in the back of

138

the car," Peter said, a huge grin spreading over his brown face. "I didn't know you had it in you."

"Any objection?" Michael asked. "We both fell in love that day you came to buy this house. You introduced me to her, remember? On the back of the motorbike. It hasn't been easy, but I've no regrets, Peter. We're going to be very happy." He paused for a moment. "You don't mind me moving in here, do you? It's what your mother wants."

"I'm very happy for you both. I've never seen her so alive and glowing. You too look different. More part of the world, if you know what I mean. There's nobody I'd like better for a father than you, Michael, and I know you'll take care of her. Next Sunday morning I'm off to stay with one of my mates in the South, near Munich. Mum will probably be upset and you'll have to tell her that it's time for me to spread my wings. So far, I've always come home because I didn't want her to feel neglected. She has been, you know. By my dad, and by me. I do love her, but she won't need me anymore. Don't make it sound as if I've only come home out of duty, though. I've enjoyed my time here. Freddy's and your friendship meant a lot to me, but now it's time to move on. You'll make it right with her, won't you?" he pleaded.

Michael nodded. "Whenever you want to come home, Peter, you just come. Your mother will understand. I'll see to that. But write to us, or she'll worry."

Peter promised and fetched several small packages out of the case. "Here's one for you," he said and threw it to Michael, who caught it in mid-air. "You're still a damned good catcher, for an old man," Peter laughed. "We'd better deliver the rest of them downstairs."

Michael rose and the two men stood for a moment, then, as if each had read the other's thoughts, they embraced. "Take care of yourself, Son. Germany is a dangerous place to be in right now. Enjoy your freedom," Michael told Peter, who looked at the man he had always admired and respected and knew he could leave his mother in his care.

The first snow fell during Friday night. Somehow it seemed fitting for Laura's wedding. She stood at the kitchen window, gazing at the trees covered in virgin white. There was no wind to disturb the stillness in the orchard and the large expanse of garden lay quiet and serene. The sweet taste of her first cup of coffee did not calm the army of butterflies in her stomach. Laura wondered what Michael was feeling. Was he up already? Peter had not come home until after 3:00 a.m. She had heard him laughing and joking with Heinz Bulger and Walter after Michael's stag party. How long had Michael stayed on?

Laura poured black coffee into a mug and made her way upstairs. There was no answer to her knock on Peter's door. The room was in darkness. She released the inner fold away shutters and her son groaned as the morning light flooded in.

"I imagine you have a few sledgehammers banging away inside your head. Here. Drink this," Laura said, looking into bleary eyes.

"Oh, God. I've been to some binges, Mum, but last night beats them all. Jochen's was packed. Just about everybody turned up to give Michael a good send off." Peter sat up and drank the hot brew his mother handed to him. "Ooh, my head," he moaned.

"Will the bridegroom be in this state as well?" Laura asked.

"I don't know. Probably. He and Freddy left about two o'clock. He was still on his feet, though."

"It's eight o'clock. I'll give you half an hour in the bathroom, then breakfast. We've got to be ready by ten. Remember, I'm getting married today," Laura said, smiling happily.

The church clock struck ten times. Erika and Peter watched from the windows for Freddy's car, while Laura sat on the settee, nervously twisting a lace handkerchief around her finger. The maroon mercedes drew up outside the house at 10:15 to take them to the Town Hall for the civil marriage. If Michael had been the worse for drink last night, he showed no sign of it this morning, as he lightly stepped out of the car to collect his bride. Erika left to talk to Freddy who whistled at her. In a new moss green suit and hat, a fox fur slung casually over her shoulder, she looked chic and very attractive.

"Oh, my..." she said, as Michael passed to go into the house. "I wouldn't mind marrying you myself. You're a handsome brute, Michael. Laura is waiting."

Peter discreetly moved into the dining room as Michael appeared. Laura noticed he looked fresh and alert, dignified in dark suit and soft hat, carrying a package wrapped in wedding paper. She rose to meet him and he held her to him for a brief moment, then glanced admiringly at the small hat sitting at a jaunty angle on the shining hair, over the heavy midnight blue woollen suit, to neat shoes and then into eyes the colour of sea mist.

"You look wonderful, Laura," he blurted out, handing her the package. "My wedding present. To wear later. I hope you like it."

"Thank you, Michael. And here's yours. With all my love," Laura said softly, picking up a small package off the table. "You look very smart," and kissed him lightly, stepping back, aware of his restraint.

Peter appeared and relieved the tension as he reminded her, "We'd better go. You don't want to be late for your wedding, Mum," and shepherded both of them out of the door.

Outside, a small crowd had gathered around the car. Katrin was trying to keep Chrissy from climbing into it because she wanted to go with her mother, Tonia and Kurt stood open-mouthed at all the excitement going on. Annie had come out from number four and was ecstatic, jumbling her words. Even Mrs. Henckler from number nine had relented and joined the others. Rosalie, her daughter, had remonstrated with her weeks ago. "How can you be so miserably mean, Mother? Don't you remember what it was like when you married Dad?" she had said.

And Mrs. Henckler had retorted, "Your father was the village plumber, God rest his soul, not a priest." She watched very carefully what went on across the road, noted that Michael only visited when he was in the company of Freddy, had come more often this week with the son in the house, but always left about eleven to walk up the hill to Freddy's place. The streetlamp outside Laura's house was most convenient. Mrs. Henckler decided the love birds had behaved very properly and she did want to go to the wedding.

Michael helped Laura into the back seat next to Erika and got in, keeping a discreet distance. After a great deal of banter and shouts of 'Good luck,' their neighbours waved them off.

The journey into town did not take long. Freddy had put his foot down once he got onto the highway close by the river. He parked in front of the imposing Town Hall. The market place had been cleared of snow and was filled with its usual rows of stalls. The large space in front of the Town Hall was empty except for a few women who regularly spent their Saturdays watching happy people getting married. Huddled into their shabby clothes, they came to remember what it had been like for them once, or dream of something they would never have, since the war had taken so many of their soldiers to rest in foreign soil. The women united in grief or regrets, but were generous enough to wish the couples well and throw a handful of rice or confetti.

Erika, Freddy and Peter got out and waited. Michael took Laura's hand into his own. "Nervous?" he asked. "You can still change your mind."

She smiled. A happy, radiant smile. "Yes, I'm nervous, but I won't change my mind. I've waited too long for you, Michael."

"Then let's go in," he said, opening the door. He helped her out and hand in hand they walked up the wide steps into the building.

The Registry Office was furnished in opulent style and the man behind the highly polished table smiled benignly. He asked them to place their wedding rings onto the velvet covered box in front of them, and began to read from a leather covered book. "We are gathered here..." and Michael remembered how he had recited the same words so many times, to join so many couples in holy matrimony and now he himself stood here to make Laura his wife. But this was only a formality. Their marriage would begin this afternoon, in his church, in the sight of God. "..Whilst thou, Michael, take..." he knew the words by heart, "..to love and to cherish... for richer or for poorer... until death us do part?"

And Michael's, "I will," came firm and clear, knowing that he and Laura would fulfil all that they promised. Laura, too, did not hesitate in her response.

"Take the rings, please," said the Registrar. "With these rings, I thee wed... with my body I thee worship..." They repeated and placed the rings onto their right hand finger. "I now pronounce you Man and Wife," the genial voice of the portly man said, thinking what a handsome couple they were.

Michael gently kissed Laura and the Registrar shook their hands. "Good luck to you both," he said and meant it. He led them to a small annex at the rear to complete the formalities and the signing by the witnesses.

"I love you, Mrs. Schiller," Michael whispered into Laura's ear.

"Thank you, Mr. Schiller. I love you to," she whispered back, smiling sweetly.

And then it was over.

Peter embraced his step-father, hugged his mother, then it was Freddy and Erika's turn and at last Michael kissed his wife properly. They walked out into the pale winter sunshine hand in hand where the women wished them well and threw confetti.

The wedding lunch at Jochen's passed pleasantly. Cornelius had kissed the bride, remarking: "I'm happy for both of you. I still think you would have made a beautiful Baroness, but I concede to the better man."

The doors to the ballroom remained firmly closed, a hive of activity going on behind the glass panelled sliding doors for the reception in the afternoon.

Erika pointed to her watch at 12:50 and beckoned to Laura. "Let's go and make ourselves beautiful, Sweetie. We'll walk home. That's the only fresh air we're going to get for the rest of the day. Don't be late, Boys."

It seemed that all of Dettingen was getting ready for the wedding. Walter was closing the shutters, the cobbler next to Jochen's had the 'closed' sign on the door and the barber shop on the opposite corner was pulling down his blinds.

""I'll say that for you, Laura. You didn't have much of a marriage before and waited ten years for the right man to come along, but when you have a wedding, you sure make up for it," Erika said, affectionately tucking her arm into that of her beloved friend.

Chapter 16

She had not enough time to luxuriate in a long bath. The gleaming gold circle reminded her of this morning's short ceremony, that she was Laura Schiller... Married to Michael Schiller, legally and forever, but for him the marriage service this afternoon would be more important...In his church, with his people...

Laura looked into her son's room and saw his suitcase on the bed, his bag next to it. He was staying with Freddy tonight and leaving in the morning. She would not see him again for another three months at least. Like Jack, her son was a very tidy visitor. It must be the conditions they lived under, economical, sparse, she thought. They brought themselves and only what they could comfortably carry and left with no more, no less...

Laura moved to the spare bedroom. Michael's belongings stood neatly arranged in the corner, his personal things in the small canvas bag Peter had left on the bed this morning. One was leaving, one moving in, but Michael's possessions had the feeling of permanence about them. Would he have to unpack his pyjamas tonight? Did he wear any?

She left the door wide open and entered her own bedroom. Mara Schumann's bed, so very big for one small person, wouldn't be quite so huge tonight, or so lonely... She sat on the edge of the bed listening to the silence of the house. That's how it had always been after Peter left, but she had known that Janus was in his room across the patio, and for a fleeting moment remembered the only time he had come upstairs to the bedroom next door. Where was he now? And what was he doing? Laura picked up the hairbrush and the gentle strokes brushed away the past.

She glanced at the silky underwear Erika had given to her as a present. Three sets. White, cream and the palest shade of grey, all of them luxuriously soft to the touch. Not the kind she normally wore. But then, she didn't have anyone to look at them. What was Michael going to make of it all? If he had never been with a woman, would he like her body? Laura paused, laid down the hairbrush and felt the firm flesh of her breasts, the flat stomach and was pleased she had retained a youthful figure. She removed the robe and stepped into the delicate garments lavishly trimmed with lace, pulled on flesh tinted stockings and fastened them to the minute suspender belt. The reflection in the long mirror of the massive wardrobe at the foot end of the bed showed a woman, happy, excited and in love.

Laura straightened the bed cover and glanced at the small clock. It was almost two. Where was Erika? She gathered the hair at the back and pinned it to the top of her head. The dressmaker had excelled herself. Not content with sketching the dress at Laura's first visit, the following week Anna had produced drawings of a lined velvet coat, reduced a cloche type hat form to half its size and covered it in the same fabric, insisting that Laura's hair was far too long for the tight fitting latest fashion. She'd have to cut it, at which Laura uttered an emphatic 'No.'

The front door opened and closed. "Laura?" echoed through the hall and up the staircase.

"In the bedroom," she answered Erika's call. "Come up." Erika bounced up the stairs and stood in the doorway, waiting to be admired. The strong colour of the softly draped cerise dress, enhancing the willowy figure, was repeated in the cloche hat entirely covered with an array of feathers. Erika held the dark blue coat open and Laura gazed in admiration at her friend. "You look magnificent. Like a bird of paradise."

Erika beamed, the blue eyes shining in the discreetly made up face. She valued Laura's opinion, her sincerity, and was glad she found the outfit pleasing. Removing the coat, she took the velvet dress, the colour of a freshly laundered summer sky, off the hanger and held it out for Laura to step into, fastening the long row of covered buttons at the back. "It's beautiful, Laura. Look," turning her to stand before the mirror.

The dress was an understatement of elegance. The fabric moulded itself to her slender body, the deep neckline was still decorous enough not to raise any eyebrows. Two slanting inset pockets, the top marked by three rows of tiny bugle beads, repeated only at the wrist. Even Laura was impressed, pleased with the way she looked. "You haven't seen my wedding present yet, have you? It's in the blue box on the dressing table. From Michael."

Erika opened the jewellery case and gasped. "Oh, God, Laura. The same stones as your engagement ring. They're wonderful." She almost drooled and picked up the necklace to place around Laura's neck. The interwoven claw-like pieces lay gleaming on the creamy skin and the square sapphire nestled just below the hollow of her throat, heightening the blue of the velvet dress. Erika gazed, a little enviously, at the glittering stone and fetched the drop earrings, an inch in length, for Laura to fasten into her earlobes, the smaller sapphires sparkling as she moved her head.

"You look ravishing, sweetie. Your husband has the most exquisite taste, for a man who's not used to giving presents to a woman."

Laura picked up the small pillbox, decorated with rows of the same minute glass beads. A very ornate hatpin, a present from Anna, secured the hat at the back.

"Anna was right, you know. I really do feel like a Princess," she told Erika, a dreamy expression on her face. "Will Michael be proud of me?"

"He should be, darling. You've never looked more beautiful. You're something out of a dream. We've got ten minutes before Peter gets here. Do you need a drink?" Erika asked.

"No, I'd better not. We had champagne at lunch and I don't want to start giggling in church. Maybe a cup of coffee, please, while I tidy this bedroom. I have company tonight," Laura said, grinning at her companion, who just uttered an astonished mock, "Oh," collected her coat and bag and hurried to make the coffee. Tucking Michael's note into the jewellery box, Laura smiled and whispered, "Michael, I love you so much." The silver edged card read, 'To Laura, on our wedding day. With all my love, Michael.'

She gently closed the box, removed her coat and took one last look around the bedroom. The only thing out of place was the white silk wrap on her pillow, a present from her son. Yesterday she had changed the well used linen on her bed for the pretty set with the embroidered corners on the pillow cases, put the matching cover over the soft eiderdown and had slept in the room next door.

"Coffee's ready," Erika called up the stairs.

Laura had convinced herself she wasn't nervous, but found her hand shaking as she held the cup at a safe distance from her dress. Was Michael feeling like this, too? she wondered.

A moment later they could hear the blast of a car horn.

"There's Peter!" said Erika. "At least Michael can't stand you up. You're married already. Come on, Pet. It's time to dazzle the natives."

Peter bounced up the steps, into the hall and stood, staring at his mother. "Great God," he stuttered. "You look wonderful. I never realised what a beautiful mother I have," pride and admiration plainly showing in his face. "Here. My wedding present. Mr Rosenstein delivered it this morning. Hope you like it."

"Thank you, Son," Laura said as she took the small package from him and opened it. The jewellery box contained a brooch, the oval gold frame held a sapphire suspended in the middle, four gold claws clasping the stone.

"Do you like it, Mum?" he asked uncertainly, as both women silently looked at the beautiful piece of jewellery.

Laura's eyes were moist as she looked at her son. "I don't know what to say. I love it, Peter. Thank you. It's perfect." The hat tipped backwards a little but did not come off as she hugged and kissed him. "I love you very much."

Erika cast an admiring glance at the young man. "You look very dignified, Peter."

Laura fastened the brooch onto her coat and pulled the hat into place, plucking a few curls over her forehead.

"You really are something to be proud of," Peter remarked to his mother, helping Erika into her coat. "I hope he appreciates you, Mum. Ready?"

"Yes. As ready as I'll ever be," Laura mumbled, picking up the dainty spray of artificial flowers.

'...There is not much choice this time of the year,' the florist had told her. "...I know one of my girls makes silk flowers and even I've got to look twice to make sure they're not real. She makes them for a fashion house in Berlin. Why don't you have a word with her?.."

Laura had, and the spray, when it was delivered a few days ago in a plain cardboard box, had taken her breath away, it looked so real. Forget-me-nots, freesia's, yellow mimosa arranged around delicate lily of the valley. It was a work of art and she knew she'd have it forever to remind her of this day.

* * *

For the first time since leaving his small parish in the agricultural region of the Eifel, thirty miles from the French border, Father Bernhard felt the symptoms of his old affliction surface. He had suffered from a nervous stomach through school and college and only found life tolerable among the simple uncomplicated farming folk. They had made little demands on him, only asking that he christen new babies, marry the couples that had to get hitched in a hurry without too much condemnation, and bury the dead. In return they fed him well, kept his house in good repair, stocked him up with winter fuel and didn't raise an eyebrow when he asked the buxom daughter

147

of Farmer Rantl to be his housekeeper. He did not interfere with their business and they considered he was entitled to his 'comfort,' particularly as he turned a blind eye to the incestuous relationships and the consequences that resulted from them. They suited each other admirably.

Today, Father Bernhard was in a panic. He had prayed all morning asking the Lord to spare him the embarrassment of having to flee the church in a hurry, or worse... THAT he refused to even think about. The wedding could not be postponed.

Father Bernhard had the uncomfortable feeling that his chaplain was hoping for him to be incapacitated. He did not care for the young man, found him too intellectual and extra-ordinarily fond of the de-frocked Michael Schiller and many speculations had entered his mind from time to time about those two. But Schiller was getting married today to a woman not of his faith. The man was a renegade and good riddance, except he wouldn't be rid of him. The church committee had already proposed to ask him to serve on it. The woman Laura was also popular and he didn't know what to make of her. She was a nice looking woman, too thin for his taste and made him feel like a clumsy oaf. Not deliberately, Father Bernhard conceded. He wasn't used to these kind of people. Much more Chaplain Dominik's crowd. He had tried to find out how this situation had come about, but Dominik never volunteered any information on the matter, answered only in general terms and refrained from any personal opinions, which irked Father Bernhard no end.

He had no luck with his parishioners, either. The affair of Michael Schiller, it seemed, was no business of a stranger. That's what he felt like here. An intruder, politely, but firmly kept out of the closed circle of loyal villager surrounding their former priest like a wall, even now...

Chaplain Dominik was more than ever convinced that Father Bernhard was not comfortable among his flock here. A good man in his way, he would never be in control. He was timid in the presence of the Baron and the Reverend Mother. Ill at ease, aware that he couldn't follow the caustic, dry humour of the people of this region, he took no part in any of the social activities as Michael had done.

Dominik knew what he wanted to be. Father Dominik, the parish priest of Dettingen. The political spectrum was worsening every year. Now that Michael was staying in this village, the two of them could work together again, as they had done before. The people here deserved better than Father

Bernhard, they needed someone stronger to lead them through the wilderness he knew was just around the corner. If that meant making his wishes known to Michael and Freddy, who in turn would ask Cornelius to work his charm on the Bishop Norbet, who might then whisper into someone else's ear, then so be it. Dominik did not want to waste years in some obscure little parish, watching the world go by. Michael had taught him well and if he could persuade the Reverend Mother to put the proposition to her cousin, the Bishop, he might make it. This place was alive and demanding and he was well liked here. With his friends behind him he could achieve as much as Michael had, in time.

Dominik went to fetch Father Bernard. He hoped that the good father was feeling better after he'd sent him off for a rest, first giving him a dose of medicine that should keep his stomach under control. Everything was ready for the wedding service.

The priest had left his bed and still felt the sickly motion churning his inside and rushed to the bathroom. He fervently wished that he'd never left his familiar, undemanding people and missed Greta Rantl more than ever.

Father Bernard made his way to the sacristy on unsteady legs and wished he'd taken more notice of his chaplain. "You don't look well Father. Would you like me to send word to Father Johann?" the young pup had asked, quitr solicitously, before suggesting an hours rest. Certainly he'd refused even to consider asking the priest from Annsberg to stand in for him. He'd be finished here, if at the first big event he was unable to conduct a service. They'd never let him forget it...

He looked at his pocket watch. 2.15. He had not been able to eat, but maybe a glass of wine might do the trick. His florid face looked pale, dark shadows showed under his eyes. He saw the bicycle leaning up against the wall and heard the clear, distinctive voice of his chaplain through the door, left open to let out the clouds of smoke from Father Johann's pipe.

"He can't go out there, Johann. You'll have to do it."

"I can't. Not without his permission. I've re-arranged duties just in case, but we'll have to ask him. There isn't much time, Dominik," said Father Johann, his soft voice just a little agitated. "What's the matter with him?"

"Nerves," Dominik replied, with a tinge of contempt.

"Oh, Lord preserve us. Go and tell him I'm taking over. This wedding day is not going to be ruined by a jittery country bumpkin. By all that is Holy. I should be mad as hell with that renegade bridegroom, but we've been friends too long. In any case, Cornelius will be out there, and Mother Agnes, so who am I to hold it against him? I'm just glad he's staying on here. I should hate to lose him."

Father Bernhard felt his stomach heaving again and gave up. He pushed the door open and simply said. "Will you take the service for me, Father Johann? I feel ill, and would be much obliged," and quickly walked back to his house, leaving Dominik and Father Johann wondering how much he had heard of their conversation. They arrayed themselves in their vestments and by 2.45 felt ready to have a tentative look into the church.

Michael, Cornelius and Freddy had arrived. So had most of the parishioners. Every pew was tightly packed, the side aisles filled with men standing and the half-moon shaped galley above overflowing with people. In the centre aisle the red carpet, reserved for dignitaries and special occasions, was laid out to welcome the bride and groom. The interior was already decorated for Christmas, but donated by the sisters, a splendid arrangement of flowers stood between the altar rails. Freddy was in high spirits and Michael looked happy, the thin face a little less strained than it had been in the last few weeks.

Father Johann, used to his own large congregation, was not in least perturbed. Cornelius attended his church sometimes, Hubert and his family come on important days in the church calendar. He was fully aware of the animosity between the brothers, but kept his own council out of respect for their father.

"You'd better go and tell Michael that I'm standing in. Tell him Bernhard's been taken ill, Dominik.

The chaplain glided out of the door, knelt and came to the altar rail, beckoning to Michael sitting in Cornelius's pew. "Johann will marry you, Michael. Bernhard is not feeling well."

Michael looked quite happy at the news. "Chickened out, has he, Dominik?" he asked, grinning at his former chaplain.

"My lips are sealed, Friend. I didn't know what else to do at such short notice," Dominik said.

"Thanks. It's fine by me," and Dominik hurried back to the sacristy, where Father Johann was reading the names of the two people he would marry as soon as the bride had joined Michael.

"Laura Michelle…" he murmured. "Unusual names. What's she like, Dominik?" he asked, never having met Laura, although he had known Peter for years.

"As unusual as her Christian names. You'll see. Michael will never desert the Lord. He's just shifted his priorities. She'll join our faith in time because she loves him very deeply, as he does her. They'll have a good life together."

They both walked out of the sacristy, knelt again and stood at the altar rail, the chaplain holding the blue velvet cushion to receive the wedding rings. Michael and Freddy also stood, waiting for Laura.

The church clock chimed three times. Two minutes later the maroon car drew up outside the main doors. Sister Andrea, waited for the signal, stopped the muted tones. Fingers poised, she heard the soft clang of the double doors below and the strains of the wedding march filled the church. Peter held out his arm and Laura lightly placed her hand into the curve. Slowly they walked the length of the red carpet. A sea of smiling, admiring faces swam before Laura's eyes, her ears filled with the music that told Michael she was coming. The solitary figure of Erika walked behind them. Today, it was Laura that held the people's attention, but Erika didn't mind.

Michael could not resist turning around to watch his bride take the last few steps towards him. He felt his throat constrict. Never had he seen her so beautiful, seen so much love in her eyes as now. And then she stood beside him, smiling that soft smile that always made him want to kiss her…

Father Johann watched the dainty slim woman walk towards them. He was a little older than Michael and like him, took a great deal of exercise. Although not quite as tall, not quite as slim as his friend, he was a man of stature. Grey streaks in his black hair and warm eyes full of compassion, he finally understood. For a moment he studied the face of Michael's bride, looking into misty grey eyes, noticed the finely drawn eyebrows and long black lashes in the up-turned face, delicate, un-lined and devoid of make-up except for the merest hint of lipstick on the gently curving mouth. He knew that had he met this woman at some other place, some other time, he too would've been sorely tempted.

"Place your rings to be blessed…" he murmured softly and watched them remove the wedding bands for the last time and lay them onto the small cushion Dominik held out for them. Father Johann could not remember the last time he had performed a marriage service with such dedication and felt the love of the people in this church enfold him, as they had embraced their former priest and his wife.

Michael and Laura walked hand in hand past rows and rows of parishioners, towards the open doors and stood for a moment, alone, looking at each other.

"I love you, Mrs Schiller," Michael said, as he had done earlier that morning.

"I love you too, Mr Schiller," Laura replied and he bent down to kiss the smiling soft lips. And then the moment passed, as the congregation rose in one mass to follow them. They would not linger and talk outside, but meet at Jochen's to celebrate the wedding in style. Father Johann and Dominik would be there, and the Reverend Mother Agnes, allowing her sisters to attend if they wished to do so.

The pale winter sunshine of the day had given way to a darkening sky, with here and there a star appearing to light the way for the night...

Chapter 17

Freddy drove the bridal pair, his father and Erika to the reception. As Laura stepped into the bar, Pauline, his mother, Jochen and Anneliese stared at the vision in blue. Michael put a protective arm about his wife.

"We have been well and truly married," he said, a wicked smile spreading over his face.

Jochen filled glasses with champagne. "Here's long life and happiness to my favourite people," he said, beaming. "To Laura and Michael."

Laura removed her coat and hat and felt a blush creep up her neck and face as a pair of blue eyes stared at her and she remembered Michael looking at her in the same way in the Summer at Peter's party. He moved towards her and stammered the same words. "You are very beautiful, Laura," and they stood as they had done then, but this time he lifted her chin and placed a tender kiss on her lips.

Cornelius roused himself. "You are indeed a wonderful sight for my old eyes, my dear," he told her, kissing the soft cheeks.

Freddy too was impressed. "You're a lucky man, Friend," he told Michael.

"I know," he said softly, "But now we've got to go and meet our guests. Come, Laura."

Taking her hand he led her through the dining room, sneaking another kiss before entering the ballroom, where Peter was shepherding the first of the villagers to their places. Under the light from half a dozen lamps the sapphires sparkled and glittered. As bride and groom shook hands, received admiration and good wishes, Michael burst with pride and happiness. And finally they let them go to their table.

Michael rose and tapped his wine glass. Silence fell over the huge room. For a moment he stood, tall and erect, a quiet, still-faced man, with the cool assurance they knew so well. His eyes wandered over the many familiar faces that used to confront him as he looked down from the pulpit. Except today, they were seated in Jochen's ballroom. It did not feel any less dignified, though. The clear resonant voice carried just a slight tremor of emotion. "My dear Friends," he said. "You'll never know how much this day has meant to Laura and me. We'll always be grateful to you for accepting us into your midst, and wish to thank you for your good wishes, but most of all for your presence here. The only way we could think of repaying the love you have shown us was to invite all of you to share this special day. Enjoy it. I know we will always remember today. Thank you for sharing it with us. God bless you," and they clapped and whistled as he sat down to take Laura's hand into his own.

Peter stood up and waved his arms about until there was quiet again. He spoke briefly. "When my mother wrote to tell me she was getting married and to who I thought she must be crazy. I had no idea, although I found out since that all of you knew. Nobody said one word to me the last time I was home. I love my mother very much, but I've never been here long enough to be of much use to her. Now I can go away without feeling guilty because she'll have the one person I respect above all others, and I'm proud to call him dad. I love them both and I know they'll look after each other." He raised his glass. "To Mum and Dad. Long life and happiness." And again there was uproar.

Cornelius added his felicitations and Freddy joked "Now Michael knows what it's like this side of the altar rail, we'll have to teach him how to live dangerously."

The Reverend Mother arrived and there was a momentary hush, but her cheerful greeting and easy smile dispelled any misgivings at her appearance. Trailing in her wake were five sisters, who, immediately they had conveyed their congratulations to bride and groom, admiring Laura's dress, made themselves comfortable among the guests. Mother Agnes too, was visibly impressed. "You look quite wonderful, my dear. Michael is very lucky to have found you."

"Thank you, Reverend Mother, but I'm the lucky one," Laura replied.

"Call me Mother Agnes, child," admitting her into the small circle of personal friends. "We shall no doubt see quite a lot of each other," and seating herself next to Cornelius.

"And what do I call you now?" asked Michael. "Mother?" his eyes full of amusement.

The Reverend Mother laughed out loud. "You are permitted to address me as usual, traitor," she said, helping herself to a piece of cream gateaux.

Father Johann arrived with Dominik who reported to Michael that Father Bernhard was almost back to normal.

"What's the matter with him?" asked Cornelius, ignorant of the misfortune that had befallen the Priest.

"He wasn't feeling well this morning, so I took the liberty of asking Father Johann, just in case," Dominik replied diplomatically.

"You mean he turned yellow?" Cornelius said, a twinkle in his eyes. They remained silent, Mother Agnes hiding her smile behind her serviette. Cornelius turned to her. "Well, my dear. I think we need a new priest. Someone who's not afraid of us. Like Dominik. What do you think? Shall we have a word with that cousin of yours?"

Dominik almost choked on his champagne.

"I believe Father Johann is quite settled in Annsberg. Is that correct, Father?" Mother Agnes asked, deliberately giving him first choice.

"Oh, yes. I wouldn't want to move. I'm quite content where I am," said the father, scotching any idea that he wanted the job offered to him. Mother Agnes smiled.

"Just as I thought. Then that leaves our young chaplain. My sisters will adore him as much as they did Michael. Are you game, Dominik?" the Reverend Mother challenged him. He just stared at her, speechless. She was the major player in this game, although he wondered why his future should be decided at Michael's reception. On the other hand, why not at this wedding? "Well, Dominik?" she asked, again.

"Yes, Reverend Mother," Dominik replied firmly. "I'm game and will serve this parish faithfully, with the help of God, Michael and Father Johann."

"Well said, young man," Cornelius remarked cheerfully. "You won't have to wait long, I assure you."

"If we leave you to honeymoon 'till January, will you join the church committee, you two?" Erika asked, grinning cheekily.

Laura retorted with good humour. "Thanks, Friend. You're very generous."

Freddy glanced at Michael and Dominik. "There's a lot of work to be done," he said.

Peter laughed and made a grimace. "Work? I'm glad I'm not going to be around. I need a holiday."

"So that's settled then, Dominik," Cornelius told the Chaplain. "I'm sure you can count on Father Johann and Michael for support should you need it."

"Of course. Any time," Father Johann said, relieved and pleased at the outcome.

"Same here," Michael added. "Welcome to the clan. You'll be fine."

The Reverend Mother had quietly consumed her second piece of gateaux and was seriously contemplating a chocolate covered round confection topped with cream and temptation proved too much. Tomorrow she would fast... "Isn't it wonderful to do business and feast so well?" she declared, spooning up a portion of chocolate cake. "Here I am at the wedding of a mutinous renegade of whom I'm very fond and admire his wife, although she's a protestant. We've just selected our new Father and I've a mind to have another piece of cake," she chuckled. "We are indeed a radical lot. Don't you think so?"

Michael answered for all of them. "We always have been, Agnes."

Jochen had thought of everything. The band arrived to play for an hour or so after tea. Hans Kohl, grinning from ear to ear, started with a waltz. He motioned to Michael and Laura to take the floor.

"Come, Laura," Michael said and took her hand as the guests applauded them. "Let's show off," he whispered into her ear.

Laura, flushed with happiness, was surprised at the ease with which he moved to the music. "Where did you learn to dance like this?" she asked.

He smiled down at her. "In my time I've attended many happy gatherings like this. My mother loved to dance. She taught me and I never considered it a sinful occupation," he said, his arm encircling her small waist a little tighter.

"I hope you didn't hold your partners as tight as this, darling?" Laura remarked, looking up at him, an impish expression on her face.

"Oh, no, my love. It would've been improper," Michael replied with mock disapproval. "But you are my wife and move with the most delightful abandon," and with eyes full of mischief he drew her closer still, much to the amusement of their guests.

Then everyone joined them. Cornelius claimed the bride, while Erika was whisked away by Michael. Laura and Michael's wedding had provided the women of Dettingen with the best excuse to ask their husbands for a new coat and dress a week before Christmas.

Pauline Hunter, resplendent in brown silk and beads held sway at the bar. Mrs. Henkler's black Sunday dress had acquired a saucy white lace jabot.

Katrin looked smart in navy and pink and Annie hid her pathetically thin figure in a voluptuous green silk. The muted colours of winter wardrobes, relieved by sparkling jewellery flashing under the bright globes of Jochen's ballroom, complimented the sober suited men as they danced.

"This has been one of the happiest days I've had for a long time, Laura," Cornelius told her as he guided her expertly through the crowd. "You look adorable. I envy Michael just a little."

"You are an old flatterer. Why have you never married again, Cornelius?"

"I had too much fun after my wife passed away. Made up for what I'd missed. Had I met you I would've stayed at home and been content," he said, a little sadly.

Laura smiled. "There's still time for you to meet somebody you can settle down with. You're a handsome man."

"Now you flatter me, my dear. I like my life, the travels, meeting interesting people and the lovely emancipated women who pause to dally a while and then move on. They are fascinating creatures, but don't know the meaning of fidelity. Unlike you, Laura." Cornelius bowed slightly as the music stopped and led her back to the table.

The Reverend Mother, Father Johann and Dominik took their leave and as bride and groom circulated among their guests, talking, laughing, no-one noticed the boy standing by the door, half hidden by a large screen to keep out the cold air as people moved in and out. Daniel had been invited, but to him his one and only suit wasn't good enough to come to a wedding. He had taken the tram to Dettingen and just wanted to have a look at them. Now he felt warm and happy, this was almost as good as being with them. He would tell Janus about it in his next letter. Then he left when the dancing started again.

Just before midnight Michael announced that it had been a long and truly wonderful day and after uncountable handshakes and affectionate embraces he and Laura finally stepped out into the cold starry night, to be escorted by a noisy crowd to the corner of Wendel and Annsberg Road.

Michael put his arm about his wife. The road was quiet, the houses shuttered and dark, the lamplight outside Laura's house a faint yellow glow. Suddenly both of them seemed a little apprehensive in the silence that surrounded them. All day there had been people and noise. Now, there was just the stillness of the night, pleasantly punctuated by the beat of the music at Jochen's.

"Do you have the key, Laura?" Michael asked.

"Peter left it under the mat."

He reached into the dark recess of the doorway, found the key on the top step, unlocked the door and then stood over her. "I believe husbands are required to carry their brides over the threshold, my Love."

Laura found herself swept up in strong arms, lifted her own around his neck and nestled against his chest. He lightly scaled the three stone steps, opened the door, then pushed it with his foot to make a soft thud as it closed and held his wife close to him in the hall, the light from the streetlamp illuminating their faces.

"I love you," he said, very softly and kissed warm lips. Standing there, holding the woman he had yearned for all these months Michael wondered at the feeling of utter contentment invading his soul. There was no torment, no desire, just a sense of peace.

"Welcome home, Michael," Laura said, as he helped her off with her coat. "We'll have a whole week to ourselves. It was nice of Freddy to let you off work."

On the low table in the sitting room stood a bottle of wine, a bottle of whisky and two glasses.

"Peter must've left them when he came to fetch his things. Do you want a drink?" Laura asked.

Michael sat on the settee, watching her.

"Not now, my Love," and held out his hand. She took it and stood before him. "I want to remove your trinkets," he said as he pulled her down to sit next to him. His fingers found the clasp of the necklace. "It looks lovely, but now I just want to look at you." He gently cupped her face in his hands and studied each feature intently. "My wife!" he said, almost in awe. "Today has been the happiest day of my life. I never dreamt that this would ever happen to me, Laura, and thank God every night for letting me have this."

"I love you so much, Michael. We both have much to be thankful for." She stroked his cheek, saw the love in his eyes and could not resist the sudden urge to kiss the gently curving lips. Like a torrent of water bursting at the banks of a stream, the kiss broke the bondage they had imposed on themselves in the past few months. Michael's arms enfolded her, pressed the slim body to him as they sank into the width of the settee. His mouth found the hollow at her throat, his hand the curves he had only tentatively explored.

He could feel her hands caressing his back, move inside his jacket and wanted to shed all the garments that kept him from touching her skin. His slender fingers moved down the soft fabric of the dress and found the exquisite sensation of silk stockings almost unbearable, the soft moans and her unrestrained plea of 'Love me, Michael,...' incited him to find the place he knew nothing of and then, as if he had been bitten by the serpent, he stopped.

Michael sat on the edge of the settee, reaching for the gold cigarette case Laura had given to him as a wedding present. With shaking fingers he withdrew a cigarillo and lit it, drawing deeply on the slim dark shape. Laura lay still, pulling her dress into shape.

"What is it, Michael?" she asked, her voice trembling slightly. He did not answer for what seemed an eternity, exhaling the blue-grey smoke. When he finally looked at her there was shame in his eyes, shame expressed in his tone.

"I'm no better than the beasts in the field, Laura. I'm sorry. Forgive me," he pleaded.

"Michael?" she said tenderly. "You could never be that, whatever you do. You're just a man, carried on the wave of wanting something you've waited for so long. I wanted you just as much. Women have needs to, darling, and nowhere does it say that you must make love in the marriage bed."

"But I wanted you here. Now," he said, still uncertain if it was the right thing to do. "It should have been beautiful..."

There was a world of understanding in her eyes as she sat up and stretched out her hand to him. He took it and looked less anxious.

"As long as there is love, Michael, anywhere is beautiful, and every place is the right place. Remember that."

"I will," he said, a wide smile making him look like a sixteen year old. "It's just..." he broke off whatever he wanted to say, looking sheepish.

"What, Michael?" Laura prompted.

"It's just..." he hesitated a moment. "I wanted to see you. I mean, all of you."

"Well, in that case you'd better come upstairs and undo all those buttons down the back of my dress," she said happily.

The house was warm and engulfed them with its comfortable silence as they walked hand in hand up the stairs. The shutters had been closed by Peter earlier and he had switched on the small bedside lamp on his mother's side. It threw a soft glow over the pretty cover.

They stood in the doorway, a little hesitant, until Michael stepped over the threshold, his hand pulling her gently towards him. Slim fingers slowly unfastened the rows of buttons down to the small of her back. Kissing the nape of her neck, he eased the dress off her shoulders and felt the slight tremor in her body. He too started to undress. Laura folded back the cover and was surprised to find him neither shy nor embarrassed.

"Your pyjamas are next door," she said, feeling rather foolish.

He smiled, a lazy sensuous smile. "No pyjamas," he said, as soft as a caress, and she stood, joyfully contemplating her husband's slim athletic body, with no suggestion of middle aged spread. Lithe, muscular and smooth. She was pleased her own was still firm and youthful. He crossed the space between them and stood before her. "Let me," he pleaded and almost reverently removed each silky, lacy garment. "God, you're beautiful," he murmured and though aroused, he did not embrace her. "Be patient with me, Laura," he pleaded again.

"Yes, Michael," she whispered as he led her to the bed and lay down beside her. His kiss was tender, fleeting, as he leant over to gaze at her body. All the paintings and statues of Eve and Venus he had ever seen had not induced a glimmer of desire in him, but he knew that the woman he married today would fill every need he would ever have, for all time.

Laura saw the intense curiosity in his eyes, aching to hold him, but lay still, trembling, as sensitive fingers traced every line and curve, reminding herself that this man had not seen a woman's body, had only acquired knowledge from a distance and other people's descriptions. She had waited ten years... what was an hour?... two hours?... He had said it should be beautiful and maybe this was what he had imagined it to be during the last few months.

Michael did not hurry. It was as if he was chartering a new course, a new destination, familiarizing himself with unknown territory, fascinated by nipples that rose from their recess to greet him, when with the utmost delicacy, he teased them with his finger. His senses lost themselves in the strange odour of her skin as he tasted the sweet, heady essence on his tongue. He listened to unfamiliar sounds from her lips, smelt the fragrance of her perfume lingering like a faint spring breeze and felt his own desire mounting as her hands caressed his body. He gazed at the tight whorls of the palest gold and momentarily rested his cheek on the softness, stroking creamy thighs and tentatively, delicately explored the mysterious place he had denied himself out of love for God. And finally understood why so many of the priests fell pray to temptation.

His mind in a delirious whirl, he retraced the route, placing feather-light kisses on slender curves and contours. At last, poised above her, Michael spoke in a low voice. "Before you came, my life was serene, with no thought of this to disturb me. But since I met you, I've dreamt of nothing else. Your body pleases me. So soft and warm to touch."

She smiled and he saw eyes that now were smokey-grey with longing, soft and limpid with desire and he lost himself in their depth.

"I dreamt too, Michael," Laura whispered. "So many times. Love me."

Michael kissed the soft mouth and abandoned himself wholly to the mounting tide and took refuge in the welcoming response of her body, breaking the shackles that had bound him for half a lifetime. The gentle motion gathered momentum and they soared to lofty plateau's, down into ocean's wild, felt torrid waves crash over them as they clung to each other, locked into an endless kiss. They cried out and floated gently on soft breezes, smiled at each other, whispering 'I love you' over and over again...

* * *

The folding shutters let in chinks of light and somewhere far off the sound of church bells penetrated Michael's sleep. A life long habit of stretching himself was impeded by the sleeping woman in his arms, and he felt the warmth of another human being next to him. Never before had he shared a bed with anyone and found it pleased him. Drawing her to him, she murmured softly in her sleep and tightened her hold on his waist. The bells still sounded and for a moment he felt guilty. Today they would not go to Mass. Laura moved and he felt the hot wave of desire stirring again as he kissed the soft lips of his wife.

161

Chapter 18

A blanket of snow cloaked the region. Endless, seamless and the gardens lay undisturbed, resting. Suddenly, only the voices of children pelting each other with snowballs echoed in the streets. Men and women hurried to the warmth of their homes.

For Laura and Michael the week had passed in a haze of ecstasy. They had ventured out to go shopping at Walter's, spent an hour or so at Jochen's and, as if by common consent, the usual jokes about connubial bliss remained unspoken. They found and tested intellectual parallels and barriers, delighting in mutual likes and dislikes and Saturday came all too soon. Laura's tentative request of giving Daniel a home had been settled weeks ago. Michael had not pressed her to explain the reason for Janus's sudden departure. There had been no need for him to leave unless he too was in love with Laura. Neither did he question her on the manner of their parting, instinctively aware that a confrontation had taken place.

They boarded a tram and arrived at the mission a little before 10:00 am. Daniel had said his goodbye's and was waiting in the empty dining hall. Laura was surprised to see Jack's old suitcase at the boy's feet. Janus must've given it to him.

"Hello, Daniel," Michael greeted the boy. "Are you ready?"

"Yes, Mr. Schiller," Daniel said quietly, looking around the hall for the last time.

Laura smiled at him. "I hope you'll be happy with us. We missed you at the wedding."

"I did come and you looked very pretty, Mrs Schiller," he replied.

"Then why didn't you speak to us?" Michael asked.

"They were all dressed up," Daniel stated, matter of factly.

Laura noticed the threadbare state of his clothes. Although clean and pressed, they were mended in several places. The boy has pride, she thought. "There's a big Christmas party in Dettingen, Daniel. A good time to get to know everyone." Noting the expression of horror on the boy's face, "You'll be fine. We'll stop at Kramer's, Michael," she informed her husband.

Michael looked at Daniel, lifted his hands in a gesture of futility. "Never argue with a woman when she's got her mind on shopping, son," and was

162

relieved to see a smile appear on the thin face. "Come, let's make her happy."

And like two conspirators they followed Laura along the narrow pavement leading to the centre of town and the market square. Michael carried the suitcase, which seemed extra-ordinarily light and held Laura's hand. Glancing at the stately Town Hall they smiled, remembering the previous Saturday. The same women were still throwing rice and confetti.

Kramer's was the largest store in town. Not exclusive, it catered for the solid and respectable middle-class citizen.

"It's been a long time since I've shopped for somebody of your age, Daniel. My son has been away from home for so long I've nearly forgotten what it's like. I'm going to enjoy this," she said, looking happy and excited. The boy and the man exchanged glances, neither of them in the habit of shopping at Kramer's.

Two hours later, Daniel looked smart in a new suit, shirt and tie, boots, cap and warm overcoat. He and Michael carried additional parcels with more clothing. Daniel wasn't sure whether he should let himself get excited in case they changed their minds when they had to pay the bill. He watched Michael's face closely, but did not detect any displeasure. A tiny spark of joy filled his starved soul, more lonely than ever since Janus had left the mission two years ago.

Laura spoke and he was startled, having watched the tall man at the cash desk. "Daniel, we don't know what you like. Will you choose your Christmas present while we're here?" she asked. "It would make us very happy."

The boy swallowed, as if suddenly a lump had invaded his throat. "But... but I've got this already, Mrs Schiller. Thank you," he stammered, looking for help from Michael, pointing to the parcels.

"These are the things you'll need. To look nice and keep warm, Daniel," Michael said gently. "A Christmas present is something you have just for pleasure," wondering whether the boy ever had anything worthwhile in his young life. "Come on, son."

Daniel liked the sound of Mr. Schiller calling him 'son' even if he meant it only as a figure of speech. It made him feel nice inside and suddenly he wasn't afraid of going to the party this afternoon. He had made sure that his body was scrubbed, his hair was washed and the clothes made him feel good.

They took the creaking escalator to the next floor and Daniel entered a Christmas wonderland. Kramer's was not a store where poor, shabbily dressed people were made welcome or felt comfortable, the shop assistants in their dark suits and dresses had an intimidatary air about them, but Daniel suddenly found them respectful towards him. There was an hour of pure delight just looking at the real thing, not standing outside in the cold, yearning to possess the treasures behind the plate glass windows.

Michael and Laura watched him carefully testing the steam engine, brass and black lacquer gleaming invitingly, his hands lovingly stroking the machine.

"Would you like that, Daniel?" Michael asked, and the shining eyes of the boy told him all he needed to know. Then his face fell.

"It's too dear," he said quietly.

Michael put his arms around the thin shoulders. "How about if we make it a present for this year and next year and maybe the year after that? Would you have it then?"

The light returned to his eyes and he nodded.

"If you put it like that I suppose it's alright. Thanks, Mr Schiller."

"We'll ask them to deliver it, but you can't open it till Christmas morning," Michael said firmly, looking for Laura, who had wandered off. They found her with a large parcel in her hand. "Been shopping?" asked Michael.

She gave him a long happy smile. "Of course. It's Christmas," but did not tell them what was in the parcel. "Let's go and eat, darling. Are you hungry, Daniel?"

A great smile spread over his thin face and the brown eyes lost their anxious expression at the mention of food.

"I'm starving," he said.

* * *

"Welcome to our house, Daniel," Laura said to the boy, dropping the parcels on the hall floor. "I hope you're going to be happy here, you'll be up in the attic. When you're older, you can move into Janus's rooms."

"Thank you, Mrs Schiller. Can I go and have a look tomorrow where he used to live?"

"Of course. Tomorrow we'll take you over to the house. Now, you've got a party to go to, and I've got to change. It's work for us. Will you take Daniel up, Michael?"

"Come on, son. Bring your case," Michael ordered.

The attic was one large room to the front of the house, another facing the garden, an open doorway connecting the two and a large dormer window in each let in the pale Winter sunshine. Daniel gazed about him, wondering what he was going to do with all that space after the little cubbyhole of a bedroom he had inhabited at the mission. The back was comfortably furnished as a den and the front as a bedroom.

"You can put your things away when we come back, Daniel. And tonight we'll talk. Just have a look round and come down when you're ready," Michael said gently. "It'll be nice having you around," and noticing a suspicion of moisture in the boy's eyes, he withdrew from the room.

"Yes, Mr Schiller," Daniel mumbled and didn't attempt to stop the flood of tears. He knew he had come home.

* * *

After a week it seemed as if Daniel had always lived with them. He was quiet, courteous and got used to Michael kissing his wife at any time, spontaneously and without the slightest trace of embarrassment. He too received a warm hug on occasions and felt quite comfortable about that. At Christmas he found the steam engine under the tree they had put up the night before. There was a thick colourful sweater from Laura and a silver pocket watch on a chain from Michael. Things he had never expected to own.

With his meagre savings from a pitiful allowance at the mission he purchased a packet of cigarillo's and two lace handkerchiefs, which were enthusiastically received. Before they set off for mass Michael handed him a package.

"You'll need some money to put in the collection box, Daniel. It's your pocket money for the week until we can work out how you'll earn your own money. We'll talk about that some other time. Today and tomorrow we'll just enjoy the holiday."

Daniel removed the paper wrapping and fingered the dark brown leather wallet and purse, saw coins and notes the like of which he hadn't ever possessed and nearly burst into tears.

"Thanks, Mr Schiller. I don't mind working. Just tell me what you want me to do." Daniel's face was a study of earnest concern and Michael smiled, placing an arm about his shoulders.

"We'll find you something to do soon. I expect you've been working hard for quite a time already at the mission."

"Since I was twelve years old," the boy informed him, seemingly proud of the fact.

"Then it's time you had a rest. You can't work in the garden for another three months. How about catching up on some schooling, Daniel?" Michael asked.

"I'd like that, Mr Schiller. Can I read some of your books?"

"Read as much as you like, son. Let's see if my wife is ready. Time to go to church," Michael said.

Chapter 19

FEBRUARY 1925

The Bonner Independent again printed scathing articles on the political front, denouncing the up and coming Nazi Party as a Dictatorship. All of them signed 'FM.' Freddy was happy and Michael, under the tutelage of Franz, found his way to places and contacts not previously accessible to him. He took to wearing less fashionable clothes, as the places he and Franz visited were mostly situated in the older part of town. Michael had no difficulty adapting to his new profession, but begrudged the late hours he had to spend away from Laura.

"I told you not to get involved in this business," Franz remarked one night at Erik's place. Earlier they had retired to the Nook, the door firmly closed by Erik as they entered and two men waved to Franz. They shook hands and Michael was introduced. He had long ceased to be surprised at how many people his partner knew and where they came from. His friends were many and varied and kept him informed on what was going on in the rest of the regions.

"What's the little Corporal doing since they let him out, Schubert?" he asked of the thick-set man, referring to the sudden release of Adolf Hitler from his apparently comfortable imprisonment.

Schubert drawled in a heavy Bavarian accent. "Gathering his forces under the nose of the Military, watched over indulgently by the police. If you want to print something really interesting, one of you had better get down South. The Communists are getting ready to have another confrontation with the pigs. We only stopped off on our way back from Berlin to fill you in, but from now on this kind of news is going to be difficult to relay openly. At least not impartially. Down there you've got to take sides and if you want to stay healthy there's only one way to go. The Communists are losing support and the Corporal is changing his tactics. He's going respectable."

"What? Standing again in the next election? Under the motherly protection of the mighty Chancellor Bismark, I suppose?" Franz remarked contemptuously.

The slightly younger man had finished his meal and in an equally heavy southern accent spoke.

"He's not so mighty any more. Sources tell me he's ailing and has to find a successor. The Corporal will keep his nose clean for the time being, fight elections and at every one he'll increase his followers. Meanwhile, his henchmen reduce the opposition by any means, even murder, to get that misbegotten Nobody into power."

"But surely, the Military aren't going to stand by and do nothing?" Michael asked.

"If the Corporal wins the support of the people by promising them a better future, then they can't find any reason to stand in his way," Mose said.

Franz agreed. "They'll probably join him and his party before he has them all shot for treason."

Ibbi Neuhaus, not particularly concerned whether the elitist Military was going to be shot, but terrified to the very core of his Jewish soul that the Corporal might be the next Chancellor, asked. "Is one of you coming down? You can stay at my house, but don't wait too long. The torches are burning very bright."

Franz sighed, a look of resignation on his face. "Michael can't go. He's just got married and hasn't got enough experience to be let loose into that particular cauldron. I'll clear it with Freddy and get down as soon as I can. Tell Miriam to keep the bed aired."

"We'll be seeing you then? It's time we moved. We've a long drive ahead." Ibbi said, rising.

They shook hands and Franz called after them. "I'll be there in a few days."

Michael liked the two men and said so, which pleased Franz.

"I've known them since the war. They're dedicated to a better future, but not with that upstart of a Corporal," he said quietly.

Slowly the snow turned into slush and by the end of February Mother Earth had re-generated herself, stretching her brown limbs towards the rays of a growing sun to dry every contour of her body. Laura and Daniel began to plan what had to be done. She remembered all that Janus had taught her last year and the boy was a willing pupil, eager to repay the two months of leisure they had insisted on. Whatever time Michael could spare, he devoted to Daniel and Laura provided huge meals to put flesh onto the thin body.

Now, Daniel looked fit and healthy. They also noticed that he was growing taller.

Franz Stahl had left for Munich four days ago. The news he sent back was not good. The forces of the National Socialists were gathering momentum and again there was confrontation between the two most dominant parties, all others reduced to the fringes, weakened by indecisive leadership and falling by the wayside.

And abruptly the news from Munich stopped. Freddy alerted every contact he knew of and Michael worried about Franz, remembering Ibbi and Mose's words the night they'd met at Erik's. Another three days went by before Freddy took the call from a woman who would not give her name, only said. "Ibbi and Franz are missing," before hanging up. He knew it was Miriam Neuhaus, he recognised her voice.

"I'm going to Munich to look for him," Freddy said when Michael reported back to the office. Mirna typed like someone possessed and looked as if she hadn't slept since news from Franz had ceased.

"That's the craziest thing I've ever heard. Don't let him go there. It's suicide, Michael," she snapped at them both.

There were not many times Michael could recall when Freddy had looked so worried.

"I'm not just sitting here on my ass hoping for some news. Franz has been with me for a long time. It's not like him not to report in every day. They've got him," he stormed.

"Then I'll have to go with you," Michael said calmly.

Freddy and Mirna stared at him, disbelief mirrored in their eyes and open mouths.

"Now who's crazy?" Freddy asked. "I'm your Boss and I'm telling you to get on with your job here. I'm going alone."

"There are other people here that can do my job. This is not where the danger is. The French are keeping the lid on things at the moment. I respect Franz and if you're going to look for him then I'm coming with you." Michael's tone had the finality Freddy remembered only too well from their time in the war.

"And what about Laura? And Daniel?" Freddy asked.

"Laura will understand and Daniel's a bright boy. He'll look after her while we're gone."

"Very well," Freddy conceded.

"If we don't hear anything tomorrow, we'll leave on Wednesday. Mirna can take over my office work and Goddart will keep the paper running smoothly. He hasn't had much to do lately. I'll ask my father to look in. Thanks, Michael. I'll appreciate your company."

"I had better go home and prepare my piece to go in on Friday. And tell my wife she's going to be a grass widow for a few days," Michael replied.

He waited until Daniel had gone up and told Laura what had happened. At the mention of the journey to Munich to find Franz her face had become still. Michael did not know what to expect, but he knew her well enough to realise that beneath that gentle, soft exterior was a woman of courage and conviction. He held her close to him.

"I have to go, Laura. Not only to find Franz, but for Freddy's sake. If it's as bad as they say it is down there, he'll need me."

"I know, Darling. I hate you going, but to let Freddy go off on his own is unthinkable. Please be careful. I don't want anything to happen to either of you. I'll have enough trouble persuading Erika to stay at home."

"You'll take care of Erika and I'll look after Freddy," he said, smiling down at her. "You are the most remarkable woman, Mrs. Schiller and I love you very much," kissing her tenderly.

The Mercedes drew up at number ten, purring softly. Freddy did not get out. He looked at his watch and waited. With both of them driving, they might make it some time around midnight. The car had a powerful engine and young Rudi had serviced every part of the machine. The time was 6:00 a.m.

Freddy reflected on their meeting last night. They had included Daniel in their plans and were surprised at the questions posed by the boy. It was almost as if he had discovered there was a world full of misery and hardship outside the mission, as well as in it. In the last two months Daniel seemed to have broadened his horizon beyond this little town, avidly reading the daily newspaper from cover to cover.

"If you run into Janus in Munich, tell him I'm fine here," he had said before going up to bed.

There had been a momentary silence as everyone stared at the boy. Michael had noticed the glance that had passed between Laura and Erika.

"Munich is not like Bonn, Daniel. It's a big City and unless you know where Janus lives, there's little chance we'll run into him. Do you know where he is?"

Daniel had appeared embarrassed.

"No," the boy had said quietly. "I don't know where he is," and wished them success in finding Ibbi and Franz.

This morning Feddy was still puzzled as to why Daniel had denied Janus's whereabouts, unless he had been instructed not to reveal that information.

Michael came down the steps, carrying his canvas bag and dressed in his climbing outfit. It would be inconspicuous so near the mountains.

"Good morning, Freddy. Are we ready?"

"Been ready for hours, waiting for you," Freddy joked and Michael laughed.

"The car drew up precisely two and a half minutes ago. Got delayed by Laura's long list of do's and don'ts. She's worried."

"It's a natural state for women, Friend," said Freddy, and started the car. "We are, after all, on a rescue mission. I hope we're doing the right thing."

"Somebody has to go, Freddy. At least we can act without having to report back and get the go-ahead. Let me know when you've had enough and I'll take over."

"I'm alright, Pal. I know the roads fairly well. Munich, here we come," and turning into the highway by the river he pointed the nose of the Mercedes south and put his foot down.

The small hotel about thirty miles from Munich offered excellent food and neither Freddy nor Michael felt like going further.

"I think we'll call it a day," Freddy remarked, downing the last of his brandy. "Miriam won't thank us for knocking her up in the middle of the night. You call Laura and I'll go and see about some beds. We'll make an early start."

"Suits me." Michael rose. "Feel like going for a walk?"

"No, thanks," Freddy said, horrified at the very idea and showing it. "I'll be in bed when you get back.

Chapter 20

They approached the city by mid-morning and both of them seemed to be in another country. The locals sported the traditional felt trilbies decorated with jaunty feathers. Under short green or grey flannel coats the men wore white calico shirts, leather waistcoats and breeches, kneesocks and stout boots. The women were mostly in longer coats, under which they wore frilly blouses, heavy flannel skirts and elaborately embroidered waistcoats, thick stockings and dainty boots. All of them seemed to have long tresses coiled about their heads.

Freddy had seen it all before, but Michael only knew of it through photographs. It was not this sight that amazed him. It was the volume of black and brown uniformed men that thronged the streets. In stark contrast to the costumes and uniforms they saw shabbily dressed groups of people carrying the Communist banners. They were peaceful, but the police presence resembled that of an army, heavy revolvers in their belts.

"It's amazing," Freddy said, astonished. "I came two years ago and it was nothing like this. There must be thousands of them."

Michael, intent on finding his bearings, remarked, "There is a tension in this town. It reeks of it."

Freddy halted the Mercedes in front of a three storey apartment block and got out. Michael followed him, through the foyer and up to the first floor. The name on the bell push said 'I. Neuhaus.' The sound of the loud ring still reverberated in their ears when the door opened and a plump, dark-haired woman threw herself at Freddy.

"I'm glad you've come, Freddy. You'll find them, won't you?" Her voice full of anxiety, dark eyes brimming over with tears. "I'm so worried."

Freddy unclasped her arms from his neck. "Let's go in, Miriam. You'll have to tell us all you know before we do anything."

She became aware of Michael. "You must be Michael Schiller," she said. "Ibbi told me all about you. How do you do." They shook hands and Michael was reminded of Mara and Josef Schumann as he looked around the apartment. It had the same feel as number ten, Annsberg Road.

"I'm sorry to meet you under these circumstances, Mrs. Neuhaus. We'll do our best to find them," Michael reassured Miriam.

"I feel better already now that you're here. Go into the sitting room while I make coffee."

She led them into a spacious room with two high windows facing the road. The two men watched as groups of people made their way towards the town centre.

"I've never seen so many brown shirts before. This town's awash with them."

Miriam asked them to sit down and placed the tray she was carrying on a long table.

"Help yourself to biscuits," and poured the strong, aromatic liquid into delicate china cups.

Michael looked around the room and found a similar type of furniture to that in his own home. Large, solid and gleaming. He wondered if this was a traditionally Jewish home, but did not like to remark on his observation as he and Freddy drank the refreshing coffee.

"Now tell me what happened, Miriam," Freddy ordered.

She sighed heavily. "Franz arrived last Monday. He and Ibbi went out every day to contacts and sent the information back to you. On Friday evening they were meeting somebody from the paper. He was going to give Franz important information. Names and places. Ibbi didn't tell me where they were going, just said they wouldn't be late. I haven't seen them since," her voice shaking with the effort of holding back the tears. "The police won't help. They just tell me Ibbi and Franz will turn up when they've had their little fling. A bored husband showing a bachelor the delights of the town, they said, and just laughed at me. Told me to go home and wait for them to come back. Ibbi doesn't do things like that and he wouldn't leave his job. Where else can I go if the police won't help, Freddy? That's why I phoned you."

Miriam started crying and Michael touched the hand of the distressed woman. "We'll find them, Mrs. Neuhaus," he said quietly. "Is there anything else you can remember?"

"No. They wouldn't tell me too much. For my own good, Ibbi said. We don't go out much any more. There's always fighting going on somewhere in the town. The thugs in the brown shirts beat up people. Men get killed. It's not like it was the last time you were here, Freddy."

"I gathered that from Franz. I think we'll pay the police a visit this afternoon."

"There is one place where they take people for interrogation," Miriam said.

"Where's that?" asked Freddy.

"Somewhere near Dachau. The old barracks. They call it the holding pen. That's where they could be," Miriam sounded hopeful.

"First we'll find out what the police have to say. People can't just disappear without them knowing about it. Come on, Michael. I'll put the car round the back and we'll take the tram. We'll be back early evening, Miriam. And don't worry," Freddy said, patting her shoulder.

Not more than three hundred feet from the imposing Town Hall, stood the equally imposing Police Headquarters. A wide flight of stone steps led up to heavy doors and into a large reception area.

"Very grand for a police station," Michael remarked.

The officer behind the desk was in his mid-forties, round and jovial, his green uniform stretched tight across his ample girth. His friendly smile never wavered as Freddy stated his business, requesting information about one of his employees, who, together with his friend, had disappeared. At the mention of Ibbi Neuhaus's name Michael thought he detected a flicker of recognition in the man's eyes. Had it been fear?

"Reporters, eh?" the policeman laughed a little. "We get legions of them coming to this town lately. They arrive and leave again. What paper did he work for?"

"Mine," said Freddy. "The Bonner Independent."

"Never heard of it. What kind of rag is it? Independent of what?"

"Independent of everything. For your information, my paper isn't a rag. It's a respectable newspaper in Bonn, which is in the Rhineland, at present occupied by the French. I expect that news has found its way down here. Now that I've given you our geographical location, why the interest in what kind of paper it is?" asked Freddy.

"It makes a big difference here," the fat man said laconically. "If your man was covering 'Births, Marriages and Deaths' he wouldn't be missing. Nor would his friend. Jews have no business to poke their noses into affairs that don't concern them."

Freddy glanced at Michael who had also understood the reference to Ibbi.

"How did you know one was a Jew?" Michael asked calmly and noticed the smile fading from the heavy countenance.

"A Jewish woman came in last Saturday. Reported her husband and his friend missing. Sounds to me like you're looking for the same men. They haven't turned up, then?"

"Not so far. Did you make any enquiries about them? They're not the kind of reporters to miss deadlines," Freddy's voice was still light and pleasant.

"So they were here on assignments? What kind?" The tone, previously patronising, now had a distinct edge to it. The bulky form of the policeman leant over the polished desk, searching both their faces. Freddy looked at Michael.

"They are both political correspondents and go wherever there's news of that kind to report. There's no law against that, is there?" Michael answered.

The policeman considered that for a moment, and his face became noncommittal. "Not that I'm aware of. At least not yet. I'll have to make a report on your enquiry. Your names, please," and taking a notebook from a drawer, he waited.

"Frederick Dettingen," Freddy said quickly. "He's Michael Schiller and works for me as well."

"Your man must be important for the two of you to come all the way down here to look for him."

"I don't like to lose people without a good reason," Freddy said. "Did you look for them?" and his tone also had an edge to it.

"When the woman came in I filed my report, had them check the cells down below. Then I made enquiries at the two main hospitals, the morgue and looked through the reports from the night before. There was nothing. We've got so many fracas going on in this town we don't even go and sort them out any more. The boys from the SA does it for us. We've two smaller hospitals where you could ask. Then there's the City Jail and the Holding Pen. It's a bit out of the way, but that's where they take the political trouble-makers."

"What and where is the Holding Pen?" Michael asked, pretending ignorance.

"The Stormtroopers Army, the ones in the brown shirts, have their barracks there, but the black shirts pull the strings. If your men are still alive,

175

and so far the morgue hasn't any unidentified bodies in residence, that's where they are."

Neither Michael nor Freddy wanted to appear too interested in the political turmoil going on in the town and diverted the officer's attention onto less dangerous ground.

"We'll check out the places you've mentioned," Freddy said. "If you'll give us directions we'll be on our way. How far is the Holding Pen, by the way? Just in case we've got to go there."

"The place is called Dachau. There's a train every twenty five minutes from the main station. You can't miss the compound when you get there. They've got two flags flying. Ours and theirs," the officer told them. "I hope you find them," he added generously.

"Thanks," Freddy said.

The burly policeman stared after them, a thoughtful expression on his face, wondering if they had any connection with Herb Graf

There was no-one of their description at either of the hospitals and the City Jail had no entry of their names. That only left the Holding Pen.

"I'm going to see Herb Graf. Maybe he can shed some light on this. He might have an idea who Ibbi was going to see," Freddy told Michael. "It's not far."

The Munich Independent Newspaper building was wedged between a furniture store and a pawn shop in a busy street. Anyone who did not know the location would have missed it. The glass entrance door was firmly locked and inside the small foyer lay empty and silent. Freddy looked at Michael, concern spreading over his face.

"That's odd," he mumbled. "I had a letter from him three weeks ago and he never mentioned giving up the business. Ibbi was still working for him last Friday. Herb had a violent dislike of Corporal Adolf Hitler and wasn't afraid to say so. He helped to put him behind bars. Now the bastard's out again I wonder if there were repercussions. The self-styled future leader of the German Nation is not known for his compassion. We'll go and see Herb at home"

They took another tram to the pleasant suburbs and got out at Rohm Avenue. The neat villa was set back from the road. An attractive fair-haired woman, dressed in black, stood in the doorway and stared at Freddy.

Michael noticed she looked pale but somehow very much in control. Too much for his liking.

"Freddy," she said, surprised at seeing him. "How long has it been? Two years? Come in, both of you."

"Hello, Eva. This is Michael Schiller."

She shook Michael's hand and embraced Freddy. Voices, quiet and solemn, carried into the hall.

"In here." Eva Graf led them to a study. "Sit down. I'll get Fanny to bring you something to drink." She left the room and they could hear her talking to someone. The two men in the study felt increasingly uncomfortable.

"Where is Herb?" Freddy asked as Eva returned. "We've been to the paper. There's nobody there. What is going on, Eva?"

"Herb is dead, Freddy. They fished him out of the river early Saturday morning. I was told he killed himself," Eva Graf's voice was cool and impassionate.

Michael could not help comparing the composed demeanour of Herb's widow to that of the genuine misery of Miriam. The two women seemed worlds apart in their grief.

"Oh, God. I'm sorry, Eva. Herb was a good friend," Freddy told her. "Will there be an inquest?" he asked.

"No. The police have a sworn statement from Franz Stahl and Ibbi Neuhaus that they saw Herb jump in. I've seen the signatures. Now they've have disappeared. Why should my husband kill himself? It's lunacy," Eva said and delicately dabbed at her eyes.

Freddy rose and patted her shoulder, while Michael sat, stunned at the horrifying news unfolding itself.

"We've got to find Franz and Ibbi," Freddy said. "Try and remember, Eva. Did Herb go to meet them last Friday night?"

"Yes. He was going to see them in the Beer Hall by the market. He left here about eight in the evening. Said he wouldn't be long. He took a lot of papers with him for Franz to take back to you," Eva informed him.

"Ibbi told Miriam he wouldn't be long. Maybe Franz was going back on the night train?" Freddy suggested.

"I'm not sure. There wouldn't be any reason for him to stay. The papers were important. Herb wanted you to have a clear picture of what was going on here and in Berlin. I expect they've got the documents back now." Her voice took on a sharpness, bordering on anger. "The Authorities shut the paper down. Nobody's allowed in there. What do you think I should do, Freddy?"

Michael had the uncomfortable feeling that Mrs. Graf was more upset about the closure of the paper than her husband's death.

Freddy said, "I don't know, Eva."

She excused herself to see her other guests and sent in Fanny. The maid, dressed neatly in black, long braids coiled around her head in the local fashion entered, carried a tray attractively arranged with food. Fanny seemed to linger, curious, and Michael felt uneasy in her presence. He did not know why, as she behaved with the utmost courtesy. He found the pale blue eyes watching them with great interest, noting everything about them.

"Will you be staying long, sir?" Fanny enquired.

"No. We have some business to finish here which shouldn't take more than a day or so," Freddy answered. He was going to add more but Michael stopped him, suggesting they have their lunch, and looked hard at his friend. Freddy was surprised, but understood the message and concentrated on eating. Fanny glanced from one man to the other and went out, leaving the door ajar. Michael moved to close it.

"What was all that about?" Freddy asked, suddenly curious.

"I'm not sure. I can't decide whether to trust the girl," Michael said, a frown deepening the crease between the eyebrows. Freddy looked startled.

"That's the first time since I've known you that you've said something like that. Amazing," he said.

"I'm living in the real world, Freddy, not the stultified confines of the church. Out here it's ugly. Maybe that's what's sharpening my sixth sense."

Freddy's eyebrows went up in amusement. "Your senses don't need sharpening and you've always known what goes on around you, old friend. Except now you're free to think and act according to your natural inclination because the rules have changed. What is it that bothers you about the girl?"

"I don't know," Michael said quietly. "Something does."

Eva Graf entered the study. "Has Fanny looked after you properly?" she asked.

"Yes, thank you, Eva. The food was excellent. How long have you had the new girl?" Freddy enquired.

"Just a few months. She's very good. I do a lot of charity work and can leave her to look after things. She cooks well, too. Something I've never been fond of."

"Does she live here?" Michael asked.

"Of course. She has the run of the house. Why do you ask?"

"Just curious. Did Franz and Ibbi come here before they disappeared?"

"Yes. On Thursday night. They sorted through the papers Herb had been working on. He was going to give Franz the rest on Friday."

"Does the girl have access to this study and the desk?" Michael enquired.

Eva looked perplexed. "She comes in here to clean and the spare key for the drawer is in that cigarette box on the desk. I don't understand."

"Your husband would hardly advertise the fact that he had vital information and was dispatching this to another newspaper. Someone must've told someone else of the meeting in the Beer Hall and what your husband was handing over to Franz. Can you think of anyone else who could've betrayed them? Think hard, Mrs Graf."

"I was the only other person that knew of it. I insisted Ibbi did not tell Miriam. She's a sweet creature, but very emotional. It's the Jewish nature. There's no-one else in the house. We never stopped talking when Fanny was in the room as I didn't think she was bright enough to follow the gist of our conversation. I can't believe Fanny is capable of taking part in the murder of my husband. Friday was her afternoon off, but she was back here by eleven. It's the time she always comes in. No, I won't believe it."

"Just be careful, Eva," Freddy said gently, and got up. "We must be going. I'll phone you from Miriam's. Tonight we'll call in at the Beer Hall. I'll miss Herb and I wish I could promise to find out what's happened, but I don't hold out much hope. The police in this town are not very helpful."

He embraced Eva. Michael shook hands.

"I'm very sorry about your husband. I just hope Franz and Ibbi haven't gone to join him. Things look bad here."

"Don't forget to call before you go home," Eva reminded Freddy and led them to the front door.

Michael could not be sure but he had the impression that Fanny was standing in the alcove next to the study and wondered if she had been listening.

The Beer Hall was big and noisy, full of men in brown and black uniforms. A sprinkling of customers in Tyrolean costumes sat on the long benches. Freddy and Michael, seated near the entrance, faced each other across the trestle table. A massive stone tankard, frothing over, stood in front of them.

"They don't do things by half here," Freddy remarked, and Michael longed for one of Jochen's thin beer glasses.

"So, what's next, old friend?" he asked Freddy. "It's been one hell of a day already."

Freddy wiped the foam from his mouth.

"At least the beer is good," he said. "As for what's next? Your guess is as good as mine. Without Ibbi we have no contacts here. There's not much we can do about Herb. Not in this town. We've got to concentrate on finding Franz and Neuhaus. As a newspaper man it galls me to admit defeat. Herb was a friend. If, and it's still a big question mark, if they've killed him, then a good man's been silenced. If, and again we only have Eva's word for it, Franz and Ibbi signed that statement, even when we find them, there's no way we can get justice for Herb."

"God, it's noisy in here." Michael lit a cigarillo and inhaled deeply, looking about him. A group of people of mixed ages and dressed in working clothes, had gathered at the entrance. He stared at them, his brow deeply furrowed.

"What is it, Michael?"

"I'm sure I just saw that maid of Mrs. Graf's. With that group over there." He still frowned in consternation. He thought he heard Freddy call out 'Miss Fanny,' but couldn't be sure as he found himself jostled from behind.

The voice that spoke in his ear was clear and distinct. "Don't look round. There's a note in your pocket. Read it and get rid of it. Eva betrayed you, too," and then she was gone.

Michael sat, stunned for a moment and felt in his pockets, then looked at Freddy, who seemed puzzled at the performance across from him. Michael shook his head and on the pretext of reaching for his handkerchief took out the note. He read and was surprised at the neatness of the handwriting. His face darkened with anger.

'Mr. Graf did not deserve to die the way he did. His wife and her Nazi lover arranged it. They made Franz and Ibbi sign the statement. I think they killed them too. Get out of this town. Eva doesn't want your friend to make trouble here, or they'll have to kill you. It's easy here, people disappear all the time. Be careful. Go home.'

There was no signature. Michael took a beermat, placed it over the note and slid it across to Freddy. His face, too, changed as he read and then stared at Michael. Freddy returned the note and made a ripping gesture with his hands. Michael tore the note into very small pieces and scattered it under the table, shouting to Freddy to drink up. The band somehow seemed louder, the voices of the people competed and feet stomped to the rhythm of the music.

The group at the door advanced, having grown in number and from the opposite end of the hall brown and black shirts mingled in one mass, swarming through the aisles. Peaceful citizens dived under the tables, to cower in terror as all hell broke loose. Freddy could neither get under the table nor get out and Michael was trapped between opposing armies.

He and Freddy did not see the heavy built police officer and a brown-shirted, good looking man raise their batons high. The force of the blows spun Freddy and Michael into oblivion.

* * *

Freddy groaned and opened his eyes. He had difficulty in focusing, but made a start with the dim light above him. A naked bulb, no wallpaper, only bricks and bars. Another iron bedstead with a straw mattress like his own. A still form lay on it. Freddy felt his head spinning, something was throbbing away like a sledgehammer. He gingerly lifted his arm and followed the track of pain to its source. There was an egg-sized swelling on the side of his head.

The Beer Hall... a fight had broken out... Michael had sat on the other side of the table... Michael... He carefully tested his artificial limb and swung it over the side of the bed. Sitting up produced the equivalent of a starburst in his head and he wondered where his walking stick was. His eyes seemed to be focussed in entirely the opposite direction and he made a strenuous effort to control his vision. The stick was hooked carefully within reach over the end of the bed. He found that almost laughable.

There was no great distance between the two beds, but it seemed like miles to Freddy as he wavered like a drunkard to where Michael lay. The faint light from the overhead bulb shone on the lean face, streaked with dark dried blood.

"Michael?"

Freddy touched the silent man and felt no response.

"Michael?" he called softly for the second time, and felt for a pulse and heartbeat, relieved to find a feeble trace of both and looked about him. The eerie silence disturbed him. If he was in the Town Jail, there should be more noise from other prisoners. A soft moan escaped Michael's lips.

Freddy's voice was more insistent.

"Michael! Wake up."

He watched as the eyelids fluttered, then opened and was relieved to see life coming back into eyes the colour of Laura's sapphires.

"God Almighty. What hit me? Where are we?" he croaked, feeling his face.

"Well, at least you're sensible enough to ask daft questions. I'd give you the answer if I knew it. The last thing I remember is sitting in the Beer Hall when that fracas started. Somehow I don't think we're in the town. It's too quiet around here."

Michael looked about his small cell, listening. It was as if they were the only occupants of whatever building they had been taken to.

"What time is it?" he asked.

Freddy checked.

"Ten past eleven."

"As far as I can tell it must've been nearly ten o clock when the girl bumped into me and gave me the note. The fighting started soon after that. Wherever we are, we haven't been here long. Why us? The place should be full of people if they arrested everybody that was in that fight."

Freddy considered that. "You're right, friend. I'm beginning to wonder if it wasn't staged just for our benefit. The question is, can we trust the girl?"

Michael pondered on that for a while, feeling the lump on his head and testing the rest of his body and found it satisfactory.

"I don't know. Mrs. Graf was very convincing, but the girl had me confused, and I can't think why. Maybe she was trying to tell us something. I wonder what happened to her?"

"We're all confused. You, me and Miriam. The only one that seemed to cope pretty well was Eva. If she has a lover and wanted to get rid of Herb, she's managed it without any suspicion falling on her. There's no reason for her to suspect Fanny of anything. Unless someone was watching us at the Beer Hall. They could've seen her bumping into you, but it was all over so quickly even I didn't realize she'd spoken to you," Freddy said. "Miriam will be worried and won't know what to think. Who's going to tell her? Certainly not the police."

"If the girl is telling the truth, then she daren't say anything to anybody. Laura will be frantic if I don't phone. God, what a mess."

Freddy looked through the bars on the doors. Only the wall opposite and a corridor stretching away either side was visible. And all of it was deathly still.

Chapter 21

Laura had spent a restless night, worrying why Michael had not called her last night. The shrill bell of the telephone reached her befuddled brain and she jumped out of bed, raced down the stairs before it stopped, her one thought was that it would be her husband.

"Hello," she breathed into the receiver, wondering what time it was.

"Mrs Schiller?" a woman's voice asked at the other end.

"Yes. Who's this?"

"Miriam Neuhaus. Your husband and Freddy are staying with me. Looking for Franz and Ibbi..."

Laura interrupted the voice with the strange accent. "Do you know why Michael didn't phone me last night, Mrs Neuhaus? Is he alright?"

"I don't know," Miriam sounded tearful. "They didn't have much luck yesterday. Last night they went to the Beer Hall in town and haven't come back. I don't know what to do, Mrs Schiller."

Laura stared at the receiver in her hand, a feeling of dread turning her legs to jelly. She sat down and tried to think, images of the most terrifying kind racing through her mind.

"Mrs Neuhaus?" She forced her voice into assumed calm. There was no point in both of them getting hysterical. "Why did they go to this Beer Hall? Were they meeting someone? Try and remember."

"I... I don't think so. With Ibbi and Franz gone, there was only Mr Graf, the owner of the Munich Independent. He's dead. They say he killed himself last Friday night. Drowned in the river. The same night Ibbi and Franz went missing."

"So why did Michael and Freddy go to this place?"

"I don't know... they didn't tell me. They went to see Mrs. Graf in the afternoon. That's all I know." Miriam sounded as if she was crying.

"Mrs Neuhaus. Please, try to keep calm. Can I get in touch with Mrs Graf? They might've said..." but this time it was Miriam that interrupted the conversation. Her voice was sharp and decisive. So much so that Laura stared again at the receiver, wondering if this was the same woman on the line.

"Don't do that, Mrs Schiller. I beg you. I can't explain over the phone. I'll try the police again and will call you later in the day. Goodbye," and the line went dead.

Laura sat, frightened and yet curious as to why she shouldn't contact Mrs. Graf. The thought of Michael in any kind of danger or even dead did not bear thinking about. Who else was there? No-one here? It had to be Munich, even if she and Erika had to go there to find them. Janus was in Munich and he had promised that if she needed help...

Laura ran up the stairs, to the attic and hammered on Daniel's bedroom door. "Daniel! Daniel, get up! I need you. Hurry," and fled down the stairs into her own bedroom to get dressed. She could hear Daniel moving about above her. Laura sat on the bed to recollect precisely what Janus had said in his farewell note...

'If you ever need me, go to the tavern...'

Had he said see Nell? She couldn't quite remember, as at the time she hadn't visualized ever having to get in touch with him. 'Daniel will take you...' it had said. She needed him now.

"Mrs Schiller?" the voice of Daniel shouted from the hall. "Mrs Schiller?" he called again, and somehow the trembling legs carried her downstairs.

"Daniel. Michael and Freddy have gone missing too. Since last night. There's no-one down there that can help, according to Ibbi's wife. Or they won't. Do you know where Janus is?" she pleaded.

Daniel was startled. "He's in Munich," was the careful reply.

"I am aware of that. Do you have an address?" Laura asked.

"No... Honestly. We write to each other sometimes, but Nell at the tavern puts the address on the envelope and posts it for me. I go there now and again to pick up Janus's letters. He never puts an address on it."

"Then we must go and see Nell. After breakfast. Janus is the only one that can save them."

Daniel wasn't sure how he should respond to her calm attitude. Mrs Schiller was not like most women. Underneath all that softness was a tough lady and he admired that. But why did she want Janus to help her? "I'm sorry about them going missing, Mrs Schiller. Maybe they're some place where there's no phone."

"Like jail, Daniel? Or the morgue?" Laura asked quietly.

"Don't even think about that," the boy answered, trying to hide his own fear. "We'd better be at the tavern just after ten. Nell's about then. I'll get dressed properly."

Laura watched him hurry back upstairs and sank into the small wicker chair by the telephone table, burying her face in her hands. She felt the tears well up from her eyes and let them flow, thinking of Michael.

Miriam Neuhaus replaced the receiver and wished for the hundredth time that Ibbi had been in some hum-drum job where he had no need for a telephone, although she had to admit that on occasions like this it had its advantages. To send a telegram with the kind of message she had just given Mrs. Schiller would be much too dangerous.

Miriam hurried into the kitchen. The kettle was steaming and she needed a strong black coffee if she was going to survive this day. She sat at the table and dropped four lumps of sugar into the scalding brew, remembering how Fanny had rung the bell just after eleven o'clock last night, blood streaming from a head wound. It had looked worse than it was and hopefully she wouldn't need stitches, but she had lost a lot of blood.

Fanny didn't need to tell her where she'd been. It wasn't the first time, nor would it be the last, as long as she was alive. Her place was not with the rank and file, but sometimes she couldn't resist the urge to join the frontline. Her task in the Communist Party was to gather information. A dangerous game, and last night she had almost got herself killed to give Michael the message. Someone had recognised her and now for Fanny there was no way back to Eva's. Where was it all going to end? Miriam wondered... why did revolutions have to be so bloody?.. Ibbi would have known what to do, now, there was only herself to get the girl out of this town...

Miriam felt better after her second cup and poured another full of steaming, black liquid, piled sugar lumps into it and walked to the spare bedroom. Opening the shutters, she watched the sleeping girl. How young she looks... and yet so old... A terrible sadness filled her soul. For Fanny and all the others like her, as fanatical in their belief as their opponents. pursuing ideologies that would end in disaster. Freddy and Herb Graf, Ibbi, Franz and Michael caught in the middle, clinging to the last shreds of sanity. Herb had already paid the price, betrayed by his own wife. Would they all have to die? Maybe she herself was on Eva's list. It didn't really matter if Ibbi wasn't going to come home again. Nothing mattered any more...

The noise woke Michael from a troublesome sleep. He had a splitting headache, something alien to him. The noise repeated itself and he assumed it must be a metal door being closed. Heavy footsteps echoed along the narrow corridor and came nearer. He could hear the jingling of keys. A blonde young man in the uniform of the new National Party looked sullen, not quite awake. Freddy too was not in the best of moods.

"There's life here after all," he said. "What is it to be, soldier? Breakfast or the gallows?" but the young man just threw him a contemptuous glance.

"I'm going to take you to the sluice room and don't bother trying to escape. My orders are to shoot you. Simple, isn't it?" his heavy Bavarian accent grated on both occupants of the prison cell.

"Message understood," Michael growled. "Any breakfast on offer? I don't suppose you know why we're in this dungeon? Do you?" contemptuous of the revolver in the young man's hand. "Or maybe they don't bother telling small fry like you," he taunted.

"This small fry only knows big Communist fish come down here. Now move. If you behave yourselves you might get breakfast."

He led them to a metal door and unlocked it. Michael had noticed heavy pipes running below the ceiling, giving off a degree of warmth. He assumed that was why they had not felt cold in the night, the heat circulated into the cells through the grilled bars of the doors.

They had passed a further six small compartments, all remarkably clean, with two beds, a striped cotton covered mattress and pillow with a blanket folded neatly at the foot end. As if by mutual agreement Freddy and Michael let the reference to the Communist fish pass. Neither wanted to get shot at the whim of this surly youth. He couldn't be more than eighteen.

The sluice room was sparkling clean, tiled from top to bottom, several wash basins, a bath and three lavatory cubicles. On a shelf above the basins lay a towel and a small bar of soap. Michael felt the stubble on his face and wished they had provided shaving tackle. The guard stood by the door, easy, but alert and did not hurry them unduly. Freddy checked his watch.

"It's just gone seven, Pal. Maybe they keep office hours here. He..." pointing in the direction of the guard, ".. he doesn't seem to be in a hurry."

"As long as somebody's going to see us. Laura will be worried sick by now. I wonder if Miriam's phoned her? I left the number by the telephone," Michael said, his face and eyes full of anxiety. "God, why us? There doesn't seem to be anyone else down here, so Franz and Ibbi must be some other place. If they're still alive. How can they get away with this? It's evil," Michael spoke softly, disdainfully getting into his stained and crumpled shirt. "I want to be home with my wife."

Freddy too had washed and struggled to get back into his clothes.

"One piece of advice, my friend. Keep the thought of our women out of your head. We're in enough trouble as it is and need to keep our wits about us. We'll be home soon. I guarantee it," he said optimistically.

The guard made a move with the gun.

"Time's up," and led them back to the cell.

He did not bother to lock the door to the sluice room and Michael wondered if that was for their benefit and how long they were going to be confined down here. He could not see any means of escape and it would be foolish to try. He would have to leave Freddy behind and that was out of the question. They sat on their respective beds, lost in silent misery, listening to the echo of the guard's boots fading in the corridor, hearing the metal clang of the door and waited...

The door clanged again and the young man in his black uniform appeared, carrying a tray. Two large enamel mugs steamed and the smell of coffee permeated the small cell. Six rolls, already cut and filled with cheese and conserve, two enamel plates and two hard-boiled eggs, still in their shell lay on the tray, which was pushed under the door.

"You don't intend to starve us to death," Michael remarked as he collected the tray off the floor. "When are we going to see somebody to sort out this mistake?"

The guard ignored the question and Michael wondered what had been his reason for joining the Fascist movement. He did not look unduly vicious. A nice simple boy without prospect of work might be drawn into the net, obeying orders without asking too many questions? If they told him to shoot them, then that was what he would do...

"Mr. Konrad will see you when he gets here," the young guard said, neither sounding pleased nor antagonistic.

Freddy had tasted the coffee and did not find it unpalatable. It suddenly re-juvenated his flagging spirits. "Just a Mr ?" Freddy called to the guard. And then addressed Michael "We're going to be interrogated by a plain

Mister, Michael. It's not fitting for two big Communist fish, is it?" then asked the youth "Haven't they seen fit to promote him yet?"

The guard did not find it amusing. He stood for a moment, a strange expression on his face and his voice held something like awe as he told them, "If I were in your shoes, I'd be civil to Mr. Konrad. He has got a rank and a uniform. He just doesn't wear it for work. It's his job to check you out and decide what to do with you," and smartly turned to stomp along the corridor. They heard the door clang again.

The breakfast tasted like a feast and Michael savoured the coffee to the last drop. "I wonder who he is?" he asked Freddy, who looked at his watch.

"Probably Intelligence if he's operating in civilian clothes. Less conspicuous. We won't have to wait much longer, I hope. This place is getting claustrophobic. How's your head?" Freddy asked.

"Better since I bathed it. Still got a bit of a headache, though."

Both men listened as the sound of heavy booted feet vibrated through the ceiling above.

"They're waking up, old friend," Freddy remarked dryly.

It was only a short distance from the tram terminus to the old barracks. A tall, slim-built man in a sober grey suit, white shirt and striped tie entered the renovated main building, called 'good morning,' to the Sergeant on the reception desk and walked lightly up the wide staircase to the first floor, along a carpeted hallway and entered what appeared to be a kind of sorting office. A young man in the black uniform of the Nazi Party was filing away yesterday's work. His desk had several piles of paper waiting to be dealt with by his boss.

"Good morning, Ulrich. I can see it's going to be a busy Friday after that fracas in town last night. How many are below this time?" the Boss enquired, the voice deep and sonorous, pleasant with a different accent from another region.

"Good morning, sir. Just two of them. The rest was the usual crowd and were taken to the City Jail for the customary treatment. One of their girls was badly hurt, but got away. Mrs Graf told her lover boy she wanted these two got rid of, but the Major's handed them over to you. I think he's a bit wary after they found Herb Graf in the state he was in. And the other two," Ulrich informed his boss.

"Bad business, that. The lady's aiming high. What about the ones below? Are they injured?" the tall man asked.

"I don't think so, sir, just bumps on the head. Gerhard had them cleaned up and they've had breakfast. People get very un co-operative when they're hungry. One of them had a slight concussion, but is alright. The other one's got a wooden leg and owns a newspaper somewhere in the Rhineland. There's a connection between him and Graf. They came looking for the two reporters. Are you alright, sir?" the young soldier asked, wondering why his boss had gone pale, staring at him in a strange fashion.

"I'm fine, thank you, Ulrich," Jan Konrad said quietly, his mind searching for a plausible excuse. "My wife doesn't sleep very well right now because of the baby. I think I'll have to move into the spare bedroom for a while."

He smiled and Ulrich understood. He had three married sisters and his brothers-in-law complained about the same thing when they were expecting babies.

"Everything settles down after a while, sir. The first is always the worst time. Here are the particulars given to the Major by Mrs. Graf."

He handed his boss two sheets of paper, typed and signed by Major E. Johannsen. Jan Konrad did not even glance at them but walked through another door to a spacious office, generously endowed with antiques and regency striped furnishings. When he had requested a less opulent work place he was told it was in keeping with his position. He had remembered the simple, comfortable home he had created in the pigeon loft and never felt entirely at ease here.

Jan stood at the high window, staring out into the court-yard for some time before he gathered enough courage to look at the sheets in his hand. He was not at all surprised to see the name of Frederick Dettingen and Michael Schiller. So the baron and the priest had come to him. It would be so easy... But Laura would still not be his wife, ever... He needed some time to think...

At nine-twenty, Jan walked into the outer office.

"Get me the Cologne files. I have some checking to do. And Ulrich.. about the prisoners. Tell Gerhard to take them to the small room next to the reception. He's to keep an eye on them until I'm through with this. If they make any trouble, he and Sergeant Berger are to lock them up again. Give them something to read. Preferably the manifesto on the National Socialist Party. That should enlighten them."

"Yes, Mr. Konrad. I'll see to it," and then handed him a large box file bulging at the seams. Jan recognized his own handwriting, the long list of names. There was no need for him to go through them. The names of the two men below were not among them. He returned to his own desk, sat in the ridiculously ornate chair and opened the file at random, looking at it, not seeing any of the names as he closed his eyes. He saw only Laura and the images rolled like a camera, the sound in his head accompanying every movement. The staccato tap-tap as she walked along the embankment, her voice echoing inside the staircase of Rema House, then the excitement as they talked about what they would do with the land at number ten, until it all fell apart that day at Peter's party, when he had seen her and the priest in the summerhouse...

Jan buried his face in his hands as he remembered that night after dinner when he had asked her to marry him and she had told him that she would never marry anyone except Michael Schiller. And he remembered that last night when they had made their bargain. She had been prepared to give herself to save them and he couldn't take her... not then, not ever... Oh, God, Laura. I'll always love you... to the end of my days...

He neither noticed time nor the moisture welling up into his eyes as he sat in his large splendid office, a lonely figure, alone with his pain. It was almost ten o'clock when the telephone shrilled.

"Jan Konrad," he said into the receiver.

"Janus, it's Nell. Are you alone? I have a message for you from Laura."

He did not speak for a moment.

"Jan?"

He made the effort to calm himself. "Yes, Nell. I'm alone. What is it?" he asked, already aware what she was going to say.

"Daniel brought her this morning. The baron and her husband have gone missing. So has one of their reporters. The last she's heard of them was from the apartment of a Mrs Neuhaus..."

"Nell," Jan interrupted firmly. "I know where they are. Tell her they'll be home tomorrow or Sunday. And that they're alright. Please, Nell, just that. I'll call you when this business is over. Tell her not to worry any more. Goodbye." He replaced the receiver, staring at the telephone for some time.

Next to his office was a cloakroom. Jan rinsed his face and the reflection in the mirror showed a lean face, the mouth wide and defined, eyes of the softest brown and a thick mass of silvery hair carefully combed back so that not one wave disturbed the smooth surface. Laura had liked it when he let it fall into natural waves after using the shower in the old washroom. Laura... Since he had left he slicked it back. It made him look different.

Jan slowly made his way back to the office, closed the file on his desk and returned it to the shelf. He instructed his assistant, "Ulrich, send the man Schiller up. It may take some time. See that we are not disturbed."

Chapter 22

Jan Konrad sat quietly, waiting for the man who had taken from him the woman he would never cease to love. Regret and hatred churned every molecule into a searing ball of pain. It was what he experienced in his nightmares, but then, in other dreams there was only love and Laura. He reached for his pipe, hoping it would calm the turmoil raging in his head. And braced himself when the knock came at the door.

"Come," he called, and watched the expression on Michael's face change from the calmness he remembered so well to one of surprise.

"Janus!" Michael exclaimed. "You're the Mr Konrad who's going to decide our fate. I had no idea you were involved with this murderous mob."

"I am, Schiller. And have the power to incarcerate you and the baron, or send you home," Jan Konrad said curtly. "Why did you come here? This is not a healthy town for people of your misguided persuasion. Sit down."

Michael did as he was told and realised that this was far from being a happy reunion with the quiet man he had met and talked to last year. He had changed.

"What misguided persuasion would that be, Janus?" Michael asked softly.

"Don't play games with me, Schiller. Answer my question."

Michael made himself comfortable, conscious of his dishevelled appearance. "Very well. I work for the Baron's newspaper and one of our reporters came down here to get the truth of what really is going on. About a week ago he didn't check in with his story at the arranged time. The wife of the man he was staying with called us on Saturday to tell us that her husband and our man hadn't come home. We waited for four days, heard nothing and decided to come and look for them. Does that answer your question?" he asked.

Jan nodded. "It makes sense," he said, a little less abrasively. "You didn't find them, of course. What were you doing in the Beer Hall last night? It's not the kind of place you and the baron frequent. Were you meeting somebody?"

Michael could not resist the taunt that sprang to his lips. "You're right. Beer Halls are not to our taste. We prefer slightly more congenial surroundings and certainly more civilized company," and saw Jan's eyes narrowing. Michael continued. "No, we didn't go to meet anybody in particular. Freddy was still upset about one of his friends here, who, according to his wife, was fished out of the river on Saturday morning."

"Herb Graf, the owner of the Munich Independent. Where did you get this information from?" Jan asked, suddenly curious.

"Mrs Graf saw fit to enlighten us; I suspect as a diversionary tactic."

"What makes you say that?" Jan wondered how much the two men knew or just guessed.

"We met somebody in the Beer Hall who told us," Michael said.

"Who was that, Schiller?"

"We've no idea. Never met him before."

The lie should at least protect Fanny, Michael hoped, and felt less guilty.

"Her," the quiet voice of Jan reminded him he need not have bothered. "You met her at Mrs Graf's. During the afternoon."

Michael controlled himself sufficiently not to show surprise at Jan's statement.

"I don't know what you're talking about, Janus."

"Mr Konrad, if you don't mind," Jan rebuffed him. "You were wise to get rid of that piece of paper Fanny slipped into your pocket. Had they found it on you, there was always the possibility that both of you might have been fished out of that same river this morning." His voice was non-committal. "The girl was injured and went to Mrs Neuhaus. Miriam took her to the station this morning and put her on a train to Prague." There was a moments silence. "I liked Fanny. She had guts and so much integrity, even if it was misplaced. She was like someone I knew once, so I let her go home."

"God Almighty. How do you know all this? How much power do you have, Janus?" Michael asked, astonished that this man knew every move they had made since leaving Eva Graf's villa.

"For your information," Jan said matter-of-factly, "Not even a mouse moves in this city without somebody leaving a memo on my desk about it. Soon, every town and village in this country will be like that. And when the Rhineland comes back into the fold, it'll happen there too. My job does not start and finish in this building. I take it home with me. But some incidents take place and there is a time gap before I'm informed."

"What about Herb Graf? Was he murdered?"

Michael did not really expect an answer to the last question and looked at Jan Konrad, who calmly re-lit his pipe, then remarked "Do you still smoke those long cigarillos? I'll send Ulrich down for some if you haven't any."

The need for a soothing cigar was overwhelming, but Michael resisted the offer. "No thanks. I'll get some when I get out of here. You haven't answered my question."

"I don't have to, Schiller, but Herb Graf was connected with the disappearance of your man. First, I need your solemn promise that none of this'll get beyond these walls. There'll be no story for the Bonner Independent. That's why I didn't want the baron here. For everybody's sake you'll have to give me your word."

Michael looked uncertain, but the face of Jan Konrad was deadly earnest. "Very well. You have it."

Relief showed in Jan's eyes, as if, in spite of himself he needed to talk to another human being, perhaps remembering the priest and not the man. His voice was firm and steady and did not betray any emotion. "I knew Herb. He was a Moderate and eventually would have had to give up the fight. Like the baron will have to. Herb was too dangerous for Eva Graf. Her sight is set firmly on the top rung of the political ladder. She had to silence Herb's voice in the paper. The baron's brother, like Mrs Graf, will have to do the same," Jan said.

Michael stared at him. "What the hell do you know about Freddy's brother?" he asked.

"I lived there, remember? I've been doing this work since 1922 and am very good at it," Jan informed him, a faint smile softening his expression just a little. Then it disappeared. "But to get back to your reporter, Franz Stahl, I was surprised when you teamed up with him. I still have my sources in Bonn and sooner or later would've asked you, by one means or another, to cease that particular activity for the sake of..." he paused momentarily, "of everybody you're connected with. I have no love for you, or the Baron, but I didn't want your names on the hit-list. Ibbi Neuhaus went to Berlin where he and his friend got hold of papers they had no right to. The Gestapo tailed them, followed them to Erik's place, where you met."

Jan noticed the blue eyes narrowing, but was not interrupted, the slim fingers pressed tightly together the only indication of anxiety. He had to admit, the grudging respect he once had for this man had not diminished in spite of... Jan forced himself to return to the more pressing business of Franz

Stahl and did not like what he must tell Michael Schiller, although he could not say precisely why.

"Fortunately for you, they didn't leave any of it behind. Eva Graf naturally saw the plans and that sealed Herb's fate. Fanny, working in the house, found them in Herb's desk. They were useful to her, working for the Communists, but she respected Herb, although they were running in different directions. Then Franz Stahl arrived and that forced Eva's hand. Those papers couldn't just disappear. Too many people had seen them, so the people had to go. You have to believe me. This particular nasty business was orchestrated on the orders of Eva Graf and her lover, a well connected Major. The war between the Communists and our movement will go on, but the killing of people like Herb is not necessary."

"What happened to Franz and Ibbi?" Michael asked.

Jan was silent for a moment, then sighed deeply. "They're dead. They were down below, signed a statement under duress and a very convenient escape was arranged. They shot them. I can't prove anything, nor do I wish to. In this case I just file their memo's. It's safer that way."

"What will happen to the bodies? And Mrs Neuhaus?" Michael asked.

"They'll come up with something. Maybe find two bodies so badly mutilated that no-one recognises them and pin the label of Franz Stahl and Ibbi Neuhaus on them. She'll be alright financially. I'll make sure of that. It's all I can do," Jan said, with a trace of regret.

"Oh, God. Is that what it's going to be like, Janus?" asked Michael, visibly shocked at what he had heard and glad Freddy was not with him in this office. He had liked Franz and felt the loss of a friend.

Jan contemplated the man he thought he hated and found he couldn't, not at this moment. Perhaps it would return later.

"This is only the beginning, Schiller. We're on a roller coaster, going up. It'll be slow, but it'll get there, make no mistake about that," he said quietly. "Anything that's in the way gets pushed over the side. What happens when we hit the down slope is anybody's guess."

Michael watched the other man with a curious sense of detachment. The image he tried to project did not sit well on his shoulders. Why was Janus here? Doing something which was not in tune with his nature. He should be working on some large estate, tending fields and livestock, as he had when he lived with Laura. Laura... Somewhere deep in his conscience a small voice told him not to ask, to let it be, but he knew he couldn't.

"Janus, why are you doing this? Why don't you come back? Maybe I could help?" and immediately wished he hadn't said that.

Jan threw him a glance so full of venom it shocked him. And the answer became crystal clear. He had guessed, but never asked Laura what had happened before Janus left and why he had gone so suddenly. His suspicion of some confrontation between them was growing stronger. He stared at the seated figure, so dignified and searched the face, but no trace remained of what he had just seen in his eyes, the quiet voice betrayed nothing of what he nursed inside his soul.

"I made my choice. There's no going back. Go home, Schiller and take the baron with you. Get out of this town. My advice to you is to stay clear of newspapers and politics. I can't keep your names off the list forever. That office out there is overflowing already."

Michael frowned, as if something was jogging his memory. "You said earlier that you've been doing this since 1922. How? Where? You must've joined them from the beginning."

"I can tell you how, but not where. I have friends to protect," Jan replied calmly. "You and I fought a bloody war that left brave soldiers in the gutter, mutilated inside and out and nobody cared. Somebody promised them a future. Not today, not tomorrow, but soon. Think about it! You came out in one piece, went back to your cosy world, fed and clothed, with rich friends. From that elevated position you and the baron could preach democracy and liberty. A noble sentiment, except it didn't do anything for the poor bastards in the missions and the soup kitchens. They gave me a reason to hope for something better than a life at the mission. I didn't understand then why the names I so carefully recorded were important, but it helped to get my brain together again. Then I met my own Samaritan..."

"I see," Michael said slowly, thoughtfully. "I didn't know."

Jan glanced at him, wondering if he had guessed, but found no indication in the blue eyes to give him an answer. "Peter became my friend and talked a lot about the people in Dettingen, about you and the baron. By then, I knew who was writing the anti-socialist articles in the paper, but couldn't betray Peter's friends. I also knew that Hubert would deal with his brother eventually, when you, Erika Behrens and anyone else involved would be without a mouthpiece. In any case, I began to think about other things."

Jan paused and filled the bowl of his pipe, seemingly reluctant to pursue the conversation further, but Michael did not intend to leave it there.

"You fell in love. With Laura," he stated calmly.

It was as if he had dealt the man sitting opposite him a physical blow. The match he held to the bowl of the pipe wavered and went out as he stared at Michael. Jan's face became still. Her image had stood between them from the moment Michael had entered the office. Silently, but at the sound of her name Michael saw the pain in the soft brown eyes and remembered his own. The months of suffering, wanting, of indecision. At last, Jan removed a match with shaking hands and put a light to the tobacco.

"Yes," was all he said. "After we moved to Dettingen I planned a different future, away from politics and the Party, to make things grow and prosper, for her. It had become less important to know what was happening on the political front."

"But it didn't work out that way, did it, Janus?" Michael asked softly. "What happened to warrant your sudden, unexplained departure? I was at the Retreat at the time and would like to know."

Jan shrugged his shoulder, evading the other man's eyes. "I just felt like moving on," came the too casual reply.

Michael had found love and gloried in its discovery. Now, another force swept through every sinew, through bones into every nerve cell in his body. Something evil and deadly. He knew Jan was lying and discovered jealousy raging inside of him, unable to banish the images that entered his mind. He leapt up. Jan was almost as tall as Michael, but felt dwarfed by the figure leaning menacingly on the desk, looming over him like the Avenging Angel. The body was shaking with rage and the blue of his eyes had assumed the colour of the night sky. Michael's voice was precise, dangerous. "What happened between you and Laura before you left?"

It gave Jan a strange, perverse pleasure to see the serenity stripped from the face and body. It was exquisite revenge and he wanted to prolong the thief's agony, because that was what he thought of him. A thief, stealing a woman's heart, the heart that should have belonged to him alone. Why should he not suffer as he did?...The face was a mere six inches away from his own. Jan's mouth fashioned itself into a lopsided smile. So, even priests had demons lurking inside them.

"She hasn't told you then?" he countered carelessly. "Why don't you ask her? She would've done anything to save your scrawny neck. Anything! For you and her friends. It wouldn't be gentlemanly of me to talk about a lady, would it?" and he did not flinch as Michael's hands came up to fasten themselves about his throat. "Some other place, some other time, priest," Jan gasped. "You wouldn't last five minutes here and this is hardly a contest."

Michael Schiller let go and straightened himself. With a superhuman effort, he subdued the rage within him, calmed the hammering of his heart. When he spoke, Jan could hear the steel of sabre blades and saw eyes that glittered like ice and in spite of himself could only admire the supreme self-control of this man. He had witnessed it once before. Last year in the summerhouse, at Peter's party. "I will ask my wife," the cold voice told Jan. "If you've used her, I'll be back to kill you. Depend on it," and they both knew he would.

"Will you have the stomach for it, though? It would make her a widow all over again," Jan taunted him. "It's a strange way of showing gratitude for your life."

"It depends on who I owe it to," Michael snarled. "Have you finished with us?"

Jan rose from the seat and walked to the window, staring down into the courtyard, not seeing the uniformed men entering or leaving the building. He felt his hate evaporating. His love for Laura would remain with him always, but once again it would recede into the deepest recesses of his mind, come alive sometimes in his dreams, or in the arms of Lotti, who never questioned him when he called out someone else's name. He felt weary and for one moment wished himself back on the embankment by the river, on that bench he had occupied for what seemed an eternity before she rescued him. How long would it go on for? But he knew the answer to that already.

Michael watched the broad back in the tailored dark suit and his own feelings transformed themselves from fury to compassion. Whatever happened last year did not matter anymore. Nothing would change what he felt for Laura. She had done whatever she needed to do to save him and now it was of no consequence. Janus had the pain of his loss to bear, while he had it all.

"Can we go, Janus?" he asked the still figure by the window.

Jan turned and became aware of the man he had hated so ferociously still standing in front of his desk, waiting to hear his fate. The voice held a note of sadness, inevitability, as he told Michael. "Yes. You can go. Leave this town today and don't come back. Remember what I said. Stay out of politics; I can't save you again. Go home, Schiller. I'll tell Ulrich to take you down."

He left the window and paused in front of the silent man, now utterly calm again. Jan stared into cool blue eyes and felt remorse. It was nobody's fault. No-one was to blame. A quirk of fate had brought them together and he had drawn the short straw.

"Michael?" he said softly. "Don't insult Laura by asking what happened between us. She obviously hasn't told you. I suggested a trade to her, because the future I dreamt of had fallen apart. I wanted her in exchange for your safety." Jan smiled, a sad smile and Michael knew the man he had met last year had not changed, only circumstance had made both of them let out the demons harboured in the darkest corner of their souls. He did not feel anger as he listened to Jan.

"Laura had the courage because she loves you, but I remembered that I owed her my life and couldn't go through with it. That's why I left in a hurry. I'm glad now. Stay out of trouble, for her sake and for Daniel's. I know he's with you and is happy there," and seeing the questioning look in Michael's eyes, he laughed softly, "I told you I still have my sources up there. You'd better watch yourself. Tell the baron to be careful of his brother. He's dangerous and he'll stop at nothing to get his hands on the Paper."

He stretched out his hand. Michael only hesitated a moment before he clasped it in his own.

"Thank you, Janus. For everything. I'll bear in mind what you've said. Goodbye."

Jan Konrad led him towards the door, paused and turned to Michael. "One favour. Make my garden grow, Michael. Give Daniel his place in the world. He needs it and will repay you with love."

"What about your place, Janus?" Michael asked quietly.

"I lost one and found another. I'm on that roller coaster going up. Slow, but sure," Jan replied philosophically.

Michael looked into the brown eyes and found them untroubled.

"What happens when it derails on the way down?"

"Ah..." Jan said, "Then I'll come knocking on your door and you can save my neck."

And at last, a warm smile spread over his face. Michael, on impulse, grasped Jan's hand again and shook it. "That's a fair bargain. I'll hold you to that. I promise to look after them both. Any message?" he asked.

Jan hesitated, then shook his head. "No, no message. Goodbye, Michael."

He opened the door to the outer office and addressed the young soldier in a firm and officious voice.

"Take Mr Schiller downstairs. He and Mr. Dettingen are free to go. They are to leave this city by seven o'clock this evening. Make a memo out to that effect. Good day, Mr Schiller."

Jan gently closed the door to his office and then he stood by the open window and waited. It did not take long. He watched the two men walk away from the building and felt the last link with the past go out of his life. Only Michael Schiller turned, scanned the windows on the first floor, and raised his hand in farewell.

Chapter 23

JUNE 1928

The kitchen table was laid for breakfast. At Daniel's place were several packages wrapped in brightly coloured paper. Today was his nineteenth birthday.

Laura, in a sleeveless shift dress, her skin golden from hours working in the garden, looked at the clock. Seven forty-five! The men had been out there for two hours already, picking strawberries before the sun got too hot. The crop was good again this year. Daniel was going to have his favourite flan today. She put the freshly gathered eggs into the pan and turned the timer upside down. Her hens were repaying handsomely for their comfortable quarters and Walter took all she cared to take to the shop. She hoped Daniel was going to like his present. He had wanted a larger telescope for some time and the stories he told about the stars were fascinating.

During the last four years he had grown in body and mind, was eloquent in what he had to say, but always it was carefully thought out. The scrawny orphan they had taken into their home was a man already and yet in some ways still a boy who could get excited over new-born chicks, tenderly restore an injured bird to health and whooped with joy when it took off. At the same time, he had cured her and Michael of their squeamishness when hens, past their best, had to be killed for food. To Daniel, everything had its place and purpose. Livestock was not there to eat food, grow fat and be petted, he told her once. It had been purchased to earn its keep, and provide food for the larder. And that meant it had to be killed. Michael could not argue with that and became as proficient as Daniel at weeding out the weaklings, killing the rabbits and chickens as quickly as the boy.

Laura took the eggs out of the pan and placed them under the knitted egg cosies to keep warm. She crossed the paved yard, leant over the gate and called, "Michael! Daniel! Breakfast!"

Her husband waved and both of them started walking towards the house. Laura felt her heart swell with pride as she waited for them. Michael, slim, brown and fit, laughing at something Daniel had said. And he too looked healthy. The sturdy body, not quite as tall as Michael, had strength and stamina. He was kind and considerate, his face neither plain nor handsome, it was nevertheless a pleasant countenance, with an assurance well beyond his years, the brown eyes looking with a calm serenity at the world. He was as much a part of their lives as Freddy, Erika and Chrissy. Somehow they had all meshed together. Daniel had taken the place of Peter, who had not been home for three years.

"Happy birthday, Daniel," Laura said, hugging him affectionately and placing a loving kiss on his cheek.

"I wish it was my birthday," Michael joked and his wife laughed.

"You get enough kissing and cuddling, darling. Today, it's Daniel's turn," and vanished into the kitchen. "Wash up, you two. The eggs are getting cold," Laura ordered.

Daniel hurried through his breakfast, eager to open his presents. Laura's shirt and tie were admired, but the book on 'The Universe and The Stars' Michael had given to him needed an immediate perusal, as did the telescope. Daniel's face glowed with happiness.

"Thanks, Laura. Thank you, Michael," hugging both of them ferociously. "They're wonderful presents."

On his sixteenth birthday they had given him permission to call them by their Christian names. It had become strange to be addressed as Mr and Mr. Schiller by someone they had grown to love and who loved them. Mum and Dad seemed inappropriate, somehow, as did the titles of Aunt and Uncle. Laura and Michael felt comfortable with the arrangement and Daniel found it quite natural.

"There is another parcel for you on the bench, Daniel. It's from Peter. Came yesterday. I kept it in case it was a birthday present. He's never forgotten, bless him," and a shadow crossed over her face. Her son had another life, away from them, marriage and a child they had not yet seen.

"No, he hasn't. Wonder what he's sent me this time?" Daniel said and started to undo the wrapping.

Michael had observed the sadness in his wife's eyes and pressed her hand. "He'll be home one of these days, my Love. You'll see," he said kindly, feeling her loss.

"There's a letter for you, Laura. From Peter," handing her a bulky envelope across the table. She looked at the familiar handwriting and wondered what was inside, a strange foreboding gripped her mind as she gazed at it.

"Aren't you going to open it?" Michael asked, watching her indecision.

Laura glanced at her husband and knew that whatever news the letter contained he would be there. "Later," she said.

Daniel held up his present, an elaborately ornate Persian dagger. "Peter says it's not for killing chickens, and that the stones are real, in case I want to buy a piece of land," balancing the sharp blade in his hand. "It's a beauty."

"Yes, it is, Daniel," Michael remarked. "Mr. Rosenstein should give you a good price for the gems. He'll replace them with fake ones and you won't know the difference."

Daniel looked at Michael as if he had suggested he should sell his very soul. "No." He sounded shocked. "I'll never sell them. I don't ever want to move away from here. Unless... unless you want me to?"

Laura left her chair and folded her arms about his shoulder. "Oh, Daniel. How can you even think about that?" she admonished him, the letter from Peter forgotten. "You belong here, with us. For as long as you want to stay. If you want to move on one day, we'll understand. Won't we, Michael?" her eyes imploring him for support.

Michael wholeheartedly agreed. "This is your home for as long as you need it. Some day you'll want to get married, have your own family. When that time comes, we'll talk about building you a house in the meadow. Right now, you belong here, son."

Daniel's face had regained its usual cheerful composure, happy in the knowledge that this was his allotted place in the great scheme of things, in which he believed implicitly.

"It'll be a long time until Chrissy grows up. Then I'm going to marry her. And a house in the meadow will suit us just fine," he said with the uttermost conviction.

Laura and Michael looked at each other, surprised.

"Chrissy?" Laura asked. "She's only nine years old."

"Well," Michael remarked, unconcerned. "If it has to be Chrissy, we'll have you for a few years yet. What about your letter, my love? I'd like to know whether that ungrateful son of yours has finally remembered he has a mother that loves him?"

Laura looked at him, a little disapproval in his eyes.

"Peter hasn't stopped loving us, Michael," she said gently. "He and Natasha have so many things to do when he gets home and the time goes very quickly. He does write sometimes. It's not like you to be uncharitable. You used to like him."

Michael concentrated on pouring more coffee for himself and Daniel before he answered. "Yes, I did. I still do, in spite of everything. It's just...I don't like the way he abandoned you."

Laura made no reply, opened Peter's letter and quickly scanned the pages. Her face was still as she stared at a page. Daniel looked up from the book as Michael asked, "What is it, Laura?"

She raised her eyes from the page and met his. "He's coming home. With the child and wants us to raise her. He says she's not safe with her own mother. That damned trollop isn't looking after our grandchild at all. She's forever going off filming or performing. God alone knows what or where..." she said, furious and very loud.

The men, speechless for a moment, looked at each other. Laura had never lost her temper before. Michael recovered and held out his hand for the letter. "May I?" and read. "Oh, God. He sounds at his wit's end." He handed it back. "Tell him it'll be alright, Laura. We'll just have a bigger family."

Daniel had not spoken and there was concern in his eyes. Laura noticed.

"Daniel? You won't mind having a little girl about the place, will you? I'll not have quite so much time to help with the work. Maybe we could get someone in for the busiest times?"

At that, Daniel seemed to brighten up again. "Are you sure you'll still want me here? I'll work twice as hard, I promise."

It was Laura and Michael's turn to look shocked.

Michael said firmly, "This is your home, Daniel. There's room for everybody. Peter won't be here any more than he was before he married that witch. We'll sort out the work. I'm sure it'll please Laura to show off the baby to all her friends and raise a pretty girl."

"Thanks, Michael. We'll manage," Daniel beamed at him.

The big coffee pot was not quite empty and still hot to the touch. Laura poured herself the third cup of the morning. The chickens and rabbits had been fed and everything else could wait. She settled down on the bench seat under the window and re-read Peter's letter, wondering what had gone so disastrously wrong as to prompt her amiable son to take such a drastic step. He must love the child as much as his father had loved him when he came home. How could a baby not be safe with its own mother? What kind of woman was Natasha to go off and leave a helpless infant?...

They would meet their granddaughter at last. Images of an angelic face, pretty, doll-like, floated in and out of her mind. A sweet little girl in frilly dresses and ribbons in her hair, just like Chrissy. It was going to be fun to show her off to the people of Dettingen, buy dolls and prams and little coffee cups and plates. Teach her how to be a lady. It would be wonderful. They must get a cot and put it in the spare bedroom. She must air Peter's bed and wash the curtains. He hadn't been home for so long that it'd be strange to have him and the child. Only two more weeks and they would be here. And she didn't want to hear the name of that terrible town ever again...

A shiver ran through her body as she remembered the four days back in March in 1925, when she had died a thousand deaths waiting for Michael and Freddy to return from Munich. After they got home that Saturday evening Freddy had told them all that had happened, while Michael just filled in about his time with Mr. Konrad. Only the barest details, telling no-one who he really was, but she and Daniel knew.

When they had been alone at last, he still did not mention Janus. She had been curious, unable to resist telling him. "I knew he'd send you home to me. How is Janus?"

Michael looked at her so strangely that she knew he must've guessed she had been to the tavern, but he didn't ask, just said that Janus had a difficult job to do.

"He is still the same man we knew, Laura," he had told her.

She had felt glad about that, remembering the night he had left her, wondering if the two men had talked about that. Maybe if she asked Michael, he would tell her.

"Did he... did he talk about anything else?"

"No," he said softly, and again he looked at her and they both knew that neither one of them could tell the truth. And kept silent.

They found a new respect for each other and said a silent prayer for the kind, gentle man that had assured their happiness. Janus was never mentioned again and if Daniel still received and sent letters from the tavern, he never said so. He was pleased when Michael had given up working for Freddy and they had started to accomplish what had been Janus's dream. It had taken two years of hard work and this year they had arrived. The Market Garden was flourishing and they had established themselves as a profitable business. If Daniel was in touch with Janus, he should be proud of him. He had given them a precise plan and they had followed it faithfully...

In between all that they still found time to be active in the church committee, had a reasonable social life and nursed Katrin through a difficult pregnancy she had not anticipated. Little Victor, a year old, was everybody's delight and did not mind being mothered by all the neighbours.

Now she herself would have her granddaughter to take care of. Michelle and Victor would play and grow up together, and there was Susanna's pretty Kirsten, also a year old. Everybody wondered what had happened in that fortnight when Luther had taken his sister and the boys to the Black Forest to heal the bruises red-haired Frank constantly inflicted on his frail wife and their two red-haired boy's when he was drunk. Little Kirsten was black-haired and had the most wonderful dark brown eyes laughing at everyone, but did not look like either parent. There would be no shortage of children for Michelle to play with...

Lost in this happy anticipation Laura had not noticed Michael passing by the kitchen window, and was startled when he placed the large flat basket she used for collecting eggs on the table.

"Maybe this'll cheer you up, my love," picking one of the luscious strawberries and popping it into her mouth. "Have you got over the shock yet?" he asked.

"A few more of these should help, darling," she remarked and selected another berry. "How will you manage out there without me when the baby arrives?"

"We have help already. The pay is fruit and vegetables for her and the boy. Guess who?" he asked, pleased with himself, blue eyes twinkling.

Laura's face was a study of surprise and astonishment.

"It's a 'she?' And works for nothing? Has she taken a fancy to you, I wonder? I'll scratch her eyes out, darling," she joked, and Michael nodded his head.

"I believe you would too, but she might turn you into a frog," he replied dryly. "The tantalizing gipsy, who parks her caravan in our meadow, wants to stay for the rest of the Summer. She came across to buy strawberries and asked how much rent we wanted for three months. She likes it by the stream. I said she could stay for nothing as long as she didn't set the grass on fire.

207

That meadow gets very dry around August. Is that alright with you? I couldn't very well say 'no', because..." he paused and leant closer to Laura. "Margharita is a very beautiful woman," he said, grinning at his wife.

"Michael, don't you dare..." she laughed, threatening him with the long bread knife. "It'll be nice to see more of our gipsy Queen and her little boy. He was so adorable last year with his lovely brown skin. He'll be handsome one day. I wonder what my granddaughter looks like?" she asked him.

"I expect she'll be dark-eyed and black-haired like her mother and will drive everybody wild when she grows up," Michael commented. "But I hope she looks like you. Then I'll have two women to adore." He kissed her tenderly. "I love you, Mrs Schiller. You'll make a wonderful grandmama," and walked gracefully out of the kitchen.

She watched him go past the window, waved as he waved to her and still wondered why this beautiful man she had married almost four years ago could still tie her inside into knots, who made love and sex into the most memorable experience of her life.

"I love you too, Mr Schiller," she whispered.

* * *

Everything was ready for them. The cot Erika brought down from her attic was as good as new after a clean-up. Laura had found a loveable teddy bear and placed it on the pretty pillow. Erika had supplied most of the bedding and the paraphernalia a one year old might need. Well, Michelle Sogar was almost one year old. In two months time they would have a birthday party for the newest member of the family. Her father would not be there, of course. Daniel and Michael were getting quite excited at the prospect of teaching the child things she ought to know, much to the disgust of Laura, who said girls did not need to play football or climb trees to be happy, dolls were more suited to fit them for the life of a lady. Michael and Daniel had looked at each other and graciously conceded that that was perfectly correct and promised to be good and leave the teaching to Laura. Michael had remarked to Daniel, with a definite cheeky glint in his eyes, that Laura was after all the best example a girl could have, at which she promptly smacked him with her serviette, still in its heavy silver ring.

The train was due in at midday. Peter had written he would travel overnight, had reserved a sleeping compartment and would only bring his personal possessions, which Laura presumed were not more than two suitcases full. Everything belonging to his childhood was still in his room here.

They waited at the station. Laura, apprehensive and nervous, Michael and Daniel as calm as always, as if this was an everyday occurrence. And promptly at 11:58 the long express drew in at the platform. Michael saw Peter before she did and steered her towards the man holding his daughter in his arms. Daniel followed to collect the suitcases. Looking at her son, Laura was shocked at his appearance. He was only twenty-six, but in almost three short years he had aged ten. A terrible hatred consumed her for a moment, hatred of the daughter-in-law she had only met once during one long weekend in 1925, when the wanton actress had alienated the women of Dettingen by flirting outrageously with their men. She had tried it on Michael and was not too pleased when he did not respond and Peter had been so besotted, that he did not notice. Nor had he contradicted her when she flaunted her political affiliations to the new Party, her admiration for the leader of that Party and the people, her friends, that surrounded him. It had been almost as much of a nightmare as Freddy and Michael's trip to that hated city a few months before. They had parted, politely, courteously and secretly hoped they would not see her again, ever...

The train drew out of the station and the platform gradually emptied of people. Daniel and Michael stayed discreetly with the three suitcases and Peter's familiar travel bag so as to give mother and son a few moments to themselves.

"Hello, Peter," Laura said gently and his free arm pressed her to him.

"I'm sorry, mum... I..." and tears welled up into his eyes.

"Not now, son. I'm glad to have you home. We all are," she said, comforted by his love. The child, its head buried into Peter's neck, two arms firmly entwined around it, had not moved and Laura assumed her granddaughter must be asleep.

"How was the journey? Did you have any trouble with the little one?" Laura asked.

"No. She's no trouble as long as I'm around," Peter replied and Laura thought she detected an infinite sadness in her son's voice.

"She'll settle down soon," she told him. "I'll take care of her, I promise. Is she asleep?"

"No, she hasn't slept for hours. She knows something's going on. I'm glad you're going to look after her, mum," Peter said, kissing her forehead, then let her go to prise away the child's arms from his neck. "Say 'hello' to your grandmother, Michelle. Be a good girl, Daddy's arms are tired."

It was as if the baby had understood all he said. The small body, clad in dungaree trousers, sandals on bare feet and a little yellow shirt, sat up in her father's arms and stared at the pretty woman smiling at her. Laura saw a heart shaped face, lips tightly pressed together, a button nose and all of it topped by a mop of short fair curly hair. The eyes seemed to change from a steely grey to the green of a raging sea, and jet black eyebrows knitted together foretold of a storm breaking. Laura stretched out her arms to take the child but it simply nestled back to bury its face in Peter's neck, arms encircling him like a clamp.

Peter looked at his mother's disappointed face and felt pity for her.

"You'll have to be patient with her. It's not you. She is terrified of all women. It'll take a little time, mum," and Laura felt her own eyes grow moist.

"Whatever happened to her, son? Did Natasha do this?" she asked, as he led her towards Michael and Daniel.

"Yes," he said quietly, and then made a brave effort to greet the two men. "Hello, Dad. It's good to see you. And you, Daniel," shaking their hands like crazy. "As you can see, I've got my hands full," he said. "This child won't let go of me."

"We'll soon fix that," Michael said. "As her honorary grandfather I'm entitled to carry my granddaughter. Come-on, Michelle Sogar, give your father a rest," stretching out his arms to the child.

Laura watched in amazement as the baby lifted its head and scrutinized Michael, who in turn stared into eyes so familiar and yet alien in their intensity. It was as if she was searching the very depth of his soul and he watched, fascinated, as the angry green receded from the irises and they became like Laura's when they made love, soft, and of the smokiest grey. They saw the mouth un-pucker itself and flicker, attempting a smile.

"Come to your grandfather, Michelle," he coaxed and was rewarded with a strange sound.

"Mch... Mich... Mitch.."

Michael studied her for a moment, puzzled. "Did they call her Mitch, Peter?" he asked.

"I don't know, dad. She's never said anything before."

"Come, Miss Mitch," and the child let go of her father's neck and let Michael lift her into his arms.

"Well, at least she's taken to somebody in the family," Laura remarked and her son placed an arm around her shoulder, knowing that his mother must feel the rejection from his daughter and was upset.

They followed the porter to the exit and in spite of herself Laura could not help laughing at the sight of Michael, the child's arms tight around his neck and Daniel making funny faces, hoping to induce a smile on the solemn face.

"I can see myself doing the work in the garden while these two bring up the baby, Peter," Laura said, a little wistfully, never realising how true that prediction proved to be and two years would pass before the child would show any kind of affection towards her.

It was Michael who became attuned to the baby's moods and wishes. Peter was exhausted from the long journey and slept for most of that weekend. Not once had the child cried or screamed and they watched, stunned, when they found her rocking furiously back and forth to relieve something inside her, some demon that held her in his grip. She struggled violently when Laura or Erika picked her up, but sat quietly in the pram watching Michael and Daniel in the garden. If they moved out of sight she would start rocking until they came and moved the pram nearer to them.

At night Mitch would rock in the cot and Laura felt helpless. Only Michael was able to send her off to sleep, murmuring softly into the tiny pink ear as he gently walked the floor with Mitch in his arms. Laura felt a twinge of jealousy creep into her soul watching them. She should be doing this, she thought, and then remembered that it was a woman that had done some unspeakable evil to this child. She was torn between hate for Natasha and gratitude that her granddaughter had found a rock to cling to. Michael would heal the wounds and then it would be her turn...

Monday was hot. Peter needed to spend time with the solicitor in town. Laura had taken the baby's lunch into the summerhouse and collected the pram from under the tree.

"Time for your food, my darling," she cooed, but already the eyes that stared at her had turned green with anger. She lifted Mitch out of the pram and was surprised by the strength as the child squirmed and pushed to get away from her. Defeated, Laura placed her granddaughter on the blanket on the floor and watched her rocking.. back and forth.. back and forth.. and could not help crying the tears the child was unable to shed.

The gipsy stood quietly in the doorway. Tall and slender, she did not need her colourful clothes to enhance her beauty. Like Michael, she had a presence that could not be ignored. The full calico skirt of a faded brown and a plain red bodice showed off her bare arms and legs, the slim feet encased in leather sandals. A red scarf was tied loosely around her jet black hair. Dark eyes watched with compassion the woman kneeling in front of the rocking child.

"I'll feed her, Mrs Laura," the melodious voice of Margharita ordered, the German attractively accented by her natural Romany language. "You sit and rest."

The gipsy knelt on the blanket, silent, waiting, and the child, sensing something strange grew quiet, staring at the woman in front of her. Laura watched, her own distress subsiding. Mitch did not object when Margharita picked her up and began to feed her, sitting contentedly on her lap.

"How did you do that? You're the only woman she's let near her," Laura posed question and statement in amazement.

"I speak the language of animals and children, Mrs Laura," the gipsy said gently. "Your granddaughter has suffered much cruelty."

Dark eyes gazed searchingly into grey ones and Laura felt a deep calm seeping into her soul.

"My son won't tell us what happened to her. He probably thinks it's for the best. It's very trying to love a child and be rejected. I don't know what to do with her, Margharita. Only Michael can soothe her. Why does she not cry like other babies?" Laura asked.

"Perhaps her mother treated her like an animal when she cried for her needs. The child associated pain with the sound and stopped crying."

"But how would she know? She's just a baby," Laura asked, mystified.

The gipsy smiled gently. "A child in her mother's womb absorbs love and hate as well as nourishment. When it leaves that place it cannot speak, but it hears, sees and feels. And never forgets."

Margharita placed a hand on the baby's head, nestling contentedly against her breast, sleepy now. "She'll be a Lion girl, with the nature of a warrior, and like the lioness, have grace, courage and a spirit that needs to be free. You won't tame her, Mrs Laura. Or make her into your pretty little doll," she said gently. "Mr Michael and Daniel will understand. One day, when she trusts you, she'll give you the love you want so much. Be patient."

"How do you know all this?" asked Laura, a deep frown between the finely drawn eyebrows.

The gipsy's handsome features were those of a young woman, her brown skin so smooth, un-lined and yet as old as Mother Earth herself. Laura looked into dark eyes, full of knowledge that spanned the past, present and future. Margharita, wife of the chief of her tribe, undisputed queen of all the fortune tellers, spoke softly. "I am a Romany, Mrs Laura. This Lion girl..." and she was silent for a moment, gazing intently at the baby's face, "..has cried too many tears already. It will be many years before someone finds the key to open the door and heal the wounds. Ramon will."

Laura stared at the beautiful gipsy. "Ramon? Your little boy?" she queried.

"Yes. It is written," Margharita said calmly.

Chapter 24

Michael was reading the newspaper after lunch. In the morning there was only time to scan the headlines. Laura had insisted he take at least an hour off to let his food settle, threatening him with dire consequences if he did not. The small girl sat next to her grandfather, drinking the last of her milk. She had grown sturdy and at first glance could be mistaken for a boy in her brief shorts and vest. Her skin was honey coloured from spending her days outdoors. Laura had fought many a battle with Mitch, trying to put pretty dresses onto a squirming body. The child would either tuck them into her knickers and when she was old enough, simply take them off. Michael had suggested, gently, to give it up.

"Mitch doesn't like the constraint of sleeves and seams, Laura. Get her something that stretches," he had said, realising that something had happened to her to react so violently to being encased by unyielding cotton fabrics.

His wife had shaken her head, abandoning the struggle and always marvelled at how he knew precisely what their granddaughter wanted. The long hair Laura had looked forward to brushing with loving care did not materialise either. The toddler would not tolerate hairbrush or comb and the growing hair looked unkempt.

Michael took the short road to end the misery. He had placed her into the chair at Hermann's and told him to cut it off. Propped up on several cushions his granddaughter sat and watched in fascination as the scissors did their work, looked at herself in the large mirror and with an expression of pure joy had ran her stubby fingers through the short curls.

"That one should've been a boy," Hermann told Michael, tickling the pink ear with the soft brush.

Michael agreed. "Laura just can't get used to it, but I think she's finally given in. The only ones that are having fun with this little monster are Daniel and me," and a small voice mimicked 'little monster' while giving her grandfather a dazzling smile. As always, his heart gave a strange lurch as they looked at each other in the mirror. Until she was eighteen months old, she would only say 'Mitch,' but had soaked up sounds like a thirsty sponge. Suddenly words tumbled out of her mouth, they became sentences in time, unstoppable, as if her mind was manufacturing them on a conveyor belt. At three years old her vocabulary was extensive and expanding rapidly.

"It's my birthday today, granpa. I'm three. Victor, Chrissy and Kirsten are coming to my party. Will you and Daniel come?" the clear voice next to him asked.

Michael took his eyes off the gloomy news of four million unemployed in Germany, the virtual collapse of a fragile economy after the Wall Street crash last year and the more oppressing prospect of the National Socialists winning the next election in September. He smiled at his granddaughter, blue eyes full of mischief. "Only if we're invited, little monster. "What about granma?"

Mitch considered this at length, cradling the doll Laura had given her this morning. She had never touched any of the others in her bedroom, but pulled the teddy bear behind her in the small cart Daniel had made for her to ferry bricks, stones and dirt about. The doll's soft, plump body was covered in pink leather. The porcelain head, its scalp crowned with long flaxen hair, possessed the sweetest face, and large sapphire blue eyes looked at Mitch with an expression of helpless vulnerability.

"The princess invites granma to the party. And you and Daniel."

Mitch looked at Laura, who sat, holding the last of her roll suspended between plate and mouth, then gazed at the child, her face solemn and still.

"We thank the princess very much and will be delighted to come to your party," he said gallantly. "Do we have to dress up?" he asked.

"Yes. I'm going to wear the dress granma gave to me as a present," Mitch said, quite unconcerned at the astonished expression on her grandparents face. No-one spoke as husband and wife looked at each other in amazement. It would be the first time Mitch was to be seen in a dress. Annie had made it and had the smart idea to remove the satin and lace dress from the doll and make a replica of Mitch's dress. Laura said a silent prayer of thanks to Annie for her innovative ruse.

"Darling, you'll look as pretty as the princess," she said carefully, hoping her granddaughter wasn't going to change her mind. Mitch slid off the seat and stood in front of her grandmother. The steady gaze of grey eyes assessed the woman seated at the table and Michael knew the child was making a decision.

The voice was soft and loving. "I love you, granma," and without touching Laura she skipped out of the kitchen. Laura felt the warm tears running down her cheeks, let them come as she felt Michael's arms about her, his voice soothing her.

"It'll be alright now, my love. You'll see. You've been so patient with her. Maybe you'll have your little lady after all."

At that, his wife started to laugh. "No, darling, she'll never be that," Laura said happily, kissing him. "Mitch will always belong to you first. If she loves me half as much as she loves you, it'll be enough."

* * *

The committee met in the Church Hall. While the Nazi Party had only just gained a firm footing in the Rhineland, as opposed to everywhere else in Germany, the neutral state of the Region under French occupation kept reasonable order on the streets. In Dettingen there were more pressing matters to discuss.

The Reverend Mother Agnes, at fifty six still as formidable as ever, tapped the table.

"So, what are we going to do?" she asked, directing her gaze at the people sitting at the table, their faces solemn and worried.

Cornelius spoke. "The only option we have is to form a Co-operative and pool our resources. Or at least as much as we can spare. The situation will not get better for some time. I propose to make your kitchen and store houses the point of delivery. Your sisters will have an intimate knowledge of what is required by our people here and should distribute where it is needed." Freddy nodded in agreement.

Walter Behrens too was in favour. "It's a good idea in principle. How do we put it into practice?"

"The mission and other charity organisations rely largely on money to feed the homeless. We don't have that particular problem here," Father Dominic said.

"What we have is men that are unemployed and can't feed their families properly."

Michael had been listening and making notes. "Can the Estate provide potatoes in quantity, Cornelius?" he asked.

"Yes, and some other root vegetables. I'll contribute a certain amount of cash," Cornelius answered.

Freddy was making notes. "I can't help with the provisions, but will make funds available," he stated.

"What about you, Walter?" Mother Agnes wanted to know.

"Like Michael's and everybody else's, business is not what it was. I'll deliver whatever is needed, though. And twist the arms of the more affluent members of our community. Most of them shop with me anyway. It's a good place to collect contributions," Walter said amiably.

"I have to fulfil my obligation to the stallholders in town and to Walter," Michael said. "Anything, apart from what we need to feed ourselves and our immediate neighbours can go towards the Co-operative. It provided the cream on top of the cake, but we'll make do with bread. What do you say, Laura?"

"That's fine by me. We're getting too fat, anyway," she remarked, smiling. "What about using the hall for a clothing centre? I don't mean jumble. Decent clothes, clean and mended, people can buy for a few pence or exchange. My granddaughter's dresses and coats and bonnets should make a sizable start. Erika will help, won't you?"

"Good idea, sweetie," Erika laughed. "Just don't give away Mitch's vest and shorts. She'll run over you with that cart Daniel so thoughtfully provided for her. Come to think of it, she'll probably bring them in herself and pick out a pair of trousers in exchange."

Mother Agnes couldn't help laughing at the thought of it. "One day, Laura, your little monster will grow up into a lovely young woman and you'll be proud of her. In the meantime, let Michael and Daniel have their fun. They seem to enjoy it."

"We do," Michael said. "She's happy and thriving. It's like having a son of my own." His comment was made without the slightest trace of regret.

"You've certainly acquired a sizable family since your marriage, Michael," Cornelius remarked, with gleeful irony. "The one that's thriving is you, my friend."

Laura glanced at Cornelius. "If Michael and my family are happy, then so am I, Cornelius. Between us we're managing beautifully," dispelling any doubts on his part that she was left out in the cold. "As Mother Agnes said, Mitch will grow up one day. In the meantime, I pretend I've got a grandson. I'm beginning to have fun too."

Freddy had been busy writing. Mother Agnes too was making more notes. She tapped her pencil on the table. "I'll ask Freddy to outline our proposal and when everybody has formulated sensible ideas, we'll meet and Freddy can give it some thought. I'd like it in print and perhaps other communities will follow our lead. Rally everybody you can, Erika, Laura. I must confer with my sisters and will let you know how best we can serve our parish. Will you talk with Father Johann, Dominik? Try and persuade him to let his rich farmers participate." She rose. "Now I must leave. Can we organise this in the next few days?" she asked, adding, "did you know the bishop is ailing?"

"What is the matter with him?" Cornelius wanted to know.

"My cousin is not well and is resting in his residence in Koblenz. He wishes to see me, but first I have another journey to make on a private matter. I'll see Bertie on my return."

In a week it had been organised and Father Dominik was going to inform his parishioners at the Sunday Service. Doctor Emil Hoffmann had offered his services to care for the old and the children of the poor free of charge, so had Paul Zweig, the dentist. At all costs, they were determined to help the Community to survive the catastrophic depression with as much dignity as they could muster. Sister Emmanuel and Sister Dominic, both capable and very forceful, had taken charge of the project they simply named 'CCA,' Community Care in Action, christened so by Sister Dominic. The Reverend Mother would be away for a week and wanted a peaceful convent in her absence. Dainty Sister Anna was delegated on all matters in her place and had strict instructions to fetch in Father Dominik to sort out any trouble she couldn't handle herself. Sister Anna always reminded Mother Agnes of Laura Schiller. Soft and sweet on the outside, but the core was rock hard. Loyal, courageous and full of hidden fire. The Sister would do well...

On Monday morning, Sister Gertrud accompanied The Reverend Mother to the station, carrying a travelling valise and a small square cardboard box, lined with a snowy white damask serviette and filled with provisions for the long journey. The train to Munich arrived and Sister Gertrud found a window seat in one of the first class carriages.

"You won't forget to change trains at Mannheim, Reverend Mother, will you? And eat your food? Ask the conductor to fetch you a drink when you need one," the sister pleaded with her Superior.

"Yes, yes, Sister Gertrud. I will. You had better leave the train. Assist Sister Anna as best as you can and don't be afraid to ask Father Dominik for help should you need it," Mother Agnes said, a little irritated by the fussing of Sister Gertrud.

"Good-bye, Reverend Mother. Have a pleasant journey."

The sister hurriedly left the compartment and waited on the platform, waving demurely as the train drew out of the station. She was quite looking forward to fetching Father Dominik on the slightest pretext. He was almost as enjoyable to be with as Father Michael had been.

The train entered and left the station at Koblenz and Mother Agnes had still not solved her personal dilemma. Was she doing the right thing?.. She had told no-one that her cousin was dying. The cancer had spread so rapidly that Bertie had little time left. Should she break the vow she had made to herself when Ira took the baby to raise as her own? Bertie wanted to see his son, be absolved from his guilt. Would Felix want to see his real father? No-one could blame him if he refused.

For thirty-seven years he had been content to be the adopted son of Count Alexander and doted on Ira as his mother, had accepted that he was a foundling, never once curious as to his parentage. Beloved by Alexander and Ira, adored by his brothers and sister, Felix had repaid them handsomely with love and loyalty. He had graduated from the Agricultural College with honours and taken the burden of managing the vast Estate off his father's shoulder. Felix knew he could not inherit the title, but was assured of his equal share of Alexander's wealth.

He had married for love and of all her grandchildren Ira had a special place in her heart for Siegfried, Felix's firstborn, affectionately known as Friedl, who, with his flaxen hair and violet eyes was the image of his father and kept the memory of his grandmother Felicia alive for Ira and the Reverend Mother Agnes.

The solemn expression on Mother Agnes's face reflected her troubled thoughts. Did she have the right to change the serenity of their lives? Impart a knowledge which had no relevance to the present just to full fill the last wish of a dying man? He had abandoned Felicia and his child without mercy. The Reverend Mother crossed herself and prayed for guidance, then settled herself comfortably to enjoy the familiar landmarks of the journey she had made so many times, looking forward with pleasure to seeing Alexander and Ira again. It had been two years since they last met.

Babette's brood were growing fast, and Ira's two youngest boy's, born during the war, had replaced Oliver and Jurgen, but Ira still placed flowers on the tomb she knew contained another mother's son. To spent some time with Felix and his family would be joy indeed.

The conductor opened the door to the compartment. "Would you like me to fetch you some refreshment, sister?" he asked politely, disturbing her memories.

The Reverend Mother would have enjoyed lunch with greater relish if her conscience had not troubled her so much. She ought to be grateful that her sisters cared for her welfare and Sister Gertrud was the epitome of what a nun should be.. kind, loving, devout and obedient, setting a shining example to the rest of her sisters.

Mother Agnes was, however, thankful that the convent did not have too many 'Gertrud's.' The thought of forty-seven Angels administering to her every need filled her with dread, as did the prospect of the future. The Church's power would be drastically curtailed. From the pamphlets that came hot from the presses of the National Socialists she knew their teaching days were numbered. They must divert their energies and resources into new channels. The small Cottage Hospital that served Dettingen and Annsberg should be expanded. Would they have time to train more nurses and doctors? Mother Agnes hoped Bertie was going to live long enough to sanction what she proposed.

The conductor returned and solicitously poured coffee and cream from silver pots.
Mother Agnes smiled graciously. "Thank you," she said sweetly. "Will you be so kind as to make sure that I am awakened before we get to Mannheim? I must not miss my connection to Riesenheim."

She offered him a shiny coin, but he held up his hands in horror "No, sister. It has been a pleasure. Say a prayer for me instead," he protested, mildly embarrassed. "You have a nap. I'll make sure you get off at Mannheim," pulling down the blinds to the corridor and closing the door behind him.

The motion of the train, food and drink all combined to induce a feeling of drowsiness in the Reverend Mother and she gave herself over to it.

Refreshed from her dreamless escape, she woke some time before the train entered the station. The long platform seemed to be filled with brown shirted men, in their black breeches, knee high polished boots and peaked black caps, heavily braided with silver. A group of them stood near the door, waiting to board the first class carriage. The steps were high. The conductor preceded her with the valise and a voice, strangely familiar, asked. "May I help you, Sister?"

It was a cultured voice, soft and kind. Mother Agnes gathered her habit and clasped the outstretched hand, negotiating the steps.

"Thank you," she said gratefully, and looked up into a face she knew so well. It had been seven years and he had grown leaner in that time. Images of the chubby baby, the lanky schoolboy and the tall, handsome student raced through her mind. He had grown into a man, and yet, he was still the same boy she had watched grow up and leave home. "Jurgen," she whispered, surprise and agony reflected in her face.

A loud voice shouted from the carriage door. "Come-on, Seb. You want to be left behind?"

She noted that he was wearing the same cap and uniform as the others and the hated armband. She put her hand on his sleeve. "Jurgen. I'm going to Riesenheim. Come with me, please. For your mother's sake," she begged.

The tall young man someone had called Seb removed his cap and she saw the familiar blond wavy hair. The blue eyes she had always told Ira looked like aquamarine and could glitter like ice on the mountains when he was angry, gave no indication of recognition, but she knew he had. Even as a boy Jurgen had been afflicted with a peculiar twitch at the corner of his right eye whenever he was apprehensive about something. She watched it now and knew for certain.

He bowed to her. "You are mistaking me for someone else, Reverend Mother. Goodbye," the familiar voice said gently and he hurriedly mounted the steps of the carriage, closing the door, cutting off the sound of her calling his name again. He did not join his comrades, but stayed by the window as the train slowly left the station.

He would never forget the look of anguish on the face of the woman they had all loved so much. Sister Agnes, who had never let her black habit stand in the way of playing rough and tumble games when they had been children, nor shirked the awkward questions they had asked as they got older. He remembered the mother he would never cease to love, the father who bore his grief with dignity and Babette, who was as pretty as his mother with children of her own, his younger brothers, Christian, at the Academy, and

Walmar not far behind. Then there was Felix, as true and loyal a son to his mother and father as if he had been their own. Seb Inkmeyer kept himself well informed and wished...

The voice of twenty two year old Scholl broke into his thoughts. "I thought your taste was more for the long-legged, racy type of blonde, sir. Nuns fascinate me, too. One never knows what delights they're hiding under that hideous black habit," he sneered, pale blue eyes cold and calculating.

First Lieutenant Seb Inkmeyer controlled his fury, well aware of Scholl's ability to ingratiate himself with high ranking SS Officers. The eyes that met the younger man had taken on a glacier-like quality, the voice was calm, hiding the contempt he felt.

"You have a mind full of sewage, Scholl. You'll go far," which seemed to please Scholl.

The Reverend Mother made her way to the rest room for ladies. Her mind was in a whirl. Had she been mistaken? No, she knew he had recognised her too. Whenever she travelled, her splendid cross of office was hidden beneath her cloak. Everyone addressed her as 'sister' but the young man had called her Reverend Mother. Only Jurgen von Riesenheim would know that. What could she tell Alexander and Ira? That she had met their son and lost him again on a train to Munich? No, that would not do. Jurgen did not want to be found or he would have acknowledged her. For his own reasons he could not go home. The hated uniform would bring as much grief to Alexander as Hubert von Dettingen's did to Cornelius. Someone had called him Seb and she wondered what his last name was...

The enormity of the consequences of what she should tell Ira and Alexander almost overwhelmed her. The Lord had not seen fit to show her the way and she made her decision.

The past must remain buried. There would be no mention of Bertie's wish to see his son or of her encounter with Jurgen. She must add the burden of her silence to all the others she carried already.

The Reverend Mother Agnes crossed herself and this time prayed for forgiveness...

Chapter 25

There had been three generations of policemen in Luther Goremann's family and sometimes he wondered if he was going to be the last. Still single, in his early thirties, he fended off the pursuing spinsters of Dettingen and Annsberg with determined charm. Luther enforced the law with a mixture of tolerance and a firm hand when necessary. He was eminently suited to the people and they to him. Socially, he was amiable and a good companion.

Luther was a big man, burly, but not fat and stood well over six feet and went nowhere without his two Alsatian bitches, Floss and Rula. They quietly kept a watchful eye on the giddy females making a play for their master. It had been said many times that there was no place for a woman in Luther's life, except for Susanna, his sister. His Chief Constable in town had no complaints and for the most part left him alone, but times were changing...

The very big kitchen at the back of the house was tidy and clean. He and the dogs had finished their supper, the table was cleared and the bowls filled with fresh water. As was his habit when at home, Luther kept up a constant flow of conversation with Floss and Rula. He did not look less of a policeman washing the dishes at the sink, dressed in a vest, his uniform trousers held up with braces, and slippers on his feet.

The dogs followed him through the middle room, large and comfortably furnished, if a little shabby. Like the rest of the house, it needed a woman's touch. The parlour at the front had long been used as an office. Two windows let in the last of the evening sun. His desk was under one, the other served for any passer by to have a congenial conversation with Luther leaning on the window sill, almost filling the space with his bulk.

It was a warm evening and not the faintest breeze stirred the pile of papers on his desk. Luther sank into the big leather chair that had been his father's and his grandfather's before him, contemplating the latest pamphlets. They were coming in by every post. His chief, already defected to the new Nazi Party, wanted to be in the frontline when they finally took power and was energetically gathering converts. Luther knew he would not be able to stand on the side lines much longer. Soon, there would be no civil police force. Central Government would rule and strangle any opposition. It had already begun. How could he serve the people here as a Nazi when the majority opposed the new Party? Who would replace him if he didn't join them? He had lived here all his life, knew everybody. Could he be of more use to them if he pinned the hated swastika pin on his uniform? Luther was still wrestling with his personal dilemma when a sweet voice intruded into the stillness of the room.

"Hello, Luther. Care for a walk? It's a lovely evening."

He saw Else, from three doors down the road and heaved himself out of the chair and leant out of the window. "Sorry, Else," he said gently to the woman gazing at him. He did not wish to offend her and felt a little guilty when her face registered disappointment. "I can't. There's a pile of paperwork waiting. Maybe some other time."

Else stoically forced herself to be cheerful. She was thirty-something. Not unattractive except for the severity of the tight curls she so carefully nurtured through the night with pins and little bits of paper. "Maybe some other time is what you always say, Luther. One of these days I'll get my revenge for all the times you've turned me down," she said, too sweetly.

"What're you going to do, Else? Drag me out by my braces? Floss and Rula wouldn't let you," he said, laughing good-naturedly.

"I know that," Else parried in return and he thought he saw a hint of malice in her eyes, but dismissed it as fancy. "I'm going to join the Nazi Party, Luther," and tripped off towards the entrance of the path to the right.

Luther stood, somewhat perturbed by her remark, wondering if Else's strange sense of humour had gone adrift or if she was serious. She was fully aware of his political convictions. She and most of his friends owed allegiance to the Conservatives. Would she defect just to spite him? A spy three doors away could be very uncomfortable indeed...

He settled himself back into the chair and scrutinized the latest demand from the chief. It was the official order attached to it that worried Luther. Stamped twice with the swastika and eagle, the directive was signed by Major J. Konrad. It was politely worded, but an order nevertheless. A dossier on every citizen was required, with his personal comments on life-style, religion, political persuasion and activity, habits, criminal records and misdemeanours by school children. He had three months to prepare the detailed files and lodge them at the new headquarters in Cologne, care of the Intelligence Department.

Luther wondered what kind of man Major Konrad was and what they wanted all this information for. On the whole his people conducted themselves respectably. Well, most of the time, anyway. Politics were an open book around here, except for the few rowdies who changed their allegiance as fast as they did their underwear. The religion was Catholic, with a few Jewish families. Luther suddenly felt hot. Moishe, the tailor, Ari from the bookshop, Simon who made and sold jewellery. All had wives and kids. There was the couple who owned the flower shop. He wasn't sure about them, but they did go with Ari to the synagogue in town. Did they want information on the convent and the sisters? How many people knew that the Reverend Mother Agnes was half-Jewish? Cornelius?... Certainly. Freddy?... Probably... Who else?.... Michael?... Most likely, but that was alright... Hubert?... If that bastard knew, it would be a disaster...

Luther decided that the convent, Father Dominik and his new chaplain were church business. They had no right to make him do this in the first place, but somewhere, deep down in his gut he knew he had no choice...

The two dogs lay sprawled on the carpet square behind him. Rula stretched herself languorously and her paw came to rest on his slippered foot. Like a child, she needed to reassure herself constantly of his affection. Luther took his other foot out of his slipper and gently rubbed her paw with it. He was never quite sure who had greater priority. The two beasts or Susanna. He loved them with a fierceness bordering on obsession, as he had loved his mother.

One day he would deal with the only thorn in his flesh. Frank, the Smithy, his brother-in-law. Drunk mostly, the red-haired sadist took great pleasure in giving hell to his sister and their two carrot-topped boys. Why she had married him he never understood. But she had guts and wouldn't make a formal complaint because of their sons. Frank was getting worse now Susanna had Kirsten, with the blackest hair and laughing dark eyes. Luther sometimes wondered if Frank suspected anything. One day soon, Frank... Luther swore to himself, as he had so many times before, I'll get you and put you away for good. They did things like that in the SS every day. He cleared his mind and dealt with the mountain of paperwork...

Luther had fed Rula and Floss, had breakfasted and was scanning the headlines of the morning papers, frowning at the accounts of more riots in the South, Berlin and some other major cities. It was spreading like the plague. He was startled by the shrill ring of the telephone bell.

"Goremann," he said absent-mindedly into the receiver, but was immediately alert as he heard the agitated voice of Cornelius's imperturbable butler.

"It's Fritz, Luther. You'd better get yourself up here fast. There's trouble. Young Rudi's belted Hubert and he's as mad as hell."

"Why did he hit him, Fritz?"

"Hubert's the only one in residence right now. He sneaked up to Delia's last night and well.. you know? She wouldn't come out of her room. Rudi went up and got the whole story. Get up here as quick as you can."

"I'm on my way," Luther said and hung up. "Come-on, girls. We've got work to do."

Luther wheeled the bike into the road, turned into the path, crossed the centre point to Quirinus Road, pedalled past the presbytery and followed the gravel lane beyond the convent leading up to the Estate, Rula and Floss bouncing ahead. Luther was very fit, in spite of his bulk, but he had to dismount half way up the hill and walk. As the lane levelled out at the top, he pedalled like fury to the mansion. Fritz was waiting for him.

"Thank God you're here. Hubert's ready to shoot Rudi," he whispered into Luther's ear.

"Where are they?" he asked, walking into the hall, the dogs at his heel.

"In there," Fritz said, pointing to the drawing room.

Baron Hubert, eldest son and heir to Cornelius' title and the estate of Dettingen and Annsberg, sat sprawled on a sofa, a bandage round his head. He was pressing a cold compress alternately to his eye and mouth while at the same time holding a hunting rifle pointed at the occupants of the sofa opposite. Luther controlled his urge to laugh as he took in the situation.

He loved the old Baron, respected Freddy, but try as he might he couldn't find an ounce of sympathy for the bloated, pitifully inadequate figure of Hubert and wasn't at all surprised his wife took herself off at the slightest opportunity. Probably in the South with some fancy man who would be younger and more attractive than her husband. With his wife and Cornelius away, it would explain Hubert's visit to Delia's room.

226

"What took you so long?" the Baron snarled at Luther. "I want him arrested," waving his hand at Rudi Waldorf, who was sitting quietly holding Delia in his arms. By the look of her swollen eyes she had cried a great deal.

"It has taken me less than thirty minutes to get here, baron. I don't have a car and it's a steep hill. Not made for bicycles," Luther said calmly. "Now, why do you want me to arrest Rudi?"

"Because I'm telling you to, Luther. He beat me up for no good reason. He's mad!" Hubert shouted, then winced. He had forgotten his split lip and hurriedly pressed the wet cloth to it.

Luther kept his face straight, trying to subdue the contempt he felt for the pathetic apology of a baron. Even the old man was in better shape. He fished out his notebook, glancing at Delia and Rudi. She looked scared to death and the young pup wouldn't mind having another go at Hubert, of that he was sure. "I'll have the details from you, baron," his pencil poised over a page.

Hubert looked sullen and hissed, remembering his painful mouth. "I had breakfast. Then got up to dress for an important meeting in town when this lunatic came storming in here and attacked me."

Luther wrote, noting the well-tailored uniform of the SS Brigade, heavily decorated with emblems of silver and felt a deep satisfaction at the blood stains down the front.

"Sir. Why should your stable lad come in here and attack you? It was in here, you said?" having observed a red stain on the corner of the marble hearth.

"It was. I came in here to read the paper. He charged in and accused me of raping her. She let me into her bed and enjoyed it," Hubert said, malice in his face and voice. "I'll see he gets put away for a very long time."

"Where's the baroness, by the way?" Luther asked.

Hubert stared at the solid figure of the village policeman and realised that Luther Goremann was not placated by his glib explanation. "She and the kids are away. What's that got to do with this?" the baron shouted, dabbing hurriedly at his lip again. "If you're insinuating what I think you are, I don't need to rape anybody. They're only too willing."

Delia burst into a fresh flood of tears and Rudi looked as if he wanted to kill the Baron.

"Delia?" Luther said quietly, soothingly. "I know it's hard, but do stop crying and tell me what happened last night."

The girl looked up at the reassuring bulky form of their friend and made a strenuous effort to calm herself, blowing noisily into her handkerchief.

Rudi let go of her. "Tell him, Dilly."

"Hanna and me did a lot of work yesterday, what with everybody away 'cept him. It was late when I got to bed as I'd wanted to finish the room we'd left. Hanna and Fritz had gone up. They sleep at the other end of the attics. I had a wash and it was so hot I laid on top of my bed in my nightdress and fell asleep. I don't lock the door and never heard him come in. I woke up and he was on top of me, with his hand over my mouth. He started kissing me and... and I couldn't get away." The look she gave the baron was full of loathing. "He raped me, Luther."

"I did nothing of the sort, you slut. You invited me in," he snarled at her.

The girl sat up, proud and straight and gathering her courage, said clearly, "I've got Rudi and he's the only one I've ever been with. I wouldn't invite you to my bed if you paid me, Baron."

"Alright, Delia, that'll do for now," Luther said kindly. "Rudi, I want to hear what you've got to say."

"Hanna didn't worry too much when Dilly didn't come down early. She knew that she'd worked late and let her sleep in. She sent Fritz up just before breakfast. He heard her crying, but couldn't get in. That's when he fetched me. She wouldn't let me in either. Fritz said to break the door down. That's what we did. Dilly was huddled in the corner of her room, scared out of her wits. Hysterical, she was. It took Hanna an hour to get her dressed and tell us what happened. It was just as she said, Luther. I swear it. Fritz stopped me from looking for him," pointing at the baron, "but I was worried about Dilly. I saw him in here after breakfast and belted him. He's a pig," Rudi said in disgust.

The baron rose from the sofa, baleful eyes directed towards Rudi. "You'll regret this. I'm making formal charges against you for assaulting an Officer of the SS Army. That'll probably cost you your head," Hubert said, menace dripping from every word. "As for you, you lying slut, I want you out of this house tonight."

Fritz had entered the room, quietly, unobtrusively. "With respect, Baron Hubert. It is your father's house and Delia works for him. I cannot allow her to leave without informing him first," the butler said firmly.

Hubert turned his anger on Fritz. "You impudent dog! I'll see you get your marching orders, too," he hissed, but found only a servile smile on Fritz's face.

"It will be most unlikely, Baron. I would suggest you call the doctor to have a look at that wound. Hanna's done her best, but one can never tell what after-effects a knock on the head might have."

Hubert was seething with rage. "Pack some clothes and get the car ready. I'm driving down to my family. As for you, Luther, I want him in jail. Just make sure he stays there until you hear from me. My lawyer will inform you of the charges. If he's let loose, I'll have your head too. Count on it." He stormed out, slamming the door.

Luther knew only too well the implications of the Baron's threat. He stuffed the notebook back into his pocket and informed Delia. "I want you to come down and see the Doc. I'll explain what happened here. Don't worry, Delia, I believe you. Were you and Rudi.. you know..?"

Delia nodded. "Yes, he's the only one, Luther. What'll happen to him?"

"I don't know. It depends whether Hubert presses charges through the civil court, which is highly unlikely because the papers will get hold of it. Maybe the baroness will persuade the bastard to drop it all. Let's hope so. A Military Court is different. Hubert's gang deal out some rough justice. When's the old man coming back, Rudi?"

The unhappy but unrepentant stable boy lifted his head, knowing full well that Hubert would have his revenge. He wished Cornelius was here.

"Not for another two weeks at least. He's in France at some Chateau or other. You know he goes off whenever he gets itchy feet. Why?"

"If Hubert goes on with this, he'll work fast, before his father gets back. You'd better get some things together and stay with me until I hear from the lawyer. I'll have to lock you up, unless you give me your word that you'll not run. Which is it to be?"

Rudi Waldorf sat up straight, his face set defiantly. "I'm not sorry for what I did to him. He deserved it. Nobody's going to mess about with Dilly and get away with it. Baron or not. And I'm not going to run, either, Luther. I promise."

"Good lad," Luther said. "You wouldn't get far anyway. Floss'll keep an eye on you. She's better than a locked cell door. I'll enjoy your company for a day or so before the storm breaks. Come on."

"I want to say goodbye to Dilly, Luther. Give us a minute," Rudi pleaded.

"Alright, I'll have a word with Hanna and wait for you outside. Get your things. FLOSS!" he spoke commandingly to the dog. "Go with him," and she followed Rudi and Delia.

Luther did not wait and made his way to the kitchen. Rudi didn't need the dog. He was too proud to slink off like a coward. Unlike that bastard Hubert.

* * *

The church clock struck seven times. Luther stretched his body in the big bed his parents had occupied and heard the plop of the newspapers in the hall. The Bonner Independent, toned down since Michael and Freddy had come back from Munich in 1925, and the Volkischer Beobachter, the mouthpiece of the Nazi Party. Luther knew how to sift out the propaganda from the real news. Everybody in the force had to take the stupid paper on the orders of the chief.

He heard the baker's boy whistling and thinking of the still warm crusty bread rolls on his doorstep, got up, crossed the landing and knocked on the door of the other bedroom. Rudi's muffled voice answered.

"Get yourself downstairs for breakfast, boy," Luther called.

Rudi grunted. "Alright... Alright."

The bread rolls made Luther feel hungry. He raked the embers in the large cooking stove and placed sweet smelling pieces of birch through the opening on the shiny metal surface. Two copper kettles full of water had stood atop all night. One he placed over the opening, which would be boiling to fill the huge enamel coffee pot, the other he took to the sink, emptied the water into the bowl to wash and shave.

Floss and Rula waited for their morning greeting.

"Morning, girls. It's going to be a busy day. Go and fetch the jail-bird," he commanded.

He smiled as both of them bounded up the stairs. Floss pulled down the handle and Rudi let out a yell. Two very heavy Alsatian bitches jumped onto him, telling him in no uncertain terms it was time to get up.

Luther had enjoyed his breakfast and was on his third cup of coffee, scanning the headlines of the Fascist paper. Rudi tucked into boiled eggs, cheese, sliced meat and crusty rolls. For a prison he reckoned Luther's would beat any other jail.

"Why do you read that bloody shit, Luther?" he asked between chewing. "You're thinking of defecting to that scum? Like that bastard up the hill?"

The paper lowered and green eyes contemplated the young man. Rudi wasn't sure if he had upset his jailer, but Luther's voice was quiet.

"I'm a policeman, boy, not the village idiot. The paper is delivered to every station on the orders of the chief. I have to read it. Between the Bonner and this one I get all the information I need."

"Freddy's paper isn't as committed as it used to be," Rudi said, a little contemptuously. "Is he getting old or scared?"

The penetrating gaze of green eyes made Rudi feel uncomfortable, but the voice of the man opposite him was devastatingly calm. "That business in Munich a few years back taught both of them not to be reckless. And you'd better take a lesson from that too if you get into the hands of Hubert's mob, Boy. Freddy isn't scared, just prudent. He's still doing his bit."

"Sorry, Luther. What'll happen to me?"

"We've got to wait. I've some errands this morning. You stay put. Floss'll keep an eye on you. Don't get silly ideas, Rudi. She'll have you," Luther remarked.

He drank the last of his coffee and rose from the table. The heavy boots stood, highly polished, on the shoe bank at the other side of the kitchen door. Luther tied them and snapped the knee high leather gaiters around his leg. He collected his tunic from the hall and fastened the row of buttons to his neck. After he had combed the luxurious mass of auburn hair, he decided not to wear the heavy police helmet. Strapping the wide leather belt around his middle, he flicked some dog hairs off his trousers, patting Rula's head.

"Alright, Girl, you're coming with me. Floss!" His voice changed to a command. "You keep him here," pointing to Rudi, engrossed in the Bonner Independent. "Don't let him out and don't let anybody in. Good Girl," and Floss immediately laid down between table and door. "I'm going to see the Doc and call on the Schillers, Rudi. Make yourself useful and tidy the place. We'll sort out your statement when I get back. I want Michael here as a witness."

Rula followed Luther Goremann to where the bicycle stood in the open shed. She watched him fasten the stiff helmet to the carrier at the back. It was the middle of July and already the sun was beating down. The dew on the long grass in his garden had long ago evaporated. Sometime he'd get around to cutting it. Right now, there were more important things to take care of. He felt hot already and wished they gave the Force a thinner uniform for the summer months. The short sleeved vest would soak up most of the sweat he could feel gathering already around the neck band.

"Come-on, Girl. Let's go visiting," wheeling the bike into the road.

Chapter 26

Laura was packing the last of the crop of cherries into flat open boxes, ready to go to market. The huge trees had yielded a bumper crop again this year. A large wicker basket stood next to her feet to take the flawed fruit. She would have at least five kilos to send to the Sisters to make jam and pies, and there was plenty left over for themselves and their neighbours. Walter had had his quota this morning and was well satisfied with the quality of his delivery. She saw one of Luther's dogs trotting elegantly towards her and knew the policeman wasn't far behind. Wiping her hands on a damp cloth, she met Rula.

"Hello, girl," and patted the blond fur, feeling foolish because she could never remember which dog was which.

"That's Rula, Laura," Luther laughed. "I'll put a label on them one day, just for you. Morning."

"Morning, Luther. What brings you here so early?"

"Trouble. I've got to see Michael."

Laura's face took on a troubled look. "Not with us, I hope. We haven't done anything wrong, have we?"

Luther never ceased to wonder at the beauty of Michael's wife. He knew she must be nearly fifty and still looked thirty. So did Michael. After eight years of marriage, they unashamedly adored each other and seemed to get disgracefully younger with each passing year. He smiled, shaking his head.

"No, Laura. It's nothing to do with you. I need Michael as a witness. Had to arrest young Rudi from up the hill. Floss is guarding him. I didn't have the heart to lock him up below."

"Good God. What did he do?" Laura asked.

"It's a long story. He beat up Baron Hubert."

"Rudi did? You're having me on, Luther. He wouldn't hurt anybody," astonishment written all over her face.

"I can't go into the details, Laura. No time. Michael can fill you in when he gets back. Where is he?"

"Up the tree. Where else? Daniel is out delivering. We're coming to the end of these. They'll have a little rest from climbing ladders until the plums, apples and pears. Shall I get him?"

233

"No, you carry on. I'll find him. Where's the monster, by the way?"

"When Ramon gets here during the school holidays, she spends most of her time with them. Whatever Michael and Daniel haven't taught her, Ramon does. I've never met a child with such an appetite for learning," Laura remarked.

"But all the wrong things, eh?" Luther said, grinning at Mitch's grandmother.

"Go on with you, you're as bad as Michael and Daniel. Ramon takes good care of her," Laura said happily. "I'm outnumbered, anyway. Two men, the boy and Margharita are just too many. They just let her do whatever she wants and Mitch is very happy."

"I must say, you're looking well on it, Laura," Luther told her and walked off towards the orchard at the far end of the garden.

The path skirted the meadow. Margharita's caravan was parked at the far end, the red and blue paint as glossy as ever. He wondered how many of the women from the villages came to have their fortunes told. Margharita had no need to walk the streets, selling pegs, or to attend fairs in the surrounding villages. From what he'd heard, she had some well-to-do clients calling on her. Must be making a tidy sum. But she was no trouble and the caravan stood on Laura's land. Rula cocked her ears as the voices of children came to her notice.

"Go, Girl. Find Mitch," he said softly, and the dog streaked off towards the clear, shallow stream. He waited for the greeting.

"Rula," a childish voice shouted with joy. "You're smothering me. Say hello to Ramon. He's on holiday."

Rula did as she was told and bounced up to Ramon, brown-skinned, black-eyed and standing precariously at the edge of the stream. Luther saw the boy and dog disappear into the water and heard five year old Mitch laughing with glee. He knew the gipsy had said something to Mitch to inflame her temper.

"It's not my fault," the girl screamed at the boy. "Rula's all wet now."

"What about me, you stupid gorgio," the angry voice of seven year old Ramon sounded across the meadow.

"You're a heathen. Mrs Henckler says so. So there," the girl shouted back and took off her vest to dry the dog.

Luther shook his head and made his way to the huge cherry trees, each with a long ladder leaning against it.

"Michael!" he called.

"Up here," came the voice from within the dense canopy of leaves. "Luther?"

"I want to talk to you, Michael," and already a pair of boots showed on the top rung of the ladder. Michael Schiller adroitly descended and stood on firm ground. "Did you hear that rumpus just now? The monster's giving young Ramon a run for his money," Luther said, and Michael grinned.

"I heard," he said, looking proud. "She's a tough little monkey and won't let anybody get the better of her. I'm ready for a drink. Will you join us?"

"Sorry, Michael. This isn't a social visit. I need you to come over to the house and witness a statement. Now, if you can spare the time."

"Alright, I'll clean up and get the bike. Who's in custody?"

"Rudi Waldorf. He assaulted Hubert yesterday evening."

Michael Schiller's face, still lean, but not as thin as it used to be, registered as much surprise as Laura's had a few minutes ago. Then surprise turned to laughter, and the blue eyes danced with merriment. "You're joking, Luther. Rudi wouldn't attack a fly and you know it."

"He made quite a mess of Hubert's face and I don't blame him. Delia says the lecherous bastard raped her. It's a mess, Michael. I'm waiting to hear from Hubert's lawyer."

The laughter had left Michael's face as he listened. "God Almighty. How can a man do that? But then, Hubert isn't a man, he's rotten to the core. How's Delia?"

"She's alright. Hoffmann had a look at her. We'd better get going."

Michael nodded. "I'll just tell Laura," and hurried to the summerhouse.

Luther whistled once and saw Rula disengage herself from Mitch Sogar's attention and streak like a flash of lightning towards him.

"Good girl," he said.

The two men wheeled their bikes out of the drive. Mrs Henckler was busy sweeping the pavement. Her lively bird-like eyes had not missed Luther going into No. 10. There was not one speck of dust in front of her house, having swept it for the ninth time.

"Morning, Mrs. Henckler. It'll be hot again today," Luther called out.

"Morning, Mrs. Henckler. You're doing a good job on that pavement," Michael said pleasantly, mounting the bike.

"Morning to you both. How's Rudi, Luther? I hope you're treating him well."

Luther was about to push off and stopped in his tracks, looking sharply at Mrs Henckler, who gazed at him over her spectacles as if to say, 'young man, you can't fool anybody...' The policeman had already guessed she had met Delia's mum at church for early morning Mass.

"He's fine, Martha. Slept like a baby and ate like a horse at breakfast," and pedalled off, Michael following hurriedly, both of them aware that by now the whole village knew that Rudi was in custody and why.

Luther and Michael wheeled the bikes up the path at the side of the police house. Floss was waiting at the gate to the garden and somewhere at the far end they could hear the swish of the sickle.

"I wish I had more prisoners like him. Maybe they'll let me keep him until he's finished the job?" Luther remarked, watching Rudi cutting a neat swathe into the knee-high grass "Let's go in and brew some coffee while I fill you in."

The kitchen had been tidied and the kettle on the stove filled and gently steaming. "Have a look at the 'Voelkischer,' Michael. Hermann Goering in Prussia and Heinrich Himmler in Bavaria sent out the blackshirts again yesterday to fight their brothers. The brownshirt lost, like last time. Between fat Hermann and sadist Heini, Ernie Roehm doesn't stand a chance. They'll annihilate him and his SA thugs. That'll leave us with the military and Hitler's private army, in their spanking new black uniforms. Did you know they've got new headquarters in Cologne?"

"I read about it in the 'Bonner," Michael answered. "What I can't understand is how the French let them get away with it."

"Simple. They're not interested, nor do they have the manpower to stop it. Don't forget, we're still a piece of Germany. This region is supposed to be neutral, but is still administered by German civil servants. Half of them have already joined the Fascists. The French are just waiting for our fragile Weimar Republic to disintegrate completely and they'll get out. It's rumoured Hitler is calling for another election in November. He doesn't want to share power with the Conservatives at any price. Goering and Himmler are stirring the pot. A few more bloodbaths like yesterday and our feeble President won't have any choice but to give power to the SS or declare martial law. I think he'll make Hitler Chancellor," Luther sounded gloomy.

Michael looked and felt gloomy at the prospect. "Then what? The end of democracy? The start of a dictatorship? They've put enough of our people away already. God knows how many so-called labour camps we've got and they're overflowing. Who's next on the list? The Gipsies and the Jews? It's going to be hell, Luther."

"I know that. It's here already. Some of our rough necks spent a lot of time in Bern's dive by the tram terminus. I can't stop them as long as they're not getting rowdy. I never did like that big oaf. He thinks he's the cats' whiskers since he took over from his father. Keeps some strange company. Frank's one of them."

"On top of his drinking, your brother-in-law doesn't need to get fired up by politics. How's Susanna bearing up?"

For a moment Luther forgot himself and threw the large spoon he had used for stirring the coffee pot into the sink, where it bounced around and finally came to rest.

"I wish..." he hissed venomously. "I wish I could get something on him, Michael. Anything to put him away. But Susi won't let me. He's killing her."

"I know. But I don't see what you can do. You can't step outside the law," Michael pointed out.

"That's not the worst of it. The chief is pressing everybody on the force to join the Nazis. Sooner or later I'll have to go with them if I want to keep my job. I was born in this house, so was my father, but it'll put me into the enemy camp. I don't know how long I can hold out."

Luther poured and they drank in silence as Michael pondered on the implication of Luther's defection. He didn't want to think about that. They had enough trouble keeping their heads above water and there was no sign that the depression was coming to an end.

"What about Rudi, Luther? What'll happen to him?"

"Depends," Luther said slowly. "In a civil court he'll get six months to a year. If Hubert gets his way, they'll take him to one of those places and throw away the key. I better get him in and take down his statement. They'll not let him stay here for much longer."

Luther sighed deeply and walked to the kitchen door.

Martha Henckler, working in Walter's grocery department five afternoons a week to eke out her meagre war pension, was replacing some of the packages in the window when the black shiny mercedes swished past and stopped outside the police house. She watched two men in the dreaded black uniform of the SS Army get out and march up to Luther's open front door. Before she could scramble back into the shop to go up the road to have a look, the men returned with Rudi, handcuffed, a terrified expression on his face. They bundled him unceremoniously into the back, got in and sped off into the direction of town. A terrible dread twisted her stomach into knots and she wondered if they would ever see him again.

* * *

To Rudi's question of where they were taking him, the sourly looking younger man snapped 'Cologne' and told him to keep quiet, proceeding to relate to his comrade the titillating details of an evening spent at the Club. Rudi felt the same dread as Mrs. Henckler had a few minutes ago, wondering what was going to happen to him.

The car turned into the road leading to the highway near the river, sped across the bridge and within thirty five minutes stopped outside the row of elegant Georgian terraced properties in the tree lined avenue. Instead of the brass plates telling people where to find Solicitors, Professors and eminent Doctors, the prominent flag announced a new era and bold brass shields displayed the names of departments. The two men pushed Rudi towards stout double doors. The sign above read 'Justice Department.' He found himself in a large reception hall.

"Another one for below, Dirk," the surly looking soldier told the clerk at the desk. "Which cell?"

The balding man glanced at the boy, his face expressing neither surprise nor curiosity as he skimmed over the document the soldier handed over. "Waldorf," he mumbled, and again he glanced at Rudi, but this time there seemed a modicum of interest in his eyes. "Take him down to number six. This one's got priority, it seems," he informed the guards.

Rudi was guided to the winding staircase leading to what had once been a dignified wine cellar but was now converted into narrow prison cells. He was pushed into a small space containing an army bed and a bucket. They left him sitting dejectedly on the bed, rubbing his wrists where the handcuffs had chafed and the clanging of the iron door reverberated around the space, invaded his head and he sank down onto the straw mattress, cursing himself for being a fool.

The naked light bulb high on the ceiling flickered now and again as heavy footsteps sounded a continuous faint thump.. thump.. thump.. Rudi could not tell how late it was and missed the cool air and fragrant perfume of the pine forest. The air was stale, humid, the bucket a revolting sight and he resisted nature's urge until he felt his bladder was going to burst. Disgusted with the soggy shirt clinging to his chest, a wave of fear dampened it still further at the sound of a pair of heavy boots on the stone slabs of the cellar. He was not sure whether to welcome the rattle of keys in the iron door. It opened and a man Rudi thought looked like a genial grandfather stood in the doorway.

"Come on, lad. You're wanted upstairs. Don't try anything foolish. You wouldn't last three seconds here. They'll just as easily shoot you as give you a trial. And I doubt whether that's going to be fair," the man in the black uniform said quietly.

"I understand," Rudi said, resignedly.

He was directed from behind to march up to the first floor. The corridor seemed never ending and human traffic was coming and going, somehow out of tune in the gracious surroundings. All of them, even the severely dressed woman carrying folders and stacks of papers had a staccato marching step.

They stopped outside a door. The nameplate read, 'MAJOR J. KONRAD.' Rudi's escort pointed to a wooden bench between Major Konrad's door and the next one. The balustrade opposite allowed an overall view into the hall below and the clerk at the desk could observe the personnel on the corridors above. They sat and waited. The door opened and a tall figure in the SS uniform, decorated with silver braid, stood listening to something another voice inside the room was telling him. Rudi found the sound pleasing, reassuring.

"I've got one more, Seb. Then I'll call it a day. Wait for me downstairs. Lotti's expecting us sometime after seven. It'll give you time to see the boys before they go to bed," the voice said.

And the man in the doorway replied pleasantly. "Will do, Jan. It'll be nice to see my godson. It's been a while."

He stepped into the corridor, closing the door and glancing indifferently at Rudi, who was startled to see a handsome man, wearing the hated uniform with a kind of redeeming grace, with eyes that reminded him of a clear blue summer sky. He watched him walk away with an easy stride. So different from the others. If they had wives and children, godsons and friends, maybe they weren't any different from the people in Dettingen, Rudi thought. Every organisation had rotten apples and they couldn't all be like the baron.

"Who's he?" he asked the guard.

"Major Inkmeyer. Nice bloke. Best policeman in the business," the old man said. "He came down from Berlin when they opened this place last year. Major Konrad arrived about the same time, only he came from Munich. Now remember what I told you. That bully at the door has orders to shoot. Wait here, lad." He rose to knock on the door, entered and returned almost at once. "You're to go in. The Major wants to see you on your own. I'll be here."

Rudi knocked and stepped into the room. The man in the SS uniform did not look up, intent on reading something on the typed pages in front of him. The thick white hair reminded Rudi of someone else. Years ago...How many?...Eight?...In Mrs Schiller's garden...Then it had been loose and floppy...Janus, the quiet man?

He waited in front of the desk and finally the man glanced at him, eyes carefully guarded.

"Your name, please?" the soft voice asked and terror left Rudi.

"Rudi Waldorf."

"Address and occupation?"

Rudi told him, remembering Luther's advice. Be penitent...civil...say as little as possible...you could get away with six months...if they're kind to you, be careful...it may be a trap...

The Major had checked and sat back in his chair, easy, relaxed. Rudi stared into a face he remembered. Still thin, a little older, it had lost the healthy glow of eight years ago. Now it had the pallor of a desk-bound person.

"I have the statement from the Baron. There's a slight variation in your account of what happened. Did you enjoy hitting him?"

Rudi considered the question. Was it a trap?

"No, sir," he answered, looking at his feet, rather than meet the steady gaze of probing brown eyes.

"Count yourself lucky the Baron's careful about his reputation. Anyone less prominent would've had you transported out of here before now. Luther

Goremann did a good job. Probably saved your life keeping you with him instead of putting you into the town jail. Doc Hoffmann's testimony on the girl's character helped. How is Delia, by the way?" Jan asked.

Rudi could not restrain himself any longer.

"It is you, isn't it? You're Janus that used to live with Mrs Schiller?"

The two men looked at each other. One curious, the other guarded, but Rudi had not missed the flicker of pain and desperation in Jan's eyes. Then it was gone. Jan Konrad spoke, his tone sharper than he intended.

"You're mistaken, Waldorf. If you have any sense in that head of yours you'll not ask me that again. I didn't hear you. Do you understand?" Again their eyes met, but now Rudi saw something else. A plea for understanding? A command to keep his secret? In return for what? A lesser sentence?

"Yes, I understand, sir," he said simply.

"Tomorrow, there's a hearing to decide what to do with you. The Baron's in a hurry," the voice of Major Konrad was brisk. "Four officers will preside. I'm one of them. I think I can persuade my friend to give you a fair verdict. The other two are in Hubert's camp and you'll get no mercy. I'll do what I can for you, but don't expect miracles. Stick to the truth and don't call the Baron names. It won't help," the Major said, then his voice took on a gentler tone. "I'll see that you get some clean clothes and have Matthias take you to the washroom and bring you something to eat. I'm afraid you'll have to stay below tonight, but believe me, it's the Ritz compared to where you might finish up. You never answered my question about Delia."

"She's alright. Hanna and Fritz are taking care of her. Thanks for asking, Janus."

"Major Konrad," Jan reminded him. "I'll see you in the morning." He rose from the chair. As he walked to the door, he paused and stood in front of the prisoner. There was an urgency in his voice. "In both our interests, you'd better forget that you think you know me. Your life, and mine, depend on it. Did you enjoy hitting him?"

Rudi threw caution to the wind and said vehemently "I did. The bastard deserved it. Should've killed him," and Jan Konrad smiled a very satisfactory smile.

Chapter 27

The Legions had marched for fourteen years along a slow road, their ranks swelled by the disillusioned, the fanatics, the arrogant and the hungry. They had flexed their muscles on the opposing forces using them as target practice. Eliminating, crucifying, killing in the name of a glorious future, their boots stained red and the corpses tagged with the label of traitors. The Caesar-in-waiting smiled indulgently.

On the thirtieth of January he climbed the pinnacle of success. His Legions, brown and black shirted, marched in triumphant spectacle, bearing the new symbol of the Third Reich. It flew from every public building. The blood-red flag, its centre a white circle with the swastika, ancient symbol of peace and luck, angular, black and menacing. The proud eagle of Imperial Prussia lay dead, mourned only by the minority who remembered the Swastika also depicted the medieval wheel of torture. Caesar had chosen well. His mighty army would crush any resistance.

The Dictator on his podium, clad in the plainest of uniforms adorned only by the Iron Cross, surveyed his generals, splendid in their brown, black and grey uniforms, row upon row of medals and silver braid glittering in the sunlight. His face set into a stern mould he spoke to the people. Of a shiny future, bread and butter for all, of a purified Germany and promised to make the Fatherland great again. The obscure corporal gloried in his dream and raised his arm to salute his people, not in a gracious wave of the hand, but with arm outstretched, stiff, harsh and unyielding.

Democracy died. Slowly. Painfully.

The salutations rose to fever pitch, drowning the screams of the victims and muted the voices of the prudent, helpless against the tide that threatened to drown them into oblivion. A hungry, disillusioned, weary nation, beaten and fragmented by war, party strife and feeble politicians, saw a new dawn and followed, proudly carrying the new flag, believing in the promised land, hoping for another noble Caius Julius Caesar. They followed a Nero, leading his people to annihilation, the long hard road littered with corpses and swimming in blood.

The air waves crackled with frantic relays of the pomp and ceremony in front of the Reichstag in Berlin. Never had the huge space been filled by so many people. The population, listening, was fired by a new hope and lifted their heads a little higher. There were to be two additional public holidays in the future. The twentieth of April, the Fuehrer's birthday and May the first, ironically the Communist Labour Day.

Dettingen, as everywhere else in the country, was glued to the radio. Already there was a noticeable change in the Parish. Over the last few months, as the vigorous campaign by the National Socialists drew to its close, the meek had been further intimidated. The waverers had been persuaded and the firm believers in Democracy hoped against hope that the remnants of the Christian Democrats would regain enough strength to reduce the power of the new Party. They kept silent. The labour camps were already full to overflowing. Their only hope were the French, who so far had prevented the open warfare between the unruly storm troopers of Ernst Roehm and the well disciplined SS troops of Goering and Himmler to fight it out on the streets in the Rhineland. Elsewhere, constant confrontation of the power struggle took place between the two rival groups.

Michael Schiller, Daniel and Laura sat in the kitchen, each picking at the food on the plates in front of them. The radio broadcast did nothing to brighten their spirits except the announcement that the new Chancellor might proclaim an amnesty for certain categories of prisoners.

"Do you think they'll release Rudi?" asked Daniel.

Michael pondered the question. "Maybe. Martha says he's bearing up and doesn't look too bad. They let her see him at Christmas. And again on New Year's Day."

"She's a strange woman. Seems to have taken him under her wing," Laura said. "I wonder if she's told him about Delia? I don't like to ask."

"She did," Daniel remarked. "When Delia stopped going last year Rudi wanted to know why and she told him. He hasn't anywhere to go when he comes out, so she offered to have him stay with her now Rosalie is parlour maid up at the house. He'll have to find work and that's going to be a problem with his record."

"Couldn't Freddy give him a job?" Laura asked Michael.

"He would, as he feels responsible for him. But he can't"

"Why not?"

"Laura," Michael's voice was solemn. "The barbarians have taken over the country. Did you read the manifesto of the Nazi Party? Did you?"

"Yes, I did. It's so full of high flying promises which you don't agree with, so I didn't take it seriously."

"Be fair, Michael," Daniel pleaded. "I don't believe what they're saying, either."

Michael sounded agitated. "Then I suggest you both read it again. Carefully. The old labour unions, mostly Communists, are finished. According to Freddy's sources, it won't be long before they're all in jail, the union halls and their properties confiscated and do you know who's going to head the new Labour Front?" he asked.

"No. Who?" Laura and Daniel asked in unison.

"Our illustrious friend, Robert Ley, Party Chairman of Cologne and personal bosom pal of the new Chancellor."

"That drunken sod! Sorry, Laura," Daniel blurted out. "Half the time he's not coherent and couldn't lead a donkey, never mind the Trade Unions."

"He won't have to. Goering and Himmler will oust him and put in their own men to tighten the screws. Trade Unions and strikes will be a thing of the past. We'll have so many new laws it'll make you dizzy just reading them. But one thing is certain. No-one will work without a Party badge. And that means us, Daniel. You, me, Freddy and Rudi."

"Michael," Laura said, soothingly. "You're exaggerating."

"Am I?" her husband asked. "Freddy can't employ Rudi for what he did to a party member, whatever the reason. Hubert would see to it that his brother's suppliers discontinue their services and the paper will grind to a halt. The same goes for me. We depend on other people for seeds to grow what we sell. Freddy and me are on the black-list already, so is Rudi. We've got no choice but to collect our party badges if we want to survive. They've declared that the streets will be free of beggars and prostitutes, the malingerers will be taught to work in the camps and we all know what that means." Michael looked at his wife and then at Daniel. "If I were single I would fight them from the pulpit, like Dominik. But I'm not. I have a wife and a granddaughter to support. Like thousands of other men I must work and whether I like it or not, I have to join the Party to keep our livelihood."

He pushed his plate to one side and got up to turn the radio off, disgusted with the constant repartee of the commentators reporting from far away Berlin. Laura contemplated the plates, with the remnants of uneaten food and found it a strange sight. Usually they would be empty. But today was a strange day and had had a profound effect on her normally placid husband. Tonight she would cook something they all thoroughly enjoyed. Chicken in wine sauce and pancakes.

"More coffee, anyone?" she asked.

"No thanks, Laura," Daniel said, looking at the clock. "It's nearly one. I've promised to go over to Mrs Henckler and finish painting the back bedroom. I'll be back for dinner."

"She says you're making a good job of that," Michael remarked.

"She's happy. Are we going to get the application forms to join the Party, Michael?"

Michael sighed wearily. "Yes, son. We've got to."

Laura placed a fresh cup of coffee in front of him, but he rose from the chair and stood looking out over the garden. The summer house roof and the top of the greenhouses were covered with a blanket of fresh snow. The earth lay undisturbed and the branches of the trees bowed under the weight of white crystalised mass, glittering in the midday sun. He could not find the spirit to admire the beauty and be thankful for the respite from long hours of toil once the ground was ready to be worked again.

Laura stood next to him, her arm sliding around his waist. "Will it really be as bad as Luther predicted last year?"

"It'll be worse, my love. Germany as we know it will no longer exist. We're on the road to hell, and its goodbye to freedom," he said gloomily.

Laura asked. "Are you sorry you're married, Michael? Saddled with a wife and her granddaughter?"

He looked down into the face of the woman he loved and smiled for the first time since the news that had shocked all of them. "Our granddaughter, Laura. I'll never regret marrying you. Whatever they take away from us, they can't obliterate the nine glorious years I've spent with you. Somehow we'll survive."

"Yes, we must. For Mitch's sake."

"That reminds me. Our granddaughter is having her music lesson with the delightful Sister Ursula until two," a mischievous glint appearing in his eyes. "We've got the house to ourselves. Feel like a rest?" his arm tightening about the slender figure of his wife, drawing her close to him.

"Yes, Darling. All this news is very tiring," Laura said happily.

* * *

It seemed that on the twentieth of April, the Fuehrer's birthday, the whole of the SA storm troopers, the SS Army, Hitler Youth and half the population were on the march, celebrating. According to the radio, parades, accompanied by blaring martial music, started at ten in the morning, would continue all through the day and finish with torch-light parades tonight, with Berlin, Nuremberg and Munich in the forefront of the spectacle.

The assembly on the village green at Dettingen set off towards the sports grounds by the river. It was a fairly small group, led by Kurt Bulger, carrying the new flag, followed by some ten youths, proud in their new uniforms. An assortment of villagers marched behind. Ed, the builder, Heini Wagner, the shoemaker and Carl Rademacher among them, looking sheepish at the few silently disapproving spectators. Hermann, the barber, stood between Doctor Hoffmann and Paul Zweig, the dentist.

Luther Goremann, his presence assuring that no fighting occurred, murmured to Doctor Hoffmann. "How long do you think we can hold out, Doc?"

"As long as we keep our mouths shut, we might weather the storm. Somebody's got to be left after the carnage to pick up the pieces, Luther," the Doctor said quietly. Already people had begun to look over their shoulder before speaking to their friends. The enemy was everywhere.

Katrin Bulger crossed the road and rang the doorbell of Laura's house. Erika opened the door. Walter Behrens had taken advantage of the closed shops and gone off to Cologne to see Leo. Fourteen year old Chrissy was in the summerhouse. She spent a great deal of her time helping in the garden, much to Daniel's delight. He had never wavered in his quest to marry her one day. Why, nobody could understand, but they accepted his decision with good humour.

"Come on in, Katrin. Just in time for a cuppa. What's the matter, pet?"

Erika had noticed the solemn look on Katrin's face. She seemed near to tears.

"I have to talk to somebody or I'll go mad. I'm losing my son and I don't know whether to be glad or sorry. What kind of a mother am I?" Katrin asked, following Erika to Laura's kitchen.

"Morning, Katrin. Haven't seen you for days," Laura said and also noticed that Katrin looked unhappy. "What on earth is wrong? You look upset," she said, placing the coffee pot on the table. "I've just taken that lot out there their coffee and biscuits, so we should have some peace for a bit. Let's have it."

She poured and pushed the plate full of cream filled pastries towards Katrin. At the sight of the delicious cakes Katrin brightened up.

"You don't know what it's been like in our house. Kurt isn't going to finish college. He's leaving home to join one of these new colleges for the SS boys."

"Can't Heinz stop him? Kurt's under age," Erika asked.

"We've asked Luther and he says if our son has sworn the oath, then he belongs to them. Apparently Kurt did. On the day when that strutting corporal was elected."

Suddenly there was fear in her eyes. Katrin clasped her hand over her mouth, staring at the two women. Frightened.

"I shouldn't have said that, should I?" she murmured. Laura and Erika exchanged glances, puzzled.

"Why shouldn't you have said that, Katrin?" Erika asked.

"It's dangerous talk and can get us put away. There's no telling who's reporting on us."

"Katrin," Laura spoke gently, but there was a note of steel in her voice. "We've known each other for a long time, and together all of us have seen good times and collectively managed to survive the depression. But times have changed. Erika, Walter and Freddy are with us, so is Mrs Henckler. You'll have to make up your mind which side you're on. We can't fight them, but we won't help them either."

Katrin looked relieved and helped herself to a pastry, considerably more like her cheerful self. "I may have a Nazi son, but Tonia and Heinz don't believe all that hogwash they're telling us. I'm glad he's going," she said forcefully. "Maybe now we're going to get some peace in our house. Kurt's been fighting with his sister ever since she started work at Kramers. They treat her well there, but he calls them filthy Jews and when Heinz told him off about it, our son said he'd report him, too. It's just too awful. What have the Jews ever done to them? I don't understand it. You know they're starting to picket outside the stores and shops to stop people from buying. Tonia is scared, but won't give in her notice on principle. She's a brave girl, my daughter, and I'm proud of her." A glint of pride shone in her eyes. "My son could send all of us to jail for siding with Tonia. I hope he never comes home again."

"I'm sorry, Katrin. I knew he was in the Hitler Youth, but hadn't realised he was that fanatical," Laura said. "We haven't seen much of him lately."

"You know where we stand, Katrin." Erika too was unusually solemn, the pert face had lost it's carefree expression. "Be careful what you say to Annie. She's caught between us and Heini and you know how she rabbits on. We all have to watch our mouths because we can't be sure of anybody now. I have to be careful with Chrissy around, Laura and Michael have the same problem with Mitch and you've got to watch what you say in front of Victor. We've got bright kids and the less they know, the easier it'll be on us. There'll be quite a few people who'll start pumping the kids for information on what the parents think. There are too many spies in this place already."

"I know," Katrin said. "I was talking to Therese Rademacher the other day and she was asking a lot of funny questions. You know her Carl is in the SA and everything you tell her is going straight to him."

"I agree," Laura remarked scornfully. "Even Jochen's bar isn't the same place as it was. It's not his fault. He's got to make a living like everybody else and can't afford to take sides. I expect the only place that'll be safe is here. We'll just have to be careful who we invite into the house."

"I want to be one of them, Laura," Katrin said. "Whatever my son is, he does not belong to us anymore."

"Have another cake, old friend," Laura invited and Katrin obliged.

Michael had been right. The constant stream of information coming over the radio was making everyone dizzy. No sooner had they got over one shock, another followed. It seemed that the administration in Berlin must be working day and night to draft new laws, amend existing ones, and feed the people with incessant propaganda. The first of May was again celebrated with pomp and circumstance in Berlin and elsewhere. They marched and carried the flag, they sang new patriotic songs and the music blared through the air waves. There was peace and tranquillity at number ten.

Michael threatened to take the axe to the radio if anyone turned it on.

Luther Goremann was making the last round on his patch before calling in at Jochen's for a night cap. Floss and Rula trotted quietly at his side, alert and sharp-eared nevertheless.

248

He turned the corner and saw them. "Go get them, girls," he whispered to the dogs.

Ari Klein's window had just been obscured by a poster telling the people to boycott his shop. The paste was still wet. Ed the builder, Susanna's Frank and Bern from 'The Stag's Head' did not have the courage to move, even though Floss and Rula stood quite peacefully.

"Why are we decorating Ari's window at this time of night?" Luther asked the sheepish looking men.

Ed and Frank remained silent. Big Bern retorted, "He's a Jew and has no business to sell books here."

"Ari can sell his books here as long as he has customers. Moishe can make his suits, which I know you've all been buying and anybody else around here is not going to have their window plastered with rubbish like that. Get it off," Luther said amiably, but his dogs made a menacing noise in their throats.

"Whose side are you on, Luther?" Ed queried defiantly, while Frank and Bern made every effort to part the poster from the paste on the window.

"I'm the law around here. Defacing private property carries a heavy fine and if I see any more of these anywhere in this village, I know where to send the summons. We've got enough of this kind of thing going on in town. I don't want it here. Do I make myself clear?" and Luther's voice was as menacing as the dog's growl. "You're at liberty to stand outside their shops during daylight and hold a placard. In silence and only until the sun goes down. I can't stop you from doing that. If you start agitating, I'll arrest you. Go home."

"They shouldn't be allowed to live among decent people," Bern said. "They're the scum of the earth," he added, hissing like a poisonous snake.

Luther was getting hot under the collar and knew he needed to keep a sense of proportion if he were to maintain his stance of neutrality.

"Have you told that to your father? He fought at their side in the last war and big as you are, boy, that old man'll whip you if he hears you talking like that."

Frank, in his usual inebriated state, found his voice. "You're not going to last long around here taking the Jews side. We'll see to it, won't we, Ed? And you can take that sister of yours and her black-haired devil of a daughter with you," he slurred, looking for support from his colleagues. But

Ed and Bern, suddenly very sober, took the bucket and brush and slunk off into the builder's yard two doors from Ari's shop.

Luther did not hesitate. His enormous fists clamped themselves around his brother-in-law's throat, and tightened. "You miserable drunken sod. I ought to kill you here and now and give her some peace at last," and then he heard Floss whining. The rage in him was burning, red spots danced in front of his eyes. He let go, but drove his fist into Frank's stomach, watching him double up in pain. Luther suffered pangs of conscience, knowing that Susanna would pay for this, but at the same time he felt satisfaction that tonight had given him an excuse to relieve his anger. "One day, Frank. One day," he muttered after retreating from the figure, still doubled up and holding his stomach. The last sound he heard before turning into Quirin Street was Frank throwing up against the wall. "Damn you. I should've killed you," Luther muttered under his breath, imagining his sister's ordeal.

* * *

The fair came the following weekend, a welcome relief to the people of Dettingen. It was the first of the season and visitors flocked from the town and villages to share the event. The Green outside the church and Convent was filled to over-flowing with carousels, car rides, chairs flying through the air, booths and stalls which spread into adjoining streets. Peace reigned until the church clock struck twelve when the cacophony of music blared incessantly all afternoon and evening, but no-one complained. This year, a great many uniformed men and boys mingled with the local population, jarring on the sensibilities of some, delighting others.

Michael had made a bargain with his granddaughter. She could ride on anything that moved, eat as many waffles and cream as she could manage and have the biggest ice cream they could find, if she would just make her grandmother happy. Laura called it bribery and corruption. Her husband laughed and said that was what life was all about and she should count herself lucky the kid was smart enough at her age to negotiate a good bargain.

"Hold still, darling," Laura implored the fidgety child, pulling the hairbrush through tight curls. "Trying to make you look like a girl is very hard work."

"Sorry, granma," Mitch said, reflecting on the nuisance of having to dress in the dark blue skirt, white blouse and cardigan once again. Once for church was tolerable. To go in your best clothes to the Fair made no sense at all. She wouldn't be able to sneak behind the rides and watch the machinery at work in case she got grease on her clothes. Maybe tomorrow? The new black shoes were much tighter than her sandals, the knee-length white socks too long, but she had promised granpa...

The little girl would be six in August. She was small, strong and sturdy, with hair of an indefinable colour. It was not blond like Laura's, or brown like her father's, more of a honey colour and when the sun came out it had a reddish tint. Lion's hair, Margharita had called it. The large grey probing eyes still changed to a dangerous green whenever she was in a rage, which was a frequent occurrence. Getting dressed for school in the mornings always brought one on. Sister Elisabeth at the convent inspected every item of their school uniform at assembly, including the freshly laundered, neatly folded handkerchief. Only the presence of her beloved Grandfather Michael kept breakfast a civilised occasion.

"There. You'll do," Laura said, looking proudly at her granddaughter. "You're such a pretty girl."

"That she is, my love," Michael remarked, surveying the two most important women in his life. "So are you," he added, his eyes wandering over the curvacious figure of his wife dressed in her navy suit, the collar of the white blouse open and showing a smooth, creamy skin. "I'll be the luckiest man at the fair to have two beautiful women for company."

"Flatterer," Laura said, a pleasing smile on her lips, kissing his cheek.

"Thank you, granpa," Mitch acknowledged the compliment politely, but the look that passed between them reminded him that she expected him to keep his side of the bargain, and wasn't fooled by any flattery.

They collected Erika and Chrissy and joined the steady stream of people from Annsberg on their way to the fair. As they turned into Dettingen Road the discordant noise assaulted their ears. Ari and Gertrud Klein, with their son and daughter, waited for Erika and the Schillers.

"We'll all be deaf by the time we get home," Ari said, having to speak louder than usual. It was difficult. He was a mild mannered, soft spoken man.

"Well, it's only once a year. At least the kids'll love it," Gertrud commented.

"We've got this for three days right here on our doorstep," Ari said, jokingly making a painful grimace, which made everybody laugh.

"I don't envy you," Michael said.

It seemed as if the whole world was at the fair. Ari and Michael dug into their pockets and both brought out a handful of coins. Michael divided his between Chrissy and Mitch, Ari handed his to ten year old Matt and seven year old Ruth.

"Chrissy, you're the oldest. Keep an eye on them. We'll wander about for a while and meet you in an hour outside the church," Michael instructed her. "I'll treat you all to waffles and cream."

Mitch grinned at him and the others whooped.

"Thanks, Mr Schiller," they shouted, disappearing into the throng.

"Do I get my spending money too?" asked Laura.

"I'll get Erika and you an ice cream," he answered in good spirits.

At the third booth on the Green they saw Luther and his sister Susanna queuing for the frothy sweet substance spooned into cornets. Luther was in his best suit and off duty. He looked at ease, but as always, alert. Susanna too had a happy expression on her face, laughing at something he had said. It wasn't very often he saw her laugh. Of Frank there was no sign. Rula and Floss had been left at home; the noise would make them irritable.

"Good to see you, Susanna. Hello, Luther. Where are the kids?" Erika asked.

"I've lined their pockets with silver and they've gone off," Luther said, smiling genially. "It'll take them a while to spend it. Then they'll be back. Are we sticking together?"

"I think so," Ari shouted. "I'll feel safer with you lot around. Too many brown shirts about for my liking."

Luther glanced at Michael. "We'll wait for you to get your ice cream and then make the rounds."

The men tried their luck at the rifle stall. Ari did not hit one duck. Luther bagged a rag doll for Susanna's Kirsten and Michael won a gaudy green umbrella for Laura.

"You should get more practice in, Ari. You're a rotten shot," Luther joked and tried again. This time he was given a pink elephant and presented it to Gertrud, who beamed at him.

"Thank you, Luther. I'll name him after you."

They were jostled by the good-natured crowd, separated and found each other again. The shouts and laughter of the people competed with the bellowing stallholders enticing the moving throng to try their luck. Business was brisk. The Ferris Wheel, proud and majestic, towered over it all. A medium sized roller coaster whooshed by, stopped, filled up and was off again. The caterpillar ride rose and fell, it's canvas covering sheltering the occupants for a few blissful rounds while lovers kissed and cuddled in the dark interior and children screamed with fright or joy.

"Fancy going on that?" Michael grinned at Laura, his arm around her. She shook her head, laughing.

They were watching, enjoying the spectacle, when Susanna's oldest son tugged at Luther's jacket, his face showing signs of a bruise. "There's some of the kids from the new flats up the road beating up Matt, Uncle Luther. I tried to stop them, but there's too many of them." His eyes watering, he bravely brushed the tears away with the back of his hand.

"Where's Ruth?" Gertrud Klein shouted, stark fear for her daughter contorting the homely face.

"They've got her, too. Behind the roller coaster," the boy said, clinging to his mother.

"Take him home, Susanna. Put some cold compress on that cheek," Luther ordered his sister. He turned to Erika and Laura. "Wait with Gertrud by the church. Ari, Michael, come on."

They followed Luther to the back of the high structure. Seven boys in brown shirts of the Hitler Youth stood in a ring around Matt and Ruth. The girl was terrified, but looked unharmed. Matt, nursing a bloody nose, glared defiantly at his captors, manfully protecting his sister.

"Jew boy, Jew boy, we're going to kill you!" the boys chanted.

Ari broke through the ring and snatched his daughter, holding her close. Luther put his great fists around the necks of the two tallest boys and Michael held on to two more.

"What is the meaning of this?" Luther bellowed above the noise as the cars rattled past. The smaller tormentors had vanished into the crowd at the front.

"They're Jews!" one of Luther's thugs spat out in disgust. "They should be put away."

"What are you going to do with them, Luther?" Ari Klein shouted, consoling his weeping daughter while at the same time cleaning the blood from his son's face.

"Nothing today, Ari. I know who they are. Tomorrow I'll see their parents," and quick as lightning he cuffed both boys around the ear, then dished out the same treatment to the other two. "Don't let me see you anywhere near these two kids again. I'll take a belt to your backside and you won't sit down for a week."

He had no opportunity to tell them anything else. They had already disappeared into the crowd. Michael carried Ruth and Ari Klein led his son towards the church.

Chapter 28

The windows in Father Dominik's study were wide open. Today he hoped to catch up on work he should have done on Monday and Tuesday, but the noise of the fair had penetrated every nook and cranny in the house. He had made a good start on the scathing sermon he intended to deliver to his parishioners next Sunday. Father Dominik was disturbed and angry that children had absorbed so much hatred already as to intimidate and threaten their former friends. He would remind his congregation in the strongest language possible from a pulpit what it said in the Holy Book about loving one's neighbour. Luther could enforce the law of the land, but his own weapons were not of the physical kind. Words and faith in the Lord were all he had to fight this evil menace with. He was not like Michael, who had seen death and hatred on the battlefield, had recovered and balanced a spiritual life with physical activities.

Father Dominik, of average height and slight of stature, mused on the probability of whether he was capable of fighting anybody should the need arise, when Clara, who had resumed her former post as housekeeper, knocked and entered the study.

"Sister Anna wishes to see you, Father. She's very upset and has a message from the Reverend Mother. I'll bring in some coffee."

"Send her in, Clara. Coffee would be most welcome."

Sister Anna, her sweet face strained with agitation, greeted the priest.

"Good morning, Father. Mother Agnes has very disturbing news from Cologne."

"Sit down, Sister Anna. Tell me what's happened."

The tiny sister sank gratefully into the large chair opposite the desk, her delicate hands nervously twisting the rosary. Father Dominik felt uneasy. He had never seen the sister in such distress. Her voice was shaking as she relayed her message. "The Bishop's secretary informed us not more than twenty minutes ago that the Fascist students are on the rampage. They're raiding Universities and College libraries, bookshops and every other library in every town for books of our greatest writers, particularly Jewish and foreign authors. They've already filled lorries with our most precious heritage since early morning. We should've been informed immediately, but with the new Bishop we are not on the priority list."

Clara entered with a tray and handed Sister Anna her cup. Not waiting for an invitation she drank hastily.

"This is sacrilege," the Priest exclaimed angrily. "Did the secretary say what they intend to do with the books?"

"Burn them," Sister Anna said.

"What about our library here?" Clara asked and the Father looked alarmed.

"Surely they wouldn't dare invade church premises?"

"The secretary didn't say. We've been instructed to move our most valuable books into the hide-out until further notice. The Reverend Mother thought you ought to know. She asked that you alert Luther Goreman, in case they get to Mr Klein's shop." Sister Anna stood up. "Thank you for the coffee, Clara. I must get back. Goodbye, Father Dominik."

The priest and the housekeeper stared at each other.

"It really is starting, isn't it, Father?" Clara asked.

"Yes. God alone knows where it will end. I don't." He drank the remainder of his coffee and rose from his chair. "I must see Luther and Ari Klein. After last Sunday he'll not be overjoyed to hear this news."

That night, the 10th of May, lorries filled with a nation's cultural heritage spilled their precious contents onto every town square. The flames consumed the names and words of great men. Karl Marx, Thomas Mann, Marcel Proust, Einstein, Freud, Wolff and Zweig joined a host of others in the roaring pyre. Freedom of speech was already a thing of the past. Now, the purging of a nation's intellect was high on the list of priorities. Berlin rejoiced at the desecration and the air waves crackled with approval. It was only the beginning.

The Reverend Mother, worried about the incident at the fair, was indecisive as to whether they should hold the Church Festival this year. Here, as everywhere, the evil had tainted the community. The free and easy bonhomie they had known through good and bad times had gone. There was fear of one's neighbour, one's friends and even of the sisters. She gazed out of the study window, but today the wonderful array of multi-coloured blooms in the rose garden did nothing to lighten her troubled spirit. Mother

Agnes wondered how long it would be before she must leave this place and retreat to an enforced retirement to Oberursel because of her Jewish blood. If Bertie had been alive they would have found a way, but the new Bishop of Cologne and Koblenz had one foot firmly planted in the Nazi camp, as had many of his priests and chaplains. She vaguely speculated how long Father Dominik was allowed to stay on. There was still so much to do... She rang the little silver bell and Sister Gertrud, demurely as ever, entered.

"May I have some coffee and TWO slices of that delicious chocolate cake, sister?"

Sister Gertrud's mouth formed an 'O' but she did not comment. The Reverend Mother must be very worried about something. It was always the same routine. Only in time of trouble or great joy did the good Mother indulge her sweet tooth.

"Yes, Mother. I'll get it," and withdrew hurriedly. Trouble, trouble, there seems to be nothing but trouble these days, Sister Gertrud mumbled on her way to the kitchen.

The Reverend Mother wrote several short notes and placed them into envelopes, some to be delivered by Sister Gertrud and one to be posted to Freddy. All contained her request for an emergency meeting of the Church Committee. Something had to be done about Father Dominik. He absolutely refused to tone down his fiery sermons, in spite of Freddy and Michael's reminder to him of their encounter with a merciless enemy. The Father continued to deliver scathing lectures from the pulpit, criticising the heathens ruling the country, deploring the strangulation of freedom of speech, lamenting the exodus of noted painters, writers, scholars and scientists. It did not stop there. He took his anger and volatile protest to the religious lessons at the school. Jimmy Stern, the Headmaster due to retire next Easter, was no coward, had received several medals for bravery in the last war. He was worried and had appealed again to Michael to tell that hot-headed Father to keep his mouth shut. He had enough trouble at the school with the members of the Hitler Youth who were constantly harassing the Jewish kids and he didn't want to finish his days in a labour camp for allowing anti-nazi lessons in his classrooms. The new Deputy Head was throwing out some very nasty hints.

In the last year the former cheerful face of Mother Agnes had acquired deep lines and she had lost her comely figure. The smiles did not come as easily as they had during the last decade. She looked gaunt, but had achieved the change-over from an excellent School of Education to a functional hospital. The west wing now served as isolation wards for children and the east wing was the best equipped maternity unit for miles around. When the axe fell, as it surely must, the school rooms were designated to become lecture halls for girls wishing to take up a career in nursing. The convent was large enough to accommodate her sisters and resident medical students if the authorities would sanction the proposal. She had excellent doctors and surgeons among her sisters to teach Medicine instead of the three 'R's. If only she could be as sure of her own future, Mother Agnes thought. A radical Father Dominik was no help under the circumstances and something had to be done.

Sister Gertrud entered the study, carrying a tray with a silver coffee pot, cream jug and sugar basin. Two large portions of chocolate gateau lay temptingly on a plate, giving some measure of comfort to the Reverend Mother.

"Thank you, sister. I'll enjoy this. Will you see that these get to our committee members in the village and post the one to Baron von Dettingen, please."

Michael Schiller read the note he had picked off the mat in the hall. A frown creased the suntanned brow. Today was Wednesday. The urgent meeting requested by Agnes was for this coming Friday. She hadn't picked a good time for him and he wondered what was so pressing as to be summoned at such short notice. Daniel would be riding into town and Laura would have to pacify Mitch. He had promised to take her and Victor to the river to teach them how to handle the two-man canoe Daniel had picked up at an auction in town. It would have to wait until Sunday. The little monster would be furious and no doubt extract the promise of at least six ice creams for her and Victor. Michael smiled. She could bargain in true gipsy style, almost as persuasive as Ramon and mostly got what she wanted.

Laura was clearing the table of the remnants of the lunchtime meal. Her husband waved the note at her. "Committee meeting Friday night. Agnes wants us at the hall at eight. Says it's urgent. I wonder if she wants to cancel the fete altogether."

"I hope not. It's small enough as it is, darling. The forecourt of the convent doesn't hold more than a dozen stalls, maybe five or six in the school hall if we're lucky. We've got to put the refreshments in there as well," Laura said, then pulled a face. "I can't go on Friday. Mitch'll be in a fine temper if you're not going to take them to the river."

"She'll get over it. I'll take them on Sunday. We can all go and have a day off. We'll have a look at that houseboat of Ari's. He's asked me again if I'm willing to buy it."

"It would be nice to spend a whole day by the water. I've almost forgotten what it's like."

Michael lifted her chin and kissed the soft lips. "Do you miss it very much? We'll buy the boat and make time to go as often as we can. On one condition, though."

"What's that, darling?"

"That you learn to swim. Agreed?"

"What? At my age? You can't be serious?"

"That river doesn't slope gently, Laura. Four metres from the bank and it goes straight down thirty feet to allow for the heavy barges and the pleasure steamers. That's a long way down and people drown if they can't swim. Are you going to learn?"

"If it's that deep I'd better. I won't get the houseboat otherwise, will I?"

"No!" Michael said firmly and kissed her again, thinking that his lovely wife was as wily as her granddaughter in getting what she wanted.

* * *

They met at the Hall just before eight. Erika unlocked the door of the annexe where they felt it was safer to discuss the political situation. Doctor Hoffmann and Luther settled themselves at the end of the polished table, Michael and Erika took their usual places. Freddy was absent, dealing with trouble at the paper and Cornelius was spending the month in the South with the Count and Countess von Riesenheim. The Reverend Mother had entrusted him with a sealed package for Ira, which he promised to deliver faithfully.

"What do you think this is about, Michael?" Emil Hoffmann asked. "Sounds as if something's come up which we haven't heard about yet."

"I've no idea," Michael replied. "Did you hear about the Vice Chancellor's visit to Rome? They've got the Church with a noose around its neck. Cardinal Pacelli signed the treaty with the Nazis and promised them not to interfere in state politics any more. In exchange His Eminence got

259

assurances that the Church is at liberty to carry on with its own internal policies. None of it will materialise, of course."

"Maybe they mean it," Luther ventured hopefully.

Michael gave a dismissive wave of his hand.

"Don't you believe it," he growled at the policeman. "They'll emasculate our clergy, remove the rebellious element as traitors and the rest will be very enthusiastic or keep quiet. Like most of our people."

"You're not serious?" Doctor Hoffmann asked, a frown on his chubby face.

"I am and I don't envy Dominik."

"Do you think he'll toe the line, Michael?" Erika queried.

"No," Michael said. "He'll die first, fool that he is, but I admire his conviction. Maybe if I was still in his place I'd do the same."

The side door opened. Father Dominik followed a sombre looking Reverend Mother to the table, their black robes accentuating the pallor of their faces.

"Good evening," she greeted them as they sat down. "I have not invited the whole committee tonight as there are delicate matters to be discussed. I gather Freddy can't be here?"

"He sends his apologies, Mother Agnes. He's got problems with one of his editors," Erika said.

"No matter," the Reverend Mother answered and smiled at the pretty woman. "You are aware of the treaty Cardinal Pacelli signed with Franz von Papen on the 20th?" Her eyes questioning everyone in turn.

"Yes, we heard," Emil Hoffmann replied and there was a nod of agreement from the rest.

"That brings me to the very disturbing news I should pass on to you. All Catholic schools and Colleges will cease to exist as such except the training colleges for the clergy. By next Easter every child of school age will be transferred to the nearest state school. Priests and nuns will be barred from teaching in these schools by order of the authorities. We are confined to Church and convents. Is that not so, Dominik?"

Apart from a subdued greeting to the committee members the priest had said nothing, his mind elsewhere. The once snug-fitting cassock hung loose about his sparse body. Michael remembered the soft-spoken, genial chaplain of ten years ago, the easy companionship they had forged between them and wondered how long Dominik could contain that fire that seemed to consume his very soul. Sooner or later he would do something that was not going to be conducive to his well-being. Luther wondered the same thing, looking at the haggard face and body of the priest and hoped he wasn't going to commit some stupid act that would bring the 'Black Maria' to the presbytery. Doctor Hoffmann knew with certainty that he must have words with his patient on the state of his health before long. The man looked positively ill. The dark eyes of the priest flashed angrily.

"Yes, Mother Agnes. We are going to be caged like wild beasts and tranquilized by the masters. Unless we join them."

"That is of course the alternative," Mother Agnes said smoothly and turned to Doctor Hoffmann. "Your son Willy, Paul Zweig's boy, Victor Bulger and the others have to leave the Priest's school in Annsberg and join the village school here. My girls too will be absorbed into their appropriate villages. Your Mitch is a bright girl, Michael, but inclined to be headstrong. The education in the state schools is adequate for most of the children, but doesn't cater for the gifted, inquisitive pupil who needs encouragement to further what talents he or she may have. We have produced many outstanding students for the universities, but it will not be so in the village school. The children from our establishments are far too advanced for their age and I'm afraid that could present a problem for the new teachers and the children."

Michael chuckled at the thought of Mitch having to sit through hours of listening to lessons she probably had a year ago and wondered how she would occupy her mind.

"Your sisters have done an excellent job educating our children. It is a sorry state of affairs, but unfortunately we have to learn to live with it," Michael remarked and Mother Agnes nodded in agreement.

"Now to another matter which I must ask you to keep confidential, you in particular, Luther. It may put you into a very difficult position. For the sake of old friendships I hope that, if you can't join in what I propose, you'll at least keep silent," she asked of Luther Goremann.

"Fair enough," was the sparse answer, but Mother Agnes seemed satisfied.

The others looked startled, wondering what other calamity had occurred. Mother Agnes drew a deep breath and looked at Father Dominik, who nodded encouragement.

"I have been in conference with Dominik all afternoon, reminding him again of his foolhardy sermons. He may be persuaded to put his oratory talents to better use. Silence, for instance."

"And pigs might fly..." Michael murmured, glancing at Erika, who shook her head, looking amazed.

Mother Agnes smiled and continued. "As some of you know I am the daughter of a Jewish father and a Catholic mother. There was never any discord about religion in my family as my parents loved each other very deeply. When the persecution began my father sold his store and the factory to a friend and took my family to America. I decided to stay here and my share of the sale was invested in Switzerland. When my cousin Bertie was alive he sanctioned the use of my own money to finance various projects at the convent. The new bishop won't allow me that liberty and would dearly like my fortune to go into the Church's coffers, but he can't force me to hand it over. I now feel that this money mountain can be used to get my people out of this country, but I need your help."

"She's mad," Father Dominik commented. The anger had left his eyes and a look of adoration had taken its place as he glanced at the Reverend Mother. "Quite mad. What she proposes is to establish a safe route for the less fortunates who have not the means to get to America direct but wish to leave. Switzerland will be their immediate destination. From there certain parties will take over. I should like your comments and contributions on the feasibility of such a plan. Whether you'll participate in this dangerous venture is a choice you'll have to make on your own. For my part, I promise to hold my peace in Church and elsewhere so as not to attract the attention of the committed SA members that live in this village. The treaty will give me a good excuse to change my ways."

Erika, Michael, Luther and Doctor Hoffmann shuffled in their seats, on their faces a mixture of surprise, horror and admiration. Luther recovered first.

"You mean, spirit them away from under the noses of the SS?"

"Why not," Michael said. "The pressure's on for them to leave, but what they're offered for stock and premises hardly pays their passage, never mind starting again in another country."

"We know that," Father Dominik acknowledged. "I've spoken to Ari Klein and Moishe. They want to go. So does Simon. They're afraid for their families but can't sell the shops, except at give-away prices."

Michael frowned, blue eyes troubled. "We need a front-man. To buy their business at the prevailing rate, re-sell them on the open market as German owned properties and let the original owners have the difference later. That takes time." He did not sound too optimistic.

"You're right, Michael," Mother Agnes agreed. "Time is the crucial factor here. What you have outlined is one way of enabling my people to start again and restore their dignity. But where will we find this giant of a man?" she asked.

"Gruenewald," exclaimed Doctor Hoffmann. "He'll do it. He's my lawyer in town. About as anti nazi as you can get. If anybody can find a way, he can. Who's going to finance this while the sales go through? It could take months."

Erika had been busy filling a page on her note pad with figures. She looked up and all eyes turned in her direction.

"We'll have to," she announced firmly. "Freddy, Michael, Emil and Walter. Not Luther. It's too risky for him to get involved. Between us we'll raise what Ari and the others have been offered for their business, which is less than half the market value and going down all the time. Once Gruenewald has sold them, we'll get our money back and pass on the difference."

Mother Agnes looked a little less strained and glanced fondly at the younger woman. "Your business sense does you credit, Erika. No wonder Walter survived the depression better than most. I'll arrange for the hand-over of the difference once our people reach Bern."

"That solves the immediate cash flow," Luther remarked, his green eyes full of scepticism. "How will you get them all to Switzerland?"

"At this moment in time they can still travel by train," Mother Agnes said, smiling at him. "How long that will last is anybody's guess. Many of them will have no means because their properties have been confiscated or vandalised. They're frightened people. The money will be waiting for them in Bern, but we'll have to get them there once visas and exit permits to leave this country are cancelled for the Jewish citizen. We must make contingency plans for this now. It cannot be done overnight."

"The river," Michael exclaimed. "There must be bargees from Holland that'll be sympathetic. And there's Captain Olaf's steamer. He'll know who can be trusted."

"Can we trust him though?" Doctor Hoffmann asked.

"Oh, yes." Erika Behrens spoke with utter conviction. "When we took Freddy's people for their annual outing up river he made his position very clear. He'll be with us. What about us?"

In the depth of his conscience Michael Schiller was already committed. To wage his own Holy War would repay in some measure for the happiness he had found with Laura. People did die for their causes, though, and he didn't want to die. He dismissed the thought and knew that he could never attempt this on his own.

"I'll have to talk to Laura before I commit myself to anything. And you have to talk to Freddy and Walter. We'll get together and figure out what can be done if it get's worse."

Father Dominik had an angry glint in his eyes again.

"The worst happened on the 30th of January when that strutting corporal manipulated his way to take his place as Chancellor of this nation. Have you any idea of how many pieces of legislation his administration has passed so far?" He glowered at everyone at the table. "Until last week we had about four hundred. They're coming out daily and its only July. By the end of the year they'll have the judiciary tied up. No Nazi badge, no job. There isn't much left. Has your Force been taken over, Luther?"

Luther nodded. "Nearly all of it. The chief was right when he told us to join them a long time ago. The ones that did are getting the promotion. I'm still at the bottom of the heap and likely to remain there. I can't promise yet what I'll do about this. Have to think it over."

Mother Agnes understood his dilemma and felt sympathy for the big amiable man who wanted nothing more out of life than to serve his community, care for his dogs and protect his sister from a drunken sadistic husband.

"It might become dangerous and you must consider that carefully. My friendship with you will not end if you refuse to take part in what is after all a high risk operation," she said graciously. "Remember, it is also dangerous to talk. Now, I must get back to my sisters. Perhaps you'll let me know when we should meet again. Goodnight, my friends. God be with you."

She rose and Father Dominik also stood up. "I'll see you across," he said quietly. "Goodnight Everyone. Think carefully before you commit yourself."

There was a chorus of 'goodnight'. Doctor Hoffmann, Erika, Luther and Michael sat in silence for a few moments, wondering about the consequences if they agreed to the proposition put before them.

Michael Schiller, a bottle of wine and two glasses in his hand, followed his wife to the summerhouse. His news was not for the ears of their granddaughter, should she wake up.

The wooden benches and trestle tables had long been replaced by stylish wicker furniture, seats and backs thickly padded and covered in pretty cotton. Mara Schumann's lanterns still hung from the beams and Michael lit two of them, made himself comfortable on the two-seater wicker sofa and patted the vacant space beside him. He filled the two glasses and they drank to Michael's toast. "To my beautiful wife, whom I shall love forever."

Laura smiled happily at the compliment, wondering what had occasioned this unexpected declaration of undying love. The reason manifest itself as Michael talked. She protested, remonstrated and finally grew quiet.

"I thought I had tamed you, Michael," she said at last.

He was not sure what to say to that, as he had never considered himself in need of taming, unless she had that near disaster in Munich in mind. He drew her closer to him.

"I hope I've been a good husband to you, Laura, but love and marriage should not kill a man's compassion for his fellow men or the desire to change events if they cause suffering and death."

She considered his words for some time, still anxious about the possible danger to him and the others.

"You've been all I ever wanted, but this..." She lifted her hands in a gesture of futility. "What you have in mind to do could result in your arrest, or worse. I know you're not afraid, but what about us? What about Mitch? She'll be in danger too."

In the pale glow of the lanterns he could see the fear in her eyes.

"I love you more than life itself and I love our granddaughter almost as much. When she gets old enough to understand what is happening right now, what are we going to tell her when she asks what we did about it all? Are we going to tell her we did nothing, stood by like so many others because we were afraid? That we did nothing because we feared for her safety?" Michael said, his features stern and uncompromising. "She wouldn't believe that and hate us for it. Mitch is a fighter and despises cowardice. I would rather be dead than face that silent contempt in her eyes."

Laura sighed. "I want you alive, even as a coward. Dead heroes are no use to anybody, darling."

"No," Michael's voice had an edge to it and she remembered that day in his study soon after they met. He had to make a decision then that was to change both their lives and had looked as determined as he did now. "Cowards have to live with their consciences every day. For people like us that too is a kind of death. Mitch is your flesh and blood and I know very well that underneath that soft shell of yours is a woman just as spirited as your granddaughter when the occasion demands it."

"That terrible business in Munich frightened me, Michael. I thought I had lost you. I understand your need to do something, but you can't save them all. Did you know that there are 200,000 Jews in Germany? Give or take a few."

Michael smiled down at her. "No. I didn't know the exact number, my Love. Agnes is not so foolish as to dream that even with her vast fortune she can save them all. But surely some are better than none at all."

"I suppose Mother Agnes and Father Dominik are counting on you to do the organising?" she asked.

"I expect so, together with Freddy, Erika and Emil. We can't involve Luther too deeply. We've already put him into an impossible situation by asking for his silence."

Laura was following the antics of a few moths zooming in on the lanterns. "You really want to do this, Michael? Jeopardize everything we have, including our lives?"

He too was watching the inevitable path of the flying creatures and wondered if all of it was pre-ordained. Maybe this was why he had left the priesthood? To live and love and be free to atone in some small measure for the barbarism of his race towards another...

"I need to do something, but only if you are with me. I can't do it without you."

"Well then..." Laura said quietly. "We had better make sure that nobody gets caught, hadn't we, my darling?"

Michael gently lifted her face and gazed at it for a moment. "You never cease to surprise me, Mrs Schiller. I love you so very much."

Extinguishing the lantern lights, he returned and took her into his arms. As always, her slender body responded to his kiss, the terrifying images of what might happen to them receded as she abandoned herself to the touch of familiar hands. The heavy scent of night stock pervaded the room and the soft breeze cooled their bodies as they whispered 'I love you'...

Much later, Laura could not suppress a giggle as she recovered her discarded clothes in the faint light of the moon.

"It's some time since we did this, Michael. I feel like a naughty sixteen year old seduced by my lover. It's wonderful."

"Any time you feel like being seduced, let me know, Mrs Schiller," Michael laughed.

The lights in the attic window suddenly blazed over the roof of the bathroom.

"Oh, God. Daniel," he murmured into her hair. "I'd forgotten all about him. We'll have to tell him."

"Will he leave us?" Laura asked.

"I don't think so. I'll talk to him tomorrow. Let's forget about it for tonight, my love."

Chapter 29

Siegburg Prison, twenty miles across the river from Bonn, was meant for seventy five, but had doubled its intake in the last few months. Light offenders were working to enlarge the small private airfield, requisitioned by the State to train future paratroopers. The farmers, whose land bordered the airstrip, had not been too pleased to give up what had belonged to them for generations past, helpless against the ruthless machinery of oppression that ground on relentlessly, oblivious of sentiment and heritage.

The Armistice promised by the Fuehrer had taken effect, but had strings attached to that generous gesture. Of the prisoners that came out of the door of the Governor's office, some waved the enrolment form to join the SA, the SS or the Military. Their one chance to wipe the slate clean.

Rudi Waldorf entered, removed his striped cap and exposed a shaven head, the sandy coloured stubble just visible. Hazel eyes showed no emotion and the pleasant looking face displayed a suitable penitence. The Governor, heavy folds of flesh straining his shirt, looked in a genial mood. Rudi became wary, remembering what Luther had told him a year ago, although he had to admit that on the whole he hadn't fared too badly.

"Waldorf?" The Governor wiped his sweaty brow.

"Prisoner 3762906497, Waldorf, sir," Rudi said dutifully.

"I see from your file that it was at the request of a Major Konrad that you were sent here. Do you know him?"

Rudi recalled Jan's words too. 'Forget you know me...' and remained servile. Not a flicker in the hazel eyes betrayed what he knew.

"No, sir. Maybe it was one of the officers at the hearing," he said calmly.

"I see. Have you learnt anything here to make you a worthwhile citizen of the Third Reich?"

"Yes, sir. To keep my mouth shut and my fists occupied with work."

"Admirable, Waldorf, and very sensible. I'll grant your parole, but there are conditions," the Governor said. "Will you swear the oath to be faithful to the Fuehrer, die for him if necessary? You'll start with a clean sheet."

Why had Janus asked for him to be at this place? Rudi wondered. So close to Bonn and Cologne when most of the prisoners had been sent as far away as possible from their home towns and families. The work was hard,

268

but bearable and the treatment fair if you did as you were told. He had nothing to lose. If anybody was going to give him a job at all he would have to join the Party anyway. He couldn't even emigrate with a criminal record.

"Yes, sir. I'll swear the oath."

"Very sensible, Waldorf. You'll be released at the weekend. Collect your clothes and a small amount of money to tide you over. Have you anywhere to stay? We can arrange for you to go to one of our hostels," the Governor said kindly.

"No, thank you, sir. I've got a place," Rudi answered, hoping Mrs Henckler hadn't changed her mind.

"Leave your address with the clerk and pick up the forms. I'll expect them to be handed in by Friday. When you're processed, we'll get in touch and find a place for you. Keep out of trouble, Waldorf. Beating up high-ranking SS Officers is not a healthy occupation and next time you might not be so lucky. Goodbye," and as an afterthought added, "Heil Hitler".

"Goodbye, sir," and Rudi dutifully executed the stiff salute. "Heil Hitler," at which the Governor lazily waved his hand in the air.

Mrs Henkler came to fetch Rudi at 10:00 am the following Saturday. She had brought him a present. The seaman's cap fitted perfectly and made him feel a rush of affection for the brusque, sharp tongued woman most people did not want to antagonize. He knew that behind that barbed facade hid a kind, warm hearted soul, too proud to let anyone see how lonely she was. The cap made him feel good as it hid the stubble on his head.

Five days later an official looking package arrived for Rudi at Mrs Henckler's house. It contained his Identity Pass, mandatory for every citizen of the country and a booklet on what was expected of every new recruit to the SS Army. Martha snorted in disgust at the array of official Nazi stamps adorning the pass and booklet. Rudi did not show her the letter from Major Konrad, requesting him to present himself at his office the following Monday at 2:30 pm. No reason was given.

Daniel Tanner had extended the hand of friendship to the ex-prisoner, as had Michael, Laura and Erika, but it was only to Daniel that Rudi confided his concern about going to Cologne. There had been a lengthy silence after Daniel had read the letter. It seemed to Rudi as if his new friend wanted to say something and then changed his mind.

"Don't worry about it, Rudi. It'll be alright. Will you have to wear the uniform when you're off-duty?"

"I don't know. I don't fancy that idea," Rudi said with obvious lack of enthusiasm.

On Monday, his suit freshly pressed by Martha, his cap set at a rakish angle, Rudi boarded the train to Cologne. This time, as he entered the graceful building housing barbarians, he did not feel threatened. The same man was sitting behind the desk. Rudi stood to attention, gave the obligatory salute, presented his pass and the letter from Major Konrad and wondered if the man would recognize him. The duty sergeant returned his greeting, glanced at the pass to compare the real thing with the photograph pasted inside the page but showed no sign of recognition.

"At ease," he said gruffly. "Wait over there," pointing to a row of chairs in the hall. Maybe he saw too many people passing through here, Rudi thought, letting his gaze wander over the simple elegance of the interior, debating with himself who had lived here before THEY had taken over. The house was made for quiet, gentle people, not strutting men and women in uniforms.

"Major Konrad will see you now, Waldorf," the harsh voice of the sergeant interrupted his thoughts. "Up the stairs, on the first floor, fourth door along the corridor. The name's on the door."

Rudi did not inform the sergeant that he knew the way.

A sudden stab of fear knotted Rudi's stomach as he stood before the door, but his knock betrayed nothing of that. It was firm and loud.

"Come," said the voice inside, reminiscent of a quieter, softer time. Like his headmaster's a long time ago, when all things had their proper place and life was certain. Entering, Rudi faced Jan Konrad.

"Sit down, Waldorf."

Rudi did and the two men studied each other in a heavy silence. Jan's probing eyes seemed satisfied with what they had scrutinised.

"I've interviewed at least a dozen candidates for this job. It's a pleasant change not to have somebody falling over themselves to make the grade. You forgot to say Heil Hitler and stand to attention," the Major said, smiling and Rudi was surprised how it changed the other man's face, made it look younger and softer.

"Sorry, I forgot, sir."

Jan noted just a hint of defiance in the apology and was relieved that prison had not broken his spirit.

"Let's cut the bull, Rudi, and get down to business. I've taken over a bigger office and need two assistants. One to do routine stuff, the other to keep an eye on him and things in general and drive me anywhere at a minutes notice. You drive already, so that's not a problem. What's more important, I need someone I can trust, who's loyal to me, not the Establishment. How committed are you to the Party?"

The two men looked at each other, taking stock and probing the depth of their convictions. Rudi spoke slowly and distinctly.

"As committed as you are. Does that answer your question, Major Konrad?" and Jan nodded his approval.

"Yes. I had a hunch that if I could save your neck you'd come in useful. Did you know the Baron wanted you in front of the firing squad? It was touch and go, but my friend is very persuasive. He owed me a favour."

Rudi felt cold at the possibility that he might be rotting in his grave by now.

"Thanks," he said with visible relief. "I didn't think that bastard would go as far as that."

"The Baron Hubert isn't fussy who he'll send down for target practice, believe me. We won't see much of him around here. How do you feel about working for me? You'll have to wear this uniform all the time, except when you're on leave. Does that matter to you?" Jan asked.

"No. To get my parole I had to swear allegiance anyway, or stay there, so I signed. But you know that already. What happens if I don't want to get involved with any of this? No offence to you."

"You've committed yourself to wear one uniform or another. If you don't, your record will stand," Jan said softly. They've big plans for a massive network of autobahns to connect every corner of this country. Four million unemployed will be happy to spill their guts for golden promises. They'll need an army just for them. You'll either hold the whip or get whipped yourself. You don't have much choice."

Rudi smiled, a whimsical smile. "I didn't think I had. Just thought I'd ask. I'll work for you, Major."

Jan's thin face registered a satisfied smile.

271

"There's time for you to put on some weight and grow your hair so you don't look like a convict. I'll notify you when and where to get measured for your kit and when to report here. In the meantime you'll get state benefit. Don't go on a long vacation, though. I need you here in about three to four weeks, maybe earlier."

"Can I ask you something, Major?"

"Of course."

"Why do you want me to be loyal to you in particular? Aren't you part of the Establishment?"

Jan Konrad looked thoughtfully at his new assistant. He picked up a small briar pipe, busied himself with filling it and lit a match to set the sweet smelling tobacco alight. The smoke drifted in a wispy cloud towards the open window. He spoke at last.

"There are two kinds of people in the new Order. The barbarous fanatic and men like me, still trying to hang on to a shred of sanity. Like you, Rudi, I was caught up in a situation and thought this was the antidote. You get trapped and can't find your way out. It's easier to stay with something you know. I'm not the adventurous type and they told me I was good at my job, but I'm not proud of what I do. That's the difference between the Baron and me. I bend the rules and need someone I can trust absolutely. If you work for me and they discover what is going on in my office we'll both be hanging in that yard below. Can I trust you?" Jan asked.

He leant back in his chair and observed the younger man sitting at ease in front of his desk, twirling his seaman's cap in a leisurely manner. He saw his face light up and a mischievous grin appear. He looked like a boy ready for a great adventure, Jan thought and hoped Rudi had understood the implications.

"I don't like fanatics," Rudi said matter-of-factly. "Let's bend the rules together, Major."

"Good." Jan too looked happy. "I'll find you a small apartment near here, but while you're in Dettingen I want you to do something for me."

"What might that be?" Rudi asked.

"Keep you ear to the ground. That hothead of a priest there has been put on the hit list. Made a lot of noise until recently. Suddenly he's quiet. Too quiet and that worries me. This Father Dominik reminds me of someone else I knew once. He too is keeping his head down and that's not natural considering all that's going on."

Rudi looked thoughtful. "Why Dettingen in particular? They're small fry, except for the Baron. You must have more important things to deal with."

Major Jan Konrad gazed at the pleasant face opposite him and drew deep from the stem of the briar. "I have," he remarked. "But Dettingen takes priority. It's personal." Jan's eyes followed the trail of white clouds on the horizon. To Rudi he seemed lost in some far-away place and he remembered the gossip Delia used to bring up to the house from her Ma. Janus, the quiet man, they had called him in the village. Hoping to step into Jack Sogar's shoes and into Laura Sogar's bed, some had said. Then the speculation started about the pretty widow having bewitched Father Michael with those misty grey eyes, so full of love he couldn't resist the temptation. And the bombshell when Father Michael had told them all that he was leaving the priesthood to marry the widow. Janus had left one night as quietly as he had arrived.

"Is it because of Mrs Schiller, Janus?" he asked quietly.

The other man's eyes left the cloud he had travelled on to somewhere and mirrored in them was a mountain of love and despair. Then it was gone and Rudi understood. Janus had loved Laura Sogar, still loved her, even now...

"Yes," Jan said softly. "I need to know what's happening there. Whether she and Peter's girl are safe. Something's not as it should be. I don't trust Schiller not to meddle in things he shouldn't. Any more than I trust the priest."

Rudi had experienced loneliness for the first time when they sent him to prison. Then he had lost Delia, although he felt no bitterness towards the girl who had married another man. Maybe their frivolous love had never touched the depth of Janus's feelings for Mrs Schiller. He seemed to harbour no bitterness either, just acceptance.

"Alright, Major Konrad," Rudi said, removing the intimacy that had fleetingly existed between them a moment ago. "It's little enough for saving my neck."

Jan looked relieved. "Thanks. We'll make a good team. One more thing. Stay close to Daniel. You can trust him. We go back to my days at the mission. Daniel was only a boy then. I asked Mrs Schiller to give him a home and I'm indebted to her for that. No-one knows he still writes and keeps me up to date. Tell him you're going to work for me, he'll understand." There was a sudden change in Jan's manner. His face took on a hardness and Rudi saw the professional. Dangerous and determined. "If you betray me to anyone I'll have you put into a place where they perfect the art of torture just for their amusement. And that's no idle threat, Rudi."

It was as if an icy breeze had entered the room and Rudi knew that this man would do precisely what he had promised and felt a chill creep down his spine in spite of the summer heat.

"I understand," he said softly. "No-one else is to know except Daniel. You have my word."

Jan left his chair. As the two men faced each other, the handshake bonded a friendship only death would end.

Chapter 30

MAY 1934

Two weeks after Easter Daniel had gone to the station to fetch Mitch's father. Peter Sogar had changed from an easy-going companion to someone seeking solitude. During his summer vacation he would devote much of the day to working in the garden and visit his friends who felt that life had dealt him a rotten card. On most evenings he would be sitting outside Margharita's caravan, watching his daughter and the boy Ramon engaged in their very serious playtime. Peter did not return to his bed until the early hours of the morning. When Margharita was not there he would get restless after a day or two and left on his motorbike to some unknown destination.

Even Michael could not reach him any more, much to Laura's distress.

"That must be a heavy load you're carrying, son?" Michael had asked Peter three years ago when communication between them took a downward turn.

Peter, his voice listless and tired, had looked into the glass Michael had filled generously with whisky. "How do you carry emptiness, dad? It weighs nothing but feels like a mountain. Let's not talk about me. How's business and my daughter?" tactfully indicating that he was not inclined to reveal whatever it was that was troubling him so greatly.

They did not pry any more after that, pleased that he found solace with the beautiful Romany. Enigmatic, graceful and serene, she was balm to the festering wounds Natasha had inflicted on him.

Daniel parked the van at the side of the house.

"You go in. I'll bring your things." Peter was told.

The times when her son would swing her about until she was dizzy, both of them laughing heartily, were long gone. Laura saw him coming through the gate and as always was shocked by his appearance. Each year he seemed to age ten, get thinner, his brown hair streaked with silver. The walk was measured now, like an old man's who had lost the spring of youth. She ran to meet him and they stood, quietly holding each other, safe in the knowledge that their love would always be there.

"It's good to be home, mum. You look wonderful. I've missed you all so much. How's the monster?" he asked, gently pulling her away from him.

"She's fine. Not growing as fast as she would like, but she's a clever girl," his mother said proudly.

Michael had come to the gate and he too was enfolded in a warm, gentle embrace.

"Hello, dad. Good to see you again. You're looking well. That work out there is keeping you fit."

"It does, Peter. Had a good journey?" he asked and felt again a deep regret at the loss of the easy comradeship they had once known.

"The liner was packed. More people are travelling now and the train was full. There are an awful lot of men in uniforms about."

"Yes," Michael said, a little sadly. "Times have changed a great deal, son. Not for the better, I'm afraid."

Daniel brought the old suitcase and travelling bag.

"I'll get on with some work. Come and see my new lodgings, Peter. I'll stand you a beer."

As they walked to the kitchen Peter looked perplexed. "Where does Daniel live now? Is it far?"

Laura laughed. "Not too far. He's made his home in the 'Loft'. Daniel's twenty five and felt like spreading his wings. Made it look nice up there..." and hesitated, glancing at her husband. "Just like Janus did."

Michael seemed unperturbed at the reference to the man who had lived there once. "Have that beer with Daniel. He's a fine lad and would like that."

"Alright, dad, I will. I'll take my things upstairs and change before I have some coffee, mum. Where's my daughter."

Laura looked at the clock. The time was 1:35 pm.

"Oh, dear," she moaned. "It looks like detention again. You really must speak to her, Michael. That's the third time this week."

Michael smiled at his wife, not at all concerned.

"I will. Our granddaughter just doesn't know how to do things the easy way. Don't worry so, my love."

"What's she doing to get so much detention?" Peter asked, a worried look on his face.

"Our little miss hasn't yet learnt that what was acceptable at the convent doesn't apply anymore. The rules have changed. It's a case of follow my leader and don't ask questions," Michael said contemptuously, then added with a hint of satisfaction. "Our monster can get very temperamental if somebody doesn't give her a satisfactory answer."

"She should be here at two. You'll have time to wash and change, Peter."

They had just sat down when the shout of 'Daddy' sounded from the terrace outside the kitchen. Daniel hastily moved his chair further under the table to avoid the crash of the door. The space was usually kept clear to allow for Mitch's explosive entrances when things had gone badly at school. Today, Peter had taken Daniel's place and Michael was safely out of harm's way on the bench seat under the window. Father and daughter stared at each other for a fraction of a second and then two arms wound themselves around his neck.

"Daddy. You got here at last. I missed you," she mumbled into his neck and there was a brightness in her father's eyes.

"My little monster," he said lovingly. "I missed you too," as he held her tight in his arms.

"Did you come on the big ship, daddy? And did you see sharks and dolphins and albatrosses? How big were the waves? As big as the ship? And what.."

"Sit down, Mitch, and have your lunch. You're late again," her grandmother chided.

"I'll tell you all about the ship later. How do you like school?" her father enquired.

"I 'xpect they told you all 'bout my detentions already?" she asked, ignoring his question.

"No," her father lied. "Nobody's said anything to me about it. Why do you have to stay behind?"

There was a short silence while she chewed furiously at the mushroom omelette, then took a deep breath.

"They're always picking on me, daddy, 'cause I get cross."

"And why do you get cross, Michelle?" her father asked, trying hard not laugh and she glanced at him at the sound of her name which nobody ever used, wondering if he was cross. But he didn't look cross.

"Well...They won't let me play football with the boys an' I've got to play silly games with girls. We can't sing 'Frere Jacques' any more and the big boys an' girls watch us all the time. They tell tales to the teachers about us from the convent. Victor an' Willy won't let me play with Rebecca an' Ruth 'cause they're Jews and we'll get into trouble if we do. An' we don't pray any more, jus' sing that stupid song at assembly an' it's so noisy in the play ground," pausing for breath and proceeding to stuff more food into her mouth.

"But, darling," Laura smiled sweetly at her granddaughter. "You didn't like praying at the convent, so Sister Elisabeth told me."

Michael and Daniel hid their amusement by chewing earnestly, while Peter looked expectantly at his daughter.

"When you're naughty at the convent, Daddy, you have to go an' pray in the chapel," she enlightened her father. "But I didn't really mind. It was so quiet in there an' the Holy Mother always smiled... you know... kind of forgiving... like granma an' granpa." There was a slight pause. "An' Daniel, 'course," and gave him a cheeky grin.

"That's a mighty long list to get mad about," her father said. "Anything else you don't like there?"

"They make you say Heil Hitler all the time. I hate Herr Hitler an' I told that to one of the big girls today. She wanted me to stand to attention jus' because she had that stupid Hitler Youth uniform on. I wouldn't an' she told teacher," forking the last of her food into her mouth.

Peter noticed the look of apprehension pass between Michael, his mother and Daniel. There was a slight note of concern in Michael's voice.

"You've only been there ten days, Mitch. It will not do. We are going to have a long talk about this, young Lady."

"But... granpa..," she wailed. "You don't want me to be a sissy, do you?" and Michael coughed to suppress his laughter, not daring to look at Daniel who was sure to be grinning.

Peter hoped he looked suitably serious, trying to suppress the chuckles that were bursting to be released.

"There are rules in every school, Mitch. If you get a reputation for a trouble maker your grades go down. You did very well at the convent and I'd like them to get better, not worse."

The girl glowered at her father. "It's alright for you, daddy. You don't have big kids yelling at you all the time, telling you who you can play with an' tittle-tattling to the teachers. An' they don't teach things like the sisters did."

Laura gathered the plates together and Daniel observed the worried look on her face.

"Mitch." He spoke so quietly that she shoot him a curious glance. "Do you know what the 'Brown shirts' do with kids that are always in trouble?"

"No," she pouted. "Beat them, I 'xpect," her face lighting up at the sight of Laura's trifles. "Goody, I love granma's trifles, daddy."

"No," Daniel said more forcefully than usual. "They take them away to a special school until they behave themselves."

Mitch was not impressed, licking jelly and cream with great abandon.

"Granpa wouldn't let me go to a place like that," she said with utter conviction.

"Your grandfather couldn't stop them, Mitch. Nobody can, if that's what they wanted to do. Your Headmaster has only to tell them you're a bad influence on the other kids and that's it. Off you go, for months and months, maybe forever."

The spoon that was halfway to her mouth stopped in mid-air. They saw a hint of fear in the child's eyes, something alien to her as she scanned the faces around the table, seeking confirmation that they were joking. Laura felt her heart go out to her granddaughter, but steeled herself and Michael pretended not to notice. Daniel wasn't usually inclined to make cruel speeches as he adored the girl, but somehow they must make her aware of the seriousness of the situation if they were to continue with their plans. Peter concentrated on his dessert, feeling the undercurrent of something that was more than an idle threat to his daughter.

"Granpa," the soft velvet voice spoke next to him, tugging at Michael's heart and his inclination was to tell her not to take any notice, that Daniel was only teasing. "You wouldn't let them take me away, would you?"

It was a small scared sound and he looked down into eyes like Laura's, soft and dark, begging him to say 'no,' but he couldn't.

"Daniel's right, little monster. I couldn't stop them," he said, feeling like a traitor. The child lowered her eyes and quietly finished her trifle.

"They will do that, Mitch," her father said firmly, his thin face showing anger. "I know they can," and four pairs of eyes stared at him, but he would not be drawn any further. "You listen to your grandpa and try to be a good girl. I've brought you a present. It's on my bed."

The tension eased as Mitch scrambled off the bench and raced through the dining room and clattered up the stairs. Michael gazed intently at Peter.

"Are you serious? Could they take her away from us?"

"They can. We'll talk about it later," Peter answered quietly. "She's found him," listening to the clatter of running feet coming down the stairs again.

"Daddy, daddy." Mitch had recovered the full volume of her voice. "Where did you find him. He's beautiful," she shouted, racing down the two steps into the kitchen and throwing her arms about her father, a strange looking doll in her hand.

"In Karun. He's a Persian Prince and his name's Rama," her father said, pleased at his daughter's rapturous expression.

"He's as brown as Ramon and looks a bit like him. Doesn't he, granma?" Mitch asked, holding the doll up for her inspection. It was about 12 inches high, with arms and legs of nut-brown smooth leather. The features were that of a youth, lean and finely contoured. He looked proud, Laura thought, the coal black eyes full of mysticism. Like the gipsy boy, when he gazed into the distance, seeing things no-one else could.

"Yes, he does, darling, except Ramon doesn't wear such beautiful clothes."

The doll's face was topped by black curly hair, thick and glossy, his costume of gold silk sumptuously embroidered with minute pearls and glittering gemstones. Baggy trousers finished just above small pointed gold slippers and a red sash wound itself around the waist. It was the three inch long dagger that fascinated the girl. Sheathed in a leather scabbard, the hilt was encrusted with many coloured jewels. She examined it carefully and Laura hoped the blade was blunt.

"It's much nicer than the one you gave Daniel for his birthday and it's the nicest present I've had from you. Thank you, Daddy," and hugged him fiercely, Prince Rama clutched in her hand. "Princess Evita will marry him and they'll live happily ever after."

Michael and Daniel excused themselves with the rueful comment that some people did have work to do and Laura started to clear the table. Peter watched his daughter unpack her satchel.

"Damn," she said under her breath and lifted the broken slate out of its cardboard cover. "Sorry, granma," Mitch ventured, looking repentant.

"What are you sorry for, young lady? For breaking the slate or swearing? I heard you well enough," her grandmother chided. "Where you learn these words I don't know. I just wish you wouldn't play with boys so much."

"Girls swear too, granma. Kirsten does, and once I heard Sister Elisabeth say that when she sat on her spectacles."

Peter and his mother exchanged glances, trying not to laugh.

"Well, don't let your grandfather hear you say such things." Laura remarked sternly. "I'll get you another slate and then it's into the dining room to do your home work. Be more careful, Mitch. You wouldn't break so many if you didn't throw your satchel about", and left the kitchen.

"Next year you'll have exercise books," her father said gently, ruffling his daughters hair. "Don't use naughty words, your grandma doesn't like it."

"But, daddy. granpa and Daniel say it sometimes," and guileless eyes looked into his. "Not in front of granma, 'course. They wouldn't dare."

"Don't you go and tell her that. They're grown men, but you're only a little girl," her father said and smiled indulgently as she pulled a face.

Laura returned with a brand new writing tablet. "Home work, Mitch. I'll come and check when we've finished the last of our coffee."

Mitch's face held very little enthusiasm, but she thought it prudent not to object and disappeared into the dining room.

Peter Sogar leant on the gate, looked at the neat plots and rows of tender seedlings demanding constant attention. The gravel path to the summer house was lined by spring flowers and behind those the roses his mother had planted over the years. He saw Michael and Daniel working on the large plot of land behind the white building and felt a little envious at the closeness of the two men. How simple life was for them? Growing food, rearing chickens and rabbits, loving each other. Each time he was home, he experienced a greater feeling of isolation. It was not their fault. Why couldn't he bring himself to talk about the despair he concealed from his mother and Michael?... They had always been able to talk freely in the past... Only Margharita understood and he wondered if she would arrive before his leave was over...

The door to the tack room stood wide open. Peter left the gate and walked into the lower part. As always, it was clean and orderly. His motorbike stood at the side of the short flight of stairs to Daniel's place. He fondly stroked the gleaming machine, now ten years old, and did not hear the soft footsteps on the terrace.

"That bike's getting a bit long in the tooth," Daniel's voice reached him from the doorway. "It's alright around here, but it's getting too old to go gallivanting across country."

"She's been a good friend, but maybe it's time to retire her. What about a car?" Peter asked.

"You can hire one for the short time you're here. I drive the van every day," Daniel said. "Your bike has given me a lot of pleasure over the years. There's a sense of freedom, with the wind and rain on your face. A car's not the same."

"Yes, I know. We'll have a look round for one of these while I'm here, before my dear wife bleeds me dry."

Daniel was shocked at the depth of contempt in the other man's voice. "Why don't you get rid of that woman, Peter? She's brought you nothing but grief. Divorce her."

"I can't, Daniel. If I don't agree to what she wants, she'll take Mitch away."

Daniel stared at his friend, a slow fury sweeping over his kind face. "How can that bitch use a child to hang on to you? She doesn't want either of you, just your money. She's no grounds to take Mitch from us."

The smile around Peter's mouth was ironic and lopsided. "You said yourself an hour ago that THEY can do anything. Natasha moves in high circles. All she has to do is whisper into the ears of one of her many lovers that her nasty husband took away her beloved daughter, to a house where Nazism is a dirty word and they'll come to fetch my daughter. Mitch'll be put with a family that's committed to the cause or, God forbid, go to one of their Institutions and finish up like her mother." Peter almost winced at the thought. "The last thing my wife wants is a divorce. I've tried that. Our Fuehrer will tolerate the numerous love affairs of his hangers-on, but won't allow a divorced woman anywhere near him. That would not please Natasha. She needs the respectability of being married and my money to keep up her very expensive life style."

Daniel, shocked to the core of his methodical unruffled soul, did not think that he alone should be made aware of Peter's plight.

"We'll have to tell your mum and dad. It'll be easier on you if you can share all this," Daniel implored, but Peter shook his head.

"No. I've carried this around with me too long. There's no point in worrying them and I want your promise you'll not repeat any of this. I'll have to ask dad to talk to Mitch so she behaves herself in school. By the way, Daniel, do you know where Janus is these days?"

Daniel glanced at Peter, taken aback by the question. "Why do you want to know about Janus?"

"I met him in Munich a couple of times at some function my wife dragged me to. He looked very smart in his SS uniform. He gave me his address and told me if I needed help, to contact him. At the time I didn't know what he meant. Later I wrote to him twice, but the letters were returned as 'not known'. Janus spoke a lot about you and I wondered if you knew where he was."

"You'd better come up, Peter. I told Michael I was going to talk to you about that bike, in case you decided to take off. We know something's bugging you and don't want you going off on a bike that's not safe. Your mum worries about you," and he ran lightly up the stairs to the loft. Peter followed, remembering the times when he used to come up here to spend time with Janus. When Life had been full of fun and adventure. He entered and was pleasantly surprised. Apart from Daniel's personal possessions it still looked the same. The floorboards were polished and the same rug was still looking good. The curtains, covers and tablecloth had changed, but the pot-bellied stove gleamed as it had then. Only the rocking chair was missing, but that had been replaced by two large comfortable leather chairs. Peter sat down in one of them.

"It feels as if Janus is going to come through that door any minute, Daniel. You haven't changed anything."

"I liked the place as it was. It reminded me of him. Is there any particular reason why you want Janus?" Daniel asked.

"Yes. He's the only one I know I can trust to keep my daughter out of the clutches of my wife. He wrote to me about the abuse Mitch was receiving at the hands of Natasha and can verify the truth in case she decides to play dirty."

"I see," Daniel said slowly. "You never mentioned any of that when you brought Mitch here."

"I didn't want to mention him because Janus loved mum, but she married dad and that's why he left. I wanted him left out of this. I just wish I knew where he was. He'll always be my friend."

Peter looked gloomy. Daniel was torn between his friendship with both men and decided that the safety of Mitch was reason enough to break his silence.

"I know where he is," and a glimmer of hope returned to Peter's eyes. "Like you, Peter, I've kept my friendship with Janus a secret from your mum and dad and if you'll respect that I'll do the same for you. You'll have to trust me on this, but I'll get a message to Janus and then it'll be up to him. We'll go to the tavern on Friday night. Nell should know something by then. Now lets have that beer I promised you."

* * *

As he walked out of the clothing store Rudi Waldorf did not feel comfortable, although the black uniform fitted perfectly and he found himself walking tall and straight. He was conscious of a sense of betrayal wearing the clothes many despised and feared. At the terminus in Dettingen, Katrin and Heinz Bulger were on the point of boarding the tram and just stared at him before hurriedly disappearing inside. Squaring his shoulders, Rudi crossed the road to the florist. The young woman, previously chatty and full of good humour, looked scared and he remembered Luther telling him that they might be Jewish. No wonder the uniform frightened her.

He picked a generous bunch of flowers from the display stand, paid and quickly waiked towards the church, where he saw Father Dominik pinning a notice to the board in the entrance.

"Good day, Father Dominik," Rudi greeted him.

"Good day, Rudi. They've kitted you out then, I see," the priest said a little sadly. "Don't forget your God. You may have need of him one day."

"I won't forget, Father, I promise," Rudi answered, thankful that the priest was still speaking to him.

He met Mrs Hunter with her new daughter-in-law Anneliese and to his greeting received only a curt response. Andreas Sachs, the football coach, passed on his bicycle and pretended he hadn't heard his name called out. Mr and Mrs Rademacher stared at Rudi in amazement, silent for once and Hermann, the Barber, standing in the shop doorway talking to Ari Klein, just nodded his head. As Rudi passed Jochen's he found Heini and Annie Wagner cleaning the window of the shoe repair shop.

"So you've joined us then?" beamed Heini and Rudi felt a sudden urge to smash his fist into the other man's face. Annie said nothing, but the expression in her eyes told him enough. The silent condemnation of timid

Annie, unable to sway her husband from his new-found political fervour, was the final insult.

"Yes. I've joined," he said, avoiding Annie's eyes.

He walked not quite so tall to Mrs Henckler's house and let himself in.

* * *

The Converted grew in numbers and the others kept silent, gripped by a fear more terrible than war. There was no cannon fire, no enemy army to face. This foe was in their midst. Father Dominik chose his words carefully to a congregation less numerous than it had been.

Help for Ari, Simon and Moishe had come from an unexpected quarter. Cornelius attended the meeting at the church hall prior to the annual fete. He placed a large package onto the table and looked pleased with himself.

"I have purchased three properties in this village," he announced smugly. "We'll be without our tailor, jewellery repairer and bookshop for a while. Until I can find suitable buyers for these premises they'll remain closed. Mr Gruenewald is attending to the necessary paper work. I hope this pleases everyone here?" looking at the astonished faces around the table.

"Why, pa?" Freddy asked. "If Hubert finds out you're going to be in a heap of trouble."

The Reverend Mother Agnes, Michael and Erika showed concern and Doctor Hoffmann didn't look too happy either. Cornelius smiled a mischievous smile, which made him look like a boy that had been on a great adventure.

"I listened very carefully to what you had in mind to do. While I'm caught between you and your brother, Freddy, I'm still a free man. I've known Agnes here..," and glanced fondly at the Reverend Mother, who smiled sweetly, "for a very long time and her friendship means a great deal to me. I can't keep on travelling and pretend nothing's happening here. The three families are leaving on the 30th of September. They'll take whatever they can and start again in America. We'll deal with any other trouble as and when it arises. Alik Gruenewald is very co-operative."

Mother Agnes, sitting next to Cornelius, placed her hand over his. "Thank you, Cornelius. I'm very grateful for your help. There'll be more people as time goes on, less fortunate than our three families. We need to be ready and I'm glad you've joined us," she said softly, a bright glimmer in her eyes. Cornelius saw it and remembered.

"How could I not, Agnes," he said and charmed her again with his beguiling smile. "After all, we're already compromised by association. I don't suppose the sixteen year old I danced with all evening back in 1890 ever thought it would come to this? It was a wonderful evening, wasn't it?" he asked, ignoring the astonished expressions on the faces of the others.

"I've never forgotten, Cornelius," she said and for a moment in time shed the burden of years and looked young and carefree.

"I fell hopelessly in love with..." she paused for just an instant, "with all of the Officers, as sixteen year old's do. It was my very first ball and Cornelius was my escort," removing her hand from his.

Freddy looked at Erika, who grinned at him.

"You never mentioned it, pa. Why didn't you?"

His father smiled ruefully. "I was already engaged to your mother, son," a tinge of regret in his voice. "Now, Michael. How's the escape route progressing?"

Michael glanced at Freddy, who nodded. "Everything's set up along the way. Around here, my house is the base. We've made access to the loft to hold six people at a time. They can come and go through the meadow and be transported in the van without being seen by anybody. Freddy's banking on his friendship with Olaf Johannsen. We're counting on the captain to make contact with his Dutch friends and that he'll take some as far as Basel himself. It works fine, in theory."

"How will the people know where to contact us?" Doctor Hoffmann asked.

"I think that Ari Klein has his own method of spreading the word through the Rabbi's. He'll not leave without setting up some kind of network. He's already made contact with Josef Schumann in New York," Michael remarked. "They are well established as a legal firm there and Josef is prepared to liaison with Agnes's people in Bern. Daniel does most of the driving anyway. He'll collect information and people without arousing suspicion. All we need is luck and God on our side."

"Amen to that," the Reverend Mother said quietly.

Chapter 31

Ludwig van Beethoven Avenue took trams and people from the Market Square to the river and across the bridge, splitting Bonn into two parts. To the north was the old town, its embankment narrow and the cobbled walk ways worn smooth over the centuries. South of the bridge they called it the promenade. Wide and paved, railings freshly painted, the University and large private properties in secluded gardens lent an air of serene old-world charm. Fashionably dressed crowds strolled at their leisure, seldom venturing beyond the four stone steps that led down to the sandy beach.

The houseboat lay close to the bank of the river. Laura and Michael had been left alone on deck, listening to the squeals and shouts of Victor, Ramon, Kirsten and Mitch. Two rope ladders had been fastened to the rails and dangled in the water below.

The voices of a multitude of swimmers and sunbathers drifted lazily on a soft breeze above the two people, relaxed and soothed by the gentle swaying of the boat. Michael, leaning back in his deck chair, long brown legs stretched out on the ledge, let his eyes wander over the slender figure of his wife, her low-cut bathing suit showing off every curve and the smoothness of honey coloured skin. As always, he felt the wonder and the heat in his blood.

"You're the most enticing woman in that costume. Pity the kids are here," he said, smiling broadly. Laura stirred on her blanket next to the deck chair, shaded her eyes from the bright light and looked up at her husband. "You're not bad yourself, darling. I love those next-to-nothing shorts. They show off your magnificent body. Very provocative," she remarked, a seductive smile hovering about her mouth.

"Be careful, woman. There are two cabins below," he threatened.

"You wouldn't dare," Laura taunted him.

"I'll restrain myself. Got to keep an eye on the kids. When are you going to get that suit wet? You promised to learn to swim, my love. Remember?"

"I did try," she said defensively. "I just don't like the water. It's so cold. But I love being on our boat, looking down at you all." She reached out and ran her hand lightly over the soft downy hairs on his thigh. "You and Mitch like it so much it makes me happy just to watch you enjoy yourselves."

Michael removed his feet from the ledge of the boat, glanced at the children below and with a swift movement joined his wife on the blanket.

"You shouldn't do that, Mrs Schiller. It gives a man ideas," he murmured, his arms holding her tight, his kiss demanding and urgent.

Laura surfaced from the spinning whirl into orbit his kiss always induced and looked lovingly into the bluest eyes she had ever encountered, gently touching his cheek. "I love you too, Mr Schiller."

Neither of them saw the girl peering between the rail of the boat. Mitch, beaming all over her face, descended the ladder again and joined the others in the water.

* * *

All through the year the Hitler Youth had pursued their campaign of harassment of the Catholic Youth Organisations. After months of stoical resistance, cowed and dispirited by bloody battles, they followed their leaders and gave up the fight. The SS Troopers had raided their halls, disbanded them by force and the Hitler Youth reigned supreme.

By order of the Fuehrer, every child at ten years of age was required to join the Hitler Youth, wear the uniform at the twice weekly meetings and events and swear allegiance to Fuehrer and Fatherland.

* * *

In October Daniel made his weekly visit to the tavern. Nell greeted him affectionately.

"There's a message from our friend. You're to come here tomorrow night. He'll be waiting in the back parlour. Didn't want to spoil your fun tonight," Nell said, a cheeky look on her face as she pulled Daniel a pint. She had got a little plumper over the years. It suited her and her acid humour had also increased. Five years ago Nell had finally given Josh the boot after finding him in bed with one of the barmaids. She had put up with his excursions to the attic, but to find him in her own bed had been too much. She had paid him off, a very handsome sum for the likes of Josh who had done less and less in the Tavern, except sit and debate the political situation with the ever increasing number of hoodlums and thugs of the new Party. Nell had cleared all of them out and her house became as respectable as anything north of the bridge was deemed to be. At first she had indulged in fleeting affairs to soothe her pride, but never let it interfere with business or her heart. That belonged to Captain Olaf. He had walked in one evening and Nell's knees had turned to jelly. He was a giant of a man, unruly black hair and beard and a voice as booming as the big bell on a Sunday morning. Except, she knew he could whisper words of love as sweetly as any lover that ever walked the earth. The black eyes of Captain Olaf would light up at the sight of her and always her heart fluttered like a butterfly on the wind.

"Alright, Nell," Daniel said quietly. "I'll be here. Wonder what's up? Do you know?"

She patted her fair hair, shook her head and glanced warningly at the two SS men that had walked into the bar. Nell did not mind the quiet ones. They would sit and talk, pay for their drinks, asking her to have one too and usually went off with one of the barmaids. She was not in the business of judging anybody's morals, but had no intention of letting her tavern get a reputation as a brothel.

The handsome face of the woman looked thoughtful.

"I don't know, Danny. Janus sent word for you to be here," she said softly. "All I know is that the Captain's coming as well. I gave him your message and he agreed. I think he's curious. Are you going to see Gerda later?" she asked and it was Daniel's turn to look cheeky.

"What do you think I come here for? She'll do me nicely for now, thanks," winking at the black-haired, well-endowed girl collecting the beer for the two SS men.

"See you later, sweetheart. Hope you're in a good mood?" Daniel whispered into her ear.

"Cheeky sod," she whispered affectionately. She liked Danny. He was kind and gentle and they laughed a lot in between drinking wine and making love. Yes, Danny was alright. Pity he had his mind set on marrying that prissy school girl he talked about sometimes. Gerda was generous by nature and hoped they would be happy. She would miss him when the time came. A fella having fun before marriage was one thing, but not after. A girl had to have some pride...

* * *

Jan and Rudi walked the length of the embankment, not wishing to leave the Mercedes in the vicinity of the tavern. Jan had dressed in corduroy trousers, thick seaman's sweater and a cap to hide his distinctive hair. In the loose leather jacket he could have passed for any sailor on a spree. He wondered if the Captain was going to turn up. Daniel and Nell had been acting as mediators between two groups of people who could not meet and were to be the vital link in the operation. Next year the exodus would really begin. So far it had been relatively easy to get everyone away on ships and trains, but the screws were being tightened day by day by the authorities.

"How are Lotti and the boys, Jan?" Rudi asked, disturbing the thoughts of his friend. "Have they persuaded her to come to the Inter-School sports tomorrow?"

Jan shook his head. "No. She won't come here, although it's a big day for Alex. He was lucky to make it to the final selection in the baseball team. Lotti doesn't like sports much," Jan said, a slight note of regret creeping into his voice.

"Why did she never come back to see Nell? She always asks about Lotti and the boys."

"I don't know, Rudi. I've asked her and offered to bring her and the boys over, but she always says no. I can't force her."

"It's a shame," Rudi remarked. "Nell's a good friend to have. She'd spoil the kids rotten."

They turned into the high archway leading to the back of the tavern and Nell's parlour. The shutters were tightly closed, only a chink of light showing at the edges. As always on his rare visits here, Jan glanced at the metal fire escape and to the attic above, wondering if Daniel went up there as he himself had done so many years ago. Poor Lotti. How different life had been then, still full of hope and foolish expectations. None of them had worked out as he planned. Had they for Lotti? They lived as man and wife and yet had remained strangers in many ways. She had the house and their sons and he was immersed in his work, but he did try and spend as much time as possible with all of them.

Jan knocked on the stout back door and was startled when it was opened by a huge figure in Captain's uniform.

"Come in," the booming voice invited them. "I'm Captain Johannsen. You must be Janus," and stretched out an enormous hand.

The slim fingers of Jan almost disappeared in the grip of the giant fist.

"I am. Glad you could make it. This is Rudi, my driver and my friend."

Once again the smaller hand of the slighter built man lost itself in a hearty shake.

"Nice to meet you, young fellow. Is he your boss?" jerking a massive thumb towards Jan.

Rudi nodded, flexing his fingers. "He is."

The Captain sank into the biggest armchair Rudi had ever seen. "Sit down. Nell's left us plenty of drinks and some food in case you're hungry."

Rudi poured the beer into glasses and sat next to Jan on the sofa. The Captain's steady gaze studied both of them for a moment.

"What can I do for you, Janus? I gather it was you that wanted to see me on some urgent matter?"

Jan took another swallow of beer. "It was," he said calmly. "How's your political affiliation?"

The dark eyes of the Captain looked hard at the other man, then he smiled. "Now that isn't something I care to discuss with a stranger. I wear the badge, as you can see," he said softly, but Jan felt that there was menace in the gentle voice. He nodded in agreement.

"A wise decision. But unfortunately we have to talk about it before we go any further." Jan looked at his watch. "Where's Daniel got to? I want him here before we discuss anything. Your boat is berthed in Cologne, I believe, Captain?"

"That's right, together with a dozen other pleasure steamers. We go on scheduled trips up and down the Rhine. It's all in the timetable, but I'm sure you know that?"

"I do, as a matter of fact. Rudi's done his homework," Jan answered.

"You're well known on the river, Captain," Rudi remarked. "And respected, but no-one knows about your political persuasions. Your engineer and second mate do, but wouldn't talk about yours or theirs. That can only mean one thing."

"And what's that, young fellow?" the Captain asked softly and Jan could feel again the menace in the gentle vibration.

Rudi had felt it too, but it was too late now to retract what had been said. "That you don't share the same opinions as your son Theo. Do you?"

Jan noted with satisfaction that the mention of Theo's beliefs disturbed the large man and was not surprised by the next question.

"Who are you?" he asked, looking at Jan with some suspicion. "What right do you have to snoop around in our private lives? I've a good mind to leave before I get mad," and rose out of his chair to tower over Jan and Rudi.

"I'm sorry, Captain Johannsen. It was necessary. Your son's views are well known at the Academy. He's in with the right people and should go far, but we're not sure about yours and we need to know."

Jan's cool voice and steady gaze seemed to have the desired effect. The Captain sat down, asking again, "Who are you?"

"Who I am and what I do is not relevant just now. I've known Nell for a good many years. We're friends and trust each other." He noted Captain Johannsen's eyes narrow at the mention of Nell. "We're no more than friends, Captain," Jan said calmly.

At the knock on the door Rudi leapt up and admitted Daniel, a little out of breath.

"Sorry I'm late. I didn't want to start up the motorbike and rode here on the bicycle. It took longer than I thought. I haven't been on a pedal bike for years and must be getting old." He shook hands with Jan and Rudi. "Good to see you again. Have you got acquainted with Captain Olaf?"

"Sort of. Not very successfully," Jan informed Daniel.

"Good evening, Captain Olaf. I'm glad you could come," Daniel held out his hand to the big man, who shook it vigorously. He remembered Daniel very well. He had come with the Schillers on the annual works outings Freddy gave his people in the summer. Whatever the boy had been before he came to live with them, Michael and Laura had done a good job of raising him. He also recalled that lately Daniel had come with Freddy, Mrs Behrens and the Schillers when they had toasted the legendary rock of the Lorelei and always there had been a lot of talk about politics in the privacy of his cabin.

"What did you tell them about me, boy?" he boomed at Daniel.

"Nothing. It was Mrs Behrens and the Baron's idea to get you here and put our proposition to you. You made your dislike of the Nazis very clear on that cruise in July. I'm only the messenger boy, Captain Olaf."

The dark eyes of the giant contemplated Daniel in a new light. There was a strength in the pleasant face he had not noticed before. The boy was like Michael. Quiet, resolute and dependable.

"And what is it that you're to put to me?"

292

Daniel looked at Jan, who nodded and took the beer Rudi handed him. He sat down. "Tell him," Jan ordered.

"Captain Olaf. For what we have in mind we need your ship and the help of some bargee's who can be trusted. The operation will be dangerous. You could lose your ship and your life. We all could."

The Captain grasped that he was invited to take part in a deadly game. "Tell me about it."

Daniel did so, without revealing the names of the major players.

"What about these two?" the Captain enquired, pointing a huge finger in the direction of Jan and Rudi.

"You don't need to know about them. It's safer that way. Janus and Rudi will supply the names and addresses of people on the list to be arrested, where and when to pick them up. We can't expect them to do any more for us."

Olaf Johannsen had already guessed at the status of the two men. "You're with THEM, aren't you?" and Jan knew it was futile to deny the truth.

"Yes," he said quietly. We're all on the same trip. If the boat sinks we'll go down with it."

Captain Olaf took a great gulp of beer "And it's my ship," he chuckled and took another gulp. "Janus. I'll be happy to join your rescue mission. Life has become tedious. It'll give me great satisfaction to outwit that Nazi son of mine. I think we can count on three of my friends who'll take some of your people on board when they lay-up for the night just before the Rock. How does Nell fit into all this?"

"This is where messages come to from Rudi and me to be relayed and acted on. She'll keep you informed. You'll have to work out your own plan of communication. My job is to move people," Daniel told the big man. He liked him. Probably about Michael's age, a wartime sailor who would know how to outrun the enemy. The face, weathered by sun and water, the hawk-like nose, gave him the appearance of a Greek god, the luxurious beard hiding a strong and stubborn jawline. Yes, next to Michael and Janus he would trust this man with his life.

Jan emptied his glass. "Rumour has it that soon all co-habitation with a Jewish man or woman, including marriage, will be a criminal offence. That's going to put a lot of people under pressure to leave." Jan checked his watch. "Think about this very carefully, Captain. Talk to Nell and Daniel. Rudi will keep in touch as I can't afford to be recognised. It's his hometown

293

and nobody'll take much notice where he goes. I've got to get back. Both my sons are in the inter-school competitions in the morning and I've got to get them here on time."

He rose and so did Captain Olaf. Jan was not a small man, but next to the bulk of Olaf Johannsen he seemed boyish.

"Goodbye, Captain Johannsen. Perhaps we'll meet again some time." He held out his hand.

"Goodbye.. er.. Janus. I'll make my decision and tell Nell to pass it on," holding Jan's hand in a grip of iron. "Are there more like you?" he asked.

"Quite a few, Captain. As Nell seems to be busy, give her my love and my apologies. Tell her we're going to thrash Bonn United. Goodnight, Daniel."

Rudi shook hands with the Captain and felt as if his wrist was wrenched from its socket. "Goodbye, Captain Johannsen. It's been a pleasure meeting you. Goodnight Daniel."

They let themselves out and the Captain settled his bulk into the armchair. "Open another bottle, boy. What have I let myself in for? he asked Daniel. "I hope you know what you're doing?"

* * *

The University had donated the vast sports grounds to the citizens of Bonn. Surrounding the baseball field were running tracks and on the periphery grassy banks to hold the spectators.

Jan, Rudi and Seb Inkmeyer took their places with the Cologne contingent on one side of the track, while the Bonn crowd sat on the bank opposite. Sunday morning was sunny, but pleasantly breezy. The dignitaries of schools, university and town council, many in brown and black uniforms, sat in the newly erected grandstand. At the far end the competing teams gathered around the clubhouse and changing rooms. The youngest of the competitors were to start the games.

"Alex should do well. He's a pretty good catcher. Put in hours of practice," Jan told Seb. "Toni isn't bothered whether he wins or loses the race. That boy doesn't like sport at all."

Seb, his fair hair ruffled in the breeze, shaded his eyes against the sun. "Takes after his mother, Jan. In three years he'll have to join the Hitler Youth and they'll make him run like hell. Sport takes priority over education and

294

religion," Seb replied, his voice heavy with sarcasm. "At least my godson is trying. Alex'll do well because he wants to succeed, like his father," and eyes like the bluest summer sky twinkled with good humour. Jan smiled, happy to see Seb out of uniform, relaxing for a change. He too felt good this morning, comfortable in slacks and sports shirt. They clapped as excitedly as everyone else when the visiting team of the under tens came marching on the field.

"There's Toni," Rudi told Jan. "He's number six."

The home team followed. Two rows of boys and girls lined up. The battle of the school heats had been fought all through the Summer and these were the best. The pride of each town was at stake. Cologne versus Bonn.

The spectators were noisy, clapping and whistling, shouting to their favourites. The starter gun announced the first race. Jan watched his youngest son finish second and felt proud.

"He's done well, Seb. Better than I expected."

The commentator relayed the name of the winner from the Cologne team when the girls lined up at the starting blocks. The gun cracked again and for fifty metres legs and arms were flying like windmills and the Bonner crowd cheered as the girl with the honey coloured hair romped home. The commentator declared Mitch Sogar the winner from the home team.

Jan sat straight and still.

"Pass me your binoculars, Seb," and held out his hand. Seb, a puzzled look on his face at the urgency of the request, handed them over. Rudi too had heard the name and made the connection. He watched as Jan scanned the crowd on the opposite bank, saw the binoculars being focussed on something and knew that Jan had found them.

Jan felt the tremor in his hands and gripped the black metal casing so tight his knuckles showed white. The blonde woman was held in a close embrace by the man at her side, pure joy making her look radiant and more beautiful than he remembered her. He felt the band of pain in his chest threatening to extinguish the breath in his body. He knew that the love he had for Laura had not faded with time and would never leave him. After the pain there came a deep sadness as he watched Michael Schiller kiss his wife.

Still curious, Seb asked, "Have you found what you were looking for?"

"No," Jan said quietly. "I thought I recognised somebody but was mistaken," and gave him back the binoculars, avoiding Rudi's eyes.

Chapter 32

MARCH 1936

He had woken earlier than usual this morning. It was going to be a very special day. Sleep had been intermittent in anticipation of the momentous events that would unfold during the day.

The pyjama-clad figure stood in front of the wash basin in his bathroom and delicately trimmed the square patch of dark hair between nose and upper lip. The lank black hair hung in untidy strands about his forehead. The flat planes of the face, skin stretched tight across a nondescript bone structure, were immobile and showed no emotion. Only the dark eyes, darting about as if triggered by some mechanism within the average sized body, shone with fanatical elation.

It had been a turbulent three years since he had stood on the podium to receive his first accolade. From Corporal to Chancellor of a nation was no mean achievement.

It had been a long wait for Paul von Hindenburg to die. Eighteen long months. Too old, too sick, the venerated gallant Chancellor had no choice but to hand over the reigns to young blood.

He had given the old warhorse a splendid send-off for the sake of the nation and the military. He could not afford to antagonise the Army Generals who had idolized the old fool. What did they know apart from honour and loyalty to the Prussian Monarchy? Well...They too had faded into obscurity and he was Chancellor Adolf Hitler. Supreme Ruler of the country and the people. They had shouted 'Hail Caesar' in Roman times...But today the people would roar his name louder than that...He could hear it already...Heil Hitler...Heil Hitler...

He attended to his ablutions with meticulous careful gestures. At noon precisely he would step onto the podium at the Kroll Opera House and deliver the news of his triumph to the Faithful...

The Fuehrer, still in his pyjamas, was ready to test the water. The neutrality and demilitarization under the Treaty of Locarno had long been a thorn in his flesh. This morning he would finally pull it out...

Seven minutes later he lifted the receiver off the cradle and gave the order to march into the Rhineland to liberate its people...

On the 7th of March the natives of Dettingen stood in clusters on the streets, bemused, shocked or elated at the incessant news broadcast coming over the air. Steel-helmeted cavalry and troops, in place since early dawn at strategic points along the border and bridges of the region, had encountered no opposition from the token French Occupation Force. The population of Cologne, Dusseldorf, Aachen and Koblenz had received their liberators with flowers and high hopes.

Martha Henckler felt the need to be with someone at this momentous time and joined the Schillers, Erika Behrens and Katrin outside Laura's house.

"Can anybody tell me why we had to be liberated?" she asked no-one in particular.

Michael, in his working clothes, hair awry from turning over the soil before planting, forced a weak smile. "Ours is not to reason why, Martha. Let's hope our French protectors won't start firing live bullets."

"Do you think they'll fight, Michael?" Erika asked.

"It depends on how much they value the treaty which kept us neutral since the last war. They're not in a position to defend the region. This is only a testing manoeuvre. Our Fuehrer has aspirations to own the world."

"Where else could he send the troops to?" Katrin enquired, a puzzled look on her face.

"To start with, wherever there are Germans living in large numbers. He'll weed out the inferior populace and make room for us to go forth and multiply."

The sarcasm was not lost on his wife, Erika or Martha, but Katrin still looked bewildered. "But what's the purpose, Michael? Who wants to 'up sticks' and go and live in somebody else's land?"

Michael seemed somewhat amused by her naiveti, but his voice was kind.

"You'll have to ask Heinz to explain the manifesto of the Nazi Party to you. There's a fat chapter on Lebensraum. That means throwing out the natives to make room for the new settlers. The Americans did it with the Red Indians, remember? They took their reservations and gave the land to the Whites. The Indians got pushed out. Where are they now?" he asked.

"He's right, Katrin," Laura said gently. "They came to liberate us this morning and it's the French who'll have to go, or fight. They won't do that."

297

"Ladies! Liberation's all very well, but it won't get the soil dug over," Michael said. "Drop in tonight, Erika. Try and get hold of Freddy."

Erika nodded and Laura excused herself to see to lunch. Martha Henckler hesitated as Michael turned into the drive to go back to the digging.

"Michael!" she called and he stopped. "Can I talk to you for a minute? It's important."

He wondered what Martha had to discuss that was so urgent.

"Come into the summerhouse," he said, and led the way. "Sit down, Martha. What can I do for you?" he asked, curious now.

Martha settled herself into a chair while Michael sank into the corner of the settee.

"It's more of what I could do for you, if you'll let me."

He gazed at the woman who would be in her early forties, but the way she dressed and scraped back the straight brown hair she looked older than Laura. Only when she talked about Rudi or Rosalie her thin face became animated and soft. His curiosity rose even further.

"And what would that be, Martha?" he asked, observing the nervous twisting of her hands.

"It's about the people that come to stay in your house. The ones Daniel takes away in the van before it gets light in the mornings. Like today," Martha said softly and noted that Michael had not moved, but glimpsed a flicker of fear in his eyes. Just for a moment and then they assumed their usual calm. "Don't worry, Michael. I'm not going to inform on you."

"How long have you known?" he asked quietly.

"I miss Rudi a lot. Since he left I don't sleep too well and stand for hours at my bedroom window, looking out over your garden and the orchard. The moon makes pretty patterns on the trees and I try to figure out what life is all about. It's beautiful when the snow covers everything. That's when I see the people running from the orchard into your house."

Michael took a long hard look into the light brown eyes that held his in a steady gaze. "You know what it means if we're found out? I don't think you should concern yourself with what goes on here, Martha."

"But I want to. I've got a reputation for a sharp-tongued bitch, as you very well know," and Michael had to smile at the apt description Martha had given of herself. "Most people don't like me very much. They're afraid of me and that makes friends hard to come by. It leaves me plenty of time to keep me well informed of what's happening in this country. I liked Rudi because we could talk. He wasn't afraid of me and your Mitch isn't either, Michael." She smiled and he was surprised, as she rarely lost the severity permanently displayed on her face. "I don't like what's going on," Martha continued. "Rosalie tells me a lot about what's been said up at the house when the old Baron isn't there. I thought it could come in useful to you and Baron Freddy. Else Gratt has given up on Luther and is now a passionate Fascist. She and the new headmaster's wife are the biggest informers in this place. For some reason they both like talking to me about the Party and what they find out when they sweet-talk the kids and their mamas. They trust me because I had Rudi staying with me and think I'm sympathetic. I want no part in what you're doing here, although I admire your courage," she said, looking intently at the man sitting quietly in his corner, a wary expression in the very blue eyes. "I always did, Michael. What I thought was that it was time to have a spy in the enemy camp. Maybe I can find out something that can be useful to you."

Michael had listened and was surprised at the composure with which she put herself at their disposal, fully aware of the risks. He was convinced of her desire to do something, be of use, even if that meant running the gauntlet with the enemy.

"What about Rosalie? Will you tell her about us?"

"Oh, no, Michael. All I want her to do is listen and pass it on as gossip. She knows I'm a busy-body and won't even notice she's given me information," Martha said gleefully. "I'll just be nosier than usual. Rosalie's not the stuff spies are made of."

"But you are?" Michael asked, still not convinced that this was a good idea.

"Of course. I have a good memory, listen to people and know when to keep my mouth shut," Martha said, grinning hugely. In all the years he had known her Michael had never seen her do that and thought she looked younger somehow. As if she had found a purpose for living and then she looked serious again. "I don't have anybody to care for other than Rosalie and she's settled up there. I'd rather go down with you and know I've done something other than sit around wishing I had."

He remembered the night when he had told Laura the same thing in this very room. 'He would rather die than do nothing' he had said and admired the woman sitting so calmly opposite him. They had lived as neighbours for twelve years and he had known her long before that, and yet, he didn't know her at all. Under that abrasive veneer, there was a caring, vulnerable soul. Rudi had found it and Mitch was never wrong in her response to people. She would be polite to most of them, but she gave her affection only to someone she trusted implicitly. And she was always at ease with Martha, as much as she was with Margharita. He made up his mind. The voice that reached the woman quietly waiting was as she remembered it from his years as a priest. Strong and firm.

"I can't deny or confirm what you've seen, Martha. What you know is already too much for our safety," he said. "You must realise that when the French troops move out, this region will be completely taken over by the Establishment. They've had to tread softly so far, but now there's nothing to stop them from carrying out the purges that have been going on elsewhere."

"They'll not waste any time," Martha said quietly. "That place Rudi's working at in Cologne is just waiting to go into action."

"Did he tell you that?" Michael asked and wondered how close Martha and Rudi had become while he had stayed at her house.

"Not in so many words. It was mentioned in confidence." She did not elaborate further, nor did Michael press the matter.

"There's a blacklist of people that stretches for miles. I'm on it, so's Freddy, possibly Erika. What we've seen so far is kid's play to what'll happen when the big guns arrive. Like Hubert on the Hill. Think carefully before you commit yourself," Michael cautioned. "I can't advise you on my own. If you're still of the same mind come over tonight. Erika and Freddy'll be there, Doc Hoffmann and maybe Luther. After nine, Mitch'll be in bed then. If you come round the back you'll find us in the dining room."

Michael stood up, still as tall and erect, his blue eyes holding hers for what seemed an eternity and she was again reminded of the priest looking down at them from the pulpit. He had only changed the clothes he wore, the man was still there. A little grey in the wavy brown hair now, his face still thin, creased around the eyes from working in the sun. It was a contented face. He had as much grace in gardening clothes than he had when he had worn the cassock. Martha rose too, stretching out her hand and he clasped it in a firm grip.

"Thanks, Michael." She had almost addressed him as Father. "I'll be there. I hope Daniel has delivered them safely."

"I hope so too, Martha."

As he watched her walk up the path and turn left into the drive he could not help but wonder that there was much more to Martha Henckler than her appearance and reputation conveyed and prayed silently that he had made the right decision.

Chapter 33

The little wooden house nestling in the fork of the huge cherry tree needed a spring clean. Mitch Sogar, in vest, dungarees and wellingtons, had diligently scrubbed the inside of her summer residence to expel the temporary visitors that had made their home there over the winter, gently brushing the assortment of little creatures into the bark of the tree. She had no wish to drown them.

At nearly nine years of age she had well formed limbs, a little on the small side, much to her annoyance. Still given to occasional bursts of demonic fury, she would, however, be full of sweet repentance afterwards, accepting tasks given to her as punishment with a grace which always amazed her grandfather. Devoid of envy or malice, her one secret desire was to be as tall as Kirsten, her only girl companion. Kirsten had long legs, although Mitch considered hers a better shape. It irked her to have to look up to her friend now and it was infuriating to watch the silly girl make goo-goo-eyes at Ramon whenever he came to stay with his mother and sister in the meadow. Why couldn't she swoon over Victor? He'd like that. The house had to be spick and span before Ramon got here...

"Can I paint it now, granpa?" she called to the man bent over the gooseberry hedge below. Michael and Daniel had divided sections of the garden with fruit bearing bushes planted close together and fruit was picked from either side of the long hedges. It had been Daniel's idea.

Michael Schiller looked up at his granddaughter, a generous smile on his lips at her foolish question.

"Not until it's dry, sweetheart. Maybe tomorrow, if it doesn't rain."

"Alright, granpa," Mitch said amiably, her legs dangling from the floor of the tree house, oblivious of the slow trickles of water finding their way through the cracks. She watched her grandfather pruning the prickly hedge and felt a deep warm love inside of her. He always reminded her of Jesus. Gentle, but strong. So beautiful, and when he looked at her with his lovely blue eyes she saw only love. He never scolded. Granma did that, although she wasn't ever really angry, just cross, which wasn't the same thing...Daddy was coming home in a few weeks and maybe he was going to stay...Granma worried about him...She had told granpa that Mr Ryker had written a letter and he was worried too...Daddy was too fond of the whisky, he had said in the letter and thought it was time for him to come home...They had stopped talking about it when she had come into the kitchen...granpa drank whisky every night, but only a little bit in his glass...He had said too much of the stuff addled the brain and ruined the liver...Mitch fervently hoped that her father was not addling his brain, as she was sure it must be very painful...

From the height of the tree house she could see the orderly plots, the hothouse behind the summer house in the middle of the garden, the lawn next to it, the freshly hoed strawberry rows and the meadow beyond...

Mrs Cros would soon be here, parking the caravan by the stream and then she would play with little Rosita, ride the big horse with granpa and Ramon would come...They would go fishing, rabbit hunting and catch butterflies...He would tell her all about the silly things they got up to in that boys school his mother had sent him to...She wished she could go there too...

Looking up into the crown of the huge tree she softly sang 'Frere Jacques', wondering how tall Ramon had grown in a year and if he had changed much...She would watch him standing in the middle of the stream, his brown skin glistening in the sunlight, his face just like Prince Rama's... Proud and haughty...But then, Ramon was a prince of the Romanies and should be looking like that...

Mitch felt a deep sadness that she couldn't tell him of the strangers hiding in the hay loft, but she had promised granpa never to tell anyone...

* * *

It was Easter Saturday. Erika and Freddy were invited to dinner at Laura's. Mitch and Chrissy had been installed at Katrin's, the usual procedure if there was business to be discussed at Michael's house. Katrin and Heinz Bulger were willing child minders, vaguely aware of something important happening at number 10, but felt reasonably safe in their ignorance.

Laura had almost finished dressing when Michael walked into the bedroom. The soft wool dress in meridian blue draped itself in gentle folds around her slim body. He stood behind her and as their eyes met in the mirror she could see the admiration reflected in her husband's, felt his arms tightening about her and the warm glow of love plainly visible on his face.

"You get more desirable every year, Mrs Schiller," he murmured into her ear and his kiss had lost none of its ardour over the years.

The dinner was a pleasant affair and only when they had settled themselves comfortably in the sitting room did Daniel reveal the latest update.

"I've made a list of everyone that's gone up the river since last year. A total of seventy eight people have been transported one way or another and reached Switzerland. That's our own people as well as Jews. I met Rudi last night and he says it'll be hotting up soon. We've got fourteen more names already."

Freddy stretched out his wooden leg to be more comfortable in his chair.

"It's a pity we can't extend this route to take more people," he said quietly. Erika and Laura exchanged a worried glance.

"No, Freddy. We can't. This is as much as we can handle for the time being." Erika's voice was firm and Freddy conceded.

"You're right, of course. It was just wishful thinking."

Michael looked thoughtful, a frown creasing his forehead. "How does Rudi get all this information, Daniel?"

Four pairs of eyes looked expectantly at Daniel.

"He's in the right place," he answered casually, while frantically formulating what he hoped would be a satisfactory explanation to four highly intelligent people. "He has access to everything that comes into that office. They've got their spies in every street, every apartment block and office and they send in their reports by the sack full. He can only select so many. It's his way of depriving the system of a few more victims, or more to the point, Baron Hubert."

"What about his boss?" Michael insisted, only partially convinced "Isn't he likely to get suspicious?"

"Shouldn't think so," Daniel answered carefully. "He's a lazy fat slob. Likes to booze and spends a lot of time in the brothel they call the Officer's Club. Don't worry about him. Rudi's got everything under control," he said, chuckling to himself at the unflattering description of Jan Konrad.

* * *

The Fuehrer's birthday on the 20th of April was also the day when promotions were made official. Major Jan Konrad had received his

304

invitation to the party upstairs to be held in two day's time. Henceforth it would be Colonel Jan Konrad. He viewed the white embossed card with some distaste, but knew he couldn't afford to turn this one down, intending to leave as soon as was decently possible. Parties at the club were not to his taste, nor was the company.

Seb Inkmeyer, having acknowledged Rudi and the junior SS soldier at their desk, knocked and entered Jan's office.

"Morning, Jan," Seb's greeting was subdued and Jan looked sharply at the tall, fair-haired man.

"Morning, Seb. If it's not urgent, leave me to get on with my work," his hand waving over a stack of papers in front of him.

"Its urgent. I need a favour, Jan."

Jan leant back in his chair, lit his pipe and decided to give his friend his full attention. "Sit down. I owe you one, anyway."

Seb pulled up a chair and opened his black attache case, took out some documents and placed them in front of Jan.

"I had to evict a Jewish couple from their house in Bruehl a few days ago. They've taken them into custody and charged them with being subversives. There's no chance of them getting out of that. You know what'll happen." Seb sounded agitated.

"We all know what they do with them, Seb. Except the population. The propaganda machine is a very potent weapon in the hands of Doctor Goebbels. Go on."

"I've applied to rent the house for the time being. It's a nice villa, secluded, well furnished and fitting for a Colonel."

"Ah... you too? Congratulations, Seb. What has renting a villa from a dispossessed Jew got to do with me? It's not my Department," Jan remarked, somewhat curious.

"But that is." Colonel Seb Inkmeyer pointed to the papers on Jan's desk, who picked them up, briefly scanning two sets of birth certificates. Both female. The first listed Hanna Ulm, German, 26, born in Dresden. The second was for Rebecca Singer, Jewish, 27, born in Berlin.

Jan hastily glanced through the rest and stared at Seb Inkmeyer. "Was the name of the couple you arrested Singer by any chance?"

The Colonel nodded. "That was very astute. Yes, it was. You'll have their files in one of your piles there. On the morning of the arrest the two solders with me searched the house, but I made the inspection of the cellar myself

305

and found the woman, one Rebecca Singer, hiding in a makeshift cupboard. I told her to stay there and that I'd be back later. Alone."

"And you went back? Why? I never took you for a fool, Seb."

"She's pregnant." Seb said quietly. "They took her husband and she doesn't know where he is. He told her to get to her parents if anything should happen to him and that's what she did. She daren't go out in case they want her as well. I just can't let them take her, Jan."

"And what in God's name am I suppose to do about that?"

"It's simple. This morning they found Hanna Ulm, better known as Rita Klein, in the river. She was a second rate prostitute, well known in the district. Somebody slit her throat last night. My job was to find out if she had any relatives to send the body to and seal up the apartment. I couldn't find a damned thing relating to Rita Klein. That didn't make sense, so I went through it again and found that lot taped underneath the dressing table drawer. She evidently didn't want anybody to know who she was. Maybe because of her family. And I didn't hand them in. I want you to do a swap, Jan. Hanna Ulm, German, for Rebecca Singer, Deceased."

"You're out of your mind, Seb. The woman's pregnant. She'll need somewhere to live and draw state benefit. The whole thing's crazy. You're crazy."

"That's why I'm renting the villa. Hanna Ulm will be my housekeeper and everybody'll think the kid's mine. I've no commitments and she'll be safe in that house with me. Will you do it, Jan?"

Colonel Jan Konrad looked at the man sitting quite calmly on the other side of his desk asking for the impossible. Except Jan knew it wasn't. It was the height of foolishness.

"Why do you have to complicate my life with this? I could denounce you for treason," he remonstrated.

"But you won't," Seb replied quietly. "I didn't want to know your motives for saving Rudi from the firing squad. You're not bent, so it couldn't have been that, but you did have a reason, Jan. I'm asking you to let this one go. She's lost her husband and her parents. I wasn't responsible for the husband, but I did have orders to arrest Doctor Gerber and his wife."

Jan did not betray his uneasiness at the mention of Rudi and wondered how much Seb knew or just surmised. Their work did not overlap. Seb was a specialist in surveillance and dealt with any unusual circumstances, both politically and homicidal, while he himself was bogged down by information and names. Sifting through the reports that were coming in day by day on the so-called enemies of the Reich. Saving some and throwing others to the wolves. Both of them doing nasty work in their own field and maybe Seb was making amends in his own way. The tentative friendship they had formed when Seb arrived here was of an intellectual kind, born out of the need to bond with another human being of a compatible temperament and both of them had buried their past a long time ago. It was never mentioned. Seb liked to come to the house where Lotti fussed over him, where they played chess and cards, delighting in being honorary godfather to Alex, forming an affectionate friendship with the boy. He and Seb were loners, uniquely self contained, content to enjoy a friendship that did not encroach on their innermost, well protected privacy, although by the very nature of this work he was fully aware of Seb's former life.

"I didn't know things like that bothered you. Always the cool and efficient policeman. Why has this got to you, Seb?" Jan asked.

"I don't know." Seb looked unsure of himself. "Maybe it's because she's carrying a new life. Save this one for me, Jan," he begged.

As far as Jan was concerned, the matter was already settled. Had he not himself pleaded for Rudi? Not only acting on instinct that the youth might be useful one day, but also to rescue his conscience before it dropped irretrievably down the dark chute to hell.

The two men sat for a long time, wrapped in their own thoughts. On the other side of the door telephone bells shrilled, voices drifted faintly into the stillness of the office. Colonel Jan Konrad finally spoke.

"Alright, Seb. If you get into trouble over this I don't want to know. Take these..." He handed Seb the birth certificate of the woman called Hanna Ulm. "We'll bury the prostitute as Rebecca Singer, Jewess. I'll change the photographs on the ID's. They're not dissimilar. Tell your.. er.. housekeeper to lighten her hair colouring. At least she's not very dark. You'll have to get the stuff for her until she can go out with a proper pass. Just don't ask me to be godfather to that child."

"Thanks, Jan. I think we're even."

"What happens if you want to get married one day and your wife thinks it's your kid? Won't that complicate things?" Jan asked and saw a flicker of something in the other man's eyes. Sorrow? Pain? Regret? He couldn't be sure as the emotions reflected there had been fleeting. So he had not forgotten after all...

Seb's voice held a note of sadness. "I'll never marry. I like my life as it is," then added in a lighter mood, "free to pursue those leggy blondes. Come over one evening and meet Hanna Ulm."

"Get settled and I'll consider it," Jan answered.

Seb rose and the handshake was firm and reassuring. "Thanks again."

Jan gazed after the retreating figure. There was no chance of Seb getting married. Even the humblest SS man and his intended bride were investigated as far back as four generations to establish the purity of the German blood. Seb would know that. Jan came to the conclusion that his friend was every bit as crazy as he and Rudi. If they got caught and one of them talked they all were as good as dead.

He promptly dismissed that thought from his mind and concentrated on the pile of papers in front of him.

Once, the first of May had the only purpose to herald in spring, when children danced around the thick maypole, colourful ribbons dangling from the highest point. It was now called Labour Day and every village green was the meeting point for the Hitler Youth and leaders to march through the town and parade on the sports grounds.

When the bells had sounded their last call to the parishioners to come to worship, the bugles announced another ritual. The verger closed the doors, but the shrill blare of the brass instruments still penetrated the calm interior of the church, jarring on the senses of Father Dominik and his flock alike. Only the young chaplain seemed unperturbed and it again confirmed the priest's suspicion that the Bishop had planted his own Judas into their midst. No doubt His Grace would be well informed of his part in giving sanctuary to the wife of the man who owned the flower shop. Twice they had wrecked the premises. The last straw had been the public exhibition of the couple on the Green, surrounded by jeering thugs in uniform, Ed, Heini, Bern and Frank among them. Luther, with Floss and Rula at his heels, had effectively dispersed the perpetrators with ruthless efficiency and guided Raul and Elisabeth Fennelbaum to the presbytery for safety, where Clara had made them drink a large brandy. Elisabeth had been terrified. Their only crime; Raul was a Jew who had fallen in love with the Catholic Elisabeth. They had both joined the list to be shipped out and were for the moment hiding on Michael's houseboat.

Father Dominik's chaplain had cringed as he listened to the scathing sermon delivered from the pulpit the following Sunday and wondered just how long the Bishop was going to let the hot headed Father remain on the loose.

* * *

The attic was ready at last.   Mitch had been determined to take possession of the two rooms since Daniel had made his home in the 'Loft'. For two years she had drawn up plans of how it should look, discarding sheet after sheet of paper on the drawing board she had requested.

Michael had rescued the rejected drawings and studied them carefully.

"Our granddaughter has a great talent for design, Laura," he had told his wife. "These are not just childish fantasies. Look," pointing to what had once been a wall and now featured a gentle curving archway, linking the rooms. Bedroom and den, flowing into each other by the un-interrupted expanse of carpet. Fitments of the palest wood lined the walls and met the sloping roof. The den had her desk, a chair and the drawing board by the window, the built-in cupboards continued into the bedroom where only the large bed and her grandmother's wicker chair occupied the floor space.

"It's beautiful," Laura had said, impressed. "I wonder who she gets it from?"

"Maybe it's the.. er.. artistic talent of Natasha? At least, this'll be more respectable than the stage. I like these. They're bold and striking, uncluttered but creating harmony and cohesion. You have noticed that carpet covers all of the floor, my love?"

"Squares aren't good enough for that young lady. It's going to cost a fortune, darling," Laura had remarked to her husband. "But as she's going to be up there for a few years yet, she might as well have what she wants."

"I think so too, Laura," Michael had agreed wholeheartedly.

"Why does it have to be such a big bed when there's a perfectly good one in there already? It was quite big enough for Daniel," his wife asked.

"Maybe she's thinking ahead to the time when she might have company," Michael had said, grinning at her. "A single bed is hardly comfortable for two people to frolic in."

Laura, a look of horror on her face, had burst out in consternation.

"Michael! How can you even think about such things. I'm surprised at you."

He had caught her about the waist and firmly sat her on his lap, kissing her soundly. "Our little girl will grow up to be a very passionate woman, Laura. Just like her grandmother," and as always, he was filled with a sense of wonder when he saw the pink blush spread over her face as she wound her arms around his neck.

Some time later he had mentioned to a dishevelled Laura, "You'll find that half that bed is reserved for the Princess and her husband, Prince Rama. You'll see," he had smiled a wicked smile at her.

Daniel and Michael had worked all through the winter, meticulously carrying out the detailed instructions Mitch gave out each day, good naturedly humouring her as the 'boss'. And the day had arrived for her to move in.

A boldly patterned Indian blanket her father had brought back for her from North America provided a grand splash of colour in the austere bedroom. As Michael had predicted, Evita and Rama sat closely together on the second pillow, the flaxen haired princess in stark contrast to the dark skinned youth, so proud and handsome.

On Saturdays Mitch was allowed to stay up and was still wide awake when she finally made her way up to the attic. It had become a ritual to pause for a few moments at the window of the den and look out over the garden. Like Martha, she stood in the darkness to enjoy the ever changing combinations of patterns the breeze and moonlight effected on the leaves below. Tonight, there seemed to be too many shadows flitting from the meadow into the orchard. The girl watched silently as Daniel emerged, leading a group of five people to the summerhouse. Was that why granma had taken the basket full of food out there at dusk?...The strangers had come again, but this time she had seen them with her own eyes...Two men, two women and a boy...She wondered where Daniel was taking them to after they had eaten...

She had woken up several times in the bedroom below and heard the van being driven away when it was still very dark. Much too early for Daniel to take stuff to the market...Once she had asked granpa, but all he had said that she must wait until she was a little older and he would explain it all to her...He had made her promise again never to go down or tell anyone...And of course she had promised, because she loved him so much...She now

310

considered herself old enough to know what the strangers were doing here, eating in the summerhouse after dark and hiding in Daniel's place and when morning came it was as if they'd never been there...

Something woke her in the middle of the night. The attic trapped the rising temperature of the warm evenings and Mitch had left the windows of both rooms wide open. The pale silver light of the moon illuminated the large clock face on the bedside fitment. It showed 2:34 am and then she heard it again. A soft melody, immensely sad, coming from the direction of the orchard. The sound wrenched at her senses. It told a story of which she had no knowledge, of heartache and loss. Mitch rolled out of bed, treading softly, remembering her grandparents in the room below. She opened one of the cupboard doors and pulled out her training suit, dressed and slipped a pair of plimsolls onto her feet. Carefully tip-toeing out of the door of the den she negotiated the stairs, reached the hall and opened the door to the terrace, following the faint, melancholy sound of the music. It came from her tree house, muted, softly, sad...

"Hello," she called up the fork of the cherry tree, keeping her voice low. Mitch did not want to climb the ladder leaning against the tree in case she frightened whoever was up there. "Hello!" she called again and the music stopped abruptly and a boy's face appeared, looking scared. He looked like Matt Klein, but she knew he wasn't. They had left a long time ago. The features were unmistakable with the black curly hair, dark sad eyes and slightly curved nose, not yet fully developed. He did not smile. "What are you doing up there? That's my house," Mitch said. "Can I come up?"

"'Suppose so, if it's your house," the boy replied solemnly.

Mitch clambered up the ladder and into the interior. The boy had brought a blanket and obligingly moved over to make room for her.

"Who are you?" she asked. "I woke up and heard music. It was so sad I wanted to cry."

"I'm Josef. That hiding place in your loft was giving me the creeps. I saw this when we came in. Do you mind me sleeping here...er...I don't know your name."

"Mitch! No, I don't mind," she said, feeling an empathy with the boy cooped up in the small space behind the hay bales, with just a skylight to let in air and light. At the same time she felt he ought to be thankful for any hiding place if they were on the run. She knew she would be.

311

"How long are you staying?" she asked, noticing the moonlight made his pale face almost white.

"We're leaving soon. That's why I couldn't sleep," the boy said, still looking scared.

"I won't see you again then? Will you play something for me?" Mitch asked.

"Alright, just for you," and put the small mouth organ to his lips, where slowly, softly he played a haunting, unfamiliar tune. Twelve year old Josef felt quite comfortable in the presence of the girl and thought it not at all strange to make music in the middle of the night to the owner of this splendid residence. He knew not if they would make it to Switzerland and safety, but he was a little less scared now, thinking that if they caught the people that sheltered them, then the girl would be no better off than him.

"I'd better get back to bed. I'm not supposed to know you're here. I hope you make it, Josef."

They shook hands very formally and the boy held out the instrument to her.

"You liked my music?" he asked sheepishly.

"Yes. Very much," Mitch answered.

"Then take it. Remember to suck and blow and the notes will come out. It takes practice. I daren't play it any more after we leave here. Will you think of me sometimes when you play?" Josef Becker asked quietly.

"Yes, I will. Often," she said generously. "Thank you for my present. I'll take good care of it."

"One day I'll come back and you can play for me," the boy Josef said, his voice full of sadness. "One day."

"I'll practice and then I'll play for you. I promise," the girl Mitch answered. "Goodbye, Josef and good luck."

"Goodbye, Mitch. Thanks for the loan of your house," he whispered after her as she climbed down the ladder, clutching the instrument.

Chapter 34

Michael had decided not to have a whole hour for his lunch, inviting Laura's comments about the danger of bending about so soon after a meal and that men of a certain age ought to have more sense. He had whispered into her ears that he would take his revenge for that last remark later and saw the smug expression on her face, which made him feel good.

Walking towards the strawberry rows he felt sure he had seen movement in the meadow and a frown creased his brow. Surely no-one would be so foolish to come here in broad daylight? The refugees were always picked up after dark and only Rudi and Daniel knew the meeting places, which they changed constantly. He carefully scrutinized the orchard and walked towards the meadow.

Zorro, Margharita's magnificent brown and white stallion was grazing contentedly in the dip by the stream. The caravan, not parked in its usual place, had a temporary appearance. What was Margharita doing here on this Whitsun weekend? She was not due for another week...

He saw Ramon, who never arrived before the long vacation from school in the summer. Something was not right...

The boy, in skimpy shorts, legs and upper body bare, had grown taller since last year and as Michael approached he set down the bucket of water he had collected from the stream, calling, "Ma. It's Mr Schiller," then greeted the older man with a wide smile. "Good day, Mr Schiller. Nice to see you again."

As they shook hands, Michael asked. "You've come early, Ramon. Is anything wrong?" and marvelled at the change in the boy's features. He was only eleven, Michael recalled, but already the strong lines of Ramon's face showed the beginning of manhood. He would be a handsome gipsy, with his mother's lithe movements and possessed of Margharita's inherent dignity. He wondered what his father was like. They had never met him and Margharita did not mention him. At that moment she descended the steps of the caravan and he was surprised to see her dressed in her traditional Romany clothes, a red triangle displaying gold coins dangling over her forehead. She was a truly beautiful woman, Michael thought and beamed with pleasure.

"Margharita," he greeted her, stretching out his hand to enfold hers in a warm, affectionate gesture. "You look wonderful. What brings you here so early?"

Though the gipsy Queen emanated radiant pleasure at seeing him again, he noticed anxiety in her eyes. "It is only a brief visit, Mr Michael. I could not leave without saying goodbye."

"But where are you going? Will you come back later in the summer?" Michael asked, somewhat taken aback.

"No," Margharita's voice was full of sadness. The knowledge that she would not see any of them again filled her with grief. "We have been free to travel in this region so far, but the French are leaving and we have no-one to protect us now. The purges of the Jews and your own people will escalate and we have been added to the list of undesirables. My people are gathering at our wintering place outside Koblenz and I must be there by tomorrow night. We are travelling in small groups to the mountains in Spain. To the Basque country. Spain itself is already at war, but there we shall be safe. If we travel over many separate routes, most of us should make it."

Michael had paled, his face full of pain. "Oh, God. You too have to flee like criminals. It's barbarous, Margharita. I'm sorry that it has come to this. Where is the rest of your family?"

"My daughter is with my husband. He did not want me to come here, but Ramon insisted that he see the Lion Girl and I was allowed to travel. Zorro should be rested by morning, ready for the return journey."

Michael gazed at the beautiful woman and felt bereft. He could not blame them for leaving. To be caged like an animal would destroy them. They had no roots except their culture, made their home any place and like a snail, carried all they possessed in their caravan.

"All of it is unjust, but cannot be stopped. We shall miss you. I'll go and tell Laura. Tonight we'll have a farewell party with our friends to wish you God speed" and then he laughed. "Sorry. Force of habit, Margharita. You must tell me what one wishes a Romany when they leave their friends."

"I will, Mr Michael and I shall look forward to the party," she said with infinite grace.

"Where's Mitch, Mr Schiller?" Ramon asked, a tinge of impatience in his voice.

"Playing football with the boys. She'll be back later. Why don't you go and join them?"

The boy glanced at his mother and shook his head. "No. I'll wait here" and turned away to fetch more water.

Margharita smiled. "He will miss her. My son is very fond of your granddaughter. It is very strange."

"I had better go and tell Laura you're here," he said, and walked back through the meadow. He too wondered about the fierce attachment that bound the boy Ramon to his tempestuous granddaughter.

Laura rushed out to greet Margharita, then invited Erika, Katrin and Martha Henckler and organised herself to hold a party at very short notice, expecting Margharita and Ramon at seven that evening.

Mitch breezed in about four in the afternoon and barely listened to what her grandmother had to say. Covered in grass and dirt, she turned tail and shouts of 'Ramon' could be heard inside the house. Laura looked at Erika, who had generously offered to lend a hand and both of them shook their heads in astonishment.

Margharita watched her son attending to the chores with more determination than usual. She was glad she had made the journey. For her friends it would seem to be a temporary goodbye until the day when she would return, but for her it was a final visit. She had grown to respect and love the former priest and the woman he adored, liked the vivacious Erika and her Baron and wished she could change the future. But she could only see it, it was not in her power to prevent events that were pre-destined. Not even the impending tragedy which would take her own secret love from her. Perhaps by the time it was all over, she herself would not want to travel again. Not to see the meadow, her friends and her lover here was a burden she would have to carry in silent grief...

She felt Ramon's bitter disappointment when the Lion Girl had not been at home. Perhaps it was a timely departure. The bond between them was getting stronger each year. A Romany Prince and a Gorgio was unthinkable, although she wished it was possible. The Lion Girl held her own heart as captive as she did that of her beloved son. A soft smile played around the full shapely mouth as she threw a last glance at the youth attending to Zorro.

It would be many years before their time would come and for that knowledge she was deeply grateful...

The stallion waited patiently as the brush strokes removed dust and loose hair from his coat. Today the boy seemed agitated and the steel needles dug in with more force than usual. Ramon felt it too, but could not give a reason why. She should have been here...But logic whispered that she hadn't known he was coming...They would not have the whole of the summer, only tonight and for a long time he wouldn't see his Gorgio...And when he did she would be grown-up, have lovers, maybe a husband and children and he would still love her...

Some of his cousins had already been paired off or were betrothed...They didn't understand why he came here every summer instead of going on the circuit...He didn't mind the travelling, but going to school was important to Ma, so he stayed at the camp with his grandmother and counted the months until the long school holiday...Then his greatest reward for waiting was to teach the hot-tempered Gorgio the ways of the Romany and as always, when it was time to leave, he would miss her for a long time.

He listened and found his heart beating a little faster as the shouts of 'Ramon' echoed through the still meadow. Zorro too stiffened his ears at the sound. The boy watched the small figure racing towards him. The hair was still that funny colour, as if it didn't know whether it wanted to be fair or rusty, he thought, all mussy and damp...She hadn't grown much since last year either, he noticed.

"Ramon," the girl called again, then saw him standing quite still at the side of the beautiful horse and stopped dead in her tracks, staring at him. How tall he had grown...

"Hola, Gorgio," the boy said softly. "Enjoyed the game?" he asked, as if he had never been away at all.

"Yes," the girl answered, still looking at him. "Why didn't you come and find me?"

"You were playing with the boys, as usual. Besides, we're leaving early in the morning and I've things to do," Ramon said, sounding off-hand and grown-up. "We've been invited to your place tonight and I knew I'd see you then."

"Oh..." was all she could think of, fierce disappointment written over her face. "I'll see you later then."

She felt he had become a stranger instead of the faithful companion who had been there every summer as long as she could remember. With some reluctance she took her eyes off the face that looked like Prince Rama and turned back to the house, without greeting Zorro.

"Are we throwing the knives tonight, Gorgio? " Ramon called after her. Her spirits rose as high as the sky. "Yes," she shouted back and fled.

Clean and scrubbed, dressed in shorts, vest and sandals, Mitch devoured her food. Michael knew she was in a hurry to get back to Ramon and Zorro. Seven o'clock was far to long to wait. He gazed at the mobile heart shaped face, with its high cheekbones and strong stubborn jaw that would stop it from being merely a pretty countenance. He loved the way the still damp curls framed the brow and delicate pink ears. He just loved all of her and silently thanked the Lord for that precious gift.

"Are you going to put on a dress, darling? It could be years and years before we see them again and they should remember you as a pretty girl, not dressed as a boy," Laura enquired of her granddaughter.

Mitch shot her a disgusted look, as if she had just been asked to climb to the moon on a beanstalk.

"What for?" she wanted to know. "Ramon and me are going to throw the knives. I can't do that in a frock. He might let me ride Zorro," and looked aghast at her grandfather, who pretended he hadn't heard.

"Have you been riding that big brute, Mitch?" Laura's voice was stern.

"Ehm..." she said, lifting soft grey eyes to Michael to get her off the hook.

"Well? Have you?" her grandmother asked again.

"Yes, granma. But only in the meadow. He's a nice horse an' likes me."

"Ramon should've more sense than let you anywhere near Zorro. He's far too big for you to ride."

"Granma. Ramon helps me up and Zorro's always very good."

Laura glanced at her husband, who was far too intent on eating his food and suspicion dawned on her.

"Michael. You knew, didn't you?" she asked

He lifted blue eyes appealingly to his wife. "Yes, my love" and Laura found her heart melting again. "She's quite safe and rides that horse like the devil," he proudly informed his wife.

He himself had ridden Zorro when Margharita had retired her faithful mare. She had exercised the lively stallion in the meadow and he had longed to get on the horse.

'Ride him,' Margharita had prompted, sliding off the broad back. 'But our horses don't have saddles.'

He had talked to the magnificent horse and the urge had been too much. He missed his gallops on Cornelius's grey, riding through the sweet smelling pine forest, but he dare not go up there since they had established the escape route.

After work he always made time to give Zorro his head. Hoisting Mitch up in front of him, the proud beast would carry them at speed through the long meadow. Michael marvelled at the extra-ordinary rapport the girl had with Zorro and sometimes he wondered if she would ever be afraid of anything. Her very fearlessness might be her greatest danger.

Laura's voice reached him and he detected a note of exasperation. "I don't know what you two will get up to next."

"I think skinning a rabbit is on the agenda," he remarked placidly.

"Michael!... Really!" Laura admonished her husband, while he winked at Mitch, delighting in the expression of pure pleasure on her face.

The people in the summerhouse listened intently as Margharita described the journey they must undertake to reach the border of France and Spain.

Ramon was getting restless. "Are you coming, Gorgio?" he asked the equally fidgety girl. "Can we take some food, Mrs Schiller?" he asked politely of Laura.

She filled a tray with sandwiches and cakes, covering it with a muslin cloth.

"What you can't eat you can give to Zorro as a treat. Don't let that horse trample Mitch underfoot, Ramon. And be careful with those knives," she advised, fully aware she might as well talk to the deaf as the boy and her granddaughter fled to the meadow.

Daniel and Chrissy took their leave too and Margharita wished them a long life and happiness and meant it. She knew they would do well. Chrissy was seventeen, as pretty as her mother but lacked Erika's vitality. She was gentle, still visited church regularly and had been appointed as trainee teacher at the village school. Daniel was her rock and everyone knew they would marry. The general opinion was that she would make the hard working young man a good wife and mother for his children, a fact Daniel had known for years.

Chapter 35

The boy Ramon carefully deposited the tray on the table just inside the caravan. Mitch watched him coming down the steps and felt a great wave of something she couldn't exactly define. He would not be here this summer. Maybe she would never see him again. What would she do without him?

Ramon's black eyes contemplated her solemn face for a moment, then he reached out and gently touched her cheek. "Why do you look sad, Gorgio?" he asked softly. "Will you miss me?"

She did not answer, as if she was afraid to tell him what she felt. The doleful expression in the large grey eyes told him and he understood when she just nodded her head.

"Come. We'll ride Zorro," and he turned away to fetch the horse, leading it towards the steps of the caravan. Zorro whinnied as he saw the girl and pranced elegantly in front of her. She took the great head into her arms and Ramon knew he would never forget that image. The Gorgio standing on the step and the beast lowering its face to be stroked. He could not hear what she murmured into the pointed ears, but Zorro seemed pleased.

Ramon took a leap and sat, proud and lofty on the broad back, guiding the horse alongside the steps and held out his hand. Mitch took it and felt the pull of his strong arm lifting her up behind him.

Laura stopped in mid-sentence and listened to the whinnying of the horse, the joyful shouts of the children on its back racing through the meadow.

"She's on that horse again, Michael," she said, looking worried.

"Let them be, Laura. She'll be fine," he replied gently.

"Ramon will look after her, Mrs Laura," Margharita assured her, smiling serenely.

It had been a fine race and both of them were hot. Zorro had galloped the length and breadth of the spring fresh meadow and would have carried them on to the end of the earth. Ramon led him to the stream where the stallion dipped his mouth into the cold water. The boy stripped off the shirt his mother had made him wear to go the party and stepped into the water.

319

"Are you coming in?" he asked the girl, splashing his chest and face to cool off.

Last year she would have removed her vest and willingly would have followed him, but now there was a reluctance to take off the garment in front of him. Instead, she sat on the stones bordering the stream and dangled her feet in the water, splashing her arms and face. She did not know why she felt like that suddenly. As she watched the slim boy in neat shorts in the middle of the stream she found him beautiful. The last of the sun's rays made the water glisten on the brown skin and dark curly hair. He moved like her Granpa, Mitch thought, as graceful as a jungle cat, not clumsy like the other boys. Ramon should be living in ancient Greece and be the son of a god...

He stepped out of the water. "We'll eat and then do some practice on the tree," he commanded, going towards the caravan.

Her grandmother had almost fainted at the sight of the hunting knife Ramon had given her three years ago, Mitch remembered. After a great deal of practice he had grudgingly given her a pat on the back the first time her throw had landed a few centimetres away from his mark. Daniel and granpa sharpened the wicked looking blade and let her practice when granma was busy indoors...The old gnarled apple tree in the meadow bore the scars of her determination to be as good as Ramon one day soon.

"Here, let's eat," the boy said, placing the food between them. He settled himself on the stones, his brown feet in the water.

"Can I give some to Zorro?" she asked, mindful of the time when he had seen her feeding chocolate to the new horse. The old mare had liked chocolate. Ramon had been furious, calling her an ignorant Gorgio and forbidding her to ever feed Zorro without permission. His mother's horses were of the finest breed, not like the old hacks that travelled with the tinkers and fair people, he had stormed at her.

"Yes. He'd like that," the boy said graciously and whistled.

Zorro nuzzled her head as she held up a piece of cake and the big mouth took it gently out of her hand. Ramon watched and smiled.

"Will I ever see you again, Ramon?" Mitch asked, holding up another piece of cake.

"Of course!" He sounded very positive. "It'll be a long time, though. There'll be war all over soon, but our people will stay in the mountains. Maybe the men are going to fight, but Ma's sending me to school in San

Sebastian in September. I've got to stay there, but if war comes I'll be in the mountains with Ma and Pa."

Are you going to be safe?"

"Nobody's going to find us there," he said, chewing on a sandwich. "When it's all over we'll see each other again."

The girl cast him an unbelieving glance. "How do you know that?"

Ramon laughed out loud, showing small white teeth. She liked it when he laughed like that. His mouth had a nice shape and the teeth were in perfect harmony with the rest of his face. Not like Willy's. His were big and stuck out like a rabbit's. Victors were alright, though, but Ramon's were the best. All of him was the best...

"I'm a gipsy and know everything," he boasted.

She bent down and scooped up a handful of water and threw it over him. "You're a show-off, Ramon. Only your Ma knows everything. You don't. I bet you can't even tell me the year we're going to see each other again. Or if we're still alive when the wars are over?" she goaded him.

Ramon looked down at her and there was something in his eyes that made her afraid and she wished she hadn't ask that last question. He looked like he did sometimes when he stared into the sky and forgot about her, as if he saw things nobody else did. His voice was very soft and sent a tingle down her spine, awakening a sixth sense she had never been aware of before.

"You're right, Gorgio. I don't know everything," and he smiled at her. "But one day, when we're grown up I'll take you to a secret place. One day."

"Will my Daddy and Granpa and Granma see you again too?" she asked and didn't know why. It had just popped into her head.

Ramon avoided her questioning eyes and stared into the water for some time. Then he laughed. "I'm not a fortune teller and I can't read the crystal. Come on. Let's go and massacre that tree before it gets dark."

Mitch Sogar remained where she was and knew with absolute certainty that he had not told her all he knew.

"Then how do you know you're going to take me to that secret place?" she wanted to know.

The boy, his head resting on the flank of Zorro, laughed again.

"Because my Ma told me," leading the horse to the tethering post. The girl stared into the water, making circles with her bare feet and wondered what it was Ramon had not told her.

They spent the time until dusk competing with each other. The flight of the blades missed their mark several times as the light faded. Mitch, as always, came off worst, but did not get into a temper, conceding to Ramon's skill. After all, he was a gipsy and older than her, she thought with an abundance of generosity. One day she'd catch him up, though...

The boy lit the lantern outside the caravan and went inside to light a lamp, but did not ask her in. She sat patiently on the bottom step. She remembered her grandfather telling her years ago never to enter the home of a Romany without an invitation, when she had let curiosity get the better of her and crept into the caravan to admire the silver and brasses while Mrs Cros had been working in the field.

Ramon came down the wooden steps, a soft cloth in his hand and seated himself next to her. He carefully polished the knives and fastened hers into its leather sheath.

"You did well tonight, Gorgio. Promise to keep on throwing. It could come in handy one day. Do you want want one of Ma's drinks?"

"Yes, please." She wondered why they were not talking as much as they usually did. Maybe it was because he was going away and there wasn't time for fighting each other.

He seemed to be gone a long time and when he finally stood in the doorway of the caravan she realized why. He was carrying a small silver tray with two tall crystal glasses filled with the pale green liquid she had so often tasted when she was with his Ma, but it was Ramon himself that startled her. Never before had she seen him in anything other than shorts or what any other boy would wear. Now he looked like a true Romany and the boy felt good as he saw the admiration reflected in her eyes.

The white shirt-blouse, elaborately embroidered, was tucked into long dark trousers, the broad leather belt fastened by a heavy silver buckle. The black and white neckerchief, sporting the signs of the zodiac, was knotted loosely around the boyish neck.

Mitch stared at the proud features and blurted out. "You're more beautiful than Prince Rama. And your clothes are just as splendid as his," wishing for a fleeting moment that she had put on her tartan kilt and frilly blouse her grandmother had given her for Christmas.

"Oh, your Persian doll," Ramon said, a little peeved at being compared with a doll. "I'll have you know I'm a real life Prince. When my father gets too old I'll lead my people and be the King," he boasted proudly.

Mitch was dismissive. "You don't have kings or palaces, only caravans and that's not the same thing."

"My Pa's the leader of our tribe and that makes him a King. My Ma was a Princess when she married Pa and is the Queen of the gipsy's," he insisted vehemently.

"Alright. But your people haven't got a kingdom, so you can't be a real Prince," she answered and then saw the disappointment in the boy's eyes. "But..." she added softly, "I'll always think of you as the most handsome prince in all the world, Ramon. I will, I promise," and was pleased to see the black eyes light up again.

"Thank you, Princess Gorgio," he laughed and executed an elaborate bow before sitting down next to her.

Mitch noticed the black shiny shoes had silver buckles on them too. She sipped her drink and imagined herself and Ramon all alone, the meadow an island where there would be no war and he would not have to go away. Three months away from her ninth birthday, she could not envisage the summers without him.

Ramon, who would be eleven a week after her birthday, sensed her strange mood. "I wish..." He hesitated a little, but then added resolutely. "I wish you were one of us. Then my Ma could speak for you and we'd be betrothed."

The girl looked into the dark face to see whether he was laughing at her. He did say funny things like that sometimes, she remembered, but the black eyes glittering in the light of the lantern showed no amusement as he gazed down at her.

"We can't be betrothed. We're too young," Mitch said earnestly. "When you get betrothed it's as good as being married and you've got to love somebody to do that. Granpa said so."

"Romanies get betrothed when they're kids. It's the custom," he answered.

"Well...I'm a Catholic, not a heathen like you and have to grow up first. I don't think I'm going to marry anybody. I'll have a caravan like your Ma and pretend to be a gipsy. Go where I like and be free." She heaved a great sigh.

"Will you get betrothed to somebody, Ramon?" she asked the boy, a wistful note in her voice.

He had that far-away look in his eyes again and it was some time before he answered. "I expect so. Ma and Pa'll arrange it. She'll have to be the daughter of an elder. I can't marry anybody else. It's the custom," he said, sounding resigned, bound inflexibly to his culture and tradition.

"So you couldn't marry me anyway," Mitch retorted peevishly. "My Daddy's never here and granpa was a Catholic priest before he married granma and my mother's a hussy."

"Who told you that?" Ramon exclaimed sharply, looking angry.

"Nobody. I heard Daniel tell Granpa once when I was in my tree house and they didn't know I was there. So I wouldn't be good enough for you anyway."

The boy considered that for a while, sipping on the cool drink. When he spoke there was a gentleness she hadn't heard from him before.

"But you're special. If you were a Romany Ma would make an exception. She loves you as much as I do."

She glanced at him to see if he was teasing her, but he looked serious and she felt a warm glow inside.

"I love you too, Ramon, and I'll miss you something awful. I'll be very cross when you marry somebody else, so don't ever tell me about it."

"Alright, I won't then," he promised solemnly and placed an arm about her shoulder. "As I can't marry you, will you be my blood-sister, Gorgio?" he asked.

"Yes. I'd like that, but first you'll have to tell me what I've got to do. Don't you have to cut your wrist, like the Red Indians, when they make a white man a blood-brother?"

Ramon shot her a look full of contemptuous disgust at so much ignorance. "They only nick it, idiot. We'll just make a cut in our thumbs."

"How big?" she asked.

"Only a little one. Just enough to make it bleed. We can't do the ceremony without blood. Unless you're scared?"

"No," she said firmly. "I'm not scared" and held out her thumbs. "Which one do you want?"

"Your left one. It's nearest your heart" he commanded and out of his pocket he took out a white folded handkerchief, placing it between them. "Ready?"

The knife looked big, but quick as lightning he made two cuts into the fleshy part and pressed their thumbs together as the blood began to flow. Mitch did not flinch as she watched the drips spreading into a dark stain on the white cotton.

"There," the boy said softly. "Now I have to kiss you."

She gave him a disdainful look. "Oh, that! Why?"

"It's the custom. Has anybody kissed you yet?" Ramon asked, a cheeky grin on his face.

"Willy tries it sometimes. He knows it makes me mad 'cause I don't like it," Mitch said contemptuously.

"You'll have to be kissed whether you like it or not. It's part of the ceremony," Ramon insisted. He carefully folded the knife into the blood stained handkerchief, placed it onto the silver tray and moved closer to the girl. "You're my sister and I'm your brother," he intoned and before she could recover from the momentous occasion Ramon bent his head and kissed her gently on the mouth, lingering longer than was necessary. Mitch found to her surprise that she liked his lips on hers. They tasted of Mrs Cros's green drink and were very soft.

Ramon moved away, but kept his arm about her. "Ma'll be pleased you're my sister. Don't ever change, Gorgio. I don't want you to grow up into a sissy girl. Promise?"

"Promise," she vowed. He took out a little phial from his pocket and poured a small amount of a yellow sticky substance over the cut in her thumb and she felt the pain go away.

"Were you scared?" he asked, a big grin on his face.

"No, I wasn't," she lied, looking him straight in the eyes.

He laughed. "Liar. Come and hold this lantern," and he ran up the steps to unhook the lamp. "We've got to make our mark," he said, handing it to her.

Ramon picked up the knife, clambered under the highest point of the shaft of the caravan and ordered. "Give me some light."

She watched him carving and presently he seemed satisfied and stood up. "Come and look, sister," and took the lantern from her. "When I look at that, I'll remember tonight," he said so gently that she felt like crying.

Mitch bent down and as he held the light she saw the zodiac symbols of two lions closely entwined around the initials of R and M. The carving was so deep it would remain as long as the caravan was in existence.

Ramon fastened the lantern and collected the tray with the glasses. He put the bloodstained handkerchief into his pocket and disappeared into the interior, presently emerging and closing the door behind him.

"Can I say goodbye to Zorro, Ramon?" Mitch asked.

"'Course," he said and took her hand, clasping it tightly in his own as they walked to where the white and brown stallion had bedded down for the night.

He nuzzled her face, soft brown eyes full of sorrow, as if he too knew this was their final meeting. There was this great pain in her chest and the knowledge that when she woke up in the morning Ramon and Zorro would be gone. Ramon felt her pain, as he felt his own and held the small body in a tight embrace. Without shame he let his tears mingle with those of his beloved Gorgio.

Mitch opened her eyes. It was still very early. Jumping out of bed she discarded her sleeping vest and pants. Hurriedly pulling on clean knickers, shorts and vest, she grabbed her gym shoes and raced downstairs, not caring if she woke her grandparents. Past the summerhouse, and already she knew they had gone. The meadow lay empty, glinting in the morning dew. All that was left of their visit was a small patch of heaped earth at the edge of the grass. Mitch exposed the top layer with her foot and felt the ashes underneath, still warm to the touch. They had boiled the kettle for tea and she stood looking down into the water, hoping to find at least a small bubble of soap Ramon would have used this morning. She didn't know any boy that washed as much as he did. There was not one speck of it left in the flowing water. All she had left were ashes...

Her eyes sought out the old tree and she saw a patch of white that hadn't been there before. She ran and found a page from a school notebook pierced dead centre to the tree with her knife. Mitch pulled out the blade and read the message, written in a neat hand.

"Goodbye, little sister. I love you" and underneath were two sets of numbers joined together by the same symbols Ramon had carved under the shaft of the caravan. She stared hard at them, mystified at first and then she knew. 1936 was this year and the lions were their birth sign of the zodiac and 1956 must be the year they would meet again.

Renewed dread added to the misery she already felt. Twenty years...They would be old and have wrinkles like Mrs Henckler and he would not be beautiful any more...

Two lonely tears fell onto the page. She could not envisage twenty years and decided to remember Ramon as he had looked last night...Tall and proud...He had kissed her...Had mingled their blood and he had looked more handsome than Prince Rama...The gipsy boy she had known for all the summers of her life had turned into a true prince...Just like a fairy tale...

Chapter 36

The houseboat looked good after a thorough clean and scrub. Michael sat back in the deck chair to admire his handiwork, a cool drink at his side. Today and tomorrow they could relax. No barges travelled on the river on Sundays. Only the pleasure steamers took people up the river for a day's outing. Captain Olaf would have left the quay at Bonn very early this morning and Michael hoped the two passengers delivered by Daniel just before the steamer slipped the moorings would get to their destination in the care of the courageous Captain.

Mitch, Victor and Kirsten had tested the water and looked set for a vigorous game of football. He felt the tension receding and cast a glance at his wife in the chair next to him, her face turned to the sun. She was still the most beautiful woman he knew and even in a pair of old, cut-down slacks and working shirt she could inflame his soul. At this moment, Michael was immensely grateful for all that the Lord had bestowed on him.

"Our granddaughter seems to have recovered her spirits," Laura said, looking over the side of the boat. "She was very upset this morning, when she found they had gone."

"She'll survive, my love. That child has the inexplicable power to disconnect herself from painful experiences and go on. She must tuck them away in some hidden corner of her soul," Michael remarked thoughtfully. "They'll be back one day, but the meadow will seem very empty this summer. I'll miss Margharita and riding Zorro."

"Martha's offered to come and help in the mornings. She could do with the money to make her life more comfortable."

"I never did pay Margharita enough, but she wouldn't take more than what she needed for food and bran for the horse," Michael said regretfully.

"I'll miss her. She was a good friend." Laura's voice too was tinged with regret. "I wonder if we'll see them again? Do you realize that life as we knew it once has come to an end? When we married there was everything to hope for. Then came the Depression and Adolf Hitler. Will there be another war for us to live through, Michael?"

He considered that for a moment. "Yes," he said slowly. "It's inevitable. All the signs point to it. When it will come is difficult to predict. Spain is only the beginning. The whole world needs a war and Hitler is playing right into their hands. It just makes me wonder if the fool knows it."

"If there is a war, you won't leave me like Jack did, will you, Michael?"

He jumped out of his chair and leant over his wife, gently placing a kiss on the soft lips. "No, my love. I won't ever leave you. I'll be too old to fight, but they'll take Daniel, though, and we'll have to work twice as hard."

"That's alright. As long as we're together nothing matters, darling. I must go and finish those cupboards below."

"Want any help?" he asked, a lecherous grin on his lean, still handsome face.

"No, you terrible man," Laura murmured, kissing the tip of his earlobe. "You have this habit of distracting me from my work," she said, putting a safe distance between them as his arms reached out for her.

Michael decided to stay where he was. He felt unusually tired. Since he had escorted Margharita to her caravan after the party he had not slept much. Her words kept going round and round in his head for most of the night. He had gone over their conversation a hundred times and still couldn't make sense of it...

"Look after Laura and the child", Margharita had said after she had embraced him, "they'll need you, Michael." He had been surprised to hear her use his Christian name as she had never done that before. "I shall be deeply grieved not to be here, but for all my powers, I cannot change destiny", she had said. "It will take its course wherever I am.'"

He had the strangest feeling that she was grieving already. 'Will there be war, Margharita?' he had asked and she had simply said 'Yes, but the girl will be safe,' without mentioning anyone else. It had been very late and he had not liked to ask her to explain it to him in view of her early departure. She had told him to stay away from the water, but what was the significance of that? he wondered. There was only this boat and it was virtually on dry land. Nor was it a fire hazard as they had no cooking stoves on board or stayed overnight, when they might need paraffin lamps. Michael could not find any indication for impending disaster and resolutely put it out of his mind. The future was in God's hands and whatever Margharita knew she had kept to herself. They all knew she had the gift of prophecy, but had never discussed the strength or the power of it, as he only believed in the power of the Lord.

The voices of the children receded and the gentle motion of the boat lulled him to sleep.

The preparation and harvesting of their produce kept them so busy that Laura had declined to take part in the preparations for the Church Fete in August. Martha, willing, but inexperienced, needed to be taught the finer points of grading, marking and packing. Laura enjoyed the somewhat caustic language of her neighbour and the feeling of trust and respect became mutual.

Michael and Daniel watched Mitch throwing her knife with increasing accuracy at the board they had fastened to the trunk of the cherry tree. The panel was thick, high and slim. She had not set foot into the meadow since Ramon left, nor did she ever speak of him. It was as if she had deleted all previous summers from her mind. Daniel was puzzled as to why, if she did not want to be reminded of Ramon, it was so important to practise with the knife.

"Bloody minded pride, son," Michael had told him. "Ramon will have told her she'd never be as good as him and she'll prove him wrong if they'll ever get together again."

Laura leant over the low wall and called 'lunch is ready' to the two men working on the vegetable patch. Daniel gave a sharp whistle in the direction of the tree house and the ragged sound of the small mouth organ the boy Josef had given to Mitch in the middle of the night came to an abrupt halt.

"She's getting the hang of it," Daniel remarked to Michael as they walked to the house.

His wife too had been listening and was infinitely grateful that they'd had no requests for trumpet or drums. She had many times tactfully suggested to her granddaughter to carry on with her music lessons, offered to install a piano or buy a string instrument, all to no avail. The shiny little harmonica had a strange fascination for the girl. Like Ramon's knife, she cherished the present from the Jewish boy and was determined to master the delicate balance between sucking and blowing, never for one moment forgetting her promise to Josef to keep on practising.

"Am I getting better on the mouth organ, granma?" Mitch asked when they were seated at the table.

Laura glanced at her two men, who were not going to help her out.

"I think so, darling, but I could judge much better if you played the piano or the violin," she answered carefully. "It's not really an instrument for a girl, is it?"

"But it's small and neat and I'll be able to play it properly soon. You can't put a piano into a tree house or a caravan. Can you, granpa?" she asked, eyes full of wicked mischief.

Laura watched her husband's fond glance resting on the child's face.

"Talking of caravans. Have you told your grandmother yet what you're going to be when you grow up?"

Laughing grey eyes shone with delight at the prospect of shocking her grandmother. "No, she wouldn't be pleased, granpa," Mitch said, grinning.

"What wouldn't I be pleased about, darling?" Laura knew it was definitely another outrageous venture that had been discussed at length between the three of them. Michael at least kept her up to date, so that she would not feel excluded.

"I'm going to have a caravan, a horse and a dog and live like a gipsy."

Michael and Daniel exchanged glances and waited for the eruption. The fork that was halfway up to Laura's mouth stopped in mid-air and an expression of disbelief played over her face. This one she had not heard about, Laura thought and her voice was a mixture of resignation and disapproval.

"I think it's about time you two..." she said firmly, looking at her husband and Daniel. "It's time you stopped encouraging our granddaughter's wild fantasies. Now that Ramon isn't coming any more, it's a good time for Mitch to stop playing with boys so much and spend a little of her energy in learning housecraft. When she gets married, her husband will expect her to know how to feed him, clean his house and mend his clothes. Mitch'll be nine in three weeks time and it's never too early to start learning these things."

The girl stared at her grandmother, then at Michael and Daniel, horror at what had been mentioned plainly mirrored in her face. Michael felt a twinge of guilt as he looked at Laura.

"Your grandmother has a point, sweetheart. You should give it some thought," he said gently to the silent girl. He and Daniel were in part to blame for the wild creature they had raised between them. It had been so much fun and he doubted if she would have become any different in the hands of women. At least they had disciplined and taught her to do

331

whatever she had a mind to do properly. As they would have had she been a boy.

Mitch had recovered from the shock of hearing Ramon's name. It had given her a pain in the chest and only now did she feel ready to speak of him.

"Ramon taught me how to catch food, granma. And clean and cook it over a fire."

"I suppose we must be grateful to him for teaching you that vast culinary knowledge, Mitch." Laura tried hard to suppress a smile.

"Thanks to Ramon I'll never starve. And as I'm not going to get married or have kids I won't have to know all that stuff. I want to be free, granma."

Laura stared open-mouthed at her grand daughter, saw the fiercely determined look in eyes that had taken on a green hue, ready to do battle. She decided to leave matters for the moment. Daniel and Michael thought it an opportune moment to make their exit. Mitch too asked to be excused. Laura remained at the table, a mixture of pride and sadness churning like a spinning top in her soul. Pride at the fiery temperament that made her granddaughter as fiercely independent and foolhardy as any boy and sadness that soon, too soon, she would have to relinquish all notions of freedom. By the very nature of things she would have to cross the border and adapt to the very ideas she despised so much. Mitch would find that boys did not play by the same rules any more and the thought of her proud and beautiful grandchild unravelling the mysteries of being Eve in a world full of amorous, hot-blooded Adams made her laugh out loud.

"Poor darling," she murmured. "You'll have to learn different tactics," and poured herself another coffee.

Michael had made love to his wife with sensuous dedication. As always, Laura nestled into his chest and drifted into the dreamy, hazy no-mans land before deep sleep claimed her. Michael too was drifting. He was a light sleeper, attuned to waking at the slightest sound and had the scream from the attic bedroom been a whisper he would still have heard it. The anguished 'Daddy, Daddy,' made his blood run cold as, already struggling into pyjamas, he pacified Laura with 'it's Mitch. I'll go and see,' before racing up the next flight of stairs.

The sight of the girl on the big bed, rocking furiously back and forth, the two dolls clasped to her chest, caused his heart to leap into his throat.

"What is it, sweetheart? Did you have a bad dream?" he asked as he sat on the edge of the bed. He noticed the swollen eyes and the damp patch on the pillow. Mitch never cried. Whatever hurt or calamity might befall the small body, not a single tear would be shed. Only the frantic rocking would betray her.

The face that looked up at him held a terrifying expression of fear.

"It...it was...it was awful," she stuttered, "so much water and...and Daddy was drowning and...and I kept shouting for him to take my hand...and he couldn't reach it and...and he drowned, granpa...There wasn't anybody else to save him and...and he didn't come up any more..."

Michael took the small body into his arms and stroked the damp curls.

"It was only a dream, Sweetheart. You haven't had a bad one for a long time now and it frightened you. Don't worry about it any more. I'll get you a nice cool drink and then you can go back to sleep."

He removed the pillow and replaced it with the dry one next to it and wondered how long she had been crying in her dream. She would not let go of the dolls, but let him settle her back in the bed. Michael hurried to the bathroom to fetch water and found Mitch lying pale and still.

Coaxing her to sip from the glass, he asked gently. "Do you want me to stay for a little while?"

The dark pools of grey looking up at him seemed full of something he couldn't define. Pain? Grief? But it had only been a dream, he thought, and then remembered that this child was not like any other. Something unspeakable had happened to her long before Peter had brought her here and it had mutilated her soul. So many times he had wished she would scream and cry like other children, had watched that silent fury consuming her instead and wanted to kill the woman who had let this happened to an innocent baby. How much did infants retain of their first few months of life? One day, he hoped, someone would reach out, nurture the damaged part of her spirit and heal it.

"Granpa? Will you tell me a story?" a small voice asked. "The one you invented about these two."

Michael's gentle voice told of the Persian prince who went to look all over the world for the fair princess he had dreamt of since he was a youth and finally found her in the cold north. He took her back with him to his land where the sun always shone and they lived happily ever after...

Her eyes were soft and she sighed. "Thank you, granpa. It's a beautiful story and I love listening to your voice. It makes me sleepy. Do you think Ramon will come and fetch me one day? He's a prince too, isn't he?"

"Yes. And a very handsome one. He'll be back some day. Go to sleep now, sweetheart. It was only a bad dream," Michael said and gently kissed her brow.

He had only reached the archway when the child's voice said, quite calmly. "Daddy won't be coming home, granpa. Not ever."

"Yes he will, Mitch," he replied firmly. "He'll be here in three weeks. Just in time for your birthday. Goodnight, sweetheart."

Mitch slept longer than usual and Laura was worried about how pale she looked. She was quiet and contrary to her normal behaviour, courteous and polite, but there was a restlessness about her which concerned Michael. Almost as if she was waiting for something...

He had not told his wife about the child's nightmare.

The telegram arrived the next day. Martin Ryker expressed his regrets. Peter and two of his men had been buried under the tons of mountain earth they had been excavating. For two days they had dug in the hope of finding them, but after a further landslide all hope was gone. He would write...

Michael and Daniel felt the loss, but it was Laura that needed their comfort. There would be no burial, no grave, no ashes...

Mitch remained dry-eyed, hugged her grandmother and walked into the orchard, climbed the ladder to the tree house and played the mouth organ. The soft, melancholy lament soldiers had sung to their dead comrades long before the strident martial music of the New Order at todays military funerals. She played hesitantly at first, but the sound gathered strength and the three people listening could not stop the flood of tears. They cried for a lost son. Daniel for someone who had been a brother to him and they cried for the girl carrying her grief inside of her without the blessed relief of hot salty tears cauterizing the wound.

Michael held his wife close to him and suddenly realized that the night Mitch had her nightmare it would have been day where Peter had been working. Could someone or something bridge the air waves to reach her?...She had known...But how?...

He knew such things were possible, but his faith dismissed them as being the Devil's work. The child had been confirmed into the Holy Church and her dream would be deemed as being possessed of witchcraft. She was strange in many ways, but never that.

Michael remembered her father whom he had known long before he had met Laura. Theirs had been a companionable friendship. And after attaining supreme happiness with the mother, her son had begun his journey to hell here on Earth. Was he himself responsible for that tragedy by marrying the boy's mother?...Had God given them all they ever desired and punished the son instead...The Lord could not be so cruel and he dare not dwell on that...He must not question...He was not a heathen like the Romanies... Margharita had known, but then, they had always accepted that she had the 'Gift'...

"I shall be deeply grieved" she had told him that last night, and something else. "I cannot change Destiny, stay away from the water" she had said...What else did she know?...He wished he had asked and then, grieving and in a state of uncertainty, he decided he must believe in the Lord or he would be lost...

Chapter 37

Time had been kind to Laura Schiller. The slender, dainty woman stood in the hall listening to the angry voices of the two children above. Uncertain as to whether to go up to the first floor bedroom, her face held an expression of apprehension and worry. At fifty five, age had not desecrated her beauty. The long hair had retained the full gleam of gold, the face was still soft and smooth with just a few faint lines at the temples.

Michael Schiller followed his wife into the hall. He looked down into troubled grey eyes and gently stroked her cheek. "Let them sort it out, Laura. They'll be friends again tomorrow," he said in soothing tones.

She gazed up at the tall, slim man beside her, relief clearly visible at his presence, then smiled. "You indulge Mitch far too much. Just listen to them!"

Michael pretended to listen, although the shouting could be heard in the street. A tolerant smile appeared around the generous mouth and the bright blue eyes were full of mischief. "Well, dear! Kirsten shouldn't have given German measles to half the kids in the neighbourhood. It's no wonder Mitch is angry. They can't go on the boat trip on Sunday, not with spots like that!"

Laura's face had regained its composure. She shook her head. "You always take Mitch's side. That child can do no wrong."

Michael chuckled and put his arm about Laura as they listened...

"I didn't wanna be at your sissy party in the first place! Granma made me go!" Mitch yelled at Kirsten, looking daggers at the pretty eleven year old.

"An' I'm never inviting you again!" screamed Kirsten at Mitch, tossing her head, two braided black pigtails flying off at peculiar angles. "You're horrible!"

"I hope your spots turn black, an' your hair falls out!" Mitch shouted back.

Mortified at the thought of her crowning glory being in danger, Kirsten screamed. "I hate you, Mitch Sogar, an' I'll never speak to you again!"

She ran out of the bedroom, sobbing all the way down the stairs. Laura Schiller stopped Kirsten in her flight to the front door, made comforting noises, said Mitch didn't mean any of it, then turned to her husband.

"I'll take Kirsten home and explain. Take Mitch some lemonade, dear."

Michael nodded, patted the tearstained face of the girl and walked through the dining room into the kitchen. He hoped the drink would soothe Mitch's temper. To catch measles five days before the long awaited river cruise was enough to make anybody furious.

Michael dropped several ice cubes into the tall glass, and climbed the first flight of stairs. He almost stepped onto the small bunch of flowers Kirsten had given her friend as a peace offering. Mitch must have hurled them after the fleeing girl, he thought. Michael shook his head, picked the blooms off the floor and entered the guest room where Laura had installed the sick child. It was empty. So was the bathroom.

Placing the flowers into the basin, he continued up the short flight of polished oak, his soft indoor shoes silent. The door to the large attic room was wide open, and inside the small figure sat cross legged on the thick carpet. For a moment he watched, glass in hand, wondering whether to intrude. Watched the compact, sturdy body facing the dormer window, the head with its mop of tawny curls bent low over the two dolls clasped in a fierce embrace, rocking, rocking... relieving the anger and frustration raging through the small body. He had seen it so often over the years.

Michael gently placed the glass onto the fitment against the wall, and glanced at the rocking figure, smiling to himself. This was where Mitch felt at ease. Not in the pretty, delicate atmosphere of the guest room below. Here she could give vent to her fury.

Michael retreated and had just reached the stairs when the soft voice of eleven year old Mitch Sogar called. "Granpa!"

It was not posed as a question. She had known who had stood in the doorway. Somehow she always did. He turned back. Mitch sat quietly on the floor, facing him, the dolls nestling in her arms. The likeness to Laura never ceased to surprise him, except Mitch would not have the slender figure or the sweet, calm disposition of her grandmother. Instead the girl would become a fascinating combination of fierce independence, determination and compassion in the next few years. The curls were like Laura's, but the unruly mop of hair changed colour with the seasons. Gold in the spring and summer, changing to bronze later in the year. Her eyes would change from a misty grey to flinty steel when angry, to that of a stormy sea, when someone regarded her as a fool or too small for some task or other.

337

Black eyebrows arched delicately over long thick lashes shading her eyes, a pert nose and the wide curved mouth already full of promise, yet it was the strong stubborn jawline that gave the face dimension and character.

Smiling at the girl, Michael ventured. "Feel better now?"

"Yes, granpa. Thank you for the lemonade!" Mitch said sweetly.

Michael passed the glass over to the girl. There was a companionable silence between them as she drank and he let his tall body sink to the floor next to her. He waited patiently, knowing that soon there would be a velvet voiced "granpa," and grey eyes full of remorse would look at him. If she were to ask him for the moon at that moment he would surely go and fetch it for her. There was a magic in her repentance he could not resist. Nor could he have loved a son of his own more than he did Laura's grandchild.

This strange small piece of humanity, who thought and behaved like a boy and would soon be caught in a tide of emotions when her physical attributes dictated that she must live in the world of women. Michael knew that he too must adjust, but perhaps then it would be Laura's turn to be the anchor of Mitch's existence. He had enjoyed their time and would be content to let her go.

Mitch sipped her drink, deliberate and slow, knowing that her grandfather would expect her to make amends for her savage attack on Kirsten. It wasn't fair that the stupid girl spread measles all over the place just because she couldn't wait to have her party. Kirsten was usually more sensible than the others in her class. She watched Michael make himself comfortable on the floor. He had the grace and power of the panther she'd seen at the zoo. Never had she seen him do anything clumsy. And his lean face always reminded her of Jesus, except the brown hair was shorter with some grey streaks here and there, a slender nose and soft, smiling mouth.

Mostly granpa's eyes were full of fun, or deeply reproachful when she'd misbehaved. The colour reminded her of the cornflowers in the meadow behind the orchard. Lately he had a few more creases around the eyes, but granma called them laughter lines. Granpa never scolded, he just waited for her to rock away the terrible fury she tried so hard to control.

As long as she could remember he had told her that tomorrow is another day, when she hadn't got something right the first time. Maybe she would learn to be like him tomorrow, or the next day. He would always be there, kind and good, loving her even when she was beastly to the girls. She adored granma but loved granpa, because they talked about important things. Not the silly things women twittered on about all the time.

"Granpa?" The pleading voice was like velvet, and Michael felt a wave of love for the child desperately needing to purge her soul of wrong-doing. He saw the grey eyes looking at him, wanting his forgiveness and absolution. "I've been cruel to Kirsten, haven't I?"

Michael smiled and nodded. "Yes, Mitch. Very."

"Will you and granma forgive me? I'm very sorry," the small voice continued.

"Of course we will, darling. But you must ask your grandmother yourself. And make your peace with Kirsten. She was very upset."

Mitch opened her mouth to make a flippant retort, thought better of it and rose, a doll in each hand, threw her arms around the man still sitting on the floor and kissed him on both cheeks.

"I'll be nice to Kirsten, I promise," Mitch said, looking angelic. "She can have the bangle that woman sent me for Christmas" and added with a theatrical pout, "I don't want it!"

"Mitch." The quiet voice of Michael's was hesitant. "If you can't bring yourself to call Natasha 'Mother', then use her stage name. Don't think of her as 'that woman'."

They had all been furious at the actress's spasmodic attempts to bribe her daughter with gifts after Peter's death. The grey eyes had taken on a hint of steel as they stared into calm blue ones. Mitch looked away first, murmuring.

"Alright, granpa," she shrugged her shoulder, "but I never think of her, anyway. I'll go and find granma an' apologize. Race you down the stairs!"

She was running like a dervish out of the door before Michael had time to get up. He heard her calling 'granma' and hoped Laura had returned from taking Kirsten home.

After a light meal Laura stood Mitch in the bath, gently sponged her granddaughter's body and applied soothing lotion to the fading rash.

"Can I sleep in my bed tonight, granma?" Mitch asked.

"We'll take your temperature first. Then we'll see, darling." Laura smiled at the sight of the disappointed face. "Alright," she said, after shaking the thermometer down. "You can go back upstairs. Granpa can bring you some fresh lemonade later and make sure you're comfortable. But leave your door open."

"Ooh, thank you, granma!" She gave Laura a tight hug. "I love you!" Mitch threw on a pair of daisy sprigged pyjamas, then skipped into the guest room to collect her dolls and the silver framed photograph of her grandparents she had taken herself, sometime on the house boat. She gazed at it for a moment, smiling.

She knew the old boat had been exchanged for tickets to America by Mr Klein from the bookshop during the Depression, but she must never tell anyone. Or about any of the others that took refuge in the room above the hay loft. So many frightened people, all in transit to somewhere else. They hid in the boat too. Some sent word that they'd made it, others were never heard from again.

Sometimes granma looked frightened, but granpa always made it right for her. If only they had the liberty granpa had told her about so many times. Instead, they had a dictator and his army of spies, watching, informing, taking people away. But where did they put them all? Even the small prison in town was overflowing with people waiting to be taken somewhere. But where? No-one seemed to know or if they did they weren't telling. People just didn't talk to each other like they used to. Everybody was careful, frightened. Nobody could be trusted anymore.

Only granma and granpa, 'Aunt' Erika and Uncle Walter next door, who weren't really an Aunt and Uncle at all, and Freddy. Erika and Freddy had something going on ever since he had come back from the last war without his left leg. And who could blame them? Walter always took himself off to Cologne every Saturday evening after he shut the butcher's shop and looked very happy when he came back on Sunday. So far she hadn't figured out the reason why, but it might have something to do with sex. The whole village knew about it and didn't make too much fuss about Freddy and Erika, as Walter had started it all in the first place. They couldn't get divorced or they would be banished from the Catholic church. She felt sorry for them and grateful to be surrounded by people she loved. Especially granma and granpa, who adored each other and loved her.

She still missed her father. Sometimes she thought she could hear his voice from the middle of the mountain, telling her he loved her. She wished they had brought him back so she could pray at his grave and tell him things. But he was with his friends on the other side of the world.

Mitch squeezed the two dolls affectionately, calling out to her grandmother on her way upstairs. "Tell granpa I'll see him later. I'll read for a bit. 'Night, granma!"

She whistled the tune of 'Old Father Rhine' with gusto and Laura smiled indulgently.

It was almost eight o'clock before Michael Schiller finished the day's work in the garden. He paused for a moment at the low wall that divided the house and terrace from the market garden. The three quarter of an acre and the large orchard needed constant attention from early March until late October. Laura attended to the chickens and rabbits. Martha was worth her weight in gold and Daniel did far more than was expected of him.

Michael walked into the kitchen. Laura was waiting, the cold supper ready for him. Washing his hands, he asked. "Where is Mitch?"

"Gone back to her own bed," and seeing the slight trace of disappointment flit over his face, she added, smiling up at him. "You two are like twins. Always needing to know where the other one is. I promised you'll bring her some lemonade later."

He sat down and ate with appreciation, then stopped suddenly, looking questioningly at his wife "Laura? Did you ever mind Mitch spending so much time with me over the years?"

There was an imperceptible pause, before she replied. "I think I did in the beginning. My vision of a granddaughter was of pretty little Michelle playing with dolls and all the usual things that girls do. I never expected a determined tomboy. She made you happy though, and I didn't mind any more."

Michael tucked into his food with renewed vigour, watching Laura eat. "Just think! You could've been the second Baroness Laura von Dettingen-Annsberg. I hope you've never had second thoughts about marrying me. Have you, Mrs Schiller?"

Laura gazed at her husband, a mischievous smile turned up the corner of the soft mouth. "No, Michael, I've never had any doubts. As for being a Baroness, I love Cornelius dearly, but couldn't have married him. He reminds me too much of Jack."

For a moment Laura stared at the plate, remembering lonely years and the husband who needed to go and conquer the world, who thought war was just another challenge and was killed by it. And her son, like his father, had to satisfy the need to explore strange territory. One careless action cost him his life. Too soon. "They're never there when you need them," Laura said softly. Then a radiant smile banished all trace of sadness. "But I see your face every morning and thank God. And when Peter brought Mitch to us, it made us complete. What more could any woman ask for in life, Mr Schiller?"

Michael took Laura's small hand into his and gently kissed the wedding ring. "I love you," his voice was tender. "To wake and feel you there is the most magical moment of the day."

Michael got up and stood behind Laura, his arms close about her. He bent down and whispered into her ear. A pink flush spread over the cheeks of the beautiful woman. The mouth softened into a warm smile despite the mock disapproval in her voice.

"Michael!" Laura said, looking up into mischievous eyes and a wicked grin. "You're impossible!"

"I know," he said. "I'll take Mitch her lemonade and have a long bath torturing myself with wild anticipation. See you soon!"

He collected the jug and glass, almost skipping up the two steps leading into the dining room. Like Mitch, Laura heard her husband whistling all the way up the stairs.

Laura stepped out of the bath, towelling her body until it glowed. She untied the blonde hair, let it fall down her back and tried to untangle the damp curls. It was useless, they simply sprang back to where they had been in the first place. The slender reflection of her body in the long mirror pleased her. Still unblemished and firm, the softly rounded breasts had retained their youthful shape. 'It must be the hours of stretching and bending in the garden', she thought.

Michael had not put on weight, either. The image of her husband waiting for her brought on the familiar longing to have his strong fingers explore and touch her. They had made love gently and quietly while Mitch was in the next room, but tonight he would be his usual ardent self again. And she enjoyed it. Never for one moment had she imagined that the tall, black robed man she had met on that cold February morning almost fifteen years ago would have so much passion in his soul. Laura slipped the silk night dress over her head, dabbed a splash of cologne on wrists and throat and walked into the bedroom.

Michael always prepared the work sheet for the next day while waiting for Laura. Meticulously executed plans kept him up to date and he moved the papers aside. Covered only by a sheet, his naked body felt the stirring of desire at the sight of her. He constantly marvelled at his own need to possess her, and wondered sometimes if that need was excessive, but she never rejected him.

He knew she wanted him too. They did not need words. Laura stood at the foot of the bed and he let his gaze travel over her. She was teasing him. Michael saw the firm outline of the breasts under the clinging garment. They had always fascinated him. Even now he still delighted at watching the nipples harden at his touch, to see the sensuous smile on her face, hear the soft moans of pleasure. And as on their wedding night, tenderness would turn into a raging inferno of desire and the world would disappear.

"Are you coming to bed, Mrs Schiller, or do you intend to stand there all night?" Michael asked, a huge grin on his face.

Laura felt the light kiss, heard the soft 'Good night, my love' and moved her head from Michael's chest to settle on her pillow. Her 'Good night' sounded as if she had already passed the threshold of sleep.

Still euphoric from his love-making, he tried to clear his mind to go over the day and repent for any small misdemeanour he might unwittingly have committed. He glanced at the clock. Eleven forty. The night was only just beginning to cool after another sweltering day. He could see the stars through the wide open window. The long delicate lace curtains had been drawn back to let the faint light of the moon illuminate their naked bodies. Michael allowed himself another few moments of luxurious reminiscence of the past hour or so, a contented smile on his face.

The sound penetrated his deliberations. It came from above. Mitch!

Michael wondered if Laura had heard it too. His wife was fast asleep. He gently left the bed and slipped hastily into pyjamas, then walked quietly out of the bedroom, closing the door behind him. As he reached the open door to Mitch's room the soft light above her head shone through the archway and showed his granddaughter sitting up in bed, the dolls clasped to her, rocking, rocking...

He stood for a moment, undecided on what to do next. Only once had he seen her cry like this. Two days before the telegram arrived saying her father was buried under the mountain he had tried to blow a hole into.

Michael still stood in the doorway when he became aware the rocking had stopped. Then he heard the familiar 'granpa'. How could she have known that he was there? He walked quickly into the bedroom, asking, "What's the matter, sweetheart?" and saw a tear stained, frightened face looking up at him.

"I dreamed it again, granpa. Just like I did before Daddy was killed. It was awful!" her voice still shaking with sobs. "I'm all alone and there's nobody to save me. The whole world's drowned!"

Michael sat on the edge of the bed, gently prised the arms clutching the dolls to her chest away from her body and placed his hands on her shoulders.

"Mitch." His voice was kind and reassuring. He wanted to cradle the girl in his arms, as he had done so many times during her childhood, but now he must be careful. She was neither child nor woman but on the threshold of self discovery. "Listen to me. You had a fight with Kirsten today and were very angry. Maybe you were thinking about that before you went to sleep. Don't worry about it," and even as he said it, the large grey eyes looked at him and he knew Mitch did not believe him.

"Granpa. I wasn't thinking about Kirsten. I was thinking about Daddy!"

"That might explain your bad dream. Think of something nice before you go to sleep. I'll wait here if you want me to."

Mitch grasped Michael's hands and held them tightly.

"I'm scared, granpa. Will something awful happen again?"

For a moment he felt a sense of unease, then smiled at his granddaughter. "No, Mitch. Nothing will happen, I promise. And I'll say a special prayer, asking God to protect us all from harm. Will that make you feel better?"

Mitch settled herself into the pillows. "Yes," she said, and a small, hesitant smile appeared on the worried face. Michael heard the velvet sound. "Granpa?" and he looked at her.

"Yes?"

There was a brief silence. "Am I too old for you to tell me a story? The one about these two!" pointing to Prince Rama and Evita.

Michael was relieved her request was not pursuing the probability of impending disasters and laughed, glancing at the clock on the bedside table. The dial showed ten minutes past midnight.

"Well, young Lady. There's no age limit to be told a story. And as it's the witching hour, a fairy story is quite appropriate. Even if I've invented it myself."

344

"Thanks, granpa. I love listening to you," Mitch said, a happy expression on her face once more.

And Michael's soft resonant voice told again of the land where the sun always shone and the people were beautiful, with skin the colour of deep amber, their eyes like black diamonds and hair a mass of black, glossy curls. And of the flaxen-haired, blue-eyed princess in her Ice Palace in the North.

Michael had finished the story and saw that Mitch's eyes were heavy with sleep. He bent over and softly kissed the brow of the girl he loved so much and heard the murmured "Thank you, granpa. Night," and saw the two dolls sitting side by side on their own pillow. Turning the lamp away from her face, he returned to his bed.

Laura had not stirred. As he crept between the thin sheet, the dream Mitch had woken from still disturbed him. The girl's uncanny perception about danger and the people she loved they had accepted a long time ago. She must have been thinking of her father and the nightmare she'd had two years ago. There couldn't possibly be anything else. They were all healthy, the business was going well and the refugees had come and gone safely on their way to the next destination. Until recently. Something was wrong and for the time operations had ceased.

The trip on Sunday certainly held no danger. Captain Olaf had taken them every year without the slightest mishap. The ship was his pride and joy and sound as a bell. This was to be their thirteenth trip. Thirteen! Michael was glad he wasn't superstitious. The only calamity he could think of was that the war everyone knew was imminent should start this weekend. How could they stop it when nations and the Church joined forces in a conspiracy of silence?

Michael remembered his promise to Mitch to say a special prayer and fervently asked the Lord to keep all of them safe. He also knew with certainty that there would be no more fairy stories.

As he drifted into that no man's land between wakefulness and dreams, faint images of a caravan in the meadow surged upwards and he thought he heard the gypsy's voice. 'Don't go on the water...'

Chapter 39

While the passengers of the Olaf Johannsen gazed in awe at the Lorelei, the train from Cologne drew into the station at Bacharach.

Two sober suited men, their faces hard and unsmiling, stepped out of the first class coach and strode toward the ticket barrier. Each carried an attaché case. The ticket collector glanced at their passes, looked alarmed and quickly uttered a clumsy 'Heil Hitler'.

The two men did not follow the laughing crowd making their way towards the town's famous attractions, but set off in the opposite direction. They turned into a side street and paused for a moment before a small guesthouse, disappearing through the open front door. In the foyer, the bulky proprietor, Krause, greeted them with a fervent Nazi salute. A large portrait of the Fuehrer hung in a prominent position above the reception desk. The men did not register, but settled themselves at a table in the corner of the dining room after ordering food and drink. Discouraged from entering into a lengthy conversation, Krause withdrew, a sullen expression on his face.

The older of the two men watched his companion flexing his fingers, a habit which irritated him a great deal. SS Colonel Inkmeyer didn't care much for the younger man. Too fanatical, too zealous.

"Will it work, Scholl?"

He never addressed his colleagues by anything else but their surname. Nor did he do them the courtesy of prefixing that by their rank.

"Yes, sir," Scholl said. "We just need Radec to put the device into place."

"Good. You're the expert. Does Radec know what to do?"

"Yes, he's one of my best men."

"What about the Captain?" queried Inkmeyer.

"Dispensable," Scholl replied curtly.

Krause appeared, a broad smile on his face, carrying a plate heaped with steak, fried potatoes and vegetables. His wife, a quiet, buxom lady who looked distinctly uncomfortable in the presence of the two men, laid the table and hurried out of the dining room. Krause fetched glasses and placed a bottle of wine on the table. Colonel Inkmeyer looked at the year, a smile softening the hard contours of his face.

"An excellent year, Krause. Thank you."

"It's an honour and deserving of this special occasion, sir!" Krause bowed. "May one ask..."

"No questions, Krause," Major Scholl interrupted. "We will require the use of a bedroom after our meal. You may leave us now."

Scholl glanced at Colonel Inkmeyer, who appeared to be occupied with filling his glass, but Major Scholl knew perfectly well that nothing escaped the Colonel, however trivial. To his colleagues Inkmeyer remained an enigma. Both men ate in silence, hungry after the long train journey.

After his second glass of wine Colonel Inkmeyer asked, "Any questions, Scholl?"

The Major's pale blue eyes met the Colonel's hard stare. "No, sir. I follow orders to the letter. The why's do not concern me," and he noticed a slight tick appearing at the right eye of the older man.

"Very sensible, if somewhat unimaginative," Inkmeyer replied coolly. "Where is the device to be situated? There are almost two hundred people on the boat."

Major Scholl hesitated a moment, and Inkmeyer noticed again the insistent flexing of the fingers. Could the arrogant Major be nervous? It would be most appropriate if he was. This was not a game to be played carelessly. Somebody was pulling very powerful strings.

"Does the number of persons worry you, Colonel?" Scholl asked.

The older man refilled his glass, offered the bottle to Major Scholl, who declined. He chose his words carefully.

"It is not the numbers so much as the method employed to catch four big fish surrounded by minnows who on the whole have no connection, except that they work for the Baron's newspaper. Many of them have joined us, yet still we cannot pin down the organisation that spirits away Jews and enemies of the Fatherland at will. Someone is desperate to put a stop to it. I wish..." the Colonel's voice tailed off.

Major Scholl seized his opportunity. "May I be permitted to ask who that someone is?"

The Colonel's face set into its usual hard mask and ice blue eyes glittered angrily at the Major. Insolent fool, thought Inkmeyer.

"No, Scholl, you are not permitted to ask. Stick to your part in the game. Where do you intend to place the damn box?"

"As you just pointed out that I should stick to my job, you will forgive me if I do precisely that. Radec will know the time and place. It is all arranged.

He only needs for me to deliver the device." Scholl paused for a moment. "If it makes it easier for you, Colonel," he said, "I have given the other passengers my consideration too." Major Scholl did not flinch from the Colonel's stare, but after a moment he looked at his watch. "I believe it is time we made ready," he said amiably, hoping to smooth over the antagonism between them.

The Colonel knew the rebuff was justified, and felt a flicker of respect for the younger man, even if it did not make him like Scholl any better. He drained the last of the wine, picked up his attache case and led the way to the reception desk, where Krause was waiting for them.

"On the next floor, Colonel. First door on your left," Krause said, bowing to the older man, ignoring Major Scholl. "Did you enjoy the meal?"

"Very much, Krause," Inkmeyer said pleasantly. "My compliments to your charming wife. The wine was excellent. Thank you!"

He watched as a smile appeared on the chubby face of the very minor official in the Nazi Party.

At the end of the street, a wide cobbled road led down to the river embankment and landing stages. The Olaf Johannsen lay berthed and the last of Freddy's jovial workforce made their way down the gang plank and milled about the pier. No-one took any notice of two men in river police uniform, revolvers at their side, who walked in the direction of the boat. Or that the younger of the two was carrying a black attache case.

"We should perhaps give them another half hour," Major Scholl said. "May I have your permission to buy a souvenir for my children, Colonel?"

Colonel Inkmeyer looked vaguely surprised. "For your children? I had no idea that you were married."

"Some of us are," Scholl replied, almost smiling. "I have a son and a daughter."

"How pleasant for you, Scholl. I'll wait on that seat over there." He pointed to a lone bench at the edge of the embankment, where he could observe the Olaf Johannsen at all times. "Take your time," he added kindly, which made Major Scholl throw him a curious glance, but he refrained from making a comment.

He watched the younger man disappear into one of the cobbled side streets that led to the town centre and realized the Major had taken the attache case with him. Somehow he felt relieved and relaxed against the railings.

Colonel Inkmeyer noticed the colourful pennants of the boat fluttering in the breeze. He had not been on a river cruise for eighteen years. The boat looked well kept and inviting. He suddenly became aware of movement on the lower deck and was instantly alert.

Two couples emerged onto the gangway. A vivacious fair haired woman in a flowery chiffon dress, slim and long-legged, had her arm through that of her companion. He walked carefully with measured steps, a stick in his right hand. Both were laughing heartily at something the other two had said. It had to be Baron Frederick von Dettingen-Annsberg, the owner of the newspaper, and Erika Behrens. The older man behind him must be Michael Schiller. Tall and good-looking, the intellect and the brains behind the covert operations. He had his arm about the waist of the dainty woman at his side.

Laura Schiller had the Colonel's full attention. Mrs Behrens was very attractive, but this woman had a beauty that would not fade with age. Her face was like a painting he had once seen, somewhere. The navy linen dress with the white large buttons showed off the slender figure to perfection, and highlighted the colour of her hair, tied back with a navy silk scarf. She swung the neat handbag like a schoolgirl, slim legs and tiny feet stepped daintily down the sloping gangway.

What were they laughing about? He felt a strong curiosity, something he hadn't experienced for a long time. It was so obvious that the older couple were still in love. Was it possible to feel like that at their age? He wanted to be with them and didn't know why. Maybe he wanted to laugh with them, feel like a human being, free and happy. Colonel Seb Inkmeyer was thirty-eight years old and had never loved anyone since he left his home. Somewhere deep inside of him there was regret that he had to witness this, today of all days.

He watched the four people walk slowly towards the town. A few minutes later he saw a young man in Captain's uniform escort a woman from the boat. Her charming features resembled those of Mrs Behrens, but this girl did not have the vitality of the older woman. She must be Erika Behrens' daughter, Chrissy, a school teacher. As far as he knew, she had no connection with any of their activities.

And for once in his long and sometimes brutal career, Colonel Inkmeyer wished he had the power to stop Major Scholl from carrying out his mission.

He felt hot and uncomfortable in the strange uniform. Conspicuous. He walked away from the railing, sat down on the bench and looked at the broad band of water, the green ripples glistening in the sun. All this reminded him of the home he had not seen for fifteen years and could not return to. It reminded him of who he had been. Of the disgrace he had brought to his family. The pain he had caused his mother, who grieved for him at a grave that held the body of a stranger.

All of it reminded him of how he had betrayed his friends in the Communist Party in 1923 and was responsible for the violence and the massacre that followed. No-one knew his real identity. He had used the name of his friend, as committed to Fascism as he himself had been once.

He had become Sebastian Inkmeyer, risen in the ranks of the Nazi Party, and did not go south again. He could not marry because he had no past, and wondered what the wife of Major Scholl was like. Would she be equally fanatical? Or a simple, kind and plump woman, like Lotti, the cheerful, happy spouse of his friend Jan Konrad? He always had the feeling that Jan, too, was not what he seemed. If that quiet, private exterior hid a secret, the brown eyes in the pale face allowed no questions. Often, when he visited Jan, they would retreat to the study and the unspoken questions hung between them, but were never voiced.

Did he also know about this operation? Jan was informed about everything. As Chief of the Intelligence Section in Cologne he had to be. Why had he not caught the former priest and his accomplices? He had exposed so many secret and subversive organisations with skill and great tenacity. Except this one. Unless...But that was absurd. Even Jan couldn't get away with that. Or could he? Seb Inkmeyer suddenly realised just how little he knew about the tall, white haired man he called his friend. The niggling thought at the back of his mind would not leave him, but he decided to put it aside when he saw Major Scholl coming towards him.

The Olaf Johannsen lay quiet and seemingly empty at the landing jetty. The two men made their way toward the ship and walked up the gangplank, where they were warmly welcomed by Radec, the second mate.

Michael Schiller's arm was still around Laura's waist as the four friends walked up to the small hotel in the main street of the town. Freddy was in high spirits.

"We're meeting an old friend for a drink in here," he said cheerfully. "You two go and look over the place. If you approve, I'll clinch the deal." He watched the bemused expression on Laura's face with glee. "Erika and me need to get away from the estate now that my fascist nephews are coming home more often. They're bringing the weirdest friends with them. Universities aren't what they used to be, eh, Michael?"

"No," Michael agreed. "Politics have taken over."

Laura had assimilated the casual reference to a place and was recovering from the shock. "You mean... you want to buy a house here? In Bacharach? Did you know about this, Michael?" she asked her husband, and knew the answer already by the amused look he exchanged with Freddy.

Erika laughed. "'Course he knew. We wanted it to be a surprise for you!" She pointed up at the gently rising street. "It's up there, looking down onto the river. I've always loved this town and the house is big enough to have you and Cornelius over to stay with us."

"Six bedrooms ought to be enough to sleep everybody in comfort," Freddy added, grinning at Michael.

"We only need one," Michael replied, and then looked at his watch. "Come on, Laura. Let's go and see if we approve," he said, tightening his grip on her waist and setting off up the cobbled street.

"Have fun!" Erika called after them. "We'll wait for you on the boat!"

Laura and Michael waved. They climbed up the hill and ten minutes later stopped before a black wrought iron gate. Beyond lay a large cream painted villa, two storeyed, with dormer windows set into the red tiled roof. They entered and followed a gravel drive, flanked by lawn. Laura left her husband to walk along the path at the side of the house and stepped onto a wide terrace.

"Michael, come and see this!" she called out excitedly.

He joined Laura and they both looked in silence at the panorama spread out before them. The river flowed majestically below, the Olaf Johannsen a white and blue speck at the landing stage. Across the water and to the right and left of them on the hillside were row upon row of vines, standing like sentinels, heavy with sweet grapes ready for harvesting. The town with its colourful roofs lay at the foot of the hill.

"It's breath taking," Laura murmured in awe. "No wonder Erika wants it so much. It reminds me of the view at Rema house where I used to live. You could see the river from our apartment for miles either way!"

"This is the finest wine growing region," Michael said. He gently placed his arm around her shoulder, drawing her close to him. "Could you be happy here, Laura?"

She looked up and smiled at him. "If I had to live somewhere other than Dettingen, this would be the place." She gazed at him for a moment, a question in her eyes. "Michael, how long have you known about this?"

"A week."

"Why didn't you tell me?" she asked.

"Freddy asked me not to. He gave Erika an ultimatum last Saturday. Either to come here to live with him permanently or he's going abroad. They've been sorting themselves out. It's a big decision for her. Last night she said 'yes'. They've been coming to this house for some time now."

"So that's why I haven't seen much of her lately, and when I did, she was so quiet I wondered whether she was alright, but she said she felt fine. What about Freddy's newspaper?"

Michael hesitated, looked down the slope and studied the narrow terraces of vines. "He's giving it up. But he wants to tell his father first. Cornelius should be back this week. Freddy wants to take over all this." Michael's hand pointed in all directions. "Maybe in time he'll blend his own wine."

Laura looked concerned. "But he doesn't know anything about the wine making business. He's running a newspaper."

"Cornelius grows grapes and brews his own wine. He'll have the right connections to give us advice until we're knowledgeable enough." Michael said carefully.

Laura glanced at her husband. "I did hear you say 'us' and 'we', didn't I, Michael?" she asked, disengaging herself from his arm.

She sat down on the wall, facing the back of the house. She noticed the wide conservatory stretching from one end of the property to the other. Inside, a large part held what looked like more vines. Michael sat down next to Laura, took her hand and placed a gentle kiss onto her wedding ring. When he spoke, his voice was quiet but firm.

"Yes, Laura. You did hear that. Freddy wants me to be his partner. Here. There was no point in discussing anything until Erika had made up her mind. They'll move in here when Freddy's settled the business with the newspaper. We'll have 'till then to decide. I would like to try it, but not without you!"

"I'll go where you go, Mr. Schiller," she said firmly. "But there's Mitch and the house and our business."

"Daniel can take care of that. If we let him rent the house, he'll marry Chrissy. He can take on a youngster and train him. Mitch will think of it as a new adventure. Kirsten can come and visit, or even stay, if Susanna will agree. Either way, it's not a long journey by train."

Michael's voice tailed off, waiting for Laura's reply. He wondered if she was angry because he hadn't told her, or upset at the prospect of leaving her home. She did not answer for some time, just sat quietly, looking out over the hills, her smooth brow furrowed in thought.

"Laura?" Michael's voice held a note of anxiety. "If you and Mitch don't want to move away from Dettingen, then I'll say no to Freddy's offer."

Laura turned and faced her husband. "You've already considered all the options. Did you think of a good school for Mitch, too?" she asked.

"There are good schools everywhere," Michael replied, taking both her hands into his own.

He looked at her for a long time as if he was not sure whether to keep the full truth until another time. They had left the house early this morning intending to have a pleasant day. The first inkling he had that this was not going to be the happiest of days was when Theo and the strange young man Radec had presented themselves instead of Olaf, then Freddy had taken him on one side in the bar to tell him that Erika was leaving Walter and that they would move to Bacharach. And he knew that telling Laura of his plans had become a matter of urgency.

"I'd like you to think that this decision wasn't influenced by other factors, Laura, but that wouldn't be the truth. There's every indication that our network has been infiltrated. We must get out now. The last three refugees only just made it to the Swiss border, with far too many problems. Things are hotting up."

Laura's face had remained so calm that he wondered if she had been listening to him. Michael was surprised by her response. "Is Mitch in danger too, Michael?"

"We all are. Now more than before. We've been lucky to survive the last ten years without detection, and Mitch can't play the innocent child any longer."

Michael looked and sounded worried. Laura spoke quietly. "Yes, we have been very lucky and I agree. The poor wretched people will have to find another way to get out."

353

She began to shake uncontrollably. Michael took his wife into his arms and held her tight. "I love you so much and want to stay alive to spend the rest of my days with you and Mitch."

Laura gently extracted herself from Michael's arms and sat up very straight. Her voice was strong and uncompromising. "I'm not afraid to die for what I believe in, but I won't have Mitch put in danger. We'll move. I'll like it here."

Michael smiled at her. "You're beautiful and marvellous and I love you, Mrs. Schiller." He kissed her soundly, then looked out over the valley, a puzzled expression on his face. "You know, I've always believed that God alone has protected us all these years, but I'm not so sure any more," Michael said, looking at his wife. "Freddy thinks it's somebody with a lot of power."

Laura, an astonished expression on her face, asked, "Cornelius?"

Michael shook his head. "No. He's got influential friends, but he's not that powerful. And it's not Freddy's fascist brother Hubert, that's for sure."

"Then who?" Laura wanted to know.

"We don't know, and it's only a hunch. I wish I did know, Laura, but something is happening. Freddy and Erika are worried. We've already sent word along the line that the operation is suspended."

Laura heaved a sigh of relief and leaned over to kiss Michael. "My love. It'll make a pleasant change picking grapes instead of apples and cherries. Let's go and look inside."

Michael placed his arm around Laura's shoulder and walked with her across the terrace to the other end of the house. A wide band of glistening gravel led them back to the entrance. He unlocked the door of the porch. The stout oak door to the hall opened effortlessly and as they stepped over the threshold Laura gasped in surprise.

"Oh, Michael. I wouldn't mind living here myself."

Admiring the open fireplace, soft leather furniture and low tables, her eyes travelled up the stairs that curved gently to the first floor landing, then on to the attics. Hall and stairs gleamed in cream and bronze Italian marble, as did the surround to the bronze hearth.

"You may have to for a while, until we find a suitable place of our own." Michael said dryly, as he picked up a note left on one of the tables and read it. "Erika's left a bottle of wine in the larder," he called after Laura, who had disappeared into the dining room. "She hopes you like the house."

"It's all so beautiful, Michael," Laura said when she returned to the hall where two glasses of sparkling wine stood on the table.

"Taste this. It's brewed specially from the grapes in the conservatory. Very good it is, too."

He handed Laura a glass. She drank it and licked her lips appreciatively. "It's delicious."

"Come on, Madam," said Michael. "To the bedrooms." He refilled their glasses and walked up the grand staircase to the gallery above. "The owner left for America two months ago," he informed Laura, who was following, playfully running her hand along the twisted bronze balustrade. Michael stopped in the doorway of a beautifully furnished bedroom and Laura gasped.

"I've always wanted to sleep in one of those. Can I try it? Just once?" she pleaded, removing her shoes.

The four poster bed stood there, wide, elegant and inviting. Laura sat on the edge, swung her legs up and laid on the cover, gazing at the canopy surrounded by frills of brocade. Her laughter echoed around the empty house. "I feel like a queen."

Michael took another drink and placed the glasses onto a side table, then leaned over her, strong fingers deftly unbuttoning her dress. "I think I'll join you, Mrs Schiller."

She protested half heartedly. "We've got a boat to catch, Michael."

He glanced at his watch, grinned and took off his clothes. "One hour and thirty five minutes gives us a lot of time," he murmured into her ear.

Chapter 40

A clear sky over the river told Freddy's people that the night was going to be warm and dry. By six forty-five that evening everyone was back on board, hot, dishevelled and very thirsty. A constant stream of noisy passengers made their way past the engine room to the cloakrooms below the bridge. Some gave a curious glance to the closed doors of the engine room and wondered who was inside there today. Certainly not Bony, Captain Olaf's second mate, or Rick, his engineer. They never shut themselves in, proudly showing off the gleaming engine and massive boiler to anyone even the slightest bit interested.

Laura and Michael met Freddy on the upper deck. Usually they would be with Captain Olaf now, but of Theo and Radec there was no sign and they presumed them to be busy on the bridge. The boat had to make the about-turn in mid-stream before gathering speed to go down river.

The man in the uniform of the River Police left the bridge and retreated unnoticed into the Captain's cabin. Most of the passengers milled about the lower deck to watch the boat slip its moorings, listening to the engine pick up speed and the rhythm of the well-oiled pistons.

"Well, what do you think of the house, pet?" Erika asked Laura, beaming all over her face.

Laura, in an affectionate gesture, placed her arm about Erika's shoulder. "I love your new home. It's so beautiful. But why didn't you tell me earlier? It certainly was a surprise."

Erika glanced at Freddy and a tender smile passed between them.

"Until last night I wasn't sure if I could leave Walter for good. "Besides." She pointing to Freddy. "That jackass threatened to go and live abroad without me. I can't let him do that. Are you and Michael going to join us?"

"Yes." Laura said enthusiastically. "Why not?"

Michael and Freddy exchanged a meaningful look.

"Just think, only grapes to worry about from now on," Michael remarked dryly, and moved closer to his wife.

Freddy turned to Laura. "Did you like the four poster bed?"

A faint blush appeared across her cheeks. "It's wonderful, isn't it, Michael?"

"Yes, and so comfortable," he said, grinning at Freddy. "By the way, did you meet your friend at the hotel?"

Erika answered, smiling. "Yes. He's the owner's solicitor and we've told him to go ahead. It'll be a good life for all of us."

Freddy was listening to the chatter of his people, the laughter. "This will be the last river cruise we'll make," he said. "They're my friends and I'll miss them."

Erika patted his hand. "Maybe the new man will bring them here next year," she said, and giggled. "We'll invite them all onto the terrace and fill them up with our own wine. How about that?"

Freddy cheered up at the prospect of having two hundred of his people squashed onto the wide terrace.

They watched as the ship manoeuvred to the middle of the river, slowly turning its nose downstream. The engine resumed its normal rhythm, a quiet, steady heartbeat. The bell to let the passengers know that the dining room would be open, rang out.

Michael put his arm around Laura's waist. "I think we'll have champagne to celebrate our future," he said, smiling down at her. "I intend to enjoy it."

"Me, too," Laura answered.

Erika took Freddy's arm and laughed, "Good idea, Michael. We'll drink to survival, freedom and the wine business."

"Very appropriate," Michael replied solemnly, then added. "I wonder if Theo'll invite us to his cabin tonight. If he doesn't, we'll take our bottle and toast the Lorelei on deck."

Freddy grinned. "We'll sit on the other side of his private deck just to let him know we've noticed!"

Theo did not join them for the evening meal, but surprisingly invited them to come to his cabin at 9:00 pm for a glass of champagne. The ship would cruise at a leisurely pace until they reached the Lorelei, then the fairy lights would be switched on, illuminating the big steamer like a Christmas tree.

She would enter the narrow stretch of turbulent water for the farewell ceremony to the mermaid.

The train for Cologne was due to leave at 6:05 pm. Seb Inkmeyer had passed through the ticket barrier and walked to the first class coach. He selected a compartment, drew the shades on the door and windows facing the corridor and removed his jacket. Back in civilian clothes, he wanted no company.

As he settled into the window seat, he recalled every detail of the afternoon with precision and wondered how Major Scholl was making out. Probably hiding in the Captain's cabin now that everybody was back on board. He pondered on the fact that he wasn't sure whether he wanted Scholl to get blown up or wished him success.

That bothered him. Was he getting old, or simply tired of the carnage? So much waste. Had he ever looked into any of the faces he helped to condemn to certain death? No! They were enemies of the Reich and in time became a multitude of nameless bodies. Awaiting trial, to be sentenced to death or put on a train to some hell hole in the heart of south and east Germany. He had heard rumours about the Labour Camps, but had never been in one. Not very pleasant places by all accounts.

He liked it here, where people still tried to lead a civilised existence, exercised their stubborn right to be themselves and got into trouble for it. An independent, quirky lot, who added French taste and culture to their own and didn't take kindly to the fierce nationalism imposed on them after the 'Liberation' of 1936.

The face of Laura Schiller invaded his thoughts. And with it another face, just as beautiful, which took him back to that cold April morning in 1933...

His orders had been to bring in Professor Gieleman, his daughter, Risla, and to search the house for anything incriminating.

The church clock had just struck six when they had arrived in the tree lined avenue. The only sound the noise of the motors of the two cars, then the hammering on the front door with the shiny brass plate. A frail old man, a black skull cap on silvery hair had opened the door and reeled back as four SS troopers marched in and began to ransack the large apartment. He had shown the Professor his pass, asked him to fetch his daughter, get dressed and accompany him to headquarters. He hoped he had been polite, but not too much so. He must not appear soft in front of his men.

Then one of the troopers pushed the girl into the room, so roughly that he wanted to tell him to leave her alone, but didn't. She had stood there, silent and dignified in a long, white cotton night gown, a shawl hastily thrown over her shoulder and held tight by small hands. He could still recall the vivid colours of that shawl. Delicate leaves, blue cornflowers, the red of full blown roses and the silken fringe around the edges of the soft fabric.

Unlike most Jewish women, the girl's hair had been like spun gold and hung in a thick braid over one shoulder. For one moment he had felt an insane desire to see it free and loose, touch it. Her face was beautiful, serene, like the Madonna in the chapel of his home. Brown soft eyes had looked at him without hatred, without fear. She had looked deep into his soul, expressing pity for what he represented. He had felt strange, wished himself far away, safe and untainted, back with his mother who had loved him so much, so long ago...

He had left Professor Gieleman and his daughter Risla at headquarters, but her face still haunted his dreams and he would lie half awake, wondering if she was alive or dead, or if he should try and find her. By the time he was fully awake, he knew that he'd do nothing. He could never face the hate that must surely be in her eyes, nor the pity: if she felt anything at all.

Colonel Seb Inkmeyer wondered if today another face would join Risla's. That of Laura Schiller, the slender woman, laughing with her husband, her hair the same colour of gold. Should he go and stop Scholl? Risk his career, his life? No. These people were enemies, after all. Breaking laws that carried the death penalty. They should have joined the Party.

He was relieved when the train moved out of the station. His mind went back to the strange thoughts he had while sitting on the embankment. Something, as yet undefined, unclear, bothered him. A strand of some shadowy web he could not fathom out. But he knew by the rare instinct that had kept him at the top for so long that it was there. The young Baron, a thorn in the flesh of his brother Hubert. Erika, his woman and accomplice, Laura and Michael Schiller, who master-minded the operations. There had to be someone who had kept them alive and safe. But who? Someone who had power over life and death. And he, or she, was not too far away. Jan? Somehow, he knew the missing piece of the intriguing puzzle was to be found in Jan's office. But how to get hold of it? He could never bribe Rudi. And then he cleared all of it away, out of his mind, as he could feel a headache coming on. Thoughts like that shouldn't fill a man's head on a hot day like this.

By 8:15 pm the dining room had been cleared of people and tables. The band had eaten well and felt ready for the next few hours of music. Rosa had transformed herself from waitress to glamorous entertainer and received a standing ovation even before singing the first of her songs. She was popular with the crowd. The band had taken up residence by the open doors of the dining room, where the breeze from the deck would keep them cool and the barmen were busy.

Chef and his staff were taking a well earned rest before preparing the cold buffet. Chef had shut himself into his cabin above the engine room, adjacent to the kitchen. He liked the faint hum of the engine below. It always sent him to sleep. The shutters above the serving counters would remain firmly closed until 10:00pm precisely. Erika and Freddy, Laura, Michael and Chrissy had remained at the Captain's table. The meal had been excellent, the conversations light hearted, though they still missed Olaf and didn't particularly want to join his arrogant son for a drink in his cabin. Chrissy excused herself to go and freshen up.

"Does she know?" asked Laura, as she and Michael had refrained from mentioning the house, not knowing how much Chrissy had been told.

"Oh, yes," Erika said. "I told her last night. She's not sure if it's a good idea but is happy for me, whatever I decide to do."

"You have decided, sweetheart," Freddy said, grinning at her. "Don't expect me to live in that big house all by myself."

"Or pick your own grapes," Michael remarked, a twinkle in his eyes.

It was almost 8:30 and after a few slow tunes the band thought it was time to liven up the evening. Amidst the noise of the music, the laughter and the singing, no-one in the dining room noticed that the engine had stopped. Chrissy felt the silence as she passed the door of the engine room on her way back from the cloakroom.

She made her way to the railings on the open deck and stood with other bewildered passengers. The ship lay silent and still in the broad river. The large number of river patrol boats they had seen that morning moored on the jetty were still there. Except one was making its way towards the ship. Chrissy hurried to the dining room and pushed through the couples on the dance floor to get to the table and Freddy.

"The ship has stopped, Freddy," she sounded worried. "There's a patrol boat coming over. From that lot we saw this morning."

"I'll go and see," Michael said. "Come on, Laura. You two find Theo and ask him if he knows what's going on."

Michael gave Freddy a warning glance and Freddy nodded, then let Erika help him up. Chrissy followed Michael, who looked concerned, holding Laura by the hand.

By now the railings had large numbers of people leaning over, as the patrol boat came closer to the hull of the 'Olaf Johannsen'. Michael saw the small craft stop below where Theo had partitioned off part of the deck outside the Captain's cabin door. A rope ladder came over the side and a man in river police uniform climbed over the railing and down the ladder to the waiting patrol boat, which immediately sped back to the river bank.

Laura and Michael looked at each other, surprise, worry and questions mirrored in their faces. Suddenly they could feel the throb of the engines again and breathed easier as the ship began to move towards the narrow entrance of the rock, wide and high and menacing in the gathering dusk.

"Let's find Freddy," Michael said and led his wife through the dancing couples.

Erika and Freddy had gone to the bridge, expecting Theo to be there. They found only Radec. To their questions he was non-committal.

"It's the Captain's business," he said curtly.

They had left as the ship began moving again and walked arm in arm back to their table. In spite of the uneasiness they felt, both made pleasant remarks to their guests, all of them mystified as to who the man was that had left the ship. Perhaps a friend of Theo's had wanted a lift down the river to join his colleagues at the bank of the village.

Freddy was not mean and would not begrudge anybody a ride or food or drink. So why had no-one seen him?

The ship was approaching the mid-way point where the customary toast took place.

"We'd better go and see Theo," Erika said to Freddy without much enthusiasm. "I'll go and get Chrissy. You go on," she said, then made her way to the open stern, where most of the passengers had gathered at the railings, drinks in hand, to salute the rock.

Chrissy was surrounded by some of her young pupils. She had forgotten about the meeting in the cabin. Somehow, after the afternoon spent with Theo, who had constantly tried to impress her with his status and his ambitions Chrissy longed for the comfortable presence of Daniel. Kind, loving and patiently waiting for her to marry him.

Erika got held up in the happy crowd, talking, not wishing to be impolite by being in a hurry. On a sudden impulse she decided to give the champagne in the cabin a miss. She felt a twinge of guilt not being with Freddy, but Theo was not like his father and would spoil the good mood she was in. Erika moved through the people to get nearer to her daughter.

Chapter 41

The bridge of the 'Olaf Johannsen' was slightly elevated, between the first and upper deck. The wide oak stairs led down to a corridor and immediately opposite was Olaf's cabin, big and comfortably furnished. The long polished table, bookshelves and chairs still left ample room for the bunk he used for a well earned rest before the return journey.

The Captain liked to entertain in style. The second door of the cabin marked 'DECK' had always been left open and passengers strolled past. Captain Olaf would have it no other way. The river was his home, the passengers his family. He was respected and loved and no-one took liberties with his privacy.

Theo Johannsen had changed the rules. He had shut them out, wanting no part of them. There was no place on the river for arrogant Captains or unfriendly second mates.

By 8:50 pm on that last Sunday in August Radec, Theo's second mate, had acquainted the young Captain of events to come. He had not revealed the final horror. Theo faced Radec across the table, his brain refusing to admit that this was real. For the first time in years he wished his father was with him to get him out of this nightmare. He noticed the revolver in Radec's hand was steady, the silencer giving it a strange shape. The man's voice was cold and brutal.

"You'll ask them to come in. If you say one word to warn them I'll blow your brains out, comrade."

"Please, Radec," Theo begged. "They're my friends. Why kill them? Why not just arrest them? At least they'll have a chance."

The menacing tone of Radec's voice sent a chill through Theo. "Friends like that get you on a slow train to the concentration camp. Remember that. I have my orders."

The enormity of what was about to happen hit Theo at last. He tugged at his jacket to pull it straight and stood tall, his voice strong. "This is my father's ship and I AM the Captain. That means I give the orders. The gun, Radec," and held out his hand.

Radec grudgingly felt a flicker of respect for this younger version of Olaf Johannsen, but only fleetingly. Then he laughed, a cruel sound, without mirth. "Major Scholl gets his orders from above. I have mine," Radec said, ignoring the request for the gun. "Somebody wants them dead. We've waited months to catch them together."

Theo's brain was racing as he glanced at the ship's clock. Nearly nine o'clock... He needed Michael here... Freddy was useless with his one leg and there would be three women in the cabin... He couldn't count on the two in the engine room, they were Radec's men... He had to stall until Michael got here before he could take the gun away from Radec...

Theo's voice was calm. "How are you going to explain dead bodies on this ship? Are you going to make them jump into the river in full view of everybody on board?"

Suddenly he became aware of the music, the singing, the laughter, and something else. The vibration under his feet had stopped. The rhythm of the engine had ceased and once again the ship lay quiet and still. He had not given orders to stop. He stared at Radec, who shrugged and said coldly,

"There has to be an accident, comrade. We've got to make it look convincing. They're important people, not just anybody."

Theo forced himself to remain calm. "What kind of men are you? My father was right. I shouldn't have listened to your bullshit. You've tricked me, Radec. Did you unhook that gangplank hoping the old man would break his neck?"

Radec smiled, cruelly, without mercy, ignoring the last question. "You wanted to believe in the glory of it all. Wanted to be part of it," he said. "We're the men that'll rule the world one day soon. Come with us."

Before Theo could answer there was loud knock at the door. Radec skirmished the table and stood behind the Captain, the gun pressing into his back. "I will, Theo. Believe me!"

"Come," Theo called, hoping to see Michael. Theo fully intended to take the gun off Radec and if he got shot, Michael would know what to do. Instead, the dainty figure of Laura stepped through the door, followed by Freddy. Both looked puzzled.

"What's going on, Theo?" Freddy asked. "This is the second time we've stopped. Are we going to have a long conversation with that mermaid up there?"

He guided Laura to a chair behind the table, while he sat down in Olaf's chair, not far from the door, where he could stretch out his wooden leg and be comfortable. Laura was uneasy in the presence of Radec, but greeted him politely, wondering why he stood so close to the Captain.

"Where's Michael and the others?" Theo asked Freddy, who detected anxiety in the young man's voice.

"Michael's gone down to the engine room to see if we're having trouble."

He saw Theo was agitated, and wondered at the reason. Freddy looked at Radec and suddenly felt sweat breaking out of every pore.

"Erika's gone to fetch Chrissy," he said sharply and was relieved to see the tall figure of Michael in the doorway, but that relief turned to fury at the sight of the two men who followed him, the guns they were carrying lengthened by silencers. "The bastards," Freddy mumbled.

"Dear God, Michael. What's happening?" Laura asked, terrified.

"What's all this about, Theo?" Michael's voice was angry as he stepped behind Laura's chair and put his hands on her shoulders. Radec moved away from Theo and Laura saw the gun, realising why Theo had not moved. She laced her hands together to stop them from shaking, felt the pressure of her husband's fingers.

"This is about treason, Mr Schiller," Radec's voice was icy. "You should be familiar with that, and the penalties. There are people who don't like what you and the Baron here have been doing for the last few years. They don't like it at all."

"I don't know what you're talking about, Radec," Michael said, and like Freddy, he felt sweat trickling down his back as he listened to Radec's callous voice.

"Unfortunately, there's little time left to give you a run-down on your activities." He motioned to one of the men standing guard at the door. The slightly built man hurried across the cabin. He disappeared through the door marked 'DECK', closing it behind him.

"Let my wife go, Radec, she's nothing to do with any of it," and then Michael rounded on the Captain, "Are you part of this?"

Theo looked at him helpless, and there was deep regret in his voice. "Sorry, Michael." I didn't know and I can't help you. There are two hundred people out there. He'll shoot them if I don't co-operate.

Freddy had remained silent, listening to the exchange of words, hoping and praying that Erika was not going to join them. For the first time in years he cursed the loss of his leg in the war twenty years ago. He wished Michael had let him bleed to death, regretted that there would not be a future for any of them. They had left it too late. Freddy then resolutely cleared his mind and assessed the situation.

The man at the door, less than a metre away from him, was broad and muscular. Freddy would have preferred the smaller one to be in his place. The big man should have been yours, Michael, he thought, but beggars can't be choosers...

He was sharp and alert now and knew Michael would react with speed and hoped that Theo had enough of his father's courage to do the same. Michael and he needed no words. They had fought too many battles together. Freddy shifted his leg to point in the direction of the man at the door. Not yet... He held the cane in a tight grip. He had to make it first time...

The explosive expert standing by the door had not moved an inch since his companion left. He hoped Major Scholl had kept his word and despatched a diver to fix the safety line from the patrol boat to the hull of the ship. With the old tub at a standstill, it should be a piece of cake. By now, Klaus would have attached the rope ladders to the railings.

He, Jasper Klein, the best in the business, had done his job rigging up the boiler so that it went through here, taking the evidence with it. He had been very careful and followed Major Scholl's orders to the letter. In the boiler room, that was. Except, he did like live people flying through the air. He had seen it once, a long time ago, and found it gave him as much pleasure as being with a woman. He couldn't always fix it that way, but this time he'd really made sure. Tonight was going to be very exciting. He wished Radec would get on with it, though.

As the music played on and the laughter of the passengers drifted into the cabin, Radec delivered his final piece of information as he addressed Theo. "You fool, you should've joined us. That partition wasn't put up out there for us to sit in privacy and drink champagne. It's our way out of here." He looked at his wrist watch. "In twelve minutes your father's pride and joy will go sky-wards."

As the implication of the callously uttered words sunk in, Theo turned to Radec, shouting. "What have you done to this ship?" He wanted to choke him, but the gun pointed at him was level with his chest.

Radec laughed. "My friend over there...," jerking his head in the direction of Jasper Klein, "... has all the expertise to make boilers fly through the air. You needed a new one anyway."

Freddy looked at Michael and the unspoken signal was understood. Freddy levered himself up on his cane, threw himself forward and in an instant his thumbs had buried themselves in the windpipe of Jasper Klein. The fat man's stubby finger on the trigger recoiled from the onslaught, while Michael pushed Laura to the floor.

"Stay there," he hissed and sprinted to the outer door and onto the deck, despatching the thin man leaning over the railings into the water with a broken neck before he had time to look up.

Theo wrestled with Radec for the gun. One bullet left the magazine and shattered Theo's arm. He heard a second shot and found himself looking at the gun in his hand. Theo saw a look of shocked surprise on what was left of Radec's face, before the man slumped to the floor. Michael hurried back and found Laura bent over Freddy.

"He's dead, Michael." Her voice was choked with tears she wouldn't allow to come. This wasn't the time for grieving. Michael felt for a pulse on the neck of the big man lying face up under Freddy's body.

"This one can't tell us anything," he said to Theo. "We have to find that bomb. Can you make it?"

"Yes, I think so," Theo said, holding an arm pumping out blood. Laura stood up, took the silk scarf from her hair and tied it round Theo's arm. Michael glanced at the clock. There was little time. He gripped Laura's shoulders, urgency in his voice.

"You have about eight minutes to get everybody to the back of the ship. There's no time for the lifeboats. The men'll have to protect the women and children as best they can."

"What about you and Theo? You can't go down there," Laura pleaded.

"If we can't find it, we'll be back in time to join you, I promise."

Michael took her into his arms and kissed her hard. "I love you," he said. "Now go!"

He left her and hurried after Theo, who was already halfway down the stairs leading to the engine room.

They did not know that most of the passengers had already crowded around the stern of the doomed ship. The band had stopped playing, as curious as everyone else about the unusual sight just a short distance upstream. Maybe that was the reason they had stopped again.

The patrol boats that had been moored on the river bank this morning, now lay at the mouth of the narrow channel, waiting. The people wondered why they were there. None of the crew made any effort to communicate, in spite of the good natured shouts that came from the 'Olaf Johannsen' and bounced off the rock as a faint echo. Erika and Chrissy felt concern and decided to join Theo after all. Surely he must know the answer. They found themselves struggling to get through the mass of people.

Laura, white faced and shaking, knew she must hurry, but first there was something she had to do. Laura took Freddy by the shoulder and rolled him over. She felt a wave of nausea when she saw the gaping bullet hole in Freddy's chest, took one last look at the still face of her friend and gently closed his eyes. Laura turned and quickly walked to the door. At the same moment Theo opened the door to the engine room. He had not noticed the thin trip wire Jasper Klein had attached to the handle.

Major Scholl was in the leading patrol boat. It was a much bigger explosion than he had expected. Jasper Klein had been in one of his playful moods again, the Major thought. Casualties would be heavy and he wondered where his men had got to.

The patrol boats moved quickly downstream. They had appeared to be manned only with two uniformed men, but suddenly were filled with a full crew. As they drew closer, the muted screams they had heard from a distance now filled their ears. From below, bundles of rope ladders were thrown over the railings, landing on top of the tightly packed bodies. Major Scholl grabbed a loudhailer and bellowed instructions to the terrified people above.

"Please be calm We're here to help you off the ship. Get men to fix the ladders to the railings," and he repeated the message again until the ladders were secure.

Four men from each patrol boat made the ascent, four stayed on board to receive women and children. Major Scholl detested rope ladders, thought them undignified, only fit for sailors to swing on. His men cleared a space for him to alight on deck. He ignored the people, the crying and the screams and moved away to survey the devastation of the ship. He'd put Jasper in the cooler for a month for disobeying orders.

There was a very large hole where the dining room and kitchens had been earlier. Where people had laughed and danced and ate good food. The Captain's cabin and most of the bridge had disappeared, taking the upper deck with it in the blast. What had not been strewn into the river had returned to the gaping hole or hit the passengers.

The ship was filling with water. She might sink of her own accord, but that would take time. Major Scholl could not wait that long. His orders had been meticulous. The dead and wounded to the hospital, identified and listed to inform relatives. The rest of the people to the large hotel in the village they had just left, to be attended to and kept until morning. He also needed to check the list that Radec had given to him. If the four traitors had been eliminated, he might be in line for promotion...

He was still staring into the dark swirling waters in the belly of the dead ship. Unlike Jasper Klein, he felt neither pleasure nor remorse, just annoyance that Jasper had gone too far again and hoped the three of them had made it back in time. According to the precise timetable, the blast had occurred at least six minutes too soon.

The Major was approached by one of his men, who kept at a safe distance from the jagged edges of the dining room.

"Sir," he called to Scholl. "Everybody's off the boat, except two women who refuse to leave. We've twenty seven dead. The wounded are being taken to the hospital."

"Very good," Scholl said sharply. "Is my boat here? And the crew?"

"Yes, sir. They're waiting for your orders. What about the women?"

Scholl was silent for a moment. The ship would have to be blown out of the water... It was now a shipping hazard... Besides, he couldn't risk leaving it here for someone to snoop around... The newspapers would want pictures... There was no telling how far they might go to investigate the accident, even at night... There could be bodies down there... Someone might still be alive... There had to be no loose ends...

"Sir?" the young man insisted. "The women?"

"I'll see to them," Scholl replied curtly. "And tell my people to come up and bring the equipment. You can go."

Major Scholl noticed for the first time the eerie silence, broken only by the sound of lapping water and distant voices. It would soon be dark... He'd have to hurry... The crowd on the narrow bank opposite the rock would have another firework display... As soon as he'd despatched whoever it was that didn't want to leave...

Major Scholl felt vaguely irritated that somebody hadn't done so already. He retreated back onto what was left of solid deck, carefully avoiding the debris, stepping around the pools of coagulating red sticky substance. He found the two women and recognised them. The older woman was cradled in her daughter's arms. They sat on the floor, leaning against the shattered railings. Scholl remembered them walking around the deck, talking and laughing with the others. The pretty chiffon dress had changed colour. A dark red obliterated the delicate flowers in places. The older of the two women stared vacantly at the devastation in front of her. He felt renewed irritation. They should have been in the cabin.

His voice held no compassion as he coldly addressed Chrissy. "You must leave, Miss." He involuntarily clicked his fingers. "My men will help you off. The doctors at the hotel can check you out."

"No," Erika screamed, but Scholl showed no emotion as Chrissy comforted her mother.

Eight men climbed over the railing, trailing thin cable behind them. Major Scholl turned and picked two of them while pointing to the women.

"Get them off. Now."

Chrissy heard the order. "We must leave, mother. There's nothing we can do here. Mitch needs us at home," she said gently, then got up and helped Erika to her feet.

The name Mitch seemed to strike a chord in Erika's numbed brain. She swayed for a moment, steadied herself on the railing and faced the Major, her voice trembling. "We're ready," she whispered.

The Major's cold eyes stared at her. "Please wait in the boat below," he said sharply. "We have some matters to attend to first."

Erika and Chrissy were helped down the rope ladder, to be received by strong arms on the patrol boat. Someone led them to the inner cabin, draped a blanket around them and a very young man in uniform handed each a glass containing a generous measure of brandy. Some time later they felt the boat move.

At nine 9:45 Erika and Chrissy ran to the open deck. Someone had pushed the handle of the detonator. On the bank opposite the rock the people watched in silence as the second explosion sent the ship to the bottom of the river. Grieving for the victims and the proud steamer. They would not see Olaf Johannsen's flag on the river again.

Major Scholl was satisfied. The explosives had worked as planned. The ship had gone down in one go, and the river would be clear for traffic in the morning. He hadn't bothered to organise a search for bodies. Their place was on the river bed. All that remained was to check the lists and report to Colonel Inkmeyer.

* * *

At Dettingen, Katrin Bulger reclined in her deck chair on the paved terrace. She was happy and pleased that the children had enjoyed the day in the garden and the party last night. She could report to Laura that Mitch had behaved beautifully, had not said one cross word to anybody and was the best of friends with Kirsten again.

Twelve year old Victor had played host to them like a gentleman and kept the two girls entertained all day. Katrin watched the three of them, sailing the toy boats they had made this morning on the big rectangular water tank halfway down the garden. It was nearly nine o'clock and time for them to go to bed. But perhaps a few more minutes wouldn't hurt them. It had been a lovely peaceful Sunday.

Katrin couldn't quite remember the exact time she noticed the silence, maybe sometime just after nine. She wondered why the children stood like statues, staring at Mitch. Curious, she left her chair and walked towards them. Mitch's face was pale, an expression of utter despair on her face as she stared into the water.

Victor spoke softly, as if he didn't want to encroach on whatever Mitch was thinking. "What's the matter with her, mum?"

As Katrin also wondered what was wrong with Mitch, she heard the quiet request. "Please, Mrs Bulger, may I go to bed now?..."

Chapter 42

Seb Inkmeyer left the train at Cologne, walked to the station car park where he had left the staff car earlier that morning and drove to the little restaurant near the headquarters. He ordered his favourite meal, savoury pancakes, saute potatoes and beans. The waitress bought him a beer. The Colonel was always polite and courteous, but never frivolous. Tonight though, he seemed to be weighed down with important matters so she left him alone.

Inkmeyer did not enjoy his food. Thoughts, terrifying thoughts, had taken over again after a short period of sleep on the train. They just wouldn't leave. On a sudden impulse he decided to call on Jan before going to the office. There wouldn't be any news until the mission was completed, but right now he didn't want to think about that.

Jan's house lay in a small pleasant village south of the town. Secluded and private. Like its owner, Inkmeyer thought, as he turned into the gravel drive. Lotti had seen the car, expecting it to be Jan's. He had taken the boys to the Zoo in the afternoon. She worried about them when they were not with her. Inkmeyer considered the boys too soft, but had never mentioned it to Jan or Lotti.

For a moment he looked at the plump, unfashionably dressed woman in the doorway. He liked her for her simple attitude to life. The boys, Jan and the house, in that order. Once it had been Jan who had been her top priority, but he could hardly blame her for clinging to her sons. Jan was not like other men. He had to fit in his family with the kind of work he did, and Lotti was not given to socialising with her neighbours, many of them prominent party members. Inkmeyer wondered again, as he had so many times before, what had drawn the two people together. So different. The enigmatic Chief of the Intelligence Section, his wife uncomplicated, loving. Or perhaps she was the perfect foil to the mysterious Jan Konrad, the man he called his friend.

Lotti greeted him with a warm smile as he left the car. "Evening, Seb. Jan and the boys haven't come back yet. They've gone to the Zoo. Will you wait?" She sounded lonely and Inkmeyer smiled.

"Just long enough for a cold beer, Lotti. I've got to be back at the office by ten."

He was led into the homely living room. "You both work terrible hours," Lotti said. "This is the first Sunday for weeks that Jan's been home. The boys had a lovely surprise. I'll get your beer."

Inkmeyer surveyed the room. It had Lotti's personality stamped all over it. Cosy and comfortable, rather than smart. Jan's place was in his study in the basement, surrounded by his work. Inkmeyer's glance rested on the long sideboard, where photographs of Lotti and the boys were grouped together. Jan was in none of them. Had that been deliberate? He wondered. Or was it simply that Lotti didn't know how to work the camera? His eyes contemplated the large wedding photo. Jan looked smart in a dark suit, neither happy nor sad, his white hair making him look older than his years. The face revealed nothing, whereas Lotti, dressed in dark costume and white blouse, her hat too elaborately decorated with veils and feathers, looked ecstatic.

Lotti placed the beer on the low table and joined him. "Jan's taken the camera with him. We'll have a few more pictures," she laughed.

"He hasn't changed much since the wedding," Inkmeyer said. "What year was that, Lotti?" he added innocently.

Lotti looked surprised. "December 1924. It was very cold in Munich. But you know that, Seb."

"My memory isn't what it was. I'm getting old, my dear." The beguiling voice of the Interrogator spoke softly. "Had you lived there always?"

He felt a twinge of guilt, but Lotti happily answered his question.

"Oh, no. We lived in Bonn. Jan came to collect me one Sunday morning. Six o'clock it was. He just told me to pack. He hadn't been to my place for months, ever since I made a funny remark about the woman who found him work and a place to live. I never saw him so angry."

Inkmeyer's mind was like a sponge, soaking up information to be sifted, stored and used at the proper time. He walked to the table and sipped his beer, hoping Jan was going to stay away a little longer. His voice was jovial as he sat down. "Jan angry? I don't believe you."

"Oh, but he was. He never came back to my room after that," and there was a wistful note in her voice. The pale blue eyes looked at him for some time. Maybe she realised she had said too much, Inkmeyer thought. He felt that for some reason Lotti had not forgotten the words that they had exchanged some fourteen years ago, or the woman. He was curious. Bonn was the place to start with.

"And you didn't see him at all before he came for you," his voice was gentle.

"Only at the tavern. He moved away from the river when his precious Mrs Sogar and her son bought a place in Dettingen, on the outskirts of town. Jan went with them to build up a market garden business."

Inkmeyer was startled to hear the name. His mind tuned in on it. Sogar... Sogar... Bonn... Dettingen... Mentally he was scrutinizing file after file. The name was on one of them. And he prompted again, friendly, laughing. "Did you ever see the lady?" he asked, relaxing, as he realised Lotti did not suspect his motives.

"Once," she replied. "I took the tram out there one afternoon. I missed him a lot and just wanted to talk to him," Lotti reminisced. "Nobody answered the door, so I looked over the fence. Jan was digging and then she came out of that big summer house and they were talking. Jan was smiling and hanging on her every word."

There was something in Lotti's voice that told Inkmeyer that the woman had left her mark on Lotti, too. There was just one more thing he needed to know. "Forgive me for asking," he said laughingly. "What did this woman look like who made such a big impression on Jan? Big as a house, with arms like tree trunks, perhaps?"

Lotti had no trouble recollecting the lady's features or appearance, and he didn't know why he suddenly wished he hadn't asked. It was the name. He felt sure the last piece of the puzzle would soon be in place. He glanced at Jan's wife, at her ample figure, rosy cheeks and straight mousy hair. She was homely and had a nice smile. He listened intently as she continued.

"No, Seb. She was beautiful. Not at all what I imagined her to be. She made me feel plain and clumsy," and Inkmeyer was surprised at the absence of envy or malice in Lotti's voice. "She was so small standing beside Jan, so slim and her hair was like sunshine. I remember she had it tied back with a dark blue scarf. I just went home again."

Inkmeyer had remained silent. Fear gripped his spine as the image of Laura and Michael Schiller coming down the gangway of the 'Olaf Johannsen' came into his mind. There was no need for more information. He had heard too much already. He suddenly felt compassion for the woman sitting there. He knew she could never take the place of Laura in her husband's heart. But why had Jan not married Laura Sogar? Inkmeyer looked at his watch.

"I must go, Lotti. It's been an interesting talk," he said pleasantly. "Tell Jan I called. I'll be in touch."

He needed to go before Jan came home. Laura Sogar... Laura Schiller... And he, Inkmeyer, was responsible for her death. As he drove back to his office, he wondered who else had the same knowledge about Jan Konrad.

The clock in reception showed 9:58pm. Inkmeyer acknowledged the salute from the duty officer and took the lift to the third floor. The young SS soldier greeted him as he entered the outer office.

"Anything important?" asked the Colonel.

"No, sir. It's very quiet tonight," the soldier said. Not for very much longer, Inkmeyer thought. He estimated it would take another hour before news of the explosion would set off speculation and rumours.

"Take an hour off, Wessler", he ordered. "I'll be in my office."

The soldier left hurriedly.

The outer office was sparsely furnished, a large desk with a row of telephones dominating the room. Inkmeyer walked through to his own office, opened a door at the far end and stood for a moment, deciding whether or not he had time for a quick shower. The room was small with a metal tube framed bed against one wall. The steel wardrobe held two sets of fresh clothing, which would be washed or cleaned as required by one of the duty valets. Inkmeyer walked into the adjoining bathroom. He decided to shower after all. It would be a long night.

Fifteen minutes later he had shaved, dressed and felt alert. He fetched a bottle of beer out of the coolbox in the bathroom and walked into his office. It was not elegantly furnished, but he liked it. Here he could work intensely, or relax when he needed to. He sat down and the big heavy swivel chair turned on well oiled bearings. Seb Inkmeyer faced the open window, looked out on the clear night sky and wondered what to do about Jan.

By 10:00 pm Major Scholl reported in. The mission had been successful. Three 'Fish' had drowned, one survived, to be dealt with later. Unfortunately there had been more casualties than anticipated. Inkmeyer listened to the cool voice on the telephone and knew that Jasper Klein had disobeyed orders again. The man was a menace.

He grabbed paper and a pencil and began to jot down figures... 27 dead... 19 seriously wounded in hospital... Major Scholl would telegraph the list of names to the outer office...

"How am I supposed to transport the people kept at the hotel back to Bonn?" the Major asked.

"I'll have a train up there as soon as I can arrange it," Inkmeyer informed him. "We'll get back to you when that list comes through."

He hung up.

No-one expected Freddy's guests to return home from their annual outing before 2:00am on Monday morning. By that time Colonel Inkmeyer had alerted the relevant police stations to get messages to the relatives of the dead, the wounded and the people left at the hotel.

Katrin Bulger had looked in on Mitch after Kirsten had gone home and Victor, quiet and subdued, had gone to bed. She wasn't sure what to do. Mitch was sitting on the floor, her dolls clasped tightly to her... rocking... rocking...

Luther Goreman, still shocked and stunned from the news he had delivered to devastated relatives, left Mitch until last. He didn't know what to do, and decided to meet the special train bringing Erika and Chrissy home. He hoped they were going to relieve him of the task. He just couldn't face it...

The train arrived at the station at 7:00am. Colonel Inkmeyer had requisitioned a fleet of cars to take the people home. He felt he owed them that at least. Major Scholl immediately commandeered one of them. The Red Cross and the police should be capable of dealing with the problem. He was tired.

Luther Goreman was looking for Erika and Chrissy Behrens, while Walter waited at the barrier. It looked as if a tide of refugees had landed on the quiet town. They walked in twos or groups, supporting each other, crying or simply stunned. Walter, too, could not believe it yet. Luther had fetched him out of bed and had driven him into town. In spite of their different lifestyle, he loved Erika and vowed he wouldn't see Leo again in Cologne. Maybe it was too late, but he'd try and make it up to her. Walter had been very fond of Freddy, Laura and Michael. He and Erika would now have to look after Mitch. He saw his wife and daughter and ran towards them, embracing both of them. They stood, not speaking, their tears flowing. There was nothing they could say.

Walter let off Luther at the police house to snatch an hour's sleep. As he watched the tired figure of his friend walk towards his front door, he almost regretted the promise he had made to Luther that he and Erika would tell Mitch of the terrible tragedy.

The house was oppressively silent as Walter led Erika into the living room. Chrissy walked into the kitchen to make coffee and to butter the freshly baked rolls the boy had left on the top step early that morning. She knew the nightmare was not over yet. Three dead in Dettingen, but there would be no funeral for them, their grave was the river. But there was Mitch...

"Do you want me to go to Katrin's?" Walter asked his wife.

Erika shook her head. "No. I'll go and change."

"You should rest, Erika," he said, his voice full of concern.

She rose wearily and he watched her go out, listening to the heavy tread on the stairs. Erika stared at the stranger in the bathroom mirror. This hollow eyed woman, her face aged by a thousand years could not be herself. Was the hair still blonde or silver? She couldn't tell, but it had strange rust coloured blotches on it, like the paper confetti they showered at each other at the carnival procession. She raised a hand to flick them off, but they stubbornly remained in place. Erika rubbed them between her fingers. They felt like dry rust. And she remembered that somewhere, sometime, she had felt a spray of warm liquid covering her, recalled someone washing her face and arms, but couldn't remember where. And the dress this woman was wearing seemed familiar, but the colour was all wrong. She herself had chosen one like it, the fabric softly clinging to her figure, the colours peach and pink, a delicate shade, which had pleased Freddy so much... Freddy... Michael... Laura... And Mitch...

For the first time that morning Erika noticed the dress with the dark patches of dried blood was on her own body. She steadied herself on the basin, took it off and dropped it into the waste bin. She bathed her face, brushed out the minute particles in her hair and changed into a dark frock, dreading the ordeal waiting for her across the road.

Erika, remembering the carnage on the ship, knew that life would not end without Freddy or Laura and Michael, but nothing would ever be the same for Mitch and she herself must live with the knowledge that because of a whim she had not been at Freddy's side. And like Mitch, had lost all she held dear.

Walter picked up the morning paper. News released from Headquarters promised an inquiry into the accident. The investigating officer, Major Scholl, would conduct the most rigorous investigation into the cause of the explosion, having been at hand and examined the wreckage before giving the order to sink the ship. A photograph of the arrogant Major accompanied the statement.

The paper had been delivered to number seven and Heinz Bulger got up from the breakfast table as he heard the flap go down on the letter box. He glanced at it as he walked back to the dining room, then stood quite still and Katrin heard the agonizing 'Oh, my God...' in the kitchen and came out to see her husband, white faced, scanning the newspaper.

"Are we at war, Heinz?" Katrin asked anxiously.

His dazed eyes met hers and he handed her the paper. A strangled cry found its way out of Katrin's throat as she read the headlines.

"It can't be... It can't be true... Oh, God! Mitch! Erika!" Katrin whispered, looking at her husband for confirmation that none of it was true. "Dear Mother of God. Not all of them?"

They could hear Victor moving about on the landing, knocking on the door of the bedroom Mitch occupied, telling her to get up for breakfast. Heinz led Katrin to the dining room, holding his sobbing wife close to him, trying to comfort her, except he could not find the words. He was dimly aware of the sound of the door bell, shrill... insistent...

Heinz moved in a world that had turned upside down, sat Katrin down at the table and hurried to the front door. He hardly recognised the woman in the dark grey dress and he wondered where the Erika of yesterday was. They did not need to speak, as he stepped aside to let her in.

Victor shouted a cheerful, "Good morning, Aunt Erika," from the landing above, but received no answer. And in the dining room Katrin enfolded Erika into plump, comforting arms.

"I'll get Mitch," Heinz said, helpless with grief.

"How am I going to tell her?" Erika wanted to know, the rivulets of her tears had left a damp patch on Katrin's blouse.

"I don't think you'll have to. She knows," Katrin said gently.

"How?" Erika asked. "Has she read the paper?"

"No. We've only just found out ourselves. The kids haven't come down yet." Katrin's voice was unsteady. "They were racing boats last night. She looked as if she was seeing something terrible in the water tank. It was strange. Almost as if she was there."

"What time was that?" Erika queried, unnaturally calm.

"Just after nine, I think," was the hesitant answer.

Erika stared at Katrin, a shocked expression in her pain darkened eyes. Eyes that yesterday had sparkled with love and the hope of a new life.

"The explosion was about that time. It took all of them. I didn't want to go for a drink with Theo. Now I wish I had," Erika said despairingly.

They had not noticed that Mitch was standing in the doorway. The face so pale that the eyebrows and lashes seemed like streaks of charcoal on a white sketch pad, the tawny colour of the hair at odds with the pallor of her skin. The girl stood still, her head held high, unapproachable.

Then Mitch walked the few paces from doorway to dining table. Erika wanted to hold her while she told her of all that happened on the 'Olaf Johannsen', but the eyes in the pale face clearly said, 'Don't touch me'. They were fathomless and grey as the sky before a thunderstorm, laden with grief, without tears.

Mitch halted before the two women, who were still clinging to one another. Erika expelled a long shuddering breath and faced the silent child in front of her. "Your grandparents are dead, Mitch," she said quietly. "There was a terrible accident on the ship. Freddy's dead, too. And a lot of other people. I am sorry."

She held out her arms. Mitch did not move and Erika dropped her hands in her lap. Katrin was quietly weeping. Mitch watched the two grieving women and wished she was part of that sorrow, could join them and let the tears wash away some of the pain that was inside her body.

Sometime in the future she would be able to talk about her grandparents, laugh again, remember the good times. As she had done after her father had died. But then they had been there to help her. Now, there was no-one...

With a gesture of deep compassion the girl placed her arms about Erika, held her close to her and whispered, "I'm sorry about Freddy. I loved him too," but did not mention her grandparents. And, as if the burden of grief had become too much, she let go and asked, "May I go now?...

Erika and Katrin cried. For Freddy, Laura and Michael. For all the others, but most of all for Mitch. Incapable of easing the pain with the healing deliverance of hot tears, cauterizing wounds no-one saw. They heard her footsteps on the stairs, and the soft closing of the door. Victor and Heinz joined them, solemn, not knowing what to do. Then the boy decided on something. They saw him leave, heard him go upstairs, heard the opening and closing of a door.

Victor stood for a moment, watching Mitch on the floor, rocking back and forth, the two dolls clasped tightly to her chest. Then he too settled himself on the floor, a little distance away from her, quietly reading a book.

Mitch was aware that the boy had entered the room, softly, like her grandfather used to do, patiently waiting, and felt comforted by his presence. She fervently wished she could pray like her grandfather had taught her to do, but there weren't any prayer words in her head any more. And she wondered where they had gone to. There was just emptiness. But God wouldn't listen anyway.

Grandfather Michael would have asked Him to keep everyone safe after she had that awful dream again. He always kept his promises, but God let them die, as He had let her father die and left her all alone now. Well, if God was so busy doing other things, she wouldn't bother him again. She didn't need him. She didn't need anybody. Or maybe just Victor. It was nice of him to be there, without fuss.

She didn't want to be touched. She wanted to be left alone with Rama and Evita...

Sister Anna knocked on the door of the study and found the Reverend Mother slumped over the desk, the newspaper relating the tragic account of the accident had slipped out of her hand and lay on the floor.

Sister Barbara, Surgeon and Physician to the Reverend Mother Agnes, diagnosed a stroke and assigned Sister Dominik to administer to the patient's every need. The prognosis was uncertain and must be left in the hands of God. Mother Agnes had enjoyed excellent health until now but Sister Barbara feared that the shock of losing three beloved friends had been too much to bear.

Tiny Sister Anna, her sweet face deathly pale, exchanged the snowy white starched wimple for the flowing mourning veil. She then assumed full control over the affairs of the convent with a ferocity that startled her fellow sisters.

Her first task was to order Sister Gertrud to the Post Office. A telegram was to be sent to the Countess Ira von Riesenheim informing her of the Reverend Mother's condition, and an invitation for an extended visit to the Convent, where two rooms would be at her disposal.

Only after that did Sister Anna write a letter to the new Bishop, assuring him that the Reverend Mother was receiving the best nursing care anyone could wish for and for the time being she herself would assume full responsibility for the Sisters and the Convent...

Chapter 43

The early morning sun played on the white table cloth, reflected on the pretty china and cutlery in Jan Konrad's dining room. At seven thirty on Monday morning the faint noises of a working day were just beginning.

Jan had breakfasted already. Lotti poured more coffee for her husband, who was busy with the morning's mail. She very seldom received any letters. The papers made the familiar 'plop' on the hall mat and Lotti went to fetch them. Jan always looked at them first. She would read them at her leisure after she had had breakfast with the boys. The radio was silent. Jan liked the morning to be peaceful and maintained he had to digest too much news during the day. He did not need it first thing in the morning.

Three different papers carried the same headlines on the disaster. Lotti watched the well formed head with its thick white hair moving up and down, from left to right, as he parted the pages of all the newspapers

He was agitated about something. Maybe war had broken out? Everybody was expecting it some time or other.

And then he was still, staring at a page, his face white as a sheet. Lotti was tempted to lean over his shoulder and read for herself what awful news held his attention to such an extent, but didn't dare. Jan was tolerant in many ways of her somewhat unrefined social graces. The few rules laid down at the start of their marriage mainly concerned his privacy and Lotti had not broken them. Looking over his shoulder to read was one of them.

She wondered if he was going to tell her what disturbed him so much in the paper.

Lotti watched the familiar figure who had forgotten about her. After fourteen years of marriage she still felt the same way about the tall, slim man as she had at the Tavern. Then he had been so brown from working outdoors, whereas now he was pale, the colour of one that spends his working day indoors.

The face was thin and lined, but at forty six still handsome, the mouth wide, curving in a pleasing way when he smiled. Dark brown eyes gave nothing away. He still moved lightly and had no suggestion of middle aged spread.

She had often held him to her, and knew the familiar contours of his body. He was a gentle lover, but she remembered the times in the early years, when he seemed like someone else. Ardent, passionate, lit by a rapacious fire she knew was not for her. Jan would whisper a name, softly, but she would hear it. Laura... Laura...

It was Laura that would have been able to reach something in Jan which was closed to her. Sometimes she felt she never really knew him at all. He was kind to them, had given her a good life, two sons and she had accepted it gratefully, because she loved him. He never spoke to her about his work, but sometimes he would talk in his sleep. She had never told him, just listened...

Jan folded the newspapers carefully, rose from the chair and without looking at his wife walked to the stairs leading down to the basement and his study. Lotti heard him close the door.

She opened the papers, read about the disaster and felt sympathy for the dead and injured but did not understand what had disturbed her husband so much until she turned the page. There was no photograph of the wreck. It was at the bottom of the river, the reporter said. It had taken twenty seven people with it.

Then followed a long list of names, headed by Baron Frederick von Dettingen-Annsberg and followed by Michael Schiller and Mrs Laura Schiller. Mrs Erika Behrens and her daughter had miraculously escaped death. Lotti stared at the photograph someone had found of last year's outing on the 'Olaf Johannsen'.

She remembered the golden haired woman from fourteen years ago and felt a wave of pity for Jan and wished she could go down and comfort him.

* * *

He left for his office at the Headquarters later than usual. His face still white, the vertical lines along the nose deeply etched. Jan placed a fleeting kiss on Lotti's cheek as she stood on the door step.

"Don't wait for me tonight. I may be late," he said gently.

Without the usual wave of his hand, he reversed the big black staff car into the road and drove off. Lotti was not annoyed, just sad.

Seb Inkmeyer was waiting for Jan in the outer office. He noticed the pallor of Jan's face and felt strangely uncomfortable.

"Morning, Jan. You've seen the news?"

There was a lot of activity this morning in the big office, sifting through every scrap of information. Full of young men, proud to wear the black uniform of the SS. The reports of the accident did not affect them any more then a rounding up of Jews or dissidents.

Except for one. He was in his thirties, of medium height, his sandy coloured hair cut short. The face was without distinctive features and would blend into a crowd, attracting no-one's attention. Rudi Waldorf watched Jan enter the office. He knew what his boss felt and wished that Colonel Inkmeyer wasn't here right now. Rudi needed to talk to Jan. Cornelius and Freddy had always been as special to him as Laura had to Jan.

Something didn't make sense about that explosion. They had to go through this with a very fine toothed comb indeed. He just hoped that bastard Hubert hadn't gone too far. He'd kill him if he had.

Before Jan led Seb Inkmeyer into his own office at the back, he glanced over to where Rudi was sitting. Their eyes met and held for a moment, then Jan told Inkmeyer. "Yes, I've seen the papers."

Jan knew Rudi was upset, but it would have to wait. First, he had to find out how much Seb knew about this business...

"That was a damned unfortunate accident up river. Have you read Scholl's statement?" asked Inkmeyer, as he sat down in one of the leather chairs.

"I did."

Jan removed his jacket, carefully hanging it onto a coat hanger on the hat stand. He took his pipe and tobacco pouch out of his pocket and sat behind his desk, methodically filling the bowl of the pipe, taking his time to light it. Inkmeyer had the oddest sensation that Jan was preparing himself for the role of inquisitor, with himself as the prisoner, and wished he'd gone back to his own office.

"What was Scholl doing up there, Seb? That's not his territory."

Jan's deceptively gentle voice made Inkmeyer uneasy. He wished he knew more about this man. They did not work together, did not know each others methods. Maybe their friendship, such as it was, had endured because of it.

Inkmeyer said casually, "He had some private business to attend to," emphasising the 'private'.

384

Jan Konrad knew instinctively that his friend was hiding something. Seb was at the top of his profession, the best in the police department and disliked SS Major Scholl intensely, but he would know why Scholl had been up there. Seb was a loner, like himself, caught in a trap. They couldn't let go of the past.

SS Colonel Sebastian Inkmeyer, the former Count Jurgen Alexander von Riesenheim, couldn't completely forget the ethics and in-bred rules of the aristocracy he had been born into, whereas he, Jan, had no problems with his background. He just hadn't been able to relegate Laura Schiller to the past.

"Why that boat? Old Olaf wouldn't have gone out with a defective boiler. That ship was his life. Why?" Jan asked Inkmeyer.

"Captain Olaf wasn't the skipper on that trip," Inkmeyer said carefully. "His engineers didn't go either."

Jan remained calm, drawing gently at the stem of his pipe and blowing wisps of blue smoke into the room. Somebody had opened the window wide, expecting another hot day, and the smoke hung in a thin layer between desk and ceiling. Seb knew perfectly well that Jan already worked out all the possibilities of why that particular ship with marked passengers on board had an 'accident'.

"Who skippered the ship, Seb?" and Jan's voice had a razor sharp edge.

Inkmeyer held Jan's steady gaze and didn't flinch from what he knew would be a showdown between them. Maybe it was time for that, and he felt relief.

"Theo Johannsen. Joe Radec was second mate and brought his own crew." Inkmeyer's voice was as calm as Jan's, but the look that passed between the two men conveyed all the knowledge one possessed and the other needed to know. "Scholl said he lost three good men."

"Not counting the Captain, of course," Jan remarked. "There were a lot of casualties. I wonder..." Jan's voice held a momentary note of sadness.

Inkmeyer felt the other man's pain and knew with certainty that what he had suspected was true. The image of the dainty golden haired woman coming down the gangplank floated into his mind. What image did Jan have in his head at this moment? He looked at his watch and rose.

"I must get to work," Inkmeyer said, then added gently "Laura Schiller didn't suffer, Jan. It would have been over instantly," then turned away as he saw the stricken look on his friend's face.

He had almost reached the door when Jan's voice stopped him. "I hope you're free this evening, Count von Riesenheim. I'll phone Lotti to have dinner ready by seven."

Inkmeyer turned and Jan saw the shocked white face, the tic at the corner of the right eye showing he was nervous. Jan had regained his composure. "We need to talk, Seb. Tonight. In my study," he said curtly.

Seb Inkmeyer just nodded and walked out of the door.

        Since he had read the papers this morning, Rudi Waldorf had gathered as much information as he dared without arousing suspicion. He had to be discreet, but as he kept irregular hours of duty as the Colonel's assistant and driver, no-one took much notice of the precise time he checked in. While he waited for Colonel Inkmeyer to leave the boss's office, Rudi sifted through sheets of papers.

Something strange had been going on yesterday. He hadn't figured it all out yet, but he was getting close. One of the SS soldiers had told another that he'd met his girlfriend at the station yesterday morning and saw Inkmeyer and Scholl getting on the express to Mainz. The young man had thought it very odd. The Colonel and the Major avoided each other like the plague. It had to be important for them to travel together.

Rudi checked the duty roster and found they had been cleared for travel at 08:20 am. Inkmeyer had checked in about 21:47 pm and didn't leave the building all night. There was only one way to find out what went on after that. He'd take the telephone operator for a pint or two... One thing was very sure. Inkmeyer wouldn't go on a pleasure trip with Scholl.

Rudi felt an overwhelming sense of loss when he thought about Freddy. He and Cornelius had always been good to him up at the estate. They'd been his family until he'd lost his temper and punched Hubert for molesting Delia. His girl. Hubert should have stuck to his wife and left Delia alone.

Major Konrad had saved his life. He could never be sure for what reason, but he owed him. And so did a lot of other people. Three of them had died last night and the boss would want revenge for somebody killing the only woman he had ever loved.

Colonel Jan Konrad contemplated the stack of paperwork Rudi had placed on his desk. He didn't feel like tackling any of it. Today he wanted to be anywhere but here, but he couldn't go home either. He must remember to phone Lotti to tell her he would bring Seb for dinner. They would eat an excellent meal and after that, the confrontation between himself and Seb would decide whether they were friends or enemies. If the latter was the case, one of them would be dead.

Right now, Jan didn't care very much who would survive. Lotti and the boys were well provided for. He had made provisions for them years ago, just in case...

He refused to let his mind dwell on the explosion and the consequences. Now he wanted to think of Laura as she had been fourteen years ago, before he left Dettingen for the South. Since his return in 1931 he'd seen her once, but only from a distance.

Jan swivelled the heavy chair to face the window and watched lacy clouds racing across the sky. He remembered how he used to watch them in the garden at No. 10. The weather had been important then. To protect the young seedlings from frost or a heavy downpour, to harvest the fruit on the right day. Laura had always laughed at him.

"I loved you so much..." he whispered. "I still do..."

He didn't hear the knock on the door. It was louder next time and with a supreme effort of control he turned the chair to face the desk.

"Come," he called out and Rudi entered, a thick wad of paper in his hands. He looked angry and came straight to the point.

"When are you seeing Inkmeyer again?" Rudi's voice was sharp.

"Tonight. Why?" Jan asked.

Rudi's light brown eyes had darkened with rage. "Then ask him what he and that bastard Scholl were doing in Bacharach yesterday."

Jan stared at him, comprehension dawning in his eyes. "How do you know they were there?"

"I just collared Wessler. He was on duty, manning the phones. Quite talkative, he was. They overhear things they shouldn't just by picking up the right earpiece. Inkmeyer came back on the 18:05 train and Scholl came down on the boat and was let off just before the Lorelei. He'd organised river patrol boats to stand by as an exercise. Everything was laid on for a disaster and they had one. The 'Olaf Johannsen'."

Jan sat in shocked silence, then spoke softly. "So they got to them after all. Just a few more weeks and they'd have been safe. That leaves us with the question as to who gave the order."

"And why?" Rudi asked. "How much does our aristocratic boy know? Scholl would have had his orders and follow them to the last dot. He won't ask questions. Inkmeyer is different. If anybody knows, he does. Are you going to play your ace, Jan?"

Jan's eyes glittered dangerously. Rudi knew the cool exterior of his boss hid a sharp mind that would have worked out already how to get the information he wanted from Seb Inkmeyer. And how much to give away in exchange. He wished he could be present tonight. Their friendship had begun the day Jan took on Hubert, who had wanted a corpse and the trust between them was absolute. But Inkmeyer was an unknown quantity. If the boss went down the road to oblivion, he, Rudi, wouldn't let him go alone. He'd be by his side and without a blindfold... staring them straight in the face... Since Delia had married the gardener up on the estate, he didn't really care about anybody, except Jan.

"It's been up my sleeve for a long time, old friend. Thirteen years and it's time to give it an airing," Jan remarked, too casually.

Rudi extended his right hand to the man in the chair, who took it into his own, and held it firmly.

"Good luck, Jan," Rudi said

"Thanks, Rudi. We need it," Jan responded.

They had both refrained from mentioning Laura or Freddy, the people uppermost in their thoughts.

Rudi turned smartly and left Jan alone.

* * *

Victor just kept on reading, now and again glancing at the girl rocking, the brown and pink dolls crushed to her chest. He knew she wouldn't cry because she was tough. All the years she and Kirsten had been in the gang, they'd treated her as one of them. When she hurt herself, they left her alone.

Once they had dared her to follow them into the middle of the river, swimming between the barges. They hadn't realised that at eight years old she wasn't strong enough to battle with two opposing swells, and she kept going under. Willi, the biggest of them had swum to her, offering to take her in. Mitch had screamed at him that she'd get back by herself or drown.

She had come in, coughing and spluttering and Willi had offered her some lemonade as a mark of respect. Willi was mean, and to part with a precious drink had surprised everyone. After that they seldom dared her to do anything.

She could fish, throw that knife of hers nearly as well as the gipsy boy Ramon had, use an air gun and play football better than some of the team, who seemed to have two left feet. In the winter she could steer the six man toboggan down the hill and she played the mouth organ when they felt like singing. Mitch was one of them, but right now he wished she'd blubber like most girls. Like his mother and Aunt Erika downstairs.

He'd never noticed before that Mitch was pretty, although her face was so white and she looked so far away. Victor wanted to touch her shoulder to let her know that he too felt crushed by the loss of her grandparents, who had always treated him like a son. They had spent many happy times in the garden and on the houseboat on the river. He would miss Mr and Mrs Schiller and wondered what would happen to Mitch now. He would have to protect her. From what, he didn't know, but protect her he would.

Victor knew that nothing would ever be the same as it had been yesterday and became aware that Mitch was still, her head bent low over the dolls. He waited for a little while and then stretched out his hand towards the girl. For a long time there was no response, then the tight grip on Prince Rama was released and hesitantly her small hand grasped his own, held on. They sat like that for a long time.

The boy felt proud and wished he was old enough to marry her.

The girl politely declined any offer by Katrin and Erika to stay with them for the time being. She wanted to go home. Chrissy decided to move into the guest room while things were being sorted out. Mitch did not object.

School did not start until another week and by that time they would have the ordeal of the memorial service behind them. The priest had arranged it for next Sunday. He had been looking for Mitch, but only found Daniel at home. Father Josef left a message that he would call again after Evensong.

Mitch, her face still pale and eyes as dark as the greyest day, allowed Victor to carry her small bag across the road. She did not go into the house, but found Daniel feeding the rabbits, much later than usual. He saw her and enfolded her in strong arms, his eyes moist as he looked down on the curly hair, his heart full of unspoken sorrow.

He had loved Laura and Michael as the parents he never knew. And now, there was only Chrissy and Mitch and maybe his own children one day. He had cried when Walter had come to tell him, but now he must be strong because Mitch was in pain and couldn't cry.

He held her hand lightly as they walked through the gate and entered the kitchen, tidy and clean, just as it always was.

Her face betrayed nothing as she took out the dolls sitting on top of her night clothes in the bag. She gathered them to her and walked slowly through the dining room and up the stairs to the attic.

"We'll have to take care of her, Victor," Daniel said to the boy.

"We will," Victor told Daniel.

Chapter 44

In Berghausen, as elsewhere, a strange quietness prevailed between the hours of six and eight p.m. Men had returned from work, washed, and the families sat down to eat. A rest restored the energy needed to move on again.

Jan and Seb arrived a little after 6:30 p.m. Lotti was waiting at the door. She had made a special effort to look nice, had cleaned the house until it sparkled and cooked the glazed goose to perfection. She wasn't sure if all that effort was just for Jan's benefit or Seb's. He always treated her well and was easy to talk to. The boys liked him too.

Jan smiled at her, greeted his sons and walked into the living room. Lotti accepted Seb's flowers with obvious pleasure and retreated to the kitchen. Seb Inkmeyer carried two packages. He handed the larger of the two to twelve year old Alec, who was very like his father. Already tall for his age, quiet, with wise brown eyes in a sensitive face and a mop of wavy brown hair.

Alec let out an astonished 'wow' as he undid the wrapping, while ten year old Toni whooped with delight at his model railway engine. Toni was chunky and took after his mother, uncomplicated, without the hidden depth of his father or brother, happy to run his engine over the floor.

Alec reverently placed his present on the low table. The beautifully carved wooden box, oblong, half the size of a chess board, was made of polished rose wood, inlaid with mother of pearl. The lid was fastened with a brass clasp and inside he found exquisitely carved ivory chess pieces. Jan stared at them and wondered where Seb had found them. The pieces depicted the armies of the Prussian and Austrian Empire, the Kaiser and the Emperor with their respective wives and Generals. The box and its contents were not new but they had been affectionately cared for.

Seb's reputation as a chess player was well known. He liked a game with Alec and the boy was getting very good, whereas when he himself played with Seb he invariably lost. Toni did not have the patience for the game. Lotti could not comprehend the moves but did play a fair game of poker.

Seb Inkmeyer pressed a little stud at the side of the box and the folded chess board appeared.

"There," Seb explained. "It's a travelling chess set, Alec. Hope you like it."

"Oh, yes, Uncle Seb. It's beautiful. Thank you."

Jan watched his friend with the boy, at ease, looking softer. He always shed his cool, remote persona when he visited this house.

"Take great care of this, Alec," Jan told his son. "Remember..." glancing at Inkmeyer, "...It might have been someone's precious possession," and the embarrassed look on Inkmeyer's face told him what he had suspected.

So it had belonged to Seb. Why had he given it to Alec?

Jan was glad when Lotti appeared with cold beer and announced dinner was ready. Usually they enjoyed her food and the company of Seb. Tonight was different. There was too much at stake for them to be at ease with each other. The two men drank thirstily, their eyes held for a moment and Jan knew that Seb too felt apprehensive.

"Thank you, Lotti," Jan said to his wife. "It smells good, whatever it is," and she looked pleased.

Jan's study in the basement reflected his personality. Neat and orderly, a work place and at the same time somewhere to sit and relax. The large window, with its iron bars to deter burglars, let in enough light, inspite of its sub-level position. Later on the roll shutters would come down and the soft light of the desk lamp would illuminate the room.

They had spent many hours down here, talking, drinking. Seb sat down in one of the wide, tapestry covered chairs. Jan settled himself in the other. There was an awkward silence between them. Neither relished the imminent confrontation. Jan opened another bottle of beer and offered to refill Seb's glass. He nodded. "What do we get out of the way first?" Jan asked quietly, lighting his pipe.

"Yours," Seb Inkmeyer replied. "I have the information you want. It'll hang us both if you use it."

"Classified?"

"From everybody, except me," Seb said. "Scholl and his men had orders to blow the ship and make sure the four traitors went up with it. Officially, we were told that they'd been operating a rescue mission for Jews for some time, but it had to be kept quiet. Three of them went down with the ship. Scholl thinks the business is finished."

"And who gives orders to you?" Jan's voice was calm but insistent and Seb Inkmeyer took a long swallow of his beer before answering.

He loosened his tie, rubbed his neck. "Hubert. Freddy's brother. He now owns the newspaper he's been after for years."

"The bastard," Jan said through clenched teeth. "Why didn't he just kill Freddy? Why the others Seb?" and Inkmeyer detected sadness and suppressed rage.

"The Baron von Dettingen has been invited to the inner circle. Freddy's activities were a threat to Hubert's ambitions and would've barred him if it became public knowledge. He couldn't get rid of Freddy alone. It still left Michael Schiller on the loose. Hubert was afraid that sooner or later a connection would be made, so his safest bet was to catch them all in one place. He knew the agenda and the customs observed on the ship."

"What were you doing in Bacharach yesterday, Seb?" Jan observed the flicker of surprise in Inkmeyer's eyes and saw him shift his weight in the chair.

"How do you know about that?"

"I have my sources, and one of them is very upset about Freddy," Jan said. "He's already figured out that Hubert is behind this. Right now he doesn't like you much either."

"Rudi?" Seb asked. Jan did not confirm it, but Seb noticed the slight lift of his friends' eyebrows, and continued. "He worked for them years ago, attacked Hubert and spent time in jail until you rescued him. Correct?"

"You always remember what's in your files, but you haven't answered my question."

"Before I do, there's something you should know, Jan." He emptied his glass, pushed it across the table for a refill. "A year ago Hubert called me to room 1A. Sound, bug and bullet proof. I was told that he suspected Freddy and Schiller of operating an escape route. I was to bring him proof and he would deal with it. My men were not to be used and nothing was to leak out because of Freddy. I was on my own, got close several times. Without the manpower, it took too long and Hubert was getting impatient. Frankly, I wasn't all that bothered about the few that got away."

"That's not the right attitude for a man of your rank," Jan chided.

"I'm not the Chief of Police and my attitude is my problem," Seb Inkmeyer replied sharply.

"You worked for Hubert," Jan reminded him.

"Earlier this year he finally got the call. That made Freddy an urgent case and Hubert started to press for results. By then I was almost sure that they had help from somebody with the right connections, the right information. Then the bastard decided on what he called a 'clean sweep' and gave me my orders. Seb paused to take a long drink. "I was to instruct Scholl and his crew, see that everything was planned down to the last detail. It took four months. I still couldn't figure out who was out-smarting me at every turn. It wasn't one of Cornelius's crowd. Dabbling with refugees is too dangerous for them. I got so close but couldn't find the missing piece."

"That must have been very frustrating for you." Jan's tone was sarcastic.

Seb Inkmeyer sat quietly, contemplating the man opposite him, realising that Jan had not given away one scrap of self-incriminating information, and admired his brilliant strategy.

"Oh, it was," Seb said. "We had the information, arrests were planned, but when we got there the birds had flown. Not all of them, of course. That would have been too obvious. The missing piece fell into place last night."

"Last night?" Jan asked, his face a cool mask. "Before or after the murders?"

"Before, but it was already too late to stop it. My orders were to escort Scholl to Bacharach, see that all was going according to plan and leave him on the ship."

Seb paused, unsure whether he should tell Jan what he had seen on the embankment, considered he was already treading deep waters and related all that had happened during the afternoon. He did not flinch from Jan's accusing stare and ended with a note of sadness in his voice. "I only saw a beautiful woman who reminded me of someone I met once. And when the memories gnawed at my conscience I became a policeman again. I'm sorry, Jan."

"You saw her?" was all Jan could say, a flicker of pain replacing anger.

"Yes," Seb said gently. "She looked like a young girl on a date. They were still in love. You could almost feel it and I began thinking about my life and the love I've never known. Then I began to puzzle over how they could've got away with their activities for so long. I thought of all the people that could have protected them and for no apparent reason your name kept going round and round in my head. I refused to even think about it, but it was still there when I called here last night. Maybe, if you'd been in I would have confronted you with it. Ironically, Lotti provided me with the link that had eluded me for months."

Jan was alert. "Lotti?" he queried. "She doesn't know anything."

Seb Inkmeyer recalled how he had deliberately used his charm on the unsuspecting woman and felt guilty. "Lotti is a generous simple woman, Jan, but don't underestimate her. She remembers that you got very angry once when she made some remark about Laura Sogar. I was looking at your wedding photo last night and couldn't recall anything about you before Munich. So I asked where you had been before that. And Lotti told me, quite innocently, all I needed to know. Laura Sogar, Rema House, your time at Dettingen. Suddenly it all fitted into place. Your wife knows you've always loved Laura, but she doesn't mind. I find that remarkable."

Jan looked perturbed and wondered why Lotti had never mentioned any of it, tried to pinpoint the occasion when he had been so angry that Lotti still remembered it so vividly. It had been in her room, more than fourteen years ago. Jan felt guilty of not loving his wife as he had Laura, but he needed Lotti then and still did. It had seemed to be enough for both of them... Lotti had been grateful to be the respectable Mrs Jan Konrad. "You have been digging deep. Where did you go? To the tavern in Bonn?" Jan asked.

"Yes. They were still shocked about the accident and not as careful as they should've been. I didn't ask for you but pretended to be looking for Lotti. Sorry, Jan," Seb said, watching the anger return to Jan's eyes. "I needed to be sure before I came here tonight. They remembered Lotti very well, told me she went off with some fellow in 1924 and hadn't seen her since. The curtain came down when I asked what you looked like. Nobody could remember exactly. You could've been anybody."

Seb noticed Jan relax a little. "So neither of us are what we say we are, eh, Seb?" He looked long and hard at the man he could so easily hate for his part in the killing, but felt instead a strong compassion for his friend. "I'd like some air. Let's go for a walk and I'll tell you about Laura..."

Upstairs, Alec and Toni helped their mother clear the dining room, hoping Seb and their father would appear from the study before bed time.

"Are they talking serious stuff down there, mum?" Toni asked

"They look worried, son. It's got to be something big," Lotti said.

She noticed the disappointment on the boy's faces. "Seb isn't on a social visit tonight. I'll ask him to drop by again, maybe next Sunday," which cheered them up.

They listened to the footsteps on the stairs, the muffled voices, but the two men did not come in. They went out of the back door and into the garden.

Lotti and her sons watched them go out of the gate and disappear into the lane. Alec and Toni rushed out to snatch another half hour with their friends on the village square. Lotti sighed and settled down to listen to the radio, wondering what she would do when the boys left her.

Chapter 45

It was still hot and the wood above the lane looked inviting. They climbed the short distance to an open clearing. A century old oak threw its shade like an umbrella over the grass. Further on it seemed that most of the villagers had taken refuge in the coolness of the dense wood. Snatches of conversations could be heard in the still air.

Jan liked the spot. It overlooked the pretty villas below and they would not be overheard. Leaning against the massive girth of the tree, he put a match to his pipe, wondered how much to tell Seb and decided that for both of them the time of secrecy had passed. He was surprised at the forthright question asked by Seb.

"What made you turn traitor? Risk your career and your life?"

"Love, Seb," Jan said gently. "And a debt owed to Laura. She gave me back my life."

"Laura? How?" Seb queried.

"It goes back a long time. I was twenty two when I joined the Kaiser's army in 1914. Not particularly patriotic, just proud to defend my country, but it doesn't take long to be disillusioned when men are dying all around you."

Jan gazed down on the village below them, remembering again the dead, the wounded, the noise of the constant cannon fire and the screams... His voice was soft as he spoke for the first time of the nightmare years.

"I had been on leave in 1915 and my family were fine. Then a year later my brother wrote that my mother had died of pneumonia and my father was grieving so much he'd got careless at work. After inspecting another railway track stretching into eternity he just didn't get off the rails as a train approached at speed." Jan stopped to relight his pipe. "The fighting was hell and they wouldn't let me come home," he continued, watching the smoke gently drifting up into the tree. "After that, my brother volunteered, joined my regiment and insisted on being drafted to my company. We fought side by side, won and lost precious wasteland and men died like cattle. Flanders was our only home. After we'd recaptured the ridge at Passchendaele in 1918 I heard my brother's screams. They told me later that I'd carried what was left of him back to the trenches and wouldn't let go of him. And for the next four years all I could hear in my head was cannon fire and screams. "My brother wasn't even eighteen years old, was all I had left." Jan's face was grim as he remembered the boy in his arms, the thin body torn to shreds.

"I'm sorry, Jan. I didn't know," Seb said.

"Why should you? When you've been there you don't talk about it."

"Where does Laura come into all this?" Seb asked, but Jan evaded the question.

"They sent me home from the hospital in 1921, except I had nowhere to go to. I vaguely remembered an old friend of my father's in Bonn. He'd opened a tavern somewhere in the old town by the river. Josh couldn't give me a home, but got me a bed at the mission nearby and let me sit all night in the tavern. I always had two beers on the house and Nell, his wife, fed me."

It was getting dusk in the copse. People were making their way home and young lovers now walked towards the woods. Seb saw a faint smile on Jan's face and wondered what Nell had been like then. Probably mothered him. He had seen her yesterday and she was still a formidable woman, although she must be getting on for sixty. Shrewd, quick witted and in charge. She had skilfully evaded his questions about Jan.

"I sat by the river all day," Jan remarked "It was the only place that gave me a kind of peace."

"Is that where you met Laura?" Seb asked.

"Yes. She asked me to come and live at Rema House. Looking after the garden and the property."

Jan was silent for some time, as if he needed to brace himself to talk about Laura. He drew in a deep breath, and for the first time spoke of the woman he met on the embankment by the river, sixteen years ago.

"Laura gave me a future, Seb. I learnt to think again. To believe in something. Loving a woman that was out of my class, but loving her just the same", and Seb began to understand why it had been impossible for Jan to forget Laura. He was still not clear on the connection between Jan and the four people, living their lives holding opposite views to what he stood for and listened intently as Jan continued.

"Two years later, Rema House was sold and became the Girls High School we now use to train our best Gestapo material. Spies, fanatics and playgirls for the Elite. Once it was the dignified home of gracious people. Well, you know what they call it now. And Hubert is its best patron."

"What happened in Dettingen?" Seb asked, stretching himself.

"1924 was a nightmare. In February, Laura and Peter found the property there and wanted me with them. She met Michael Schiller on that first day." Jan said calmly. "He looked into a woman's eyes and after serving his church for half a lifetime he was as lost as I was. The irony of it all was that she was free, and so was I. I deluded myself that if I made a success of the market garden we'd planned, she would grow to love me. But Michael renounced the Church and that killed off any chance I might have had."

Jan paused to put a match to his pipe. Seb noticed that the hand holding the match was trembling slightly, but Jan's voice was steady. "I turned more and more to the Party, began to sift through boxes containing names, addresses, information, and started on the road to where I am now. What I had on Freddy and Father Michael would've marked them as subversives even then, so I suppressed it."

"Why?" Seb asked.

"I don't know. I was very angry, hated him and couldn't stop loving her. And I wanted her so badly it was driving me crazy. The thought went through my head that I could blackmail Laura. I tried it and it didn't work."

Seb could see the pale outline of Jan's profile looking down at the village. It was getting dark but neither one seemed anxious to leave the clearing. The thought of Jan even contemplating blackmailing the woman he loved so much was out of character. But then, he had never loved anyone so deeply, had not experienced war and the traumatic aftermath as Jan had. What might he himself have done under these circumstances?

"What happened, Jan?"

"Laura would have made any sacrifice to save him and the others," and Jan told of the day in September 1924, the shame of it etched forever into his soul... "I couldn't take what she was prepared to give. I owed her too much," Jan said softly. "And for what she did for me once I protected them all. Had I denounced Freddy and Michael, she would have suffered. I know it sounds crazy but I came to respect both men and many times wished I was on their side. I never stopped loving her, but learnt to live with it, except I can't control dreams. That's where she haunts me still. Call me a traitor, Seb, but I have no regrets."

SS Colonel Sebastian Inkmeyer, odd man out at Gestapo Headquarters, feared by most, admired by some, had listened intently.

It was all very neat, precise, like Jan. He had methodically placed his informants in the right place. Rudi, whom Rosalie provided with information about Hubert, Daniel close to Laura, and had got away with it for years. But he, ignorant of what Jan felt for Laura Schiller, had been instrumental in causing her death.

Seb too looked down on the pretty roofs of the affluent villas, windows ablaze with lights. He felt a strange longing to be someone else, almost envied Jan his futile all-consuming love. Felt again a sense of dissatisfaction at what his life had become.

"Thank you for telling me. I think I understand, Jan," he told his only friend. "How long have you known about me?"

"Since 1924. Soon after I got to Munich. They gave me the job of sorting through mountains of information. It was only by chance that I spotted it in a pile of old newspapers. Let's go back to my study and I'll show you," Jan said, getting up.

Both men walked away from the quiet wood, immersed in their own thoughts, down the hill, Jan's pipe gently blowing smoke.

Disappointed, Toni and Alec had gone to bed. Lotti had prepared a tray of sandwiches for the men and settled down on the settee to listen to her favourite radio programme.

She was faintly curious as to what they might be talking about, but knew better than to ask. It couldn't possibly be about Laura Schiller. All that had been so long ago, although it must have been a shock to Jan to read about it this morning. He had acted strangely when he'd read the paper. And all morning she'd wondered if he still loved her, even now. No man could carry a torch for a woman that long, but then Jan was different from other men.

Maybe now she was dead he would forget about her. She heard the gate open and shut, heard the back door and hoped they might stay and keep her company. Jan and Seb came in and she could tell that business was going to take them downstairs again.

"I've cooled the beer and food is on the tray," Lotti said amiably.

"Thanks, Lotti." Jan sounded apologetic. "We'll take it downstairs. Seb and me have some things to sort out. Don't wait up."

"The boys were disappointed not to see more of you, Seb. Will you come over again when you're free? Maybe spend the day with us next Sunday?" Lotti asked. "If that's alright with you, Jan?"

"I'm not sure what I'll be doing. It's too far ahead, but Seb can come if he wants to. You're always welcome", looking intently at the other man, who understood and felt grateful.

"Tell the boys if their father is busy, I'll take them out for the day. Always providing nothing urgent crops up," Seb told Lotti.

Jan collected the tray of food. "Bring the beer, Seb. We've got unfinished business to get through."

Jan did not close the wooden roll shutters completely. The windows were left wide open inside the room. The narrow slots in the shutters allowed enough ventilation into the study to cool the room. Seb opened two bottles of beer and poured them out while helping himself to a sandwich.

Jan took a long drink and asked. "Tell me why, Seb. Or should I call you something else?"

Seb looked thoughtful for a moment. "No. Seb'll do fine," he answered. "There isn't much to tell, really. Mine was a typical aristocratic upbringing, much like Freddy's. Except that my father was a bit higher in the social stakes. My mother doted on all of us, but I was the baby and got more attention than the others and I adored her. I still miss them."

Jan found it strangely comforting to hear the longing in his friend's voice as Seb continued. "I went to University and made a lot of friends in the Communist Party. I liked their ideas in a superficial way, but in my last year many of us changed sides to the new Fascist Party. They really pulled out all the stops with their recruiting methods. After we graduated I didn't go home but stayed at Seb Inkmeyer's apartment. He was two years older, well off, with no family that I knew of."

"That explains why he could disappear without anybody looking for him," Jan remarked.

"Yes. He was a true fanatic and hated the Communists more than Jews. And like a fool I gave him the names of all my friends. I didn't know until that rally in '23 that he had marked them all for target practice. Well, you know what happened there. It was a blood bath. Then I found Seb and some of my friends after it was over. Maybe it would have been better if I'd been killed. It was a marvellous piece of propaganda and I knew it'd make the headlines for days. I also knew I couldn't go home again. Not just because of the disgrace to my family. I had betrayed my friends and felt responsible for

401

their death." Seb paused and took a long swallow of beer. "How did you find out?"

"I'll show you."

Jan walked over to the end wall covered entirely by a heavily carved fitment. He bent down to open one of the lower doors in the centre and reached inside, withdrew a key and unlocked the tall door at the end of the unit. Seb was surprised to see Jan's uniform, dress suit and formal uniform hanging in the space. The inside of the door had a full length mirror, the floor held an assortment of high boots.

Jan pushed the uniforms to one side, pressed a switch and the well-lit space revealed the back of the compartment. Jan removed the back panel and exposed narrow shelves with binders and files.

"That's ingenious. Who knows about that?" Seb asked, impressed.

"Only Rudi. He built it. And you, now."

Jan reached inside the space, lifted out a folder labelled 'Seb' and placed it on the low table. He sat down and took a long drink before opening the green folder. It contained a sheet of personal details. Rank, name, date of birth. Place of work, which Jan handed to the man sitting opposite him. Then he removed a sizable stack of newspaper sheets and put them on his lap, flicking through them. He selected two and opened them out on the floor.

"Have a look," Jan invited Seb, who got down on his knees, immediately recognising the pictures.

One was of two rows of opposing factions, still orderly, but the tension distorting their faces was plainly visible. In the line of uniformed bodies two faces were ringed.

Seb recognised himself and the man standing next to him. Of the same height and build and fair-haired, like him. Sebastian Inkmeyer. They could have been brothers. He was holding the new banner, but his own hands were also around the flag pole. There was no mistaking the large unusual signet ring on his hand, heavily embossed with the family crest. "Now look at this one," Jan said.

Seb did so and he saw himself kneeling by the mangled corpse of Sebastian, lying in the road. His left hand was lifting the dead man's arm. The ring could clearly be seen again, and Seb looked at Jan.

"Do you still have it?" Jan asked, but Seb looked incomprehensibly at his friend.

"Have what, Jan?"

"The ring. You're a very good policeman, Seb. But in my job you've got to have an eye for detail. You should have put that ring on his finger before you sent him off to be buried at your place as Count von Riesenheim."

Seb was still staring at the pages, his face revealing a distress Jan had never seen before. He understood only too well what Seb must be feeling.

"That ring was the only tangible reminder of who I was. It never entered my head to part with it." Seb's voice was full of sadness. "I still have it," he said, getting up. "Why didn't you tell them?"

Jan did not have to think twice before answering. "I decided every man is entitled to keep his own secrets, as long as they don't interfere with his work. And you've been the best in your job for as long as I've known you."

Seb looked intently at Jan, while making a decision. "I'm grateful to you. There is a favour I want to ask. It may be awkward for you, though."

"Well, you can ask," Jan said calmly.

"I have a package at home, and a letter to my parents. I'll write a second letter telling them what I've asked you to do. If you agree, I'd like you to keep the letters and the package in that place there." Seb pointed to the open door of the fitment "If anything happens to me, will you send my body home? Please, Jan."

"What the hell should happen to you?" Jan exclaimed, surprised at the suggestion.

"I don't know, but I don't trust Hubert. He'll have a lot more power if he gets to Berlin. And I'm the only one who knows what he's been up to," Seb said.

"But what can he do to you? What about your connections?" Jan asked.

"They'll be too busy saving their own skins to worry about me, believe me," Seb snorted.

"I don't think anything will happen to you. It'll most likely be me that'll get shot or hanged if any of what I've told you ever gets out," Jan said ruefully. "As for your request, if it ever comes to that and I'm still around, I'll take you home, friend", and held out his hand, which Seb took firmly.

"Send those two pages with the letters. They'll recognise me. At least my mother will," Seb commented as Jan gathered the newspapers together and returned the file to the hiding place, arranged the uniforms tidily, and locked the door. He returned the key and made himself comfortable.

"Let's have another beer and finish Lotti's sandwiches. And you can tell me what it was like at your home before you went to University and got corrupted by the Great Leader," Jan said, a hint of sarcasm in his voice.

Seb looked happy to oblige.

Chapter 46

No-one attended Evensong in the church at Dettingen that Monday. Father Josef did not hold it against his parishioners. He was used to seeing the same old lined faces during the week, but even they had deserted him today. He knew the whole village was mourning the loss of their friends.

Chrissy opened the door to him at No.10 and he was glad to see her. She led him into the dining room. The table had not been cleared and Father Josef was happy to accept her invitation to stay and eat. He liked the teacher and hoped that she and Daniel would decide on a wedding soon. Chrissy made a point of telling the inquisitive Father that she had temporarily moved into the spare bedroom while looking after Mitch and Daniel. It satisfied him.

"How is the child bearing up?" Father Josef asked, devouring the remains of the chicken Chrissy had cooked for the evening meal. He also enjoyed the cider she fetched from the wine cellar.

"She is very quiet. Victor managed to persuade her to eat something."

Victor had spent most of the day with them, helping Daniel in the garden. He wanted to be close to Mitch and only reluctantly returned home to sleep, promising he would be back in the morning to feed the livestock.

Mitch had wandered aimlessly through the garden, expecting her grandparents to come along one path or another. She had gone to her room and stayed there, staring out of the window, seeing nothing. The silence in the house was all-consuming, as if the very structure was numb with grief. Like herself. She felt nothing. The talking and the laughter had stopped.

"Where is Mitch?" Father Josef asked Chrissy, remembering the reason why he was there. "I'd like to see her. We must pray."

"I'll fetch her," Chrissy said and left him to finish his meal, which apparently took priority over Mitch's soul. The Fathers did alright on their visits, it wasn't surprising they all got fat, Chrissy thought, hurrying up the stairs. It seemed irreverent to shout for Mitch, irreverent to disturb the mourning of the house itself.

The girl was sitting in the rocking chair she had asked Daniel to bring up this afternoon. Chrissy remembered Janus had made it when he moved into the large pigeon loft he had converted into his home.

Janus, the reserved, white haired man who had come with Laura and Peter to start the market garden. Her own mother had been intrigued by him, always said that he loved Laura with a passion he hid behind that silent exterior. Then Laura and Michael had kept the whole village on tenterhooks with their forbidden love affair and one Sunday in September 1924, Janus was gone, as quietly as he had arrived. Chrissy wondered what had happened to him and where he was now.

"Father Josef wants to see you, Mitch," Chrissy said gently, loath to disturb the girl staring out of the window, clutching her dolls.

There was no movement or answer and Chrissy wondered if she had heard. Mitch got out of the chair, walked through to her bedroom and placed the dolls, very gently, onto her pillow. But the voice Chrissy heard was as cold as a steel blade.

"I hope the ugly Father doesn't ask me to pray with him for my grandparents. They don't need it. If there is such a thing as heaven, then they're already there."

Chrissy stared at the girl's face. It was still a child's face, but what she saw in the dark pools of her eyes frightened her. She saw nothing, and yet everything that anyone had ever suffered. But Mitch's vehement remark about the Father shocked Chrissy to the depth of her being. How could anyone not want to pray? It was their duty. The girl must be ill. Maybe she should take her to Doctor Hoffmann. Yes, she would, but Mitch was a law unto herself. Always had been. Only Michael had possessed the gift of reason and persuasion to steer her in the right direction. Oh, God, if Mitch had lost her faith, what would become of her?... Chrissy felt the moisture rising in her eyes as she followed the girl downstairs to see Father Josef. She didn't give much for his chances of making her pray if she didn't want to. Or couldn't...

Father Josef neither inspired confidence, nor did he have the handsome features of Michael Schiller. With his bulbous nose and slight squint, short and rotund body he had almost no redeeming graces to make him likeable, except to the old folks. They were more concerned with getting to the pearly gates and didn't much care who got them there. She wondered why the Bishop had called Father Dominik to serve as his secretary and sent them this ugly priest. Chrissy hurriedly made the sign of the cross, repenting her uncharitable thoughts. But he was ugly, everybody said so...

All that week it seemed as if some strange cosmic blight had settled over Dettingen. The village on the south border of the town still looked the same, but the people had been silenced. Only the school playground noises jarred the stillness. Women still shopped at Walter's, their voices as sombre as their clothes. They had discarded their bright, colourful dresses for muted greys and blues.

The men called in on their local drinking places, stayed for a while and went home again. There was no football practice, not one game of cards was played and rifles stood quietly in their places waiting to aim at targets. The talk was subdued, asking why it had happened, and how best to help Daniel at this busy time.

They discussed what Father Josef had told someone, who had told somebody else, who in turn told another. He had come to believe that the girl was going crazy with grief, as he'd been to see her for the obligatory prayers for the deceased and she had told him she couldn't remember any words to pray with and gave no responses to what he'd read to her from his prayer book.

Father Josef had been in a right state and didn't know what to do about her. He would have to confer with the Bishop before the child became a heretic, and someone pointed out that the Father didn't know much about anything, never mind dealing with a strong willed girl like Mitch.

Mitch spent her time rocking in Janus's chair, or sitting in the tree house, pulling the short ladder up after her. She remembered Granpa Michael joining her, his long legs dangling over the floorboards because there was not enough room inside for all of him.

They had talked about all she ever wanted to know. He had always answered her questions, never lied to her, but now there was nobody to teach her. And she wished fervently that she could be like the other girls, talking about boys and hair and giggling about everything. She was glad Kirsten had called after school, although she too had a tendency to prattle on and on, but Victor was quieter, soothing, nice.

Next week they had to go back to school and maybe she'd start feeling again.

Father Josef had pinned up a large notice on the glass covered notice board next to the church door. It changed the time of the early Mass to 9:00

a.m. as there would be no Holy Communion at the 11:00am memorial service for Laura and Michael.

Chrissy had attended, but Daniel and Mitch declined, saying one Mass on a Sunday was quite enough. They had breakfast instead. She watched Daniel tucking into his bread rolls, his light brown hair tussled. He had a nice face, she thought. Kind brown eyes and a stubby nose, like a boy's. A soft mouth, which had a permanent smile hovering around it and nice teeth. Strong and even, biting off a big chunk without any trouble at all. He was quite big and sturdy, but not clumsy. She didn't like ungainly people. Father Josef was clumsy, and ugly, and had messy eating habits.

She wondered if she could talk to Daniel now that Granpa wasn't here anymore? What she liked about Daniel was that he didn't evade the issues, talked to her like a grown-up. There was something she needed to know. Would the people who used to hide in the hay-loft and the houseboat still come? To be fed, change their clothes and leave at dawn? She had seen them often and Daniel must know about them. Did Chrissy know, too? It had been quiet lately and she wondered why.

Daniel stopped eating, conscious of Mitch's eyes on him. He put aside the sheets of papers covered with writing and figures and returned her gaze. "What is it, Mitch?" he asked gently. "Are you worried about the service?"

"Just a bit. It's not like a funeral, where you walk behind the coffins to the cemetery. You know they're inside and you can go and talk to them. But my granma and granpa are at the bottom of the river."

Daniel looked at the face that expressed nothing. He could only guess at the awful emptiness inside of her. She had been the same when her father was killed, but Laura and Michael had been there. Now it was up to him and Chrissy to see her through. It was hard enough to cope with their own grief and Chrissy had Erika to comfort as well. His voice was tender as he tried to put his own feelings into words.

"I know, and when you're ready I'll take you to where they went down and we'll say goodbye there. I always thought of them as my parents and loved them for giving me a home, caring for me. I never did tell them I loved them in words, but tried to be a good son to them. Right now, I don't know what to do either, Mitch. I'm grieving as much as you, but I've got to carry on with your grandfather's work.

"I know you loved them and they loved you. I'm glad I've got you, Daniel," she said softly, rose from her chair and for a moment stood, just looking at him, then placed her hand on his shoulder in a gesture of comfort. "I've got to get ready. Maybe we'll talk about going up there, soon. Thanks," and she walked out of the kitchen.

Daniel felt proud and humbled at the same time and wanted to cry, but instead cleared the table.

At 10:45 the bells called again. This time there was no joyous mingling of sound as the big bell boomed over the village. Like a giant heartbeat it called the people to pay homage to the friends they had lost.

Walter Behrens had not gone to Cologne. He escorted his wife to the church. Chrissy, Mitch and Daniel followed. Like them, dark suited men and women in black dresses walked silently along the wide streets towards their meeting place. The double doors of the church were wide open and the soft tones of the giant organ floated out into the still air, away over the Green and up towards the forest.

Today there was no segregation. They all sat tightly together in the pews. United, their eyes on the bier, with its black cloth and four wreaths resting on top, each one trailing two wide silk ribbons with black writing on it.

Mitch knew which one was hers. Yellow tea roses and blue cornflowers entwined with the green. Gold for Laura's hair and blue for Michael's eyes. And while they waited for Father Josef, she wondered if they had written what she'd wanted on the white silk ribbon. Erika had said it should be spelled properly, Chrissy had said 'Grandmother and Grandfather' was more appropriate, but Daniel, bless him, had said 'Granpa and Granma' was what they'd always been called by her and that it should be good enough to put on a wreath.

She gazed at the Madonna and Child, hoping for some message to fill her empty mind. Father Josef was droning on, but she didn't hear. The people stood, knelt, prayed or sang and Mitch, by habit, stood or knelt, but did not pray. The words had gone and even the sweet voices of the nuns made no impact.

Her eyes contemplated the banks of wreaths and sprays and she wondered what Aunt Erika had told Father Josef to do with them all. They had no grave to leave them on. Mitch thought of a lorry heaped full of flowers going up to the Lorelei and being dropped into the river. Why

409

not?... Daniel could drive the van... Maybe not all of them. There were so many...

Mitch noticed Father Josef was climbing the steps to the pulpit.

He'd babble on about granma and granpa as if he was going to miss them, she thought. What did he know about them? He never concerned himself with anything. Left it to the church committee to come up with good ideas. They did all the work. Maybe now her grandparents had gone he'd have to do his job properly.

She was staring at a small wreath, almost the shape of a posy. It was the colour that held her attention and she wondered who had sent it. Red roses, deep red, some a little brighter, but not pink. A lover's posy. Something granpa used to send granma on her birthday from the florists with lots of ribbons. He would write the card himself and paste down the envelope, and Granma was always delirious with happiness.

Mitch could not take her eyes off the roses and felt as if they were sending a message, wanting her to know of someone's pain. The sensation was so strong that she felt the urge to turn around and scrutinize everybody's face. Someone in this church was suffering as much as she was. But who?

Erika and Walter's wreath, in the shape of a cross, lay on top of the bier, so did Chrissy's and Daniel's. There was a large one from Baron Cornelius, and her own. She was aware that Father Josef had come down from the pulpit and Mass would soon be over. The nun's were singing again, then the final Lord's Prayer and Chrissy whispered that they must leave first and follow Father Josef to the door.

"You go with Daniel. I want to stay here by myself," she whispered back and Chrissy looked shocked.

"But you can't," she pleaded. "It's not paper."

Daniel had heard, squeezed behind Mitch and took Chrissy's arm and stepped out into the aisle to follow the Priest. Walter had enough sense to guide Erika out of the pew to follow Daniel and Chrissy. As the church gradually emptied some of the men furtively wiped the tears from their eyes.

Mitch had stood in front of the bier and felt nothing. The roses seemed to draw her. As she moved near to them, someone else's grief overwhelmed her and she turned to see a man's figure in one of the last pews, his head bent low. All she could see was thick white hair.

She wanted to go to him, but at that moment he rose and walked to the small side door leading out into the garden and to a path behind the convent.

Mitch bent down, picked up the small wreath and walked quickly through the men's aisle and the side door. There was no-one in sight, but a car engine started up not far away and she wondered if it was the man and who he was.

Quite tall and slim. From what she had seen of his face in the dim light of the church, it was a thin face, but not so old as to warrant white hair. She looked down and read what had been printed on the white silk band. The black letters said only: 'To Laura, J' and Mitch stared at the silk ribbon. It was to her grandmother. But who had sent it? The tall man in the last pew? She had felt his pain. Had he loved her a long time ago? Did he still love her?

Mitch did not want to meet anybody and turning away from the church, followed the path that criss-crossed in between the houses and led to home. She carefully carried the red roses, feeling a kinship with the unknown man in the church and wished she could meet him.

Chrissy and Daniel had gone to see Father Josef to let him know that they would collect most of the wreaths after Evensong to take them up river tomorrow. Mitch wanted it, Daniel wanted it and Erika was going as well. They would throw them off the nearest ferry to float past where the 'Olaf Johannsen' had sunk.

"Isn't that somewhat unusual, Daniel," the priest asked. "They should be distributed to the convent."

"Not these, Father. She wants them in the river, by the Lorelei and I'm taking them there first thing in the morning," Daniel said quietly, giving neither Father Josef nor Chrissy time to think of any objections.

Erika called at No. 10 after lunch. She found Mitch in the wash house. The wreath was carefully arranged over a bucket of water, the ribbons draped above to keep them dry. The woman stood in the open doorway, watching the girl staring at the red roses, some still in bud, others just beginning to open.

"Why did you bring that here, Mitch?"

"I wanted it. Someone sent it who loved my granma," Mitch said, looking at Erika. "Read the message, Aunt Erika."

The woman stepped into the cool of the wash house, her face pale and drained from the ordeal of this morning's service at the church. She held the white ribbon in her hand, read 'To Laura. J," her brow furrowing with concentration. Her mind was slow, as if part of it had been obliterated. For fourteen years there was only Michael. Before that there had been a man, with white hair who had lived here.

"Janus?" Erika whispered.

"Who's Janus?" asked Mitch.

"He came here with your grandmother and your father from Rema House and lived in Daniel's place. When your grandmother told him she was going to marry your grandfather, he left. No-one's seen him since," Erika said, letting the ribbon fall across the red roses.

She stepped out into the court yard and leant over the low wall.

"What did he look like, Aunt Erika?" Try and remember," Mitch said gently, fully aware of Erika's sudden lack of concentration. Chrissy was worried about it and hoped it was only temporary. "It's important," and she felt an overwhelming wave of compassion for this woman who only last week had been vibrant and alive, like her grandparents. Erika's face was contorted with the strenuous effort to remember.

"He was tall, slim, but had broad shoulders, he worked hard in the garden and got very brown. Janus had a nice face, didn't talk much to anybody except your father. His hair was all white when he got here and he couldn't have been much more than thirty then."

"I saw him this morning in the church. Not close, but it was him. I felt his grief, it's still here, in the roses. That's why I brought them home. Tell me about him, Aunt Erika. Please."

And Erika told Mitch what she knew of Janus Konradewski.

* * *

They made the journey. The van, filled with wreaths from floor to ceiling, travelled on the highway along the banks of the Rhine. The rock called the Lorelei lay bathed in sunshine, beautiful and majestic. Daniel, Erika and Mitch did not talk much.

The 'Auto-ferry' halted in mid-stream and every passenger reverently let go of a wreath until the very last one floated down stream. Mitch threw the red roses after the others and watched them go. There seemed to be a flotilla of flowers floating past the rock. The people on the ferry stood in silence.

The Captain hooted three times on the whistle, as a last farewell and the small tug went on its way across the river.

They sat in the van. Daniel held Mitch to him, tears silently making their way down his cheeks. Erika, reliving the nightmare of a week ago, was sobbing into Daniel's shoulder as if her heart would finally break.

The ferry returned and they hadn't noticed. Gently, the Captain asked if they were all right and they took their seats in the front of the van and drove off, away from the rock.

* * *

Dettingen slowly settled back to normality. Victor escorted Mitch to school. He did not dare mention her grandparents. She had stopped in the middle of the road one morning after listening to his praises of them. Her voice was icy, her eyes like steel.

"I'm glad you're my friend, Victor. If you want to stay that way, don't mention my grandparents ever again. They're dead and gone."

She had left him and walked alone to school. They spoke of other things after that. He had told Daniel and word got around. No-one spoke of Michael and Laura in Mitch's presence.

413

Chapter 47

A month had passed. The first Saturday in October was still warm and sunny, although the dew stayed longer on the grass in the mornings.

Chrissy had cleared the table after lunch, bringing the coffee pot and setting it down on the pretty cloth. Mitch wondered why Daniel was not in his working clothes.

"Mitch," Daniel said. "Chrissy and me are going to get married at the end of the month."

"Congratulations. It's about time. You won't have to sneak over to Daniel's place any more," Mitch said dryly, looking at Chrissy, who blushed.

"And how do you know about that, young lady?" asked Daniel, trying to be serious.

Mitch was silent for a moment, a flicker of pain crossing her face. "I sit in the rocking chair for a long time at night, thinking of them. I miss them so much," she said. "That's when I hear you go over there. It's alright. I don't mind, really."

Chrissy and Daniel exchanged a glance, wondering whether this was the right time, when Mitch asked, "Where will you live?"

"That's what we need to sort out, Mitch," Daniel said.

"Why don't you move in here and let off your rooms to somebody that can help you in the garden. I'd like the sitting room and my attics. You can have the first floor to yourselves."

Chrissy's face brightened up considerably. "Wouldn't you mind us living here? We had thought it could be a solution to all our problems, but didn't like to mention it," she said.

"Why should I mind? We can share the kitchen and dining room. You can do what you like with the furniture upstairs. I'll have granma's desk, though, and some of granpa's bits and pieces. It'll be nice."

"Thank you, Mitch," Daniel said gently. I've always felt at home here with your grandparents. Oh..." He paused for a moment, looking mysterious. "There was a letter from the solicitor three weeks ago asking me to call. I went to see him. It was about your future."

"What did he say," Mitch asked, curious. "Is he going to stick me into some orphanage? Or maybe send me back to my long lost mother?"

"Don't be silly, Mitch," Daniel said sharply. "Why should he do that?"

"I can't live here all by myself, can I," she queried.

"No, you can't." Daniel looked at Chrissy. "We've got to talk and this is as good a time as any," and he saw a worried frown appear on Chrissy's brow.

"Fire away," the girl said.

Mitch made herself comfortable on the bench seat. She watched Daniel's face, it reminded her of when her grandfather wanted to talk to her seriously. There was kindness but also determination that whatever it was that had to be said, would not be put off. She liked that. Chrissy was like granma, loving and kind, but Daniel would have to do the important bits. That was alright with her.

Daniel spoke tenderly, as Michael would've done. "Victor told me that you don't want to hear anything about your grandparents. He was upset about that. Everybody talks about them, except you. Listen to me..." he told Mitch as she shot a furious glance at him. "People here loved and respected them and the greatest honour anyone can do for the dead is to remember them with affection. That way they live on. Life goes on, Mitch, but we'll never forget them. You'll have to talk about your grandparents sometime. There are legal matters to be settled."

"What about? Me and the house?" Mitch asked quietly, and Daniel was pleased that at least she was listening. He felt they had overcome the first hurdle.

"Yes," Chrissy said gently. "You're a minor, and a Guardian has to be appointed. Your Grandfather made provision for that a long time ago. After your father died."

"Why should he do that? Was it because of what they did?"

Chrissy looked mystified. "What do you mean?"

Mitch glanced at Daniel, who shook his head very slightly, but she noticed. She felt he was suddenly on edge and realized that Chrissy had no knowledge of the activities her grandparents, Freddy and Erika had taken part in. Daniel had been involved, as the refugees had been hiding in the loft next to his quarters and she had heard them talking in his living room many times. She had seen them leave with her grandfather or Daniel. Maybe it was because Chrissy was the schoolteacher and had to work with the Nazi pigs that they'd kept her out of it.

"Er...I mean...They did keep me out of the clutches of my 'dear' mother," Mitch said lightly, hoping Chrissy was going to be satisfied with that.

"Oh, I see," Chrissy said and Daniel looked relieved. "Yes, they became your legal Guardians. They loved you and didn't want to give you up."

"I know they did and I loved them, too," she said, stumbling over the words, looking at Daniel. He smiled encouragingly. Mitch took a deep breath, then said firmly. "What did my grandparents arrange, Daniel?"

He looked again at Chrissy, who smiled happily at her future husband.

"Well, whether you like it or not, you have two new Guardians until you come of age. For the next ten years you'll have to put up with them," he said smugly.

"Tell me the worst. It's not Walter, is it?" Mitch asked.

"No, Dear." Daniel's fatherly voice sounded just like her Grandfather, Mitch thought. "Your new parents are..." he paused deliberately and Mitch squirmed in her seat, "us..." he pronounced solemnly.

"You?" Mitch asked, astonished, and scrambled off the bench to hug Chrissy, then Daniel. "Bless granpa and granma for giving you to me."

Daniel disentangled himself from two arms wound tightly round his neck, blinked once or twice because there was moisture in his eyes. "Can you live with us and be happy, Mitch?" he asked the girl.

"Yes, I can live with you, but it'll take a little time before I can be happy again. I promise to be good."

"I'll remind you of that when you step out of line, girl."

Daniel tried to look stern, failed and burst out laughing. Mitch laughed, too. It was only a small sound, but a beginning. Chrissy wiped her eyes and held out her arms and Mitch let herself be embraced. Daniel hoped it was the first tentative step to heal a tormented soul.

"We have to get married in a hurry and everyone will think the worst," Chrissy wailed. "We'll have to tell everybody it's for your benefit. I'll try and be a mother to you. We do love you, don't we, Daniel?"

He nodded and knew it would work out fine.

* * *

The wedding of her only daughter was Erika's salvation. It would be at Jochen's. Jochen, now plump and jovial, was a culinary artist and the decorations would be splendid, even at this short notice. Everyone was convinced the spinster school teacher had got herself pregnant and months would be counted very carefully.

The men gave up their evenings to get the market garden and fruit orchards into shape, so that the newly-weds could spend a week in Cornelius' lodge in the Black Forest, his wedding present. A car was at their disposal, as Cornelius felt that the van was not the proper vehicle to go on honeymoon with, and commented that the servants at the lodge might disapprove. They were a loyal lot, but tended to give themselves airs and graces.

Erika burst into tears when they showed her the letter from the Baron and knew that he too was facing life again without Freddy.

On the last Saturday in October at 2 p.m. in the Parish Church, Chrissy Behrens became Mrs Daniel Tanner.

* * *

The Gestapo headquarters in Cologne was busy, but Seb and Jan felt that somewhere a new impetus had been added to their daily work of sifting through the persecution processes. The targeting of Jewish residents was gathering momentum. Rudi felt it too and promised to keep his ear to the ground. Which meant taking Wessler for more beers.

"Something is brewing, Jan."

Seb seated himself in a deep chair in Jan's office. Since they had confided their innermost thoughts to each other, Seb often dropped in.

"I know," Jan said. "I can feel it, but I can't put my finger on it. The troops are restless. You've heard nothing at all?"

"No. Hubert was my main source of information and let a lot of classified stuff slip when I was working for him. He's gone to Berlin and I'm not too well endowed with friends around here. The Baron does not keep me informed of what he's doing," Seb commented wryly. "Maybe he doesn't trust me anymore and picked himself another henchman. Around here, only one fits the bill."

"Scholl?" Jan asked, looking a little worried at the thought of it.

"Scholl!" Seb confirmed. "In which case no-one gets to know anything until it's about to happen. We don't know who his people are. They'll be as fanatical and tight-lipped as he is. I wish I knew, Jan."

"Maybe we're both over-reacting. Or getting old, and that usually means scared. Unless you're like Scholl."

"How about Rudi? Can't he dig up something?" Seb asked.

"He might come back with something important. Rosalie from the Estate left a message with Daniel Tanner, which he delivered to Nell at the tavern. Rudi's gone to find out. I'll let you know when he gets back here. Now go and do something useful and let me get on with my work. It's all right for the likes of you who're free to come and go as you please."

"I'm going. There's a distinct lead I have to follow up. One of our lesser officials has brought in a pile of trivia on his neighbours. If Scholl gets there before me he'll have them all sent to Dachau. See you," and strolled out of Jan's office.

The noise of the outer room invaded the quietness as Seb opened the door. Then it was gone and Jan's glance rested on the patch of sky visible through the window, clouds chased each other with greater speed as the Autumn winds grew colder and stronger. As so often happened, he remembered Laura, but the pain that had crushed his heart for weeks, had turned into a softer ache, bearable, and could be ignored as he worked. Now and then, as he paused, she would flit through his mind and he could almost forget the way she had died.

Sometimes he thought about the child he'd seen in the church, holding his wreath as if she knew and wished he'd gone to speak to her. He wondered how she was coping with her grief. And Erika Behrens. Her daughters wedding should've eased the pain. Somehow he must try and find a way of giving Daniel a suitable present without compromising himself or the others. It was all in the past and hopefully forgotten.

Rudi had to knock twice before he received an answer. Entering, he walked towards the desk and stood in front of it. Jan knew he didn't want to hear what his friend was going to tell him. If he had good news he'd sit in the armchair, when he was angry he stood or leant over the desk. Today was bad news day. Rudi stood in front of him, stiff as a ramrod.

"Nell gave me the message. Hubert is up at the Estate. Been talking to his sons. Something's planned for the ninth, that's the day after tomorrow. Rosalie couldn't find out what, but it's big and all over the country," Rudi said, relaxing just a little. "I wined and dined Wessler, our telephone man and need more petty cash, Jan. He eats and drinks like a pig," and a note of disgust crept into his voice.

"I'll arrange it," Jan promised, picked up his pipe off the stand and put a match to the tobacco. He drew deeply. "What's the news?"

"He's not sure exactly, but said the same thing. The ninth of November is fireworks night, whatever that means. Have you noticed that our streets are full of uniformed men?"

"I've noticed. There are more of them than police, so something's afoot. Seb's as mystified as I am. Maybe we've been blinkered by what happened on the river. It's time I paid more attention," Jan said determinedly.

Rudi sat down at last and leant against the back of the chair, deep in thought. His sandy coloured hair flopped over his brow, the hazel eyes looked troubled.

"There's something else." Rudi's voice held a note of anger. "Rosalie thinks Hubert is going after Erika. She's overheard them talking about the 'one that got away'. One of the boys, the younger one, told Hubert to leave her alone, but the bastard said he'd like nothing better than to drop her into the river too."

The only noise in the office came from the staccato sound of the pencil in Jan's hand, his gaze fixed on the racing clouds outside, his brain evaluating what Rudi had told him.

"If something big's going on the day after tomorrow, Hubert'll use it as a cover if he wants Erika put away. I've missed something, let my personal feelings interfere with work." He was talking to himself. Rudi kept quiet, shifting his position to be more comfortable. It could take some time. "We can't go there, but Seb can," Jan continued, then faced the young soldier in his immaculate black uniform. "The girl could be our excuse. She's technically an orphan, has property and the State is entitled to see that she's cared for. Get the file and I'll brief Seb. Bring the standard forms for requisition and I'll sign them."

"What do I tell Daniel? He's just come back from his honeymoon," Rudi asked, looking doubtful.

"Yes, I know. But we don't have much time," Jan reminded his driver. "Get a message to him. Tell him to trust Seb and raise no objections, whatever is proposed. Ask him to pick me up at the tavern at 10 pm on Wednesday night. Not in his van, it's too conspicuous. On the motorbike. Tell him I want to see Erika. It's time she was told who murdered Freddy." He opened a drawer of the desk, took out a wad of notes and placed them at the edge. "This'll keep Wessler in food and beer for a while, Rudi. See what else you can dig up."

Rudi picked up the money and grinned. "They don't pay me enough to feed that pig, but he's useful," he said and walked to the door.

"Find Seb for me and ask him to come over," Jan called after him.

Chapter 48

Wednesday, the ninth of November started like any other day. It was the time when autumn slid into winter without anybody noticing. The rain felt cold, the winds began to have an edge to them and the children going to school in the mornings wore raincoats with hoods.

Today, the playground was infested with the uniforms of the Hitler Youth League. Chrissy felt uneasy and tried to remember if there was some special occasion they had to celebrate, but couldn't think of one.

"Is something going on in town?" she remarked to one of her male colleagues.

Dieter Wagner, who took the boys in the sixth form, grinned a secret kind of grin. "There's a big rally in the sports arena down by the river. There'll be fireworks tonight. Should be good."

"I don't know anything about that. What's it in aid of, Dieter?"

"Nothing in particular. We're going to have some fun, so we're told. You should join us, Chrissy, you're far too passive."

"I've just got married and am working out my notice. After that, all I want to do is look after my husband and the business," Chrissy smiled at him, careful not to antagonize him. Dieter and his cousin Heini held ranks well above the run of the mill citizen sporting the same outfit.

She was curious about tonight's visitor. Daniel had asked her to prepare some food and to invite her mother, but not Walter. They weren't sure what to do about Mitch. Hopefully she would be fast asleep. Daniel hadn't said who was coming, only that it was somebody important. Her mother would recognise him and he had information about Freddy.

Chrissy was far too concerned with her shopping list to give much thought as to the purpose of the intended rally.

School finished at noon. Mitch had been excused from attending the rally by the Headmaster, resplendent in his brown SA uniform. She had pleaded successfully that the appointment with the solicitor was very important on account of what was going to happen to her in the future. The large grey eyes looked troubled and he relented, giving the usual admonishment about failing in her duty to the Fuhrer by not attending.

'Even junior members of the Hitler Youth must accumulate their good behaviour badges to become worthy citizens of the Reich,' he'd said, and didn't see the satisfaction in her eyes at being let off from what she considered the most boring chore she could think of. She had better things to do with her time, but the sports sessions were almost enjoyable. Victor caught up with her as she skipped down the steps into the yard.

"Going on your bike to the rally?" he enquired.

"No. Going to the solicitors in the van," she said, grinning.

"Cheat," Victor pouted in disgust. "Did he let you off without a fine?"

"Yes. I looked ever so helpless and worried and he fell for it."

She gave him a demonstration and Victor laughed out loud. "You're a witch, Mitch Sogar. You nearly fooled me."

They arrived at their homes and Mitch called after him. "Come over later and tell me all about it."

"I will," he shouted back, before disappearing into the doorway at number seven...

Victor cycled the long road to the river, crossed the highway and followed the wide gravel lane below. Just before it merged into the broad embankment on the south side he veered off to the left, followed another lane and saw the sports ground and stadia ahead, heard the martial music and began to whistle to the melody. He liked the music but couldn't stand all that marching, couldn't keep in step and didn't like flinging his arms about. He had made up his mind. There wasn't going to be any foot slogging for him. He was going to fly in aeroplanes, but for that he needed all the merit badges he could lay his hands on until they'd accept him as a cadet at sixteen. Maybe he'd be lucky and get in before war broke out.

He stopped on the slope and looked down onto the vast arena and couldn't believe that this town had so many people in uniforms. Where did they all come from? He wondered what it would be like in big cities? Was all of Germany going to march? It looked like the rallies they saw on the newsreels in the cinema from Berlin or Munich. The music was blaring, flags and banners waved above the standard bearers head. Orderly rows of men, students and children began to form. And then a strong voice told them to assemble, began to speak of duty to the Fuehrer and Fatherland.

Victor hurried to the cycle stand, locked up the bike, ran to his unit and fell in line. The voice droned on and on. Victor wasn't paying much attention standing next to Willi, admiring the neat hunting knife his friend had been given by his father.

They sang the National Anthem and the voice told the younger children to be dismissed and go home. The others closed ranks and sang again to the music. It was 2:00 pm. Victor and Willi collected their bikes and decided to spend an hour in town. Once past the market square in the narrow street leading down to the river were the old curiosity shops, where they liked to spend hours browsing about strange objects from all over the world. The old men with the long beards and skull caps always made them welcome and explained the origins of everything. They enjoyed each other's company, and forgot about time listening to Mr Goldstein...

They thought the older boys dressed in the same uniform as themselves were just letting off steam, until the first brick came hurtling through the window and they heard the mob on a rampage chant...Jew...Jew...

Mr Goldstein and Mr Cohen urged Victor and Willi to go quickly. The old man thrust an ivory handled hunting knife into Victor's hand and led them to the side door in the alley where they had left their bikes.

"Go home, boys," he instructed them and locked the door. The street was filled with men and youths, filled with hatred, voiced in obscenities at the terrified objects of their hatred, the gentle Mr Goldstein and Mr Cohen. Further down, more doors and windows smashed. And in front of each shop lay the contents, to be carried to the square ready to receive the baptism of fire.

Victor and Willi, terrified, pushed their bikes in between uniformed bodies carrying goods and possessions, stared in disgust at the policemen standing idly by to watch the orgy of destruction, and rode their bikes like fury along the embankment, leaving behind the shouting, the music and the men still marching towards town.

At 1:00 pm Daniel and Mitch got into the van. They had an appointment with Johann Glaser, the solicitor. There were forms to sign and he wanted to tell the girl what was going to happen to the market garden. Michael and Laura had made provision for Daniel to buy the business, but not the house. The money, together with their savings, was to give their granddaughter the opportunity to choose whatever she wanted to study for as long as was necessary and provide enough to live on.

The office was in a dignified building just outside the town centre near the river. Well known and long established law firms resided in the elegant structure. Daniel parked the van and they both listened. Below them, on the sports ground, martial music blared and voices tried to compete with the insistent beat of drums. Daniel felt uneasy and hurried Mitch inside.

Johann Glaser was waiting for them. They shook hands, but the solicitor did not ask them to sit down. He was gathering papers into his briefcase, while talking to Daniel.

"I'm sorry, Daniel. I'll have to see you both some other time. Take Mitch home."

The man in the dark suit sounded agitated, frightened. He was about Daniel's age, and he'd taken over the practice from his father. Johann was half Jewish. His mother had defied all convention to marry the man she loved.

"Has something happened at home? Is your family alright?" Daniel asked, worried now. They had been friends for many years. Old Mr Glaser and Johann were fully aware of the dangerous lifestyle Michael and Freddy had pursued in the past.

Mitch thought it prudent to stay silent. Whenever she had delivered messages here, they had always been kind and looked away while she un-pinned the envelope concealed in her pants. Granma would fasten the safety pin and remind her to give it only to one of them, no-one else. Granpa hadn't liked it much, he thought she shouldn't be put in danger, but she had told him she wasn't afraid of anything and rode over here on her bicycle. She had enjoyed the secrecy and felt important, but never asked what she was carrying.

The telephone bell startled everybody. Johann listened, his face grave, drained of colour.

"The whole town is in uproar. They're having a purge on the Jewish shops. The police just stand there and let these barbarians wreck every premise, particularly book shops. They're making bonfires already. My father is due at the synagogue this evening. That's where they're going to next. I've got to stop him." He grabbed his coat and hat.

"My God, Johann. Where is it all going to end?" Daniel was angry. "I'll take you home. If what you say is true, it's not safe to go on a tram. Come on, you two."

"Thank you, my friend. I'm sorry, young lady. There's no time today for hot chocolate and biscuits," Johann said ruefully to Mitch, as they hurried out of the office. He locked it and followed Daniel and Mitch to the van.

In the distance, from the direction of the town centre, shouting could be heard. Many voices, angry, venting a mindless fury on the innocent, while passive bystanders looked on, either too frightened to intervene or glowing with satisfaction. Daniel drove like somebody possessed to the small villa by the river to drop Johann and then back to Dettingen, a strange feeling of impending disaster constricting his chest.

He finally grasped the meaning of the bonfires Rosalie had mentioned.

They passed Walter's shop and saw them. Two big cars outside number 8 and 10, black and sinister. Daniel's heart sank. Women were standing in the road or leaning out of their windows. Silent, terrified. 'The miserable cowards,' Daniel cursed. He drove through the gate and secured it with a heavy chain, telling Mitch to go and see if Chrissy was alright.

"What about Aunt Erika?" she asked.

"I'll go there when I've seen Chrissy. She'll be scared," he said as he hurried after the girl shouting 'Chrissy.' Her voice answered from the dining room.

"In here."

Mitch and Daniel stood and stared at the man leisurely getting up from the sofa. He was tall, dressed in a well cut grey suit, blue eyes that could glitter like glacial ice friendly now. He stretched out his hand to Daniel.

"Colonel Inkmeyer," the man introduced himself. "You must be Daniel Tanner? I've put your wife's mind at rest that I'm only here on business concerning this young lady," and he held out his hand to Mitch. "Don't be afraid, it's nothing serious," as she briefly held his.

Daniel had moved to the side of his wife. He was surprised to see her calm and quiet. "You alright?" he asked.

"Yes. Will you go and see what's going on next door. There are four of them with my mother, but Katrin's with her. The Colonel says he can't interfere as it's not his jurisdiction."

"No, I'm afraid it's not my business," Inkmeyer said, eyes looking hard into Daniel's, who understood. "Go and see your mother-in-law, Mr Tanner. I'll be here when you get back."

"Would you like more coffee, Colonel?" Chrissy asked pleasantly, hoping her mother wasn't going to be arrested and wondering at the real reason for his visit.

Inkmeyer accepted his cup with an easy grace and Chrissy was impressed by his manners. At least he conducted himself like a gentleman, she thought. Mitch had retreated to the kitchen for lemonade. She too wondered what the man wanted. Somehow he didn't look as if she should be afraid of him.

"Mrs Tanner," the Colonel said quietly. "If I'm not mistaken, the officer who is with your mother will begin to wonder what a staff car is doing here. He may want to investigate. Say as little as possible and tell the child to do the same. Would there be any incriminating evidence at your mother's house?"

"On what, Colonel? She's never done anything in her life to make her a danger to the State", Chrissy retorted angrily.

Inkmeyer sipped more coffee, studying her. He presumed Major Scholl to be next door, going over every inch of the premises with meticulous care on Hubert's orders, and hoped Erika Behrens had not been careless in leaving things about the house Scholl might find useful.

"I just wondered, Mrs Tanner," he said pleasantly. "Let's hope they'll find nothing", and leant back against the sofa.

"What should they find? What would they be looking for?" her voice held a note of anxiety. "Do you know, Colonel?"

Inkmeyer concluded that the teacher was unaware of the life-saving network the Schiller's, her mother and the Baron had operated for years and did not think that this was the right time to impart his knowledge to her. He was saved from giving a plausible reply by the insistent ringing of the doorbell.

Chrissy stared at Inkmeyer, fear in her eyes. Inkmeyer's voice took on an officious, urgent tone. "Bring the child in here. And please, trust me. Whatever is said."

"Mitch," called Chrissy to the girl in the kitchen. "Stay with Colonel Inkmeyer", and hurried into the hall, as another loud ring sounded through the house. She opened the door.

Major Scholl asked politely if he might come in. Chrissy did not argue with the man in the black SS uniform, decorated heavily with silver braid.

She stood aside as three young soldiers pushed past her, stood and waited for orders.

"What's happened to my mother?" Chrissy asked sharply. "Is she alright?"

"Of course, Miss Behrens. We have met before. On the boat," Scholl informed her. "There has been a complaint made against your mother about activities detrimental to the Reich and we must investigate every one of them. You understand?" and she could feel menace emanating from this man. She remembered their encounter on the 'Olaf Johannsen' very well.

"Yes," Chrissy answered, reminding herself to stay calm. "What do you want here?"

"Just routine, as you are related. We would like to inspect your premises so we can cross you off the list", and he nodded to the three soldiers, who had stood at ease, silent. "I have already spoken to Daniel Tanner who lives here. Perhaps we may go and talk somewhere? My men know what to do."

Two of the brutish looking soldiers made their way upstairs, one moved to the cellar door.

"Shouldn't I go with them?" asked Chrissy, visibly annoyed. "Have you got a search warrant, Officer?"

"I'm Major Scholl and do not need a warrant if I think State security is at risk."

"State security?" echoed Chrissy. "I'm a teacher and my husband works the market garden. Since when does that threaten the State?" She glared at him.

"We will not be long. If you co-operate my men will be careful and leave everything in its place. Those are my instructions, Mrs...?" he asked.

"Tanner," Chrissy snapped at him. "You'd better come in here", and led the way to the dining room, where Colonel Inkmeyer and Mitch had been listening to the exchange of words. Major Scholl followed and faced Inkmeyer, writing on an official looking form. He barely looked up at the Major.

"Scholl? What brings you to this sleepy backwater?"

"I might ask the same of you, Colonel. I had official business at the house next door," Scholl said, somewhat taken aback by Inkmeyer's presence.

Chrissy sat primly on one of the dining chairs, but did not offer the Major a seat. Mitch stayed silently in the other corner of the settee, following the orders of the Colonel. They both felt the antagonism between the two men.

"I trust you completed your task at number 8 to your satisfaction. What reason do you have for sending your..." and there was an imperceptible pause before the Colonel continued, "...your men searching this house?"

"Simply a matter of elimination, Colonel. Mrs... er, Tanner is the daughter of Mrs Behrens. We wish to make sure that no traitor teaches in the school."

"Admirable, Scholl. How did Mrs Behrens fare?"

"Nothing was found, but naturally it has made her aware that we have our eyes everywhere."

"Naturally," Inkmeyer repeated the word with chilly contempt. His glance rested on the ceiling where footsteps went back and forth, the third soldier from the cellar had joined his comrades and clattered up the next flight of stairs. They could be heard talking, opening doors and drawers. Daniel was hurrying through the kitchen.

"What is the meaning of this?" he addressed Major Scholl. "What have we done?"

"Hopefully nothing to warrant a return visit, Mr Tanner."

"How's my mother?" Chrissy asked her husband.

"She's alright. Katrin is still there, clearing up the house. Are you going to leave her in peace now?" he asked Scholl, who just shrugged his shoulders.

"I expect so," he said coldly.

"Scholl," Inkmeyer put the wad of forms on the table and rose. "I am not here to partake of coffee and biscuits. That I can do at my office. I'm here on business and your men are scaring these people. I have a delicate task to perform and would like them to answer my questions lucidly. Perhaps you recall the accident on the river?"

Daniel stepped closer to Chrissy's chair, putting his hands on her shoulder, pressing reassuringly while looking at Mitch.

"Yes, I remember, Colonel. Why?" Scholl looked puzzled.

"Mr and Mrs Schiller's granddaughter now owns a market garden and this property. She is a minor. The State requires assurances that she's well cared for. You and your men are interfering with my work," Inkmeyer's voice was icy. "I should be obliged if you would remove yourself from these premises. I want to get back to Cologne. There are matters to attend to tonight. Do I make myself clear, Scholl?"

"Yes, Sir," Scholl answered coldly. "I'll see to it," and walked out into the hall. The sound of a shrill whistle pierced the quietness of the afternoon. Three pairs of heavy boots stomped down the stairs.

"We found nothing," the squat soldier said, disappointment written all over his face.

"What about this?" asked the good looking young storm trooper that followed him, his mouth cruel, eyes shining with satisfaction. "Somebody loves black vermin", holding Prince Rama by the throat.

Major Scholl eyed the boy doll with disgust, took hold of it by thumb and forefinger and held it away from him as if afraid of contamination. He returned to the dining room, not bothering to knock, and addressed Mitch.

"Is this yours, girl?"

She stared in horror at Scholl. "Take your filthy hands off him!" she shouted and dived around the table before anyone could stop her. "He's mine. Give him to me!" she screamed, trying to retrieve her doll.

The Major looked distinctly ruffled and Inkmeyer watched, a gleam of satisfaction in his eyes at the prospect of his sub-ordinate being attacked by an eleven year old girl. Prince Rama was held high above and the Major shouted, "Ringer," and one of the soldiers appeared in the doorway. "Get rid of this," Scholl snarled and threw the doll to him.

A whispered 'No' escaped Mitch's lips, then blind fury erupted. Two small, hard fists struck the Major in the region of his solar plexus, rendering him speechless as she screamed again.

"I hate you, Nazi pigs. I hope you rot in hell," and dived out of the door, where the two stormtroopers grabbed at her.

The foot that could boot a football into the back of the net with some force, connected with his private parts and his comrade licked his hand where sharp teeth had drawn blood. The crunching of black boot on the brown doll felt as if someone was stamping on her own body. Daniel and Chrissy had rushed out to the terrace, but it was already too late. The soldier straightened up, a smug expression on his face, satisfied that nothing was left of the offending affront to the Aryan Race.

The flower pot, still filled with earth, hit the back of his head and he stumbled. Before Mitch could despatch another missile, Colonel Inkmeyer's hand took it from her, his voice stern. "That's enough, child. Go inside."

The soldier, still nursing his head, heard Major Scholl as if from far away. "Wait for me in the car." The cold, merciless voice then addressed Daniel. "You had better control that vicious animal you call a girl or I'll see to it that she's placed into a Correction Camp. I would ask you to make a note to that effect on your questionnaire, Colonel."

He left, followed by the two stormtroopers in the hall. Inkmeyer wondered what would have happened to the girl if he had not been there and retreated discreetly to the dining room, hoping to talk to her. He watched by the window as Chrissy shook the torn silken garments free of what remained of the beautiful doll and Daniel swept the pieces away. He nodded as the young woman rushed into the dining room, excused herself and fled up the stairs, tears streaming down her face.

She saw Mitch sitting on the floor, Princess Evita clasped to her chest, rocking, rocking...

Chrissy Tanner paused at the bottom of the stairs, wiped her eyes and caught the last sentence of the conversation in the dining room.

"...and I can't see how you can keep all this from your wife. You must tell her." Inkmeyer's voice sounded urgent.

She entered the room and the Colonel rose from the sofa. "How is the child, Mrs Tanner? Crying her eyes out?" he queried.

"Mitch never cries, Colonel Inkmeyer, more's the pity. And what am I supposed to be told, Daniel?" she enquired of her husband, who exchanged a meaningful glance with the man gathering up his papers.

"I must be going. Jan is waiting for me at the office. He'll need to know what's happened here. He asked me to remind you to pick him up at ten," Inkmeyer said pleasantly.

"Who's Jan?" Chrissy asked, knowing Inkmeyer had deliberately diverted attention from her question. "Is he a colleague of yours, Colonel?"

"Yes, Mrs Tanner, and my friend. Treat him kindly, he's suffered much in the past few weeks. I hope we meet again under more pleasant circumstances."

Inkmeyer held out his hand, took hers and placed a fleeting kiss on the back of it. Chrissy felt flustered. No-one had ever kissed her hand before.

"Goodbye, Colonel Inkmeyer," she stammered.

"Goodbye, Mrs Tanner. Take care of your mother. She's a very courageous woman. I should like to meet her sometime. Goodbye, Daniel."

The two men shook hands warmly and walked through the hall and out to the waiting black car.

"I wish you luck," Inkmeyer said as he turned the key and drove off.

Chrissy was brewing fresh coffee. She needed it and prepared herself to ask her husband some searching questions, wondering what the Colonel had meant by referring to her mother as courageous. What did he know about her if he'd never met her? But then, they knew everything about everybody. She hoped Mitch was going to be alright without her beloved 'Prince Rama'. How could they do such a thing? It was only a doll, after all.

Chrissy Tanner, long time village school teacher and Christian, had not, unlike her mother, lost all faith in human nature. She still believed that if she prayed hard enough God would intervene and lead the savages towards the path of righteousness.

Eleven year old Mitch did not believe any such thing anymore.

Daniel faced his wife, his voice strong and firm. "There is much you don't know, Chrissy, about me, your mother, Michael and Laura. But now is not the time to explain. Tonight you'll have all the answers. Don't look so worried." He took her into his arms, gently kissing the top of her head.

"It's all so confusing," she said. "Why was the Colonel here? He didn't do or say anything important. And the remarks he made about my mother? I don't understand any of it, Daniel," leaning against his broad chest.

"Darling," Daniel's tone was tender. "I've got to go and see to Mitch. Talk to her. Michael always did when she got upset. Be patient, Chrissy."

She felt a comforting glow as she watched her husband hurry out and up the stairs, then a frown appeared on the smooth brow as she wondered again why the high ranking officer of the Gestapo had paid them a visit. And who Jan was...

Dettingen became quiet again after Major Scholl and his men departed. Erika had not been taken away. The women withdrew into their houses waiting for Katrin to spread the news

Seb Inkmeyer did not drive through the town, but skirted the villages towards the river and the bridge. It was getting dark and he could smell smoke. He cursed loudly. Tomorrow they'd start the never ending processing of Jews taken into custody. He was tired of it all but had nowhere to go. He could flee abroad but they would find him. The network of spies was world-wide and very efficient. He should know, he had helped

431

Jan to set it up years ago. There was no place on earth that did not have a cell operating a direct line to Berlin.

The Mercedes nosed along the empty embankment. Smoke filled the car and he shut the window. He glanced to his left along the wide road leading to the bridge. It was filled with marchers, bearing torches, going into town. Inkmeyer turned right and sped along the bridge to the highway on the other side.

Jan hadn't picked the best day for visiting, he thought, and then changed his mind. Maybe it was the best day. They'd be tied up for weeks and Scholl would be in his element deporting as many Jews as he could lay his hands on to the labour camps. A smile hovered around Inkmeyer's lips at the prospect of telling Jan what had happened this afternoon. Scholl would never forgive him for witnessing the humiliation the girl had inflicted on him.

It would be interesting to watch her grow up. She was hot headed. If she wasn't afraid to hit Scholl now, what would she be like at fifteen, sixteen? Would she then tackle the world or be like a young Mrs Tanner, unwilling or unable to see what was going on around them? Like the ones he'd noticed behind the flimsy curtains, watching, waiting, doing nothing.

Somehow Seb Inkmeyer couldn't envisage the girl doing that. She'd be more like Mr. Behrens. And again he felt a curiosity about the woman he had seen only once. Taller than Laura Schiller, who had held his attention with her timeless beauty. Erika Behrens had exuded an appetite for life, her willowy figure swathed in some flimsy dress, he remembered. Fair-haired, long legged, she and the young Baron had been an attractive couple.

Seb Inkmeyer smiled again, thinking that she'd made the ideal Baroness. Or a Countess... then switched off his momentary day dreaming, remembering that he had helped to dispatch Erika Behrens' lover and her friends, as well as the innocent people on the boat, to the bottom of the river. He had called Scholl a cold blooded, ruthless killer, but what was he? His hands were not clean, either.

As he approached the city, the glows of the bonfires lit up the sky in the gathering dust and Seb felt the waste of it all settle like a heavy weight on his shoulders.

Chapter 49

Jan Konrad stood at the high window of the front office on the second floor. Since dusk he had watched the bonfires springing up in all directions over the City. He could feel the elation buzzing through the room. The streets swarmed with uniformed men and youths, carrying their torches and banners, rampaging through the town. The police stood and watched, fire engines waited, but did not put out the flames. Arrests were made, the protesting Jews bundled into Black Marias, packed in like sardines. He felt an overwhelming desire to leave it all behind, but he was trapped, like Seb. He was getting worried about him.

After taking several detours Inkmeyer walked into Jan's office at 5:27 pm. "I need a drink. It's bloody insanity out there," he said, sinking into one of the easy chairs, watching his friend pour out a whisky. "Neat, and make it a double."

"How did it go, Seb? Are they all right?" asked Jan, opening a bottle of beer.

"As far as I can tell. Scholl and three of his bastards tried to scare Mrs Behrens, but she held her own. Didn't panic. Tanner evidently had warned her. It's the young girl that worries me."

"Why?" Jan looked puzzled. "She's only ten or eleven."

"That one's too old for her years. Knows too much. She punched Scholl, booted one of his boys where it hurts, bit the other one and threw a plant pot at the hooligan in the yard stamping on a brown doll dressed as an Arab. It all happened so fast we didn't have time to stop her," Inkmeyer said.

Jan's face had disbelief stamped all over it. "You *are* joking, aren't you?" he uttered, in amazement.

"No." Seb held out his glass for a refill. "You should've seen Scholl. When he'd finished with Mrs Behrens, her daughter was next on his list. He was surprised to find me in the dining room filling in the forms you gave me. All would have been alright if that thug hadn't found the doll. The girl went berserk. You'll have to talk to Tanner about her."

"I'm not surprised she went for him. Daniel told me years ago that she was obsessive about those dolls. The Sheik was a present from her father. He

433

brought it for her from Persia. That stupid idiot who trod on it can think himself lucky she didn't throw a knife," Jan said.

"Bloody hell." It was Seb's turn to look astonished. "Is that what Schiller taught her?"

"Yes and no," Jan said slowly. "He loved that kid and never stopped her from doing whatever she wanted, but taught her to do it well. She's not your average sweet little Miss. Mitch was like a son to him."

"Did you ever meet her real mother?"

"Oh, yes." The face of Jan betrayed the disgust he felt for Natasha Sogar. "She sold herself to the Party for a career, destroyed Laura's son and treated the child like an animal. She boasted that she tied it to the legs of the cot with a rope long enough for it to get food and water until she got back. When she was filming and couldn't get home she left Mitch with a friend of hers. The madam of a whore house. Some of the girls cared for the baby better than her own mother."

"How do you know all this?" asked Seb, astonished.

"I had to go there sometimes..." Jan saw the blue eyes of his friend widen in surprise, saw a grin on his face. "No, I didn't go there to have a good time. They needed health certificates and some doctors cheated when Madam paid them well. It was sometime in 1927 when I saw the baby for the first time and wanted to know whose it was. Madam was very evasive at first until I threatened to shut her down. After that I made it my business to keep an eye on Peter's wife. He had been my friend, and was still working abroad to keep Natasha in luxury. Peter was a good man and didn't deserve that woman."

"What did you do?" asked Seb curiously.

"I wrote to him, and in 1928 he severed all ties with Natasha and came home with his daughter. They never divorced. She's a cruel calculating bitch, uses everybody and moves only in the highest circles. The evil roles she plays on stage and in the movies aren't an act. She plays herself. I'll talk to Daniel, in case that she-devil wants her daughter back, now the girl has property and a thriving business. She needs legal guardians in a hurry, for her own safety." He picked up his briefcase, stuffing it full of papers. "I've got to hurry, if I'm to get to Bonn in time. Are you going home?"

"No," Inkmeyer grinned. "I'm going up to the club to pick one of our girls to keep me company. I fancy the blonde with the long legs. The world's gone mad out there and tomorrow we'll be counting the victims. I need a night out." He paused for a moment and they exchanged a look of despair at what was waiting for them in the morning. "A piece of advice, my friend," Seb said quietly. "Take Rudi with you. At least as far as the tavern. That mob out there is out of control. And keep away from the river."

"I'll do that. Thanks for going this afternoon, Seb."

"Oh, I enjoyed seeing Scholl squirm. Let's hope there'll not be any repercussions. He's a malicious bastard." He downed the last of the whisky, rose and walked to the door. "Give my regards to Lotti and the boys."

It was 9:15 pm when the reception desk phoned to tell Jan his driver was waiting with the car. The city lights had lost their familiarity as landmarks as a pall of smoke obscured the sky. The car smelled of wood smoke in spite of the closed windows. What they had witnessed from the window of the office was only a minuscule part of the mayhem that raged over the whole of the country. To the glow of the bonfires had been added the blaze of each synagogue and the mindless destruction of priceless documents and holy scripture, the flames serving to fuel a hatred induced by incessant propaganda and fear. Kind, terrified people stood helpless behind their curtains, weeping and ashamed of their cowardice.

The Fanatics and Believers joined in the merry dance around the bonfires, delighting in the tinkling of glass and swarming with drunken victory to join the seething mass of uniformed thugs.

November the ninth was to have a pretty name when the papers recorded events for posterity the following morning. 'Crystal Night' they called it. The sound of shattering glass and the weeping of the innocent could be heard all over the country throughout the night. The roar of the flames drowned out the futile prayers of the victims.

Jan Konrad, travelling away from the city of Cologne towards the town of Bonn, painfully aware that events would inevitably take their course, felt helpless. They crossed the bridge and stopped to let the long line of marchers pass. The torches, held high, snaked towards the town centre. Smoke hung thick in the air and rowdy, hoarse voices rang out, competing with the crackling of fires and the breaking of a multitude of windows.

The tavern was quiet. Only a few locals with no taste for head hunting had remained. The rough-necks and fanatics were out with their torches marching into town. Nell saw Rudi and Jan, beamed all over her face and moved her ample figure to embrace both of them. The false smile she reserved for her uniformed customers had disappeared and pure joy spread over her features.

"It's good to see you. How's Lotti? And the boys?" she asked Jan, while Rudi walked over to Daniel's table.

"They're fine, Nell. Alex is getting big and Toni's full of nonsense."

He had never understood why Lotti refused to visit the tavern when they returned from Munich. Nell had been good to her and still asked after her when he came back here to see Daniel. He knew Nell was hurt by the snub and felt sorry for her. It had never affected their relationship, though. He had not forgotten her kindness to him when he needed it most.

"Beer, Janus?"

She never called him anything else and it made him feel good. Jan looked down into the plump face, the laughing blue eyes full of pleasure at seeing him again and regretfully shook his head, extracting himself from arms like tree trunks. "Sorry, sweetheart. I've serious business to attend to. Gotta keep a clear head. I'll see you when I get back."

"I'll have Rudi to tell me what's happening while you're over there." Nell gently touched his face. A shadow crossed over her own. "Be careful, boy. There's enough devastation going on in town without you landing yourself in trouble. See you later." She noticed Rudi had already made a play for the new barmaid.

Daniel and Jan shook hands and left through the side door, where the motorbike was parked. The alley at the side of the tavern was lit by a street lamp and Jan saw the bike. Daniel watched his friend and wondered whether to let him drive it. There was a strange expression on Jan's face.

"Do you want to drive?" Daniel asked.

Jan hesitated, then shook his head. "No. It's been too long."

Daniel pushed the heavy machine into the road and mounted. A lacy curtain of smoke hung over the river, the glow from fires illuminated the town on their right, but the south embankment on the other side of the bridge lay deserted. Jan buttoned the leather jacket he wore over a thick high-necked fisherman's sweater, pulled a black corduroy cap over his hair and swung a long leg clad in cords over the pillion seat. Daniel started the motor and followed the wide embankment along the river.

Jumbled thoughts raced through Jan's head as he passed the small bench he'd sat on so long ago. He glanced to his right and the stone steps leading up to Rema House were still there. Every window in the place was ablaze with light. The high hedge that used to screen the property had been removed, or cut low. He couldn't be sure which. And then memories flooded into his head as Daniel branched off and took the same route he himself had covered so many times in 1924, when he'd still had his dreams.

Mitch had gone to bed, read a little, then got up again to sit in the rocking chair, the flaxen haired doll clasped to her chest. She had cherished the two dolls for so long that now there was an empty space in her arms and it felt strange.

She was frightened, wondering what was the matter with her. It had started when she had sat here after dinner and remembered the heavy boots crushing Prince Rama's face. She'd felt a lump in her throat and her body had started to shake. Tears had streamed out of her eyes. They tasted salty and wouldn't stop. Strange noises were coming out of her mouth and the silk dress of Princess Evita was very wet. She had wanted her grandparents so much that it started all over again.

'I'm crying', Mitch thought. Like all the other girls, like Chrissy and Aunt Erika. It didn't make her feel any better and she didn't know whether to be glad or mad.

Mitch held the doll in front of her, scrutinizing the face. She was so pretty and Prince Rama had been so handsome, but now he was just dust. Ashes to ashes, dust to dust, she recited. Why had she cried tears for a doll when none would come for her grandparents, her father or Freddy, whom she had loved as much as Aunt Erika? She remembered waking after the nightmares and her pillow had been wet. Maybe she had done her crying in her sleep?

Hugging the doll she tried to apply logic to the vexed question and wished she could talk to Granpa. He'd explain it all to her. Mitch sniffed and found it very unpleasant.

The rocking chair was wide and deep, built for big men. She gave it a push and jumped off as the momentum brought the chair forward, then walked purposefully into her bedroom. The small wicker chair stood empty and she placed the doll on the cushion, spreading out the damp dress. She knew that Princess Evita would not comfort her any more. She was getting too old for dolls anyway.

As a last gesture of affection she knelt in front of the chair, looked at the doll's sweet face for a long time. Mitch placed a kiss on both cheeks and walked away, murmuring, "Goodbye, Princess..."

Mitch thought she'd heard the motorbike. Daniel had gone into town and must be back. Maybe he knew something about the awful stories Victor had told her when he'd come back from town. She knew Aunt Erika was downstairs and he'd be sure to tell her.

Daniel drove along the path by the stream and nosed the machine into Annsberg Road, past the market garden. The bike came to rest in the gutter of the pavement and Jan dismounted. "Go round the back, they're expecting you," Daniel said, securing the machine on its stand.

Jan saw that the narrow path by the house had been widened to accommodate the van. He opened one gate and looked into the darkness. The summer house gleamed faintly in the night. The terrace was lit by a bright glass lamp above the kitchen window. Jan smiled. His lamp. He'd fixed it soon after they'd come here. He looked through the window and noted that only the decor had changed in the kitchen. Everything was just as he had left it. He felt a sense of homecoming and at the same time, a terrible loss, knowing she would not be there. And wondered for a moment if it had been wise to come here at all. He squared his shoulders and knocked on the kitchen door, stepped inside and quickly mounted the two steps into the dining room.

The thick woollen socks made no noise on the stairs. Mitch reached the bottom of the stairs and stopped. The dining room door had been left open. She heard the stranger's voice, deep, pleasant. "Hello, Erika. Remember me?", he said.

Mitch did not move. She had not heard the man speak before, but knew that she had seen him. Erika Behrens called out "Janus," and the girl heard the amazement in the woman's voice. Her mind went back to the memorial service, the posy of red roses, the white haired man at the back of the church. She had felt his pain and remembered the print on the silk ribbon, 'To Laura. With my love. J.," and knew it was him.

The streetlamp and the light from the patio illuminated the hall. Mitch sat down on the stairs and listened.

Jan recognized Erika and was shocked by her appearance. The change was drastic and recent. Freddy's death had taken the life force from her and his voice was kind. "Hello, Erika. Remember me?" He took off his cap, the thick white hair springing back into soft waves.

Erika Behrens stared at him, surprise and confusion mingled in rapid motion on her face, and she called out in amazement. "Janus! What the hell are you doing here? Where've you been all these years?"

"Here and there," Jan said, smiling, as they shook hands. He turned to Chrissy. "Mrs Tanner. I've heard a lot about you from Daniel. It's nice to meet you at last," and offered his hand, which Chrissy took hesitantly. All she knew about this man was his rank and name and hoped the news he had for her mother was not going to upset her any further. It was hard to see her suffer so much.

"I'm pleased to meet you, Colonel. Unfortunately I can't say I've heard anything about you until this evening.

"Colonel, eh?" queried Erika. "Colonel of what, Janus?" Her eyes suddenly alert, questioning. Daniel had come in and saved Jan from an immediate answer.

"Give the man a drink, Chrissy. We've just left a town full of lunatics on the rampage. You'll read all about that in the paper tomorrow. Now, we've got other business to discuss. What'll you have, Jan?"

"Beer'll do fine."

He was pleased the dining room was also much as he'd left it, except for a change of some delicately patterned wallpaper. That would've been Laura's choice. Jan wondered for a moment where his rocking chair had got to. He was sure Daniel had told him it had stood by the stove all these years and that Michael had liked to sit in it. He took the chair next to Erika, who leant back in the corner of the settee, studying the man she had known as Janus.

"You haven't changed much. Look older, of course, but still very handsome. But then, you always were." Erika smiled at him. "What are you Colonel of, Janus?" she asked sweetly and he felt relieved. There was still the old Erika somewhere under that mountain of grief.

Chrissy brought two beers and poured more cider into her mother's glass. Jan looked intently at Erika, formulating his words carefully.

"SS Colonel Jan Konrad, Chief of Intelligence Sector at Gestapo Headquarters in Cologne, at your service, Mrs Behrens," he said, raising his glass to her. "Prost."

Erika contemplated his face, a calculating look in her eyes which he did not miss. "Jan Konrad, is it? I like Janus better. It's more You," she said and showed little surprise at his rank. "So that's where you disappeared to fourteen years ago. Were you by chance responsible for the visit to my house this afternoon?" Her voice had an edge to it, which he didn't miss either.

"No, but I knew it might happen. That's why I sent my colleague. It could've been worse otherwise."

"He was very nice and polite," Chrissy said, smiling at the memory of the attractive man kissing her hand. "He told you what happened?"

"In detail. Inkmeyer's a friend and knows what's been going on here the last few years. You know what I'm talking about, Erika?"

Daniel looked up at his mother-in-law, refraining momentarily from biting into another sandwich. Chrissy looked puzzled and Erika narrowed her eyes as she faced Jan. "No, I don't know what you're talking about. Enlighten me," she said carefully.

"May I, Mrs Tanner? They look very inviting", casually helping himself to a sandwich off the platter. "You'd better tell them, Daniel."

Opening two more bottles of beer, Daniel Tanner spoke softly, informing his wife and her mother of the part he and Jan had played in the rescue of the Jewish men, women and children, of the political refugees and the dissidents. He spoke of the danger Rudi and Rosalie had faced, of Nell, who provided a neutral territory for them to meet in, of Captain Olaf and all the other participants in a game of life and death. Not once did he mention Hubert von Dettingen. To reveal his hand in the murder of Freddy, Laura and Michael was not for him to disclose. That he must leave to Janus. Chrissy listened in silence, a new esteem for her husband shining in her eyes. Erika listened and lost her guarded look, as she gazed thoughtfully at Jan.

And the child at the bottom of the stairs listened intently, so many pieces of the incomplete puzzle falling into place.

Daniel reached for his wife's hand, held it tenderly. "I've been tempted so many times to tell you all this, but it was too dangerous. You understand?"

"Yes, but I'm glad it's over." Chrissy squeezed his hand and leant over to kiss her mother's cheek. "No wonder Colonel Inkmeyer thought you were courageous, mum. I didn't know what he was talking about, then."

Erika patted her daughter's thigh. "Just don't tell anybody what's been said here. They can still put a noose around all our necks," and then faced Jan. "I always knew you loved her, but didn't realise how much. It was you that sent the roses, wasn't it?" she asked softly, then took his hand. He nodded.

"Yes. I've always loved her. But in time I came to respect Schiller and Freddy for their beliefs and couldn't stand by and do nothing. I thought I'd paid my debt by telling Mitch's father how I'd found her and felt righteous when he brought her here. I knew Laura would care for the child. So would Schiller. When I came back to Cologne in '33 and found out from Daniel what you were doing, I just couldn't leave it there. I was still hooked."

Jan had spoken quietly. He let go of Erika's hand and suddenly there was anger in his face. He raked his fingers through his hair in a desperate gesture, his voice shaking with rage. "Just a few more weeks and Freddy would've given that degenerate pig of a brother what he wanted most of all. The newspaper. To spread his putrid propaganda. But he couldn't wait because they called him to Berlin. So he had them killed. You two should've gone with the others. The bastard sent that henchman this afternoon to scare you." Jan emptied the remaining beer in one long gulp, his hand shaking.

For a moment there was utter silence in the room as three pairs of eyes stared in horror at the dejected man, his own grief intruding again in the familiar surroundings that could have been his, if fate had not sent the priest into this parish, or if Laura had not moved. If... if... if... It was all so long ago...

Daniel's face had disbelief written all over it, while Erika's seemed deathly still, the dark pullover accentuating her paleness. Chrissy sat in her corner, quietly weeping. Jan finally looked at Erika and saw something manifest itself in the blue eyes. Hatred, and a hunger for revenge. She found her voice, rasping at first, then getting stronger. The old Erika would have been devastatingly frivolous in order to get her information. Now he saw a woman wounded and dangerous. He too wanted revenge and could use an ally.

"Jan?" Erika said, slowly and distinctly. "How was it done?"

"I was told after the 'accident' that Hubert had given orders to rig the boat so it would blow up in that place and at precisely the time you would all be in the Captain's cabin. He gave the order, but we'll never prove it."

Daniel rose from his chair, still in a state of shock. "Oh, Jesus. I need something stronger than a beer", and fetched a nearly full whisky bottle out of the unit, poured a large amount into three glasses and handed one each to Jan and Erika. He filled a smaller glass with brandy and gave it to his wife, who sipped gratefully. Erika and Jan took a deep swallow. Still dazed from the news, Erika tried to light a cigarette, but Jan had to steady her hands holding the lighter. He felt his own shaking as he lit his pipe.

The woman in the corner of the settee inhaled deeply. He felt her composure returning and knew he had to be on his guard if he was not to implicate Seb Inkmeyer. Erika Behrens would want to know who carried out Hubert's orders. She would be persistent.

"Who gave you all this information, Jan? You haven't been playing a double game by any chance?"

He had not expected her to think along those lines and was momentarily taken aback. Erika was recovering rapidly, he thought.

"No. I haven't," he said calmly, as if it was the most natural thing in the world to be accused of double dealings. "I don't want to answer your first question tonight. Maybe some other time."

"How can anybody do that? There were more than two hundred people on that boat. What kind of man murders his own brother?" Chrissy asked, her voice still shaking.

"There are many ways of killing, Mrs Tanner. Signatures on a piece of paper are just as lethal as a gun or a bomb," Jan said, glancing at the woman in the corner. She appeared cool, but that was more like the old Erika he'd known. She gently blew smoke towards the ceiling, then looked at him.

"We had no idea that you and Daniel knew each other. He's as much of a dark horse as you used to be. I'm grateful for all you did in the past. Perhaps it makes..." she paused for a fraction, "...makes the signing of papers more bearable," she said softly. "I'm not sure if their death is any easier to bear knowing what I do." Her eyes held his. "It will be an incentive to face the future."

Jan saw the hatred and knew it would be her driving force from now on.

"Don't be a fool, Erika." His voice was suddenly hard. "We can't bring them back. Don't endanger the lives of your daughter and the child."

"What are you talking about, Jan?" asked Daniel, aware of an undercurrent passing between his friend and Erika.

"Revenge, Daniel. It's too dangerous right now," Jan said firmly. "You'd better keep an eye on your mother-in-law. We don't want her to be arrested. I'll have to sign the deportation order if she's going to go after that bastard."

Chrissy had listened with growing concern to what had been said. "What had you in mind, mum? Go up there and shoot the Baron? You must be crazy even to think about it. Promise you won't do anything, mum, please?"

Erika blew more smoke up to the ceiling, a smile playing around her lips. It was the first time Jan had seen her smile and he did not like it. Her eyes told him that it was by no means over. He let out a deep sigh.

"Promise me you'll wait, Erika?" he asked, then added gently, "Revenge is sweet. I'd like to see him hang as much as you do. But he's too big and powerful. We'll talk again some other time. Daniel knows how to reach me. What has been settled about the child? We don't want that bitch in the South to get her hands on her. She is still her legal mother."

"We were at the solicitor today, but he couldn't see us. He's half Jewish and got worried about his father when they started marching into town. Chrissy and I will be Mitch's legal guardians when the papers have been signed," Daniel told Jan, who seemed pleased at the news, then looked at his watch.

"You'll do a fine job. Now, I've got to go. If you have a problem, get in touch. My lawyer will handle it, but don't wait. And tell that young lady to keep her temper under control. They'll put her away if she goes around attacking the elite troops of the Reich."

In spite of his serious tone, he couldn't help smiling as he remembered what Seb had told him. "I wish I'd been here to see it. I'd like to meet her sometime," and he spoke to Erika. "Maybe you'd both come and have dinner with me one day in Cologne. I can't be seen here just now. It's not wise." He collected his cap and held Erika's hand for a moment. "It'll do you good."

"I'll think about it, and thanks for coming. It's good to see you again, and I won't forget what you did for us, or what you've said. Goodbye, Janus."

Jan said goodbye to Chrissy. "Look after your mother, Mrs Tanner."

"Chrissy, please. Can I call you Janus?"

"Of course, although not many people do these days. It'll be nice."

Daniel and Jan left the same way as they came in.

The girl on the stairs had heard enough and like Erika Behrens, her eyes too had become hard and glinted like steel with the need for revenge.

It was almost 1:00 am when Erika returned home. Walter had not gone to bed, but fallen asleep on the sofa. He was snoring softly, his head laid back against the cushions. There was a vulnerability about him when he slept.

Erika gathered the cardigan around her to stop the chilling of her body. But her mind was locked in a frozen lake of despair, waiting for the warmth of satisfaction at seeing Hubert dead at her feet. Only then would she be able to start living again. Now, she needed an ally to get to the murderer and maybe Jan Konrad, as he called himself now, was just the man. He knew who'd carried out Hubert's orders.

Erika turned out the lights and climbed the stairs to her own bedroom. She stared for a long time into the dressing table mirror. It was time she took herself in hand. The eyes that looked back at her from the mirror were cold, and she wished it was not so. But then, she was cold inside.

The girl crept back up the stairs, as silently as she had come down earlier. The heating was still on and she had not felt cold, but she shivered as all she had been listening to went round and round in her head. A cold hatred churned inside of her, choking, twisting...

Her body nestled in the rocking chair, her arms clasped around her chest as if to stop herself from disintegrating, and she rocked, staring unseeing out into the night, while wild imaginings of killing the murderer that had robbed her of all she loved raced through her mind. She would get him, but it would take time. And she must learn patience...He liked them very young, but not eleven years old...The bastard chose from the fourteen to sixteen year olds at the Rema Academy...She knew that because Kirsten had told her...She had three years in which to grow up and learn to be a woman...And she needed somebody to teach her...Kirsten knew a lot...Aunt Erika knew much more...She'd know what he wanted them for and what he did to them.

Mitch Sogar had made up her mind. She had to attend the meetings of the Youth League diligently, win all the merit badges she could get, study her subjects at school and be among the best. That way they couldn't refuse her entry into the Academy. She'd make her body into something the Baron would want to have, but would never get, because she was going to kill him first. How?...She'd work that out when the time came. He would pay and wasn't going to die in a hurry. It'd be slow, and painful, and she'd watch him, telling him of her grandparents and Freddy. But first she had to grow up...and fast...

There was a precise map in her head of what she had to do...

* * *

It was nearly two in the morning when Jan decided to go to bed. He had sat in his study pondering on what had happened. The meeting in Dettingen had displaced all the assumed rationality he had disciplined himself with over the love he still felt for Laura. Her death had not diminished what he felt and time had not lessened the memory. Whenever he allowed himself the luxury of a journey into the past, when there had still been hope of a future with the woman he loved and always would love, he dreaded sleep because he knew there would be dreams of love or the nightmare of rejection.

Lotti was reading when he entered the bedroom. It was an unusual sight as she was rarely awake when he retired. He noted the soft pink of a lacy bodice covering her ample bosom, the hair carefully arranged into curls. Jan undressed and slid into bed.

"Your hair smells of bonfire, Janus. I heard about it on the radio. Was it bad?" she asked.

"It was awful," he replied, surprised at the note of compassion in her voice.

They never discussed any events that had political connotations. He stretched and placed his hands behind his head, trying to relax, and still the feverish activity raced through his head. Lotti sensed the tension. She turned towards him and he felt her soft hands gently caressing his body, felt the warmth of her through the thin material of her nightdress. There was an urgency in Lotti's movement. Tender, yet demanding, as if tonight she needed confirmation of his loyalty. Jan gave himself over to the sensation, floating back to that night when he had held Laura in his arms, absorbing her very essence. He could still taste it...

And he made love to his wife with the uncontrollable ardour he always felt whenever he thought of Laura.

445

When it was over, he felt guilty that it was not so at any other time. She looked up at him and the pale blue eyes held a faint trace of condemnation. "Will you ever stop loving her, Janus?"

He stared down at the woman he had lived with for fourteen years and foolishly remembered their wedding vows. She had pledged her love and had given it to him, generously. He had said he would love, honour and cherish her, but had never once told her 'I love you.' She knew he cared for her enough to have remained faithful. He honoured her as the mother of his sons and provided all she ever wanted. The sex they shared was gentle, companionable, fulfilling the needs of the body, without the raging fire he experienced when he dreamed of Laura. Only then could he savour the elation lovers should feel when the tide of passion had spent itself and they rested in each other's arms. With Lotti he could pretend, but as always the reality faced him afterwards.

Jan moved his body and leant towards his wife, and she saw the sadness reflected in the depth of the brown eyes. An infinite, helpless regret as he realised that she knew. Had always known.

"I don't know, Lotti," he answered softly. "I don't know. Go to sleep, dear. It's late. Goodnight," and he placed a tender kiss onto her forehead.

Jan turned away to escape the sight of disappointment he knew would be in her eyes. Maybe one day he could tell his wife that he loved her.

His last thoughts centred on Mitch Sogar. He had failed Laura, but he would not fail her granddaughter...